ETHEREAL

A Long Way Home Novel

RAYMOND S FLEX

BEGINNINGS

A SUDDEN AND UNSOLICITED JOURNEY

TREVOR HARRISON swung his sandwich bag as he traipsed between the gravestones in Rutsley Church and Burial Grounds. Although the sun shone brightly through a thin layer of wispy cloud, the air had an early November bite to it. The scent of days-old flowers, scattered along the graves, wafted up his nostrils.

He considered whistling to himself, but thought that might be just a little disrespectful, taking into account the decomposing bodies only a matter of feet below the soles of his shoes, so he just gave his sandwich bag an extra swing, for good measure. The plastic felt smooth in his hands and he savoured the sensation of it spinning in his grasp—almost as much as he savoured the thought of consuming his sandwich in a few minutes time, when he located an appropriate spot.

On the other side of the burial grounds, he spotted a sturdy wooden bench. It sat beneath a tree which was in the midst of shedding its last-remaining, browning leaves. As he made his way over to it, he noticed there was a skip in his step—an actual *skip*! He tucked the tail of his overcoat beneath him as he sat on the bench and then slid his sandwich out of its plastic wrapper.

Trevor considered the events of the morning. He played them back out in his mind's eye. Everything had happened so quickly, so fast that he'd hardly had time to absorb it all.

He took a bite of his sandwich. Mustard, cream cheese and mayonnaise. His favourite. That just rounded the whole day off, made it better than perfect. If he got hit by a lorry this afternoon, on his way back to the office, then he would die a happy man.

That morning, his boss, Jeremy Anderson, had strutted up to his cubicle, with a sly smile either suggesting he had some wretched task to dump on one of his minions or that he was holding back a surprise—something that would bring out a strong reaction.

Luckily, for Trevor, it had been the latter, and a good surprise, in the same class as the one where he would get home after a hard day's work to find a good ale already poured and waiting for him on the kitchen table.

He chewed up the sandwich, taking the time to dab the mustard right into his tongue, to get a bit of a sting from it, then he swallowed.

Jeremy had rested his hands on the edge of Trevor's cubicle and a gleam had passed over his eye. He made a comment about how long Trevor had been working at the office, how he was an example to follow, and about how he was integral to the whole company. And then Jeremy's sly smile had faltered. He had started talking about cutbacks, that belts were being tightened, impossibly-tough decisions made, lambs being brought to the slaughter.

As Trevor bit off another chunk of sandwich, he couldn't help humming to himself, taking time to appreciate all the colours of the day—the beauty of nature.

Next, at the office, Jeremy had slid an envelope into Trevor's hands, given him a nod, then moved onto the next redundancy case. That was the worst moment, the waiting, the period before opening the envelope. He had thought he had been finished, that he would be out on his arse, in his mid-fifties and without a hope in the world. And then, when he had actually read the letter, a matter of seconds later, his whole body had shaken from the shock—the number typed out there, all the details.

He popped the final piece of sandwich into his mouth and, still grinning, patted the inside pocket of his overcoat, unsure where or not the events of the morning had really happened. He reached in, for good measure. The envelope was still there, nestled in the pocket. It felt weighty and substantial, like the paper realised the importance of the information which it conveyed.

When he had told his fellow employees that his employer was offering him an early retirement, they'd looked at him with mellow eyes, consolation etched on their faces, as if this were truly the worst possible scenario for a human being. But that was because they had no plans. And Trevor *did* have plans.

As Trevor got up from the bench, tightening the belt of his overcoat round him to see off the chill, he admitted to himself that he had needed something like this, a kick up the backside, to get himself moving on with what he really wanted in his life. What he had wanted, always wanted, was to open a modelling shop, where he could sit round all day painting aircraft made of plywood, tanks of cast iron and soldiers of plastic. He was sure he would make some friends who shared his interests, rather than having to go into the office all day and drown in chit-chat and small talk. Goodness, he had had enough small talk for a lifetime.

He trod along the path, glancing at the various names engraved on the stones. Being in a place like this, having come here almost every lunch break for the thirty years he had worked at the office, he had never thought of its significance, that it might bear some sort of warning. Today, though, he did see the meaning, that he was wasting his life, that he had to treasure the precious few years he had left and enjoy the time he had here on Earth. Because, soon, he would be sharing the same soil as these fellows.

He gave the church a once over. He'd never had much use for religion, to be fair he'd never had any time to give to it. For the first time in his life he had the chance to consider, to look back at, how work had dominated everything—hardly leaving time for anything else. He had always argued with himself that he needed to work, that he was the breadwinner of the family. But his kids had gone through university, got their own jobs, and his wife had her own comfortable side-business ironing clothes for the neighbours. It was fair to say that now was his time to take advantage of his freedom, to open his shop and enjoy the remainder of his life.

As he strode along the path, he noted a plaque on one of the church buttresses. Feeling in an inquisitive mood—now that he had his freedom he had time for flights of fancy—he peered closer to examine it.

The plaque had once been black, but its colour had drained as it had been weathered over the years, and now it appeared as more of a mouldy green. The writing itself was difficult, almost impossible to make out, as it too had eroded over the course of time. He stooped over, leant closer and reached out to run his fingertips over the lettering.

The plaque was ice cold and sent a shiver round Trevor's collar. Perhaps he should've taken that as a warning, but, having come this far, he decided that he must know what the plaque said, why it was there. And so he brought his other hand round to aid in his reading of the engraved words.

He closed his eyes to concentrate on what his fingers felt and he read, in his mind, the following:

Rutsley Church kindly thanks Mrs Bridget Donoghue for her generous donation to the general upkeep and maintenance of the grounds. 20——.

Trevor frowned to himself, thought about how the plaque had got itself in such a state over such a short period of time. When he opened his eyes, examined it further, he realised that several fingerprints covered the veneer. He wondered whether it had been youths who'd come here, committed this act of vandalism. But, if it had been youths, they must've been patient, come here every day for months and months to do that kind of damage. And wouldn't they have 'tagged' it somehow with a marker or a can of spray paint?

As Trevor considered this strangeness, he tried to draw his fingers away from the plaque, only to find that they were stuck. At first he thought it was his brain, something blocking his fingers from leaving the surface and then he realised that he was physically attached to the plaque, that no matter how much force he exerted in prising his fingers free, he just couldn't. And that was when he panicked.

He bellowed, at the top of his lungs, hoping that the church vicar might hear his cries or someone passing by on the street might overhear him. But, before he could take notice of his efforts, he felt a hot sensation pass from the plaque, through his fingertips and through his whole body. The next thing he knew, the whole world was fading, retreating from him. It was like being stuck in the middle of a roundabout, being hurled round at warp speed. He let out a nauseous groan.

The whole world filled with a blinding white light and his eyes burnt with the effort, so he squeezed them tight, hoping the sensation would subside, that he would escape from whatever episode he was having. And then, all of a sudden, without warning, the world ground to a halt and he was back on solid footing. He opened his eyes and absorbed the scene.

He was still in the graveyard or, at least, some version of it. When he looked above he noted the purple sky and when he looked round he noticed the gravestones, dotted out as far as the eye could see. In the distance snow-capped mountains rose up and, he was sure, that he could make out the sturdy forms of gravestones speckled up their sides.

Where in hell was he?

He backed away from the plaque and made his way out, among the graves. His body still tingled from whatever journey he had just passed through, and he felt quite faint, light-headed. In front of him was a stone building. He thought that a good place to make an inquiry.

The door was wooden and there was a bell with the sign: Rin fur Atenshun, scrawled onto it. Always having been somewhat of a grammar snob, Trevor couldn't resist a delirious snigger as he held it down.

There was a dampened *dong* from within the building, as if someone had taken down one of the church bells, covered it in a bed sheet and struck it with a hammer. Looking back at the church, Trevor realised that it had been reduced to rubble. A shudder ran through him. Perhaps whoever was here now, in the churchyard, had pillaged the bell from the destroyed church. Despite Trevor's indifference to religion itself, something about desecrating a church seemed wrong to him, taking pieces of it and using it for something new. Judging from the grammatical state of the message he had just read beside the bell it must've been a couple of yobs hanging out here. In fact, it would probably be better for him to clear out quickly.

With that in mind, he backed up from the door, already thinking about returning to the plaque. Surely it would just be a case of touching it again to bring him back to the graveyard, the *real* Rutsley Church.

However, just as he got a few steps away, there was a shuffling of feet from behind the door. A few muttered words later and the door swung inward. A little midget with a mop of tangled blond hair squinted up at him, a permanent frown fixed on its lips. "What you want?"

"Oh, uh, I was just leaving," Trevor said.

"What do you mean leaving?"

"I think I've come here by mistake."

"'Mistake?'" the midget said.

"That's right."

The midget brightened somewhat. "Yes, that happens all the time." He glanced round Trevor. "Divus?"

Trevor looked behind him to see another midget standing there. His heart bobbed in his throat and he almost leapt out of his skin. He held his hand to his chest. "You frightened the life out of me!"

Divus remained serious. "What's he want?"

The first midget rolled its eyes. "Says he's lost, that he's heading back off where he came from. That he got here by accident."

"Accident?" Divus said. "Happens a lot."

"That's what I said," the first midget said.

Trevor felt his brain expanding and contracting, like a sponge soaked with hot water being squeezed.

The first midget continued, "Well, you might as well give him a look round the place, you know, since he's managed to get here. Be a bit cruel to send him back totally baffled."

Divus sighed. "I've got a whole humanity of gravestones to get through. Do I look like I have time to give tours?"

The first midget glared at him.

Divus relented. "Fine, but if Frank complains about the state of the gravestones round the turn of the ninth century, then tell him to sod off and employ a proper tour guide, all right?"

"I'll tell him that, shall I? Verbatim?"

Divus gave him a loose-wristed wave then turned to Trevor. "All right then, follow me, if you want to see what this is all about. If my tone comes across as somewhat drab don't take it personally. You'd probably be rundown too if you'd spent the better part of eternity here."

Seeing his way into this baffling conversation, Trevor

managed a faint smile. "I think I know how you feel. I just took an early retirement from work."

"'Retirement?'" Divus said, spitting the word as if it were a profanity. "That'd be nice, I can tell you. Not going to happen, though. Not for me." Once they had walked out of earshot of the first midget, he said, "That was my wife, Doris, by the way. She just about completes my misery round here."

"Oh come on now, really, it must be nice to work with your wife."

Divus stopped dead, reached out and rested his hand on Trevor's forearm. He met his eye. "Trust me on this one, okay?"

Trevor decided to drop the theme there.

They proceeded through the gravestones, Trevor keeping an eye on the plaque emblazoned on the buttress as if it might sneak off if he didn't watch it closely. "Um, I'm terribly sorry, but I think I'd better go off back home. You see, I'm supposed to get back to the office in a couple of minutes. Last day, and all that. Don't want to let the boss down on my last day."

Divus snorted then produced a cloth from the waistband of his trousers. He wiped his nose then blew it noisily. Still twitching his nose as he returned the cloth to his waistband, he said, "No need to worry about that. This is the End of Time, see? When you touch the plaque you'll return to the time when you first touched it."

"That's handy."

"Isn't it?" Divus said, marching onward, through the gravestones.

They continued walking along the path, with Divus stopping every so often to point out a particular gravestone, explaining to which part of human history it referred, where it would send him if he were to touch it.

Needless to say, after twenty minutes of these matter-of-fact observations, Trevor was rendered stunned. "So, you mean, that I could bring people through the plaque then transport them to any time at all in history?"

"*Human* history." Divus said it as if the words bit his throat. "And, no, that sort of thing wouldn't be allowed. Frank wouldn't let you get away with it."

"Who's Frank?"

Divus rolled his eyes. "This is turning into a complete tour, isn't it? Better be getting a decent tip."

Trevor wondered whether Divus was joking. He had only brought small change and wasn't quite sure how the End of Time had affected inflation. Maybe money would be like an artefact here, a valuable keepsake. But, somehow, if Divus had access to all history then surely anything held just about as much value as anything else.

Divus lurched forward and scrubbed at a tombstone, clearing the muck gathered over the name. "Frank's the Master of Time."

"Right, and what does that entail exactly?"

"He's kind of a glorified security guard, but don't tell him that you heard it from me."

"I know how to keep mum."

"Good."

As they headed up into some foothills of the End of Time, Trevor noted a gate off to their side. It attracted his attention because it glowed several colours, neon shades of green, yellow, pink and red, alternating. Several trees poked out over the fence surrounding the area.

"What's that?" Trevor said.

Divus looked back over his shoulder, then crept closer, in conspiracy. "Another world. Want to take a look?"

Another world? That sounded rather intriguing. Trevor had come this far, so he might as well. "All right."

Divus withdrew a key on a chain from beneath his shirt and fitted it to the lock on the gate. He looked round again and then gave it a shove.

The gate buckled back on its hinges to reveal a whole other world of gravestones.

Trevor followed Divus inside.

Divus looked up at Trevor. "Gotta be fairly quick in here, okay? This is another plane of reality, another world entirely."

"You mean to say that these worlds just go on and on, more and more gates, one after the other?"

"Exactly."

"All graveyards just like this one?"

"Uh huh."

Trevor ran his eyes over the gravestones in wonder. All sorts of lettering that he had no hope of making out. Once he had been on holiday with his wife, to Paris, and he had just about been able to cobble together phrases with his rough knowledge of school Latin. But this was a different matter altogether because there were no letters he recognised. "What's the name of this world?"

"Ethereal," Divus said, giving him a sidelong glance. "Actually, Earth is a derivative of this world. Your common language, English, is almost identical. Only Ethereal, like all originals, quite frankly, has a much superior system of notation."

"I . . . I don't understand any of the words on the gravestones."

"No, I don't suppose you do."

Trevor took a little offence at Divus's tone, not quite liking how he was doing down his breed. There was a certain smugness to the way he spoke, like a magician smirking in wonder at an audience's astonishment at a simple sleight of hand.

One gravestone, a foot or so ahead of Trevor, began to glow blue. He stared at it, expecting some strange being to burst from it at any second, but the glow soon subsided. He stepped closer to get a better look. As he took in the strange letters on the gravestone, he felt them drawing him in, calling him to touch. And, after a brief bout of resistance, he gave in and reached out and brushed the stone with his fingertips.

Divus cried out, but the damage was done.

When Trevor attempted to whip his hand back from the stone, he found it was now performing the same trick the plaque had pulled on him, keeping his hands firmly in place. He stared at Divus, wanting him to save him from wherever the stone was sending him.

Another blinding light, blue this this time, consumed Trevor's vision and he felt himself tumbling backward. Alice falling down the proverbial rabbit hole.

LOCKED UP

ALEXIS SAT with her back pressed up against the dungeon wall. The bricks dug into her spine and the constant *drip-dripping* of a broken pipe somewhere was driving her to distraction. The air carried a stench of dank soil and made her shiver all through her body.

She turned her attention to Prince Courtney, who had brought her here from Earth, who was playing an improvised game of checkers with their cellmate, Sydney, using some vaguely white and black pebbles they'd gathered from the floor.

Courtney had been one of her classmates at school and then, one day, he'd asked her whether she'd like to go on an adventure. He'd brought her here, to Ethereal, and they'd mounted an unsuccessful attempt at dethroning Courtney's apparently usurping uncle, King Fredrick. Obviously Fredrick had not taken a positive view of this attempt of his would-be nephew striding in and taking his place, and so now they were here. Down in the dungeon.

She really had no idea how long had passed, how long she had been trapped here. It seemed like years, indeed it had been. She timed the days by their morning gruel but had given up after a thousand. Despite Courtney's reassurances that no time would pass on Earth while they inhabited Ethereal, she couldn't help feel that she was wasting time here. Some days she hoped King Fredrick would decide to lop their heads off, just for a change.

Courtney slapped his pebble across the board which he'd drawn in the dirt. "King me!"

Sydney shook his head. "That's not even your piece."

"What're you talking about?" Courtney said. "It's clearly white."

Alexis drew her knees up to her chest and held her head in between them, applying pressure to the sides of her skull. That sometimes gave her a bit of a head rush, made this place disappear for a few seconds. To think that she had been drawn here because she'd found Courtney attractive, indeed been dazzled by his handsomeness. Whoever invented the expression: 'Absence makes the heart grown fonder,' had been onto something—if logic held that the reverse was just as true.

Sydney continued to remonstrate. "There's no way you're getting a king for that. I told you it's my piece."

Courtney giggled inanely. "No, no it's not. I can swear on my sword that it's my piece."

"You don't have a sword."

"I will do once I'm back in my rightful place."

Alexis scrunched her eyes shut. These arguments always went round in circles. First Courtney would bring up his supposed claim to the Throne of Ethereal and then, pretty soon afterward, Sydney would make some remark of his superior intelligence. Before Sydney had been incarcerated down here with them, he had been known as the Bald Poet—one of the King's entertainers. According to Sydney's story, he had briefly got himself into the King's affections, only to blow his big opportunity in front of some visiting nobleman. He never did go into much detail about it.

She peered upward, toward the ceiling and watched the water drip from a notch in the tiles for a few minutes. Once that got old, she stood up, stretched and then resettled herself on a patch of straw in the corner of the cell—what was known as 'the sleeping straw.' In fact, now might be a good time for a nap.

"Alex?" Courtney said.

Alexis wrenched open an eyelid.

"You've been watching the game, haven't you?"

"Not really."

"I mean to say, you've seen whose pieces are whose, haven't you?"

No way was she getting herself involved in this. It would only lead to one of them glowering at her for the foreseeable future. In a cell this size two was certainly a crowd—three had all the ingredients for murder.

"Alex?" Courtney said.

She hated it when anyone masculinised her name—it gave it a chummy ring. Despite herself, she still felt some affection for Courtney, and it only served her dislike for the intimacy they had shared for so long.

"Alex?"

It looked like she couldn't ignore him much longer. But she could try. She rolled over to face the wall, giving him her back.

She heard his footsteps pad over the cell and then felt his form looming over her. He dropped his voice to a near whisper —that husky tone which sent shivers through her veins. And she hated herself for feeling that way toward him. He stroked her neck. His warm breath warmed her throat. "Alexis, are you all right? You've been awfully quiet over the past few days."

"Yeah," Sydney said. "It's almost as if you've lost all hope."

That was what she hated most about this arrangement, that there was always two pairs of ears listening into everything.

Alexis told herself to ignore them both. If only she could have the opportunity again, to not go with Courtney, to not have followed him on this absurd quest. Weren't there any worlds with happy bunnies hopping round, clouds made of marshmallows, that kind of thing? From what Courtney had told her over the years in this cell, she supposed there might well be.

Courtney's nimble fingers drifted south, toward her collarbone and stroked her bare skin there. "I'll get us out of here, I promise. When I'm King—"

At some point it was inevitable, but right then, Alexis snapped. She had simply had enough of all this and wanted to go home. She shoved Courtney away from her, got to her feet and glared down at him. "Just leave me alone, you wretch! Why can't you just face up to the facts and realise that we're going to die here? You got us into this mess and you're constantly making promises about getting us out, but I never see any action!"

She punched one of the iron bars. It reverberated with a *thwong* and pain flushed through her arm. Partly out of agony, partly out of frustration, tears drooled down her cheeks and her voice went up a pitch. "How're you going to save us, huh? You're supposed to be this great prince, but all you are is a conman, a third-class liar."

"Alexis, please?" Courtney said, with his woozy voice and slight smile.

She held up her finger. "No, you're going to listen for once. I think I'm speaking for both me and Sydney when I say we've had enough listening to your nonsense. We don't care how you're *one day* going to be King of Ethereal. We need solutions now, otherwise we're going to die here!"

There was a long silence broken only by the scuttling of a rat, wandering off somewhere in the darkness. Lucky rat.

She stood her ground and glared at Courtney, bringing herself under some sort of composure. "What're you going to do, then? What's your master plan to save us?"

Courtney gave a sheepish grin, then exchanged glances with Sydney.

"I knew it!" Alexis said. "You've got nothing, absolutely nothing. All the boyish charm in the world can't save you now."

Another silence, and then Courtney stepped forward tentatively. "Dear? I can promise that someday—"

"No! No more 'somedays' or 'once-upon-a-times.' I'm done with all that crap. I want what's real, what's going to help us out right now." She blew out her cheeks then chewed on her lower lip. "What we need now is pragmatism. Someone to think through how we're going to get out of this dungeon."

Throughout this dressing down, Sydney had kept his eyes firmly fixed on his bare toes. Only now, when he was sure that the tirade had reached an end—or at least a natural pause—did he volunteer to throw in his two cents. "I think I might have a plan."

"And?" Alexis said. "No point being dramatic about it. Go on, spit it out. And I can't promise not to be pissed off if it's something you could've told us years ago."

This made Sydney even more unsure. His eyes wandered away from Alexis, to a particularly interesting brick sticking out of the wall.

"Poem boy," Alexis said, jabbing her thumb up at her face. "I'm up here."

Reluctantly, Sydney turned his eyes to her.

"Tell us, then," Alexis said.

Sydney licked his lips. "This might sound a tad dramatic, but, please, bear with me, hear me out."

Alexis made a mock bow, then slumped back against the wall, thoroughly fed up. "You've got all the time in the world, Your Majesty."

"Right," Sydney said, still looking utterly unconvinced of what he was about to say, "so, this plan. If there's one thing I recall about King Fredrick—"

"*Prince* Fredrick," Courtney said. "Let's not indulge this pretender."

"Would you shut up?" Alexis said.

Courtney skulked back into his corner of the cell.

"Continue," Alexis said to Sydney.

"As I was saying, Prince Fredrick has a certain weakness when it comes to women. In fact, he has—what is said to be— quite a harem."

Courtney sidled up to Alexis and laid his hand on hers. "I

promise that the first thing I'll do once I'm king is do away with that horrid thing."

Feeling all tired out from shouting, Alexis let the comment pass.

Sydney continued, "What I propose is that the next time they bring us gruel, tomorrow morning, you should ask the server whether you might be considered for *Prince* Fredrick's collection of maidens."

Alexis pinched her nose between thumb and forefinger. "That's the most revolting thing I've ever heard."

Sydney hunched his shoulders, like a scolded puppy expecting a rolled up newspaper to soon find its way onto his head, with no small amount of force.

"But," Alexis said, "that's the only feasible plan I've heard the whole time we've been in here."

"Hey!" Courtney said. "What about my plan to knock out the man who brings us gruel, steal his keys and storm the castle from within?"

Alexis sighed. "Because, first of all, we don't know whether or not the server actually has the keys. We've never seen him open the cell door. And, secondly, and most importantly, there are armed guards swarming the entire castle. Only one of us has ever held a sword"—Courtney beamed—"let alone swung one," Alexis finished.

Courtney frowned. "I don't like this plan at all. Won't you be the only one that gets out?"

Alexis rolled her eyes. "I believe the idea is that once I'm out I can help you two get out too."

Courtney's frown lines deepened. "And how would you do that?"

"First, I'd earn the trust of King Fredrick—"

"*Prince*—"

"Do you comprehend the words 'shut' and 'up?'"

Courtney closed his mouth.

"Once I have *King* Fredrick's trust then perhaps he will allow me on a looser rein, and then I can plan on how I'm going to get you two out of the dungeon here. Agreed?"

Courtney and Sydney nodded glumly.

"Good," Alexis said, settling down on a patch of hay, looking to get some sleep before she had to put her plan into action.

Despite the impending plan, fraught with risk and a quite palpable danger of having her head detached from her shoulders, Alexis slept well. So well, in fact, that she almost missed the server in the morning. She woke to see him retreating from their cell, having delivered the three bowls of freezing gruel.

She straightened up and called out to him. "Hey, you!"

The server flinched then looked round, as if whoever had called surely couldn't be speaking to him. His eyes slowly found hers.

Alexis rose and padded up to the bars. She wrapped her fingers round the cold metal. "I've got a proposal."

The server hovered at the stairs leading up out of the dungeon. "Sorry, I'm not supposed to speak to prisoners."

"Just wait, okay? What I've got in mind might well interest your king."

The server grinned. "He's your king too, you know."

Alexis decided to leave this little side swipe for now. It would only waste time to explain the intricacies of where she came from, that in the United Kingdom she really did have her own monarch to look up to. "Right," Alexis said. "Do you think you could tell the King that I would like to become part of his harem?"

The server's grin widened. "You wish to become one of the King's maidens of your own free will?"

"Yes."

"Impossible."

"Why? Why's it impossible?"

The server pouted and gave a shrug. "The King doesn't simply accept applications for maidens, he selects those that catch his fancy. It is an honour to even be considered. What makes you think that he would be interested in taking a traitor into his private quarters? How would he know that you're not just going to stab him in the ear while he sleeps?"

A shudder passed up Alexis's spine. The server was already getting too close to where her real intentions lay. Granted she had no ambition of killing the King, or even putting Courtney on the throne, but she did intend to escape. She hadn't merely decided to make a more bearable life for herself here in Ethereal —something more bearable than being stuck in the same cell as Sydney and Courtney anyway.

She glanced back over her shoulder, where she saw Courtney and Sydney still twitching away in their sleep. One thing about never seeing daylight was that it messed up the body clock. She turned her attention back to the server and managed a smile. "Couldn't you put a word in with the King? Let him know that I would be willing? That's all I ask."

The server considered, his features creasing up and his lower lip jutting out further and further. Then, with a single flash of his eyebrows, he disappeared up the stairs, going back up into the castle.

Alexis clung onto the bars as she heard the sounds of a stirring sleeper behind her: the profound breaths, the groaning stretches and then, finally, the smack of the lips. If there was anyone else in the worlds who made as much of a racket upon waking as Courtney, she really didn't want to know about them.

Courtney strode up behind her and laid his hands on her hips. He brought his lips so close that they brushed her earlobes. "Morning, gorgeous."

Subtly, Alexis shrugged her way out of Courtney's attempted embrace, making for her bowl of gruel. She scooped it up and stared down into it. All those stodgy, grey oats. Earlier on in her incarceration she had toyed with the idea of not bothering to eat, starving herself to death, but that phase had passed, especially now she had a plan to get out—something to concentrate on. She just hoped that the server would go through with her request. They really couldn't get her out of this cell soon enough.

A DAY IN THE LIFE OF A GROTESQUE

JOHN STONEFIELD rose from his bed of straw to the smell of bacon wafting in through from the kitchens. He yawned then stretched his enormous, bloated limbs. As he stretched his hands, more like pancakes, clattered against the roof. His fingers were more like sausages. Just another day in the Damned Forests.

He tiptoed his way round the sleepers, curled up on the floor. They all had their deformities. There was one woman with seven arms and three legs, she was called Deborah. Then there was the older man called Severus whose entire face was consumed by wrinkles—so much so that he had to lift the flaps of skin in order to see or talk. They were several feet underground, in a kind of burrow nestled beneath the tangled roots of an old oak tree: a home they dubbed Witney Branches.

He headed on along the corridor, inhaling the earthy smell which dominated the entire place. It smelled just like home.

When he reached the kitchens, Susan stood at the stove. She was completely covered in hair, so much so that John had heard cruel Grotesque children chiding her with remarks about being an ape behind her back. But she had been his savour. The one who had brought him here, taken him in when even his own family had shunned his deformity, the curse a witch had cast upon him.

She turned and looked him over, a hand resting on her hip. "About time one of you got up. Thought I'd have to go in there, start busting some skulls to drag you up from the Land of Nod."

John rubbed his aching temples, still reeling from his nightmares from the night before. It was always the same, just with slightly different iterations. He would arrive at his parents' house, walk in through the back door, enter the kitchen where his mother would be hanging up clothes or chopping vegetables, and then she would turn round to scream right in his face. Then his father and John's two older brothers would run in, clutching scabbards. Just before they would run him through he would wake up in a cold sweat.

He took up a hastily-nailed together stool at the kitchen table, which consisted of several planks of wood resting on rotten logs. As the stool took his weight, it creaked.

"Feeling especially reflective this morning or what?" Susan said.

He thought of telling her about the dreams. She had helped him with so much. When he had come here, aged twelve, after being cursed by the witch and pushed into exile by his family, she had taught him how to use his enlarged body. He had hardly been able to speak when he arrived, but now he felt normal—just like he had been before. But he would never be able to re-join normal society and that stung him more than anything.

"Yes," Susan said, giving him a sidelong glance. "I know reflective when I see it." She sighed. "Remember what I always say:"—as she spoke the words he mimed along with her —"Forget the past, you can't change it. Make the most of the time ahead of you.'"

How could he ever forget about his past? He decided it might be time for him to broach the subject. He stared at the back of his monster's hands. "Susan?"

"Hmm?"

"Have you ever thought about, you know, leaving the Damned Forests, going out to discover the world outside?"

Susan shovelled several rashers of bacon onto wooden plates. "Why would I want to do that? I've got everything here." She looked at him face on. "My family's here."

"But, don't you ever miss your real family? The one out there, in Ethereal?"

For a second, John was sure that he saw Susan's eyes go all watery, but she turned away before he could be sure. She continued about her task of serving out the bacon rashers. When she spoke again, her voice was near a whisper. "Forget the past, you can't change it. Make the most of the time ahead of you.'"

After a substantial, if meaty, breakfast, John headed out through the tunnels with Horace, his de facto best friend among the Grotesque. Horace had one giant eye in the middle of his face.

The eye took up so much space that his mouth and nose were just about squeezed onto his chin, while his ears were almost shoved onto the back of his head.

They had the responsibility of scouting out the terrain, working out whether there might be any honey boars or blood bears in the area. Funnily enough, the blood bears were little more than a nuisance, their favourite past time being digging up tree roots and scoffing them. This, of course, would have disastrous consequences for Witney Branches.

On the other hand, the honey boars had sharp fangs and were quick on their feet. Although they only came up to shin height they could chew through all manner of skin, muscle and bone before the victim could so much as cry for help.

At the first meeting which John had attended, it had been decided that he and Horace would make something of a balanced scouting team—considering John had the build to see off all but the meanest of creatures and Horace had the sharpest vision of any man ever to be born in Ethereal.

John plodded through the undergrowth, kicking at loose stones, sending them hopping along the damp ground which was covered in decomposing leaves. Up above he could see little dashes of blue sky, and he supposed it to be a wonderful day—not that that impacted at all down here, in the thick of the Damned Forests. Despite Susan's words, he had been unable to get the idea of escaping this place off his mind and so he decided to broach the subject with Horace. "You don't ever think of leaving here?" John said.

Horace took some time to consider the question. He stared off through the trees and, for a moment, John thought he might've spotted something up ahead, a threat, but Horace turned back. "Didn't you tell me that your family near enough killed you when you went back to them?"

"Yeah."

"Then doesn't that answer your question? You're a monster, you'll always be a monster wherever you go, so what's the point of leaving the Forests? This is our home now."

John scuffed his foot against a pile of leaves. He uncovered a rabbit hole. He crouched down, lay on his front and reached his arm into it, feeling for a nice tasty bunny to take back for brunch. One thing about being his size was that his mind wasn't often far from the subject of food. Just as his fingers brushed something furry and shaking, he felt a quiver, right through the earth. A profound vibration. He straightened up and looked to Horace. "You feel that?"

"Feel what?"

John noticed that Horace had been looking off in the direction of the Witney Branches, no doubt attempting to get a peek into one of the windows, where Tirana, a Grotesque with an exceptionally curvaceous body, would often take showers without any regard for who might be watching on.

"That vibration," John said. "Like an earthquake."

Reluctantly, Horace turned his attention back to John. "Nah. Nothing like that."

John slipped his arm back into the hole and felt round, but the rabbit had gone. Either his touch or the vibrations had spooked it. He withdrew his arm and sat back, feeling the soft ground beneath his oversized buttocks, and thought about how he had to get away from the Damned Forests, even if it was just for a day. He had to see the outside world again.

And then, there was a great big, enormous jolt. Unmistakable this time. The tops of the trees shook and birds squawked out high above them, some taking flight, soaring up into the azure sky. John and Horace exchanged glances.

The vibrations halted once more, but it was clear that when another arrived it would be even greater. So they both ran for Witney Branches, like a pair of school boys. When they reached Witney Branches, Susan was just coming out of the entrance. She looked over their faces from beneath her hairy face. "What's got you two all hopped up?"

But there was no need for them to reply because, just then, another huge tremor passed through the earth.

John's heart rapped against his ribcage. "We have to get everyone out."

"Whatever for?" Susan said.

"What do you think?"

"It's probably just a thunderclap. In any case, you two need to stop behaving like frightened pre-schoolers. Supposedly you're our first line of defence against intruders."

"Uh," John said, "yeah, but only if they're my size. You know, even being overgrown as I am, I'd struggle with something the size of a tree. Which is what that sounds like."

Horace stood his ground, staring into the trees with his cyclopean eye. "I . . . I think I can see something."

John sidled up alongside him as if he might have a chance of being able see what Horace could see, far in the distance. "What is it?"

"There, on the hillside. I can make out something. Some movement."

"Movement? That's a bit vague."

Horace scowled at him. "If you think you can do better then go ahead and take my place."

Susan stepped up between them. "Do you keep up this bickering while you're out on watch? Then it's no wonder no one ever comes close to our home—"

Another tremor broke off her words.

John looked expectantly at Horace. "Still can't make anything out?"

"No, not really. Just a blur ever so often. It's the trees, they're getting in the way."

"Yes," Susan said, "occupational hazard of living in a forest, I suppose."

John continued to stare along with Horace, determined to see something there. They waited a long time, perhaps ten minutes or more, there wasn't another vibration.

Susan clucked her tongue. "Looks like that's the end of that."

However, John wasn't so sure.

"You must be hungry, big fella," she said, patting John on the bicep.

Horace turned away from surveying the terrain. "John almost had us a rabbit."

"Almost?" Susan said.

"It escaped down the hole."

Susan turned back toward the entrance of Witney Branches. "Well, can't promise that my snails will compete with that, but they'll be a nice appetiser for the main course. Pickled ducks eggs."

Throughout their exchange, John continued to stare into the distance, not convinced—as his friends were—that whatever had been making those tremors had really gone. He glanced back at them, parted his lips as if to say something, then thought better of it and just jogged off, into the forest. Over his shoulder, he heard snatches of the conversation between Horace and Susan.

"Off again, is he?" Susan said.

"He'll be back when he's hungry," Horace replied.

John paid no attention to them. If they didn't believe that Witney Branches was truly under threat then it fell to him. He had to take whatever might be happening seriously. His friends —his family—depended on him for that.

He skirted tree trunks and shimmied over exposed tree roots with well-won practice—a practice only possible from a childhood spent in the forest. He kept up his pace until he heard sounds, men speaking, and he slowed down to a walk before crouching down, getting low in the undergrowth. If there was one thing which was sure to draw attention, it was a giant. From experience, on sighting a giant, John knew that people usually resorted to throwing spears and shooting arrows before dialogue.

From where he stood he was on raised ground, just over-looking a clearing. He could see three men standing round, all wearing checked blue and white robes. He had no need to rummage his mind to work out who they were. Those were the colours of Fredrick, King of Ethereal. He stayed low in the tall grass as he listened in.

There were three bay horses tied up to one of the trees, all of them swaying gently in their sleep, like an out-of-sync pendulum. One of the men, almost bald with ragged clumps of hair on either side of his head, was chopping at a tree with his long sword.

"Wouldn't do that if I were you," a second man said. He had a razor-thin moustache. "You'll only blunt the blade."

The first man seemed to see sense and sheathed his sword at his waist.

The third man had a large gut. And, as he stooped to light a fire, it spilled out over the edges. He glanced up to speak. "Wouldn't want to get jumped by a Grotesque out here without a weapon in full working order now, would you?"

The first man sneered. "I don't care. I don't believe in all that rubbish. Fairy tales and magic, what a load of crap."

"Aye," the third man said, "they all say that until they get themselves cursed."

As if to confirm this the first man's eyes darted round the camp, looking into the trees, briefly resting on where John lay, before moving on.

John thought about backing off. These men were part of the King's army and it would be better to just leave them to whatever it was they were doing. After all, one of the great defences of the Grotesque was to remain unnoticed, here in the middle of the Damned Forests. But that was just it. John was certain that whatever these men were doing, the power they possessed, however they had caused the tremors, would put the Grotesque in great danger. He had to gather all the information he could before returning.

The second man rose his head and looked off down the trail. "What's happened with the machinery? I was led to believe we'd have got through this lot by nightfall."

"It's hard going, my lord," the third man said. "Whenever we hit the roots it gets difficult to bring them up, almost always breaks the mechanism."

The second man, who John now recognised as being the superior of the group, a lord no less, shook his head and kicked at a clump of dirt. "The King will not be pleased. He ordered that the Forests were to be cleared by next week, that all trace of these foul creatures be destroyed."

"Aye, but that's easier said than done," the third man said. "Like I said, it's tough going."

The first man, who had been beating up a tree with his sword, cast a glare round the clearing once more, obviously looking for something to slaughter, an unsuspecting rodent perhaps, that looked just about all he could manage. And then he picked out John. "Hey! Who's that? Up there!"

There was a scraping of metal as swords were unsheathed and waggled in the air.

The lord stepped forward, eyes blazing and lips peeled back in a snarl. "Identify yourself or shall we have to come in there and get you?"

John's pulse sped up and his muscles tightened. He looked back over his shoulder, to the forest stretched out, the route back home. If he leapt up right now he could run and the men would never catch him. But if he did go then he would never find out what the King was up to in the Damned Forests, never get a look at this 'machinery' they were using. Looking over the group he was sure that he could handle them. If they tried to get up here, to his ledge, he could be out of sight before the first had got halfway up. Now was his time to be brave, to stick up for those that had taken him in when no one else would.

He swallowed back the last of his anticipation and stood tall so that he was in clear sight. He checked them for any sign of bows and arrows and found none. That had been his only other fear.

The first and third men's expressions turned from hardened resolve to gaping wonder. Their swords trembled in their grips.

This reaction was all too familiar to John. It brought him back to when the witch had cursed him, back at her house, and then when he had returned to his family they had been too afraid of his physical form to even give him the chance of an explanation.

Unlike his inferiors, the lord held his ground and, in fact, his features darkened, as if an old and known foe had just presented himself to him, one which he had expected all along. "Are you alone?" he said, his voice hard and sure.

"Yes," John replied.

The lord jabbed his tongue into his cheek and then muttered something to the first man, who set off running immediately.

John watched him go, now becoming anxious. He would have to keep his eye out for any attempt at a sneak attack.

"Where did you come from Grotesque?"

John flinched slightly at such a direct address. Of course he was in no doubt as to what he was, since he had grown up among them, been one of them, but, among themselves, they hardly mentioned that name—the name they went by in Ethereal. He composed himself and stared the lord down. "What? So you can go burn it down?"

The lord gave him the sliver of a smile. "Precisely."

Anger filled John as never before. Even when he thought of the witch he never managed to poke himself into a fury, but now faced with this man who quite openly declared he was going to destroy the only home John knew, he found himself clenching his teeth.

"Why don't you come down here, Grotesque? Face me like a man."

John snorted a laugh. "Like a man? You've got a sword."

"And you could break any one of my limbs like a twig. Seems a fair fight to me."

John considered the challenge. Now he was riled and he felt like he could do this man physical harm and not feel terrible about it. He looked off into the clearing, trying to establish whether enforcements were on their way. He really could've done with Horace at this point.

"Well?" the lord said.

John blew hot air out from his nose and descended the slope, slipping and sliding down the loose earth. When he reached the bottom, he stood up straight, still eyeballing the lord. "What do you want with the Forests?" John said.

The lord sneered. "The King's sick and tired of all the mystery, wants them gone. You have no reason to know why."

"So you don't know?"

"The King tells me just what I need to know, nothing more. All I know is that my loyalty to the King outstrips any sentiment I might feel for the Damned Forests, which just crawl with evil creatures."

"What makes you think we're evil?"

"It's a hunch. When I was a young boy my father always told me to kill whatever was different, and it's worked out quite well for me thus far. Or so my knighthood would claim."

"Your knighthood doesn't claim anything, other than you're a cowardly murderer."

The lord gave him one long, self-satisfied grin and then sheathed his sword. "Lord Eversham, pleased to meet you." He raised his finger into the air, as if to signal something. "I'm sure we'll grow to be great friends."

"What do you mean?" John said.

A large net, held by dozens of hands, swooped over John's head and brought him down to the ground with a *thud*.

MISTAKEN IDENTITY

TREVOR FELL into a large patch of grass. As he lay there, coming round from yet another, dimension-bending trip, he patted his overcoat pocket just to check that his envelope detailing his early retirement package was still there. It was, which meant this wasn't a dream. Or if it was a dream, it was an especially realistic one.

He looked about him and recalled how he'd got here, how he'd touched that gravestone, no, how it had drawn him in, almost argued with him to reach out and touch it. Surely this would just be a simple case of finding another gravestone like it, touching that one, and he would be right back at the End of Time. Divus would lead him right back to the plaque, send him back to his own world. No harm done. Only one problem with that plan. There was no gravestone in sight.

There was, however, a very pretty, crystal clear stream burbling along beside him. As he raised himself to his haunches to get a better look, an almighty migraine stabbed at his temples and he had to sit back down a moment to get over it. When its intensity had passed, he dared to move again. Maybe he'd find a pharmacy around here somewhere—get something to kill it.

The stream was like nothing he had ever seen. It had an iridescent sheen to it, but not from where, as Trevor originally thought, an oil spill or a campsite upriver. The water had an overly wholesome aura to it. He dipped his fingers in. It was freezing cold. Fresh from a spring. He recalled going up to Scotland when he had been younger, and he'd had time for holidays. He had come across a stream like this and it had fascinated him, so accustomed as he was to the gritty city water he'd lived with almost his whole life.

Still, now wasn't the time to be standing round musing about channels of water, no matter how beautiful. He lugged himself into an upright position and examined his surroundings. Curious, really. There seemed to be no landmark of any sort in sight. Just hills and hills, rolling this way and that. He peered closer and made out what he believed to be a path, winding up and down the slopes. Well, that might be a start, but what would really be welcome was a gravestone to send him right back to where he'd come from. Then again, after all Divus's posturing, doing down the human race, he supposed that someone from the *enlightened* world of Ethereal would know just how he could get back to the End of Time. And so he got up, double-checked for a gravestone and, finding none, made his way along the path to ask someone for directions.

He paced on for about twenty minutes without coming across any sign of life whatsoever. Already he was having doubts about having left his point of entry beside the stream and he wondered whether he should've just waited there. Maybe Divus would be along shortly to guide him back. He turned round and held his hand up to shield his eyes from the sun. He couldn't see any figures back where he'd come from and he would surely need a spot of dinner soon, so it only made sense to push on, before it got dark.

After several hours of trekking, and now regretting not having had a little drink from that stream, he reached a tumble-down shack. Years upon years of being stuck in the office hadn't been kind to his fitness so when he reached out to rap his fist against the door, he was giddy with exhaustion.

The door was no more than a pair of castoff wooden planks, stuck together with what appeared to be mud. It looked like a light breeze would bring it down without too much bother.

Not getting any response, Trevor knocked again.

This time there was muttering from within. The door drifted open and a incredibly tall, skinny man peered out. He wore thin-framed glasses, perched on the ridge of his nose and he had white hair with jet-black, bushy eyebrows. "Yes?" the man said.

"I've been walking for hours. I . . . I just arrived here, I'm not entirely sure how. I was at the End of Time, you see, and—"

The man glared at him then slammed the door in his face.

Trevor considered how he had approached that introduction. Perhaps it wasn't quite as Divus had insinuated. It seemed that these people of Ethereal were just as ignorant of the End of Time as the people of Trevor's world, Earth. He put himself in the man's shoes. If he had lived way out in the sticks he would probably be rightly cautious about sweaty nutters rolling up outside his door, babbling nonsense about the 'End of Time.'

Trevor had to approach this with tact, because, with the sun dipping over the horizon, he needed to find some shelter and preferably some food before continuing his journey—wherever that was headed . . . in the direction most likely to find someone who *was* in the know about the End of Time.

He took a long, cleansing breath and then knocked again.

Predictably, the door didn't open immediately.

He waited since he really had nowhere else to go.

About twenty minutes passed before the door open a crack and the man peered out through the gap. His eyes wandered all over Trevor, pausing when they reached his shoes. He snapped his attention back up to Trevor's face and said, "Go on. Get out of here. You're on private property, don't you know?"

"Sir, I'm terribly sorry for coming across as rude before. It's just that I've found myself stranded out here and I'm looking for somewhere to rest for the night. And, preferably, something to eat."

"No, no," the man said, shaking his head with resolve. "Can't help you. You'll just have to keep walking. Can't risk anything, not out here, not being an old man like I am, being here all alone."

"Please, I really have nowhere else to go. I can hardly keep on walking along the path at night. I'll collapse from starvation sooner or later."

"Can't be helped, no, can't be helped."

Maybe now was the time to just come out and say it, now he'd managed to calm the man down somewhat. "I . . . I'm not from round here. I don't know how I got here. I'm lost and don't know anyone."

The man looked him up and down. "You've got a lowlander's accent."

Trevor took this revelation on board. "Oh, yes, I suppose I have."

After a brief pause, the man opened the door to reveal a dagger he held at his chest. Its blade was curved and its handle made of some kind of bone. The man remained poised, ready to lurch forward at any sign of provocation.

"Erm, may I come in?" Trevor said.

The man's grip tightened on his dagger then he stooped backward, into the shack. Trevor took this as his invitation to enter, so he did.

The shack smelled of hazelnuts and cream. Trevor wondered at it for a moment before he caught sight of a wooden mixing bowl sitting on a table. There were no seats so Trevor picked out the most comfortable-looking patch of dirt and sat down.

The man fussed his way through various jars and wooden boxes, muttering to himself as he went. He had to remain in a permanent stoop so his scalp wouldn't brush the roof of the shack. Being that this shack looked to have been constructed by the man, Trevor wondered why he hadn't thought to make it a couple of feet taller on the inside so that he would be more comfortable. But, being the guest, and treading on thin ice as he was, Trevor hadn't the gall to inquire.

The man rustled up a hard loaf of bread and a jar of water, which he handed over to Trevor without a word.

Trevor took it with a word of thanks.

The man took up his place opposite Trevor. He dusted off a battered, hardback book with yellowing pages and continued from where he'd left off. When the daylight ceased to penetrate the shack, the man lit a paraffin lantern. Around what Trevor supposed to be eight o'clock at night, the man extinguished the lantern, rolled over on the ground and promptly went to sleep.

Trevor sat there in the darkness, not quite sure what to do next. He had managed to get himself in the shack, get down a bit of bread and have a drink, and he felt somewhat refreshed. Now, however, he did feel the tug of sleep drawing him in, weighing on his eyelids, and, after a minute or so, he could no longer relent and drifted off into his dreams.

The next morning Trevor awoke to something throttling him over the head. He cracked open his eye to see the man standing over him, a wildness in his eyes, as he brought a wooden spoon down on him over and over again, crying something in a language strange to him—what he decided must be a local dialect. He had no doubt as to its meaning, however, and he shuffled to his feet and made for the already-open door before the crazy old man could pull the dagger on him and give him something to really worry about.

Back on the dirt path, Trevor assessed his options. He could return to the stream, where he had come from, where he might find Divus, looking fed up, but otherwise obliging in taking him back to the End of Time, or, on the other hand, if he did return and Divus wasn't there, then he would have to trek all the way back to this shack. And since it had taken him a whole day to get here in the first place, he would have to walk through the night, and only to arrive back here where the man awaited—this time fully-prepared to stab him.

There was only one way to go, and that was forward. He had

to keep moving. Someone, somewhere in this world, would know how he could get back. Wouldn't they?

He proceeded along the path, checking back over his shoulder every so often, worried that the man might have snuck after him, planning on doing away with him then throwing him into one of the ditches which lined the road. About what he reckoned to be midday, with the sun as overhead as Trevor could imagine, he came across a signpost. He couldn't read what it said, of course, but it pointed off in the direction in which he was travelling. Surely it meant there was a village up ahead? And, the chances were, that not everyone in the village would be a geriatric, dagger-wielding maniac. Not that Trevor held out any hopes.

It was approaching sunset as he reached the village. The steep roofs reminded him of German houses—not that Trevor had ever been to Germany, but he recalled some image from a TV programme. Here, each house had a wooden porch, painted in all variety of colours: peach, maroon, purple, orange, turquoise, green. Strange as it seemed, the village did something to revive his mood, put him back on a positive footing. It was impossible to be pessimistic in a place like this.

He paced along, what he presumed to be, the main street of the village, taking in the fronts of the houses, and beginning to wonder where all its people were. Perhaps they did share something in common with that man, that they stayed indoors and hated to be bothered. He might as well give up if that were the case because he would never be able to reach another village without needing a drink of water. He was parched.

And then, through the smooth twilight sky, a bell stuck six doleful times. He halted and waited, in ominous expectation.

Up ahead, there was a larger building that stood out against the rest of the homes. All at once, its doors peeled back and children rushed out, followed by a group of mothers chatting among themselves, then came the fathers, all of them bearing enormous handlebar moustaches—some of them hung down to their waists, while others kept them braided.

Trevor examined the building a little more and noticed a large mustard-coloured stone embedded just above the doors. As the people passed beneath it, they writhed their hands, hunched their shoulders and appeared to blow raspberries with their lips. The whole scene struck him as one of devotion and, the building ahead, a church. He would wager that he'd stumbled across something of a religious community. Now he would really have to take care not to step on any toes. So he put on his best mild face and approached the nearest woman to him.

She had her hair tied up in a shawl, an apron hanging down over her front and she spoke rapidly to her children, bobbing their way along the path, tripping one another up, punching each other and generally acting like children.

Trevor thought he recognised the dialect to be the same as that of the man in the shack, but he couldn't be sure. He was no expert of the English language, let alone ones that didn't even have phrasebooks.

He held out his hand. "Oh, sorry?"

She beamed at him. "Yes," she said, with a strong accent.

"I . . . I'm looking for someone who knows about the End of Time. You see, I'm not from this world, and I'd quite like to get back to mine."

The woman didn't scream out for one of the men to slaughter him or give him an odd glance and shuffle off after her children. Indeed, if anything, her smile widened and she tilted her head to one side. "Of course. You must be the hero."

Trevor had no idea what she was talking about, but far be it from him to disappoint. She looked so delighted that he'd arrived. "Erm, yes, I suppose that's me."

The woman pivoted and called to one of the men, who had an especially shaggy moustache, in their language, and he broke off from his friends and approached them. He held out his hand for Trevor to shake, while the other men, the whole village, really, gathered round them. "A pleasure," the woman's husband said. "An absolute pleasure."

The last time Trevor could remember getting such a warm welcome was when he'd been summoned to a give a seminar to a bunch of foreign businessmen up in Swadditch. He had no idea which country they'd come from—although by their faces he would've wildly guessed somewhere in the East—but they'd brought him all manner of gifts and gazed at him with genuine admiration as he'd flashed through his presentation. When they'd gone out for a drink in the hotel bar, the last night of the seminar, a good-looking female member of the group had made advances on him. He had been so shocked that he had turned her down on reflex—in retrospect he was glad that his sense of marital fidelity had kicked in.

Trevor accepted the man's handshake and remained fixated on the moustache. He had always looked down on facial hair, believed it to be somewhat unhygienic, that one would spend hours combing out all the bits of food. In fact, when he'd been called upon to conduct job interviews, he had turned down several applicants on the basis of 'excess facial hair,' although not officially, of course. But this man's moustache seemed to be well-kept, pristine even.

"Yes," the man said. "Very nice to meet you at last. We have been waiting for so long."

Trevor wondered whether he might have been mistaken for some religious figure of these people, but he felt he had gone on too far with this misconception to turn round and tell them that he was really just boring, soon-to-be-retired Trevor Harrison. They might kill him.

"We shall prepare the feast, at once."

"Feast?" Trevor said, thinking that this was getting better and better.

As if someone had shot a gun in the air, the people dispersed to their houses, apparently to make preparations.

The man continued to grin at Trevor. "I must introduce myself. My name is Gyt."

"'Git?'"

"No, 'Gyt,' with a 'y.'"

"Ah, I see."

"And this is my wife, Goyt. I am Mayor of Gotnot Town."

Trevor really had seen his luck change. Not only had he got shot of that man in the shack but he was finding himself taken under the wing of a mayor, and being given a feast in his honour. For the first time since he had left Rutsley Church behind he was feeling like he might've made a good decision to do some wandering, to take a little longer than normal in inspecting that plaque on the church buttress.

Gyt showed Trevor to a spare room in his house, with the bed already made, and told him to take some time to wash and relax. Trevor did just as he was told, making ostentatious use of the steaming hot water to get himself clean after a couple of days trekking and a night spent on a dusty floor.

When he emerged from the bathroom, all scrubbed up, he found a spare set of clothes set out on the bed. A clean, white shirt with a pair of beige trousers. There was also a light-blue jumper for the evening nippiness. He ditched his work clothes, leaving them in a pile beside the bed, half-hoping that when he returned to his bedroom they would be washed and ironed, ready for him to put on once again.

Trevor emerged into the street to see that tables had sprung up from nowhere, and tablecloths had been smoothed down. Presently, children bucked about wildly, tying multi-coloured balloons anywhere there was space for a string. Delicious smells filled the air: pork, beef, lamb, chicken, herbs, spices. He really had no nose to pick out the intricacies, but, at that moment, only having ingested a loaf of bread and a couple of glasses of water in the past forty-eight hours, he realised how deeply he cared about food.

Gyt helped him into a chair at the head of the table.

From where Trevor sat, he could make out the whole of the village, their faces smiling back at him. The women had been seated to his left, while the men sat to his right. So his left field of vision was consumed with the shawl-headed, rosy-cheeked wives, while the handlebar-moustached men consumed his right.

They all looked him with so much expectation, as if he was meant to make a toast, or something. Children wandered up the table, pouring out a wheat-coloured liquid into glasses. They served everyone else before, finally, reaching Trevor.

Gyt grinned as the boy topped off Trevor's glass, then took the boy by his arm and ruffled his hair. "My son," he said.

Trevor returned the grin. "He's very fine."

"Yes," Gyt said.

Seeing the food laid out before his eyes was killing him. He had to stick his fork into that succulent pork, its skin just sizzling away, or get his knife into one of those joints of beef, with its colour of tanned blood sending his stomach into fits of gurgling.

Gyt made a short speech in the local dialect and then announced, for Trevor's benefit—in English, that they may commence the feast.

Trevor got through all the food presented to him, offered him by the wives, in record time. Only by his fifth helping of beef, fourth of lamb and third of pork, with a little half-serving of chicken, did he turn down a serving. He was stuffed.

Gyt clapped his hands together and, all of a sudden, the villagers withdrew from the table, as if controlled by strings dangling down from the sky, and set about collecting up all the dishes, taking the scraps of meat back to their houses. Once the food had been taken away, they whipped the tablecloth off and then, with that done, removed the table. Finally, they took Trevor's stool too, and he was left standing there, waiting to be told what to do next. Secretly, he was hoping he would be allowed a nippy retreat to his comfortable bed, to sleep away his exhaustion. But, somehow, he got the feeling that more might be expected of him. That he had to provide entertainment of some sort.

Indeed, as he had expected, the villagers all returned, stood outside their homes, eyes all turned on him. One of the wives produced a sword from somewhere and brought it, resting on a velvet cushion, up toward them. She stopped when she got to Gyt and presented it to him with a curtsey.

Gyt took the blade in his hand and passed it over.

Trevor took it from him, attempting to hide his confusion with a look of graciousness—and he was gracious, because he hadn't dined like he had just now, well, ever. The sword was heavy, substantial in his hands. He thought he might drop it and seized it tighter to prevent it slipping from his grasp.

After he'd stood there for what seemed like hours, with the villagers' adoring gaze on him, Trevor leant into Gyt and asked, "Uh, sorry to be a little behind, but what's this for exactly?"

"This is to slay the monster."

"What?"

"The monster, we dare not speak its name," Gyt said, laying a strong hand on Trevor's shoulder. "Don't worry, all heroes have to start somewhere. We'll get you off on the right track."

This seemed like the right time to come clean, so, feeling terribly awkward, Trevor handed the sword back to Gyt. "I'm awfully sorry, but I think there's been a mix up. See, I'm not really a hero. Actually, I'm about to retire, so I'm a little adverse to danger."

Gyt frowned. "What do you mean you're not the hero? You've come from Earth, have you not? You travelled through the End of Time to aide us?"

"Erm, yes, well sort of, you see it's really all a mistake that I came here. I touched the wrong gravestone, you see."

Gyt studied him a few moments longer, then broke into a smile. He clapped Trevor on the back, a little too hard, then let out a throaty laugh.

The villagers joined him.

Gyt brought his lips close to Trevor's ear. "If you're not the hero then I've just made a fool of myself in front of my people. Do you think they would forgive such a mistake? No, if you claim not to be the hero then you might as well run me through with that sword, or just give it to me and I shall do it for myself."

A bloody nightmare. That was what this whole trip was turning into. A bloody, bloody nightmare.

GETTING OUT

ALEXIS DOZED her way through the day, doing her best not to overhear Sydney and Courtney's frivolous conversations as they ploughed through game after game of checkers. If she ever managed to get out of this place she would never, ever be able to look at a checkers board the same way again—or a black and white tiled floor, for that matter.

Whenever she turned to look at the game, she managed to catch Courtney's eye. She had no idea how he did it, knew that she was looking, it was like he had some sixth sense for women, how to keep them ensnared in his ridiculous good looks.

Her ears pricked up to the sound of feet slapping their way down the dungeon staircase. Her stomach told her that it was still a long way off her morning gruel, and so there was only one other thing that could possibly be happening. Either it was some minion to announce their imminent execution or King Fredrick had accepted her request.

Mercifully, Sydney and Courtney broke off their game of checkers to watch the scene which was about to unfold.

The server of their morning gruel skittered down first, to be followed by the man who Alexis recognised to be the head of the King's house. Jenson, that had been his name. She had overheard it while Courtney had been in the process of tying the noose round their neck—getting them sent down here to the dungeons.

Jenson had hard eyes and a side-parting, which gave him a boyish air, despite being well into his sixties. When he walked, he bent his knees, almost mincing. He kept his hands held behind his back, as if he were merely passing time while waiting for a bus or train or, perhaps, in an Etherealean-context, a horse-drawn carriage.

He cast his eyes over their cell, literally looking down his nose at them. First he considered Sydney and Courtney, the latter of whom had screwed up his eyes and mouth like someone who'd only read about scowling in books. Then Jenson turned his attention to Alexis and pursed his lips. "Madame prisoner, from what I understand, you would be willing to become one of the King's maidens?"

As she considered her answer, she felt Courtney's eyes burning a hole in her neck, appalled at what his future queen was doing—that a woman might actually have a chance of saving his skin. She stepped forward so she caught a whiff of seasoned pork on Jenson's breath. It had been so long since she had eaten anything with flavour that she could've licked the traces off him right there and there. But it was hardly the appropriate time, so she stuck with a simple, "Yes," in answer to his question.

Jenson nodded, somewhat glumly. He considered his slippered feet, which had a little splatter of mud on the toe, presumably from his journey down the staircase, then said, "And to what do we owe this sudden change of heart?"

To the best of Alexis's knowledge *she* had never been given the option of whether or not she would join the King's 'maidens.' She puffed out her chest and steeled her shoulders to show she was the one in control. "I'm bored of this place. I don't want to live out the rest of my life down here, in the gloom." She cast a glance over at Courtney and Sydney. "With this pair of reprobates."

"Hey!" Courtney said.

Jenson gestured for him to be silent and, against all odds, he did as he was told—perhaps some deep-set survival instinct telling him to hold his counsel, that whatever this bimbo was up to, she could well save his hide. Jenson studied Alexis's face, tutting to himself. "You'll need some serious work before you can be presented to the King."

"That's fine," Alexis said.

"And if there's any sign that you're anything other than completely obliging, submissive to the King's intentions then you'll be back in this dungeon with these"—he grinned —"'reprobates.'"

Courtney smouldered away, but said nothing.

"I understand," Alexis said.

Jenson clapped his hands twice. "Very well."

There was the sound of more footfall on the dungeon staircase and two enormous guards emerged. Both of them wore black hoods, with eyeholes torn through. Between them they carried, what seemed to be, many feet of heavy iron chains.

Alexis felt a tingle of fear at the pit of her stomach. "Uh, what're those for?"

Jenson gave her a snarky grin. "I thought it wise to take some precautions, so I've arranged for your companions to be fully-restrained until such a time that I can be sure you're one-hundred-per-cent compliant."

One of the men produced a bulky key ring, selected one of its keys and jammed it into the lock. As he twisted it, the whole mechanism squawked. Both men entered the cell.

Courtney and Sydney backed up against the brick wall, hands drawn up to their chests. Although Courtney had often declared all the heroics he would commit if he were to find himself in a situation like this, with the cell door open. But all it had taken was a bit of muscle to send him into a quivering mess.

Alexis watched on as her cellmates were cuffed and dragged by their chains over to the wall, where the bulky men strung each of them up by their ankles, before chaining their hands below them.

Courtney's blond hair dangled down, brushing the tiled floor. He addressed Jenson while he attempted to puff his fringe out of his eyes, which was more difficult than it seemed. "Is this really necessary?" he said.

"Oh yes," Jenson said, as he slunk into the cell and offered his arm to Alexis. "Please, my dear, if you'll allow me."

Alexis gave Courtney and Sydney a final look, as the large men put the finishing touches to their bindings, tightening up the chains to keep their ankles in place. As they picked their way up the spiral staircase, away from the dungeon and up into the castle, she turned to Jenson. "You're not going to hurt them, are you?"

"That all depends. If you co-operate fully, there's a good chance they'll be fine. But, if you displease me or, gods forbid, the King, then I might well have their heads taken off."

With that gruesome thought weighing on her mind, Alexis hushed up and allowed Jenson to lead her onward, to her new quarters.

Alexis had no real concrete idea of what she had been expecting. All she had hoped for, in her wildest dreams, was a battered old mattress in the corner of some room she shared with a dozen other 'maidens.' But, instead, what she discovered was an expansive bedroom, with a four-poster bed and floor-to-ceiling windows looking out on the castle gardens. The room smelled faintly of raspberries and when she stooped to touch the cream-coloured bedspread, it felt as fine as silk.

For a long time, after Jenson had left her alone—with a guard on the door, of course—she had just stood there and stared. In all the years she had been in the dungeon she had forgotten places like this existed. It was almost enough to make her cry. Almost.

As she lay back on the silk sheets and stared up at the cloth panel which hung above her, she thought about Sydney and Courtney, down in the dungeons, hanging upside down because of her. Despite all of their individual annoyances, how being in their company had nearly driven her crazy, she felt bad for them —knew that she was responsible for getting them out. But that didn't mean she couldn't enjoy herself while she worked on a plan.

Once she'd contented herself with the fact that the bedroom wouldn't disappear, that she wouldn't blink a couple of times and stir from a dream, still be down in the dungeon, she levered herself up off the bed and strode over to the wardrobe, which she flung open, just as she'd seen princesses do in films.

Frocks of all materials and colours were nestled inside. As she fingered her way through them, she noted that the King had a certain taste for low cut bodices and hems that rode up on the thigh. Then again, she recalled, despite all this pretence, the beautiful bed, the grandiose room, she was little more than a whore—one of the King's 'maidens.'

"Satisfied?"

The voice caught Alexis off guard, so much so that she dropped the frock which she held in her hands. The flimsy crimson frock, with an especially low neckline, slid through her fingers and rustled onto the floor. She crouched to retrieve it, while glancing back over her shoulder to the woman standing at the door.

The woman wore a sea-green frock. She had silver hair and a beauty spot, which might've been painted on, pocked on her left cheek. The way she held herself, with her chin slightly raised and her hands clasped at her belly, suggested that she might be in charge round here. "So they got you out of the dungeon quite safely?"

Cheeks a little flushed, as if she'd been caught in the act, doing something forbidden, Alexis hung the frock back in the wardrobe, then turned to give the woman her full attention. "Yes, they brought me up here and told me to wash and rest."

The woman stepped into the room. "My name is Henrietta, and I'm in charge of the King's maidens. It is my responsibility to hold you to the high standards the King demands." She closed one eye as if judging the impurities and imperfections shrouding a precious stone. "You look like you could do with a wash."

Alexis couldn't help but let a giddy giggle escape her lips. "Yes, well, I really haven't had a chance to bathe since I was sent down to the dungeons."

"We'll see to that," Henrietta said, circling Alexis and picking at her hair, spots on her skin, then she took a step back and sighed. "All we can do is work with what we've got. But, if I don't say so myself, I think we'll turn you out to be quite respectable for the King. You are naturally beautiful. You have that girlish sheen to you."

Despite the circumstances, the fact that this woman would technically be getting her in shape for the King's whim, Alexis couldn't help a slight glimmer of pride. Only later did she consider that Henrietta might say the same to all new recruits, in an attempt to keep morale high.

Henrietta rested her fingers in the crater in her chin and hummed to herself. "There are three simple words that I demand all my girls keep in mind: etiquette, obedience and glamour. If I find you to be defective in any of those categories then we must work to correct it at once, otherwise . . . otherwise, we shall have no choice but to send you back where you came from."

Alexis made a note to bear that in mind, although she really had no tangible grasp of what each of those words meant to Henrietta—surely it was up to her how to interpret them.

Henrietta curled her hand round and inspected her fingernails. "I also tell the girls that I've been in their same position. I, too, served as one of the previous King's maidens, and so I shall hear no complaints or allegations of injustice." She looked up suddenly, shooting Alexis an icy glare. "That I have no idea of what it means to serve the King."

Alexis saw her opportunity. "You knew the previous King?"

For the first time in their acquaintance, Henrietta smiled. "Certainly."

"Then you must know about Prince Courtney, one of the prisoners I shared the dungeon with."

Henrietta's smile faltered. "I'm afraid that King Fredrick demands that the previous regime be forgotten." She batted a hand, as if to dismiss the whole matter. "It's all history now, in any case. Irrelevant to the modern era."

Lowering her volume, Alexis said, "Is it true that King Fredrick took the throne unrightfully?"

"Rightfully, wrongfully, what difference does it make in the end? The fact is that he's the King of Ethereal now, and his authority is beyond question." She plucked an eyelash with her thumb and forefinger. "You'd be best-advised not to mention the past anywhere else in the castle. Of course you may speak with me about everything and anything, but, outside of this room, idle talk will not be tolerated. It might cost you your head."

"I'll keep that in mind," Alexis said.

Henrietta made to leave the bedroom, but, before she did, she hovered in the doorway, and then waved her hand off to indicate a door on the other side of the room. "You'll find a bathroom in there where you can freshen up. I'll be by in around an hour or so to call you down to dinner, where you can meet the rest of the girls."

Before Henrietta left, Alexis managed to ask the question

which had plagued her mind throughout their encounter. "Henrietta?"

"Please, call me' Hen,' all the other girls do."

"Right, Hen, do the other girls have bedrooms as nice as this one? It's just that I don't feel like I deserve this. That I've done nothing to earn the right to sleep in such a wonderful place."

"There are five bedrooms for the King's maidens, all up in this, the North-East Wing, and they all have identical rooms— anything else would breed jealousy, as you must realise. You'd be better served getting used to this pomp. Play your cards right and you shall be held highly in the King's affections for many years to come." Unexpectedly, tears surged to Henrietta's eyes. "And you'd be best-advised to enjoy it, because if there's one thing I can promise, it's that it won't last forever."

Alexis stood stunned, watching Henrietta hitch up the hem of her frock and skittle out of the room, closing the door behind her with a wooden *slap*.

———

After she'd discarded her dungeon clothes and bathed, Alexis felt like a new woman. With a towel wrapped round her waist, she examined her choice of dresses, not wanting to pick out something which would be too ostentatious, but, at the same time, not wanting to come across to her fellow maidens as dishevelled. In the end, she settled on a fairly anonymous light-green number. As she thrust herself into it, she realised that the dresses might be a couple of sizes too small. Then again, she supposed that wearing skimpy, tight-fitting clothing really came with the territory.

A knock at her bedroom door and a muttered word, through the wood, informed her that it was now time to take dinner. Alexis plunked her feet into a pair of scratchy slippers, which matched the dress, and headed out.

The guard who watched over her door looked her over then arched his eyebrows. "Blooming heck, you scrub up all right, don't you?"

Thinking to herself that if she'd been anywhere else other than Ethereal, and warned to act on her best behaviour lest she lose her head, she would've given the guard a smack on the cheek, she managed to force a faint smile.

The guard led her up and down stairs, round tight bends, through expansive hallways.

She presumed that King Fredrick's castle wasn't so much lovingly-planned as haplessly-improvised as each whim took its ruler. Knowing Prince Courtney more thoroughly than she would ever have liked, she could only imagine what damage someone with an equal lack of brainpower matched with a surplus of money and power could exert.

As they descended deeper into the castle, down an impossibly long staircase, lined with statues of, what she presumed to be, past Kings of Ethereal, pleasing scents of roast beef and creamy soup stroked her nostrils, sent pangs of hunger through her belly and her mouth watering. She could hardly control herself as she turned the corner.

The King's other four maidens sat at the table, with Henrietta perched at the head. They all had their bowls of soup set before them, steam rising up. Sliced beef sat in the middle of the table, all ready for serving. The maidens' cutlery remained untouched and their faces expressed an insurmountable patience, as if they would have waited forever for Alexis to join them.

Alexis took up the only free place, which she deduced to be hers, while the guard stood at her shoulder, with his back to the wall, spear pointing up at the ceiling.

There was an extended, almost reverential silence until Henrietta deigned to speak. When she did, she introduced Alexis, mentioning nothing about her coming from the dungeon—which Alexis was somewhat thankful for—then she went on to present her to each of the maidens individually. Almost at once Alexis forgot all their names, partially because she was so intensely focussed on the meal spread out before her, and partially because she just naturally had a terrible memory for names.

As she gorged herself, the maidens made polite conversation, talking round Alexis as if she weren't even there. It reminded her of a time when she had joined the Brownies as a young girl, and she'd found herself left out by all the cliques, all the girls who already knew who their friends were and were unwilling to make new ones.

However, not having to respond to the usual ice-breaker questions meant that she could take in the girls one-by-one. She noted the distinct variation, and saw that the King kept his harem in such a way that he would never get bored. One of the girls had curly red hair, cute freckles dotting her cheeks, and a buxom bosom, another was a stick-thin blond with a pointy, catlike face, while another had tanned skin with dark-brown hair and clear blue eyes. The final one had a frail, teenage body and stunningly-white hair. Alexis wondered whether it was dyed or natural.

Last of all, Alexis considered herself, her sleek black hair and slightly rounded figure, and wondered whether, had she been any other mixture of features, the King might've passed her over, ignored her request. Or perhaps it was purely personal, a means to get one over on Courtney for his audacity in attempting to oust King Fredrick. All that mattered right now to Alexis was the next slice of beef and taking another slurp of the full-bodied wine.

When the feast had reached its end, Henrietta rose and dismissed the rest of the maidens with a curt nod, while holding Alexis back. Once the others had gone, Henrietta also dismissed the guard, after much argument, as it seemed the guard was under orders to keep Alexis under twenty-four hour surveillance. All this only served to fill Alexis with apprehension, or perhaps it was indigestion.

Henrietta gave Alexis a weak smile. "The King has asked to see you."

MEANWHILE . . . IN THE DUNGEON

SYDNEY WOULD'VE THOUGHT he'd get used to being chained upside down after an hour or so. But, no, he hadn't at all. His ankles felt chilled to the bone, and his feet had been lost to numbness long ago. At the other end, his hands felt bloated and unwieldy. If one of the guards let him down right now, not that they would, he was sure that he would be unable to run, that he would simply collapse into a heap and foam at the mouth.

Beside him, Courtney sobbed away, his eyes wrinkling up and snot dribbling down onto his forehead. It was quite a disgusting sight, but, other than shut his eyes and reflect on his pounding headache, there was really nothing Sydney could do about it. What could he say now that, for all that he and Courtney knew, Alexis was being touched up by a lecherous king.

The guards stood with their backs to Sydney, mumbling

among themselves, playing a game of slapsies, each taking turns to slap the back of the other's hand, leading to lots of *oohing* and manly grunts of pain. Sydney supposed it didn't take much in the way of academic credentials to become a castle guard—their muscles and gigantic frames more than qualified them for their jobs.

Sydney tried to move himself in his chains, to get some kind of feeling back in his legs. But the guards had tied him down tight. He wondered whether this might be doing any kind of lasting damage, and then realised that might not matter since 'lasting' might only mean till morning. Would the King have them killed after all this waiting? He hoped not, as he was trailing Courtney 5,693 to 5,687 in victories at checkers. He couldn't die losing to an idiotic prince, what would the gods say to that? They'd probably just laugh.

After giving up on loosening the chains by wriggling about, he decided that the only way he was going to get more comfortable was to have one of the guards see to him. He reasoned that the guards had no authority to kill him, only to cause him discomfort. And it didn't follow that the King would have them killed if he was using them as leverage with Alexis. Also, he had the feeling that the King would be enjoying the satisfaction of possessing what Courtney thought was rightly his, and if he killed Courtney he would lose that.

So Sydney bucked up his courage, took a deep swallow—since being upside down did nothing to keep his throat moist and ready for action—and then said, "Oi! Can you give me a bit of slack?"

Slap. Grunt.

One of the guards landed a hefty slap. The one who had struck turned round to face Sydney, his features contorted, a sneer stuck on his lips as if he could hardly believe Sydney had had the audacity to actually speak. Sydney noticed there was a little black dribble on the guard's chin—meat juice, most likely. "Wha?" the guard said.

Sydney noted that Courtney had stopped his sobbing—at least he'd achieved something. He blinked a few times, to cast off the haze affecting his vision, blurring the guards into four figures. "Could you loosen my chains, just a bit? I'm having a hard time breathing."

The guards exchanged glances, then the guard who had spoke before sneered at Sydney. "No," he said, before promptly returning to the game of slapsies.

Courtney sniffed. "Great going," he said, keeping his voice low. "You're just going to make it all the worse for us."

Sydney rolled his eyes. "Won't you take care of these two when you're King?"

"Oh, shut up, fool."

"I'm a poet, not a fool."

"What's the difference?"

Sydney couldn't quite believe he was having this conversation while upside down, having to make his most common of defences to a mental defective. He did his best to sigh, but it caught in his throat and led to a series of spluttering coughs. Finally, he did get a hold on himself. "A fool turns cartwheels, stands on his head, and tells fart jokes and limericks. A poet, well, recites poetry."

"Don't you do limericks?" Courtney said.

Sydney would give his right leg never to hear that word again.

That was exactly what had got him into the King's favours in the first place, and then, once he had established himself, he had got it into his head that a bit of epic poetry might be on the King's level. The King or, more accurately, Jenson had not agreed—somehow taking the poem to be a slight on the King's sexuality. As Sydney had turned the lines he had lovingly written in less than half-a-day over and over in his mind during his incarceration he had, begrudgingly, come to see evidence for that interpretation.

Courtney snorted. "Go on then, poet, give us a limerick."

"Nah, I don't do that," Sydney said. "Not anymore."

"It'll cheer me up."

Courtney already seemed plenty cheered up. As he saw it they were both in fairly neutral moods now. All a limerick would serve to do would be to make Sydney miserable and Courtney happy. So, Sydney would lose out on the net mood index.

"Not going to happen," Sydney said, and as he did he noticed that something about the atmosphere in the dungeon had changed. The game of slapsies had halted, and the two bone-headed guards were concentrating on him and Courtney.

One of the guards stalked forward, up to the bars of the cell. He poked his chubby hand through the bars and pointed vaguely at Sydney's chest. "Tell us a limerick. Haven't heard one in ages."

The other lughead sidled up beside the first. His pudgy fingers wrapped round the bars. "Yeah, give us a limerick."

Before he knew it, Sydney was bombarded on all sides with pleas for him to indulge his public. Now he knew how it must feel to be a magician at a six-year-old's birthday party, being bothered for yet another balloon poodle. Still, the protesting was effective, because after approximately ten seconds of protest he had had enough.

"All right, all right!" Sydney said. He met one of the guard's eyes. "I'll tell you a limerick on the condition that you turn us the right side up after."

The guard's lips formed a straight line. "No."

If Sydney had had use of his arms at this point, he would've crossed them over his chest and smirked. But, as he didn't, and it took just about all his extra energy to stay conscious, he settled with saying, "Then no limerick."

The other guard was more reasonable. He nudged his companion in the ribs and whispered something in his ear.

His companion, however, didn't see the funny side. "We've got our orders. No one's to be let down. You're to be held like that, wrong side up."

"Who says?" Sydney said.

"Jenson."

"And that's it, is it?" Sydney said. "Just because Jenson tells you it makes it so?"

"Uh huh," the guard said. "It's called following orders, being loyal, not that you'd know much about that, eh, Bald Poet?"

A sharp tingle ran through Sydney's veins at that name. He had just about erased it from his memory. Sometimes he wondered whether he still had the ability to write and recite poetry. This dank dungeon had a knack for killing creative buzz. He'd tried to write poetry in his head the first week here, but it had been so gloomy, every stanza had ended with a synonym of 'death.'

Sydney tried to open his mind up again for diplomatic discussion. If a limerick was his bargaining chip then he would have to make the best use of it that he could. "Tell you what, if I tell you a limerick, and you laugh, will you turn us the right way up?"

"No," the guard said, finally.

"Oh come on, it's not like Jenson's going to be coming down here any time soon, is it? I mean, he's got his two best men on the job, hasn't he? What's he got to worry about?"

Courtney pitched in with, "Yeah, or at least his two best-fed men!"

Sydney shot him a scowl, and Courtney seemed to recall what exactly they were trying to achieve with the guards here.

The guards, however, remained unmoved. Apparently they got that comment quite a lot—it wouldn't have surprised Sydney if they'd got it right from the King's mouth, after all he shared genes with Courtney.

The other guard cupped his hand round his companion's ear and whispered quite loudly, so loud that Sydney could almost make out every word he said. The way he seemed to have learnt to whisper was to speak the first syllable quietly and then, after that, just speak like normal. Nonetheless, the words didn't matter all that much, because once the other guard was through, his companion looked decisively swung, not that he was going to show his hand right away.

The guard chewed on the inside of his cheek then glared at Sydney. "Okay then, that's a deal, if you can make both of us laugh we'll pop you back upright."

Something of a veteran to bargaining with half-wits, Sydney wanted to make the terms crystal clear before he loosed the first line. "And you have to leave us the right way up until someone tells you otherwise, a superior, someone like that."

The guard grimaced because Sydney had seen through his masterstroke. "Fine," he said. "We'll leave you that way until someone tells us otherwise."

Sydney allowed himself a grin.

"But you've got to make us laugh first."

Sydney shut his eyes and tried to separate his thoughts from the blood pounding through his skull, making his brain feel like a soggy sponge. Although he was rusty, he trawled his brain and brought a limerick he was certain would do the trick to the forefront of his mind. He licked his lips in anticipation and noticed the looks of cautious excitement on his public's face, even Courtney. "There once was a man in a bucket, and one day he found a golden nugget, but that nugget didn't shine, not even after a sip of wine, and his wife told him it was sh—"

Footsteps hammering their way down the dungeon staircase cut off the end of Sydney's limerick. The server of gruel appeared at the base of the stairs. He glanced over the bulky guards who, by now, had turned to see what the fuss was about. "Fattie Number One," the server said. "Jenson wants you upstairs right away."

"I've got a name, you know?" the guard said.

The server didn't miss a beat as he turned to the other guard. "Fattie Two, go with him."

"My name's Clive, not Fattie Two," the other guard said.

"Right," the server said, flashing his eyebrows, as if the guards' identities were one more thing that he had to bother himself with. "You've got your orders."

The guards exchanged glances and, for a second, it seemed like they might be readying to clobber the scrawny server between them. But, as always with the employees of the castle, the fear of Jenson won out. The two guards skulked off up the staircase and out of sight.

Sydney tried not to let his hopes die completely, but he had been sure that, if the guards had been given time, his limerick would've at least raised a chuckle. And now, here they were, back where they started—still upside down.

The server paced in front of their cell, his eyes moving from one to the other. "I was sent down here to let you know that your liberated companion shall be enjoying the company of the King tonight."

Courtney let out a long, spiralling howl.

The server grinned. "Thought you might be glad to hear it. Just because you're down here, in the basement, upside down, don't think that you've been forgotten completely."

As the server turned to head back up the staircase, Sydney summoned the courage to challenge, him. "What about us, isn't anyone going to keep an eye on things here?"

The server shrugged. "You're chained and upside down, what kind of plan are you exactly going to hatch?"

Annoyingly, the server had an excellent point.

With a final look of disregard for the two prisoners, he disappeared back up the staircase.

Sydney stared long and hard after the server had disappeared. Every joint pulsed with blood and his muscles felt like a single touch might be enough to snap them in two. He flexed his fingers to try and keep the numbness out of his hands, but it didn't really help.

Courtney seemed almost unaffected by their ordeal, as if he was quite indifferent to being hung upside down in chains. "Fancy a game of checkers?"

Sydney squeezed his eyes shut, not wanting to detail the various logistical problems they would face unless one of them had a well-hidden psychic ability to move pebbles round on the floor of their cell.

"Sydney?" Courtney said. "Did you hear me?"

LEAVING THE DAMNED FORESTS

J OHN CAME ROUND with a great big ache stabbing away in his brain. The last he remembered was the net descending over his head, and then someone—he supposed the lord—had struck him with the hilt of his sword.

A canvas hung down all round the room which was just about big enough for him to breathe. As he tried to get to his feet he stumbled and thudded into the canvas which covered something hard. He reached out to touch the canvas and realised that it covered a set of bars. He was caged.

He steadied himself by taking hold of the bars and rooting his feet. Wheels squeaked below him and bounced through ruts in the road. He crouched down and lifted the flap of the canvas to look out. He caught a cloud of dust right in his face and coughed. As he regained his senses, he realised that a horse must be drawing him in carriage. When he checked out the back side of the canvas he saw the road slipping by from underneath him.

Already the outside world was lighter—they were coming to the end of the Damned Forests.

A cocktail of emotions descended on him. First there was the panic at leaving his family behind, after all he had heard of the men claiming that they were going to ransack the Damned Forests, tree-by-tree, the fear at what might be about to happen to them, and then he felt a slight excitement at leaving.

He did try to break through the bars a few times, but they were made of iron and, even with all his strength, he could do nothing to shake them, let alone bend or break them. In the end, he just sat back in the middle of the cage and waited, knowing that, sooner or later, he would have the opportunity for escape.

Unfortunately, John's patience failed to pay off. John had presumed that if only he could get one of his captors close to the bars, he could grab them, threaten to snap their arms off if they didn't free him. However, when his captors stopped sometime in the afternoon, they took extra special care not to get close to him. One of the men passed him a joint of beef on the end of a very long wooden pole, which he poked through the bars.

John did manage to seize hold of the pole, but there was very little he could do since his movement was restricted. And when the man drew his sword and started waving it about, he thought it wiser to surrender for the time being.

And so he sat back as the day slipped into night. He even managed to get some sleep, telling himself that he needed to conserve energy and search for his opportunity.

John was woken with the aforementioned pole, which one of the men jabbed into his ribcage. When he peeked out he saw that the canvas which had covered his cage had been taken down and he could once more take a three-hundred-and-sixty view of his surroundings. He was inside a castle. He saw turrets above him, crossbowmen pointing their weapons down at him, eyes staring along the sights.

When he absorbed what had been his caravan he was a little dismayed to see that only a man and four horses had drawn his carriage, while there had just been another man—the one who had fed him the food and prodded him awake just now—accompanying him through the Forests. If he had just made a little more fuss, shaken his cell further he might've been able to escape. Now, however, it was dawning on him that it would be another matter entirely to escape a castle. But what did they want with him? Why hadn't they killed him when they'd had the chance?

The men who had fed John was speaking with an official-looking member of the castle who had a side-parting and constantly shot looks over to the cage, sizing John up as if he were a cut of meat.

Finally, they broke off their conversation and the man who had taken John approached the bars, even dared to stick his face between them.

John had the urge to rip his skin off, right there and then, but the crossbowmen made him more wary, made him reconsider how he should act. In any case, he denounced all violence—the idea of hurting someone else made him sick to the stomach.

When the man spoke, he enunciated every word, as if John wouldn't be able to understand what he was saying. "We're leaving you here, all right, lummox? Got to get back to our job taking apart your home now." He flashed John a grin then reached inside the cell and patted him on the knee. "You take care."

John suppressed all his rage and it took all his self-control not to break the man's fingers like toothpicks. He watched the man go, doing his best to memorise his appearance—the leather vest, an animal skin hanging from his belt. The matted grey hair brushing the backs of his shoulders. When he escaped the first thing he would do would be to secure Witney Branches, and then he would search that man out and punish him. He hoped he would find him alive.

The two men shuffled out of the square with their horses, leaving just John in his cell. A pair of burly men, big for humans but about half the size of John, emerged from within the castle, took hold of the front part of the cage and wheeled it toward the large, dark entrance.

John sniffed the air, taking in all the smells of ash, smoke and raw sewage. After he had spent so long living in the Forests he had forgotten about the damage men were capable of inflicting on nature. To think that only this morning he had dreamt of leaving the Forests, seeing the world outside. At least he had got what he'd wanted for once.

They wheeled him into the castle, along several long corridors which were filled with stone statues, what he supposed to be representations of past kings of Ethereal. And then they rolled him down a slope. He presumed they must be taking him down to the dungeons. He quite fancied that prospect, since he liked his chances of being able to break out of some flimsy bars given enough time to do so.

However, when they reached their destination, and John

took in the spears, the swords, the scabbards, the hefty steel shields and the maces welded to the walls, he realised that they had brought him down to the armoury. But why? Why would they bring him here.

The two burly men wheeled him out to the centre of the grand room, its ceiling towering upward for what seemed to be ten storeys, and then they stepped away from the cage, standing sentry at his side. John was about to ask what he was to expect next, when a man, with his hair clumped into braids and all dressed up in armour with a purple sheen strode inside. He had the man from outside lingering on his heels, the man with the side parting.

John stuck his head between the bars and glared out at the two men as they drew closer. Both of them wore concerned expressions, like they really had no idea quite what John was doing there. He hoped he might have the opportunity to argue for his freedom, for them to simply to turn him loose outside the moat so that he could make his way back to the Forests.

The man with the braids's eyes rolled back in their sockets as he absorbed the sight of John. "Allow me to introduce myself, Grotesque."

Once more, the familiar quiver at hearing that name tickled John.

The man continued, "I am Alderney Frum, General of the King's army."

The man with the side parting stepped forward. "And my name is Norman Jenson, the King's Special Aide and Head of the Castle."

John's eyes moved between the two of them, knowing that if they just let him free he could tear each of them apart, limb-by-limb. He wouldn't even need any of the weapons lining the walls of the armoury.

"It's my understanding," Frum said, "that you were intercepted in the Damned Forests when you ambushed one of our clearing parties."

There were some technicalities to the matter, that he had been the one who'd been ambushed, but John decided it was better to stay silent for the moment, let them think he was some mute giant, and allow them to underestimate him.

"I say," Jenson said, "can you hear what we're saying, or are you deaf as well as dumb?"

John grunted.

"Better," Jenson said.

Frum pursed his lips. "Let me be straight with you, Mr Giant, the only reason I've not turned you over to my swords, had you shredded into several pieces and fed to my dogs, is that we believe you might be somewhat useful to us."

Jenson narrowed his eyes. "I'm sure you've faced discrimination throughout your entire life, felt that there was no place for you in the real world, in Ethereal, outside of the Damned Forests. But I have news for you, there might well be, if you're willing to declare your loyalty to the King."

Although John knew that he should've been solely focussed on what was happening back at Witney Branches he found his attention drifting, interested in knowing what these two might have in terms of an offer.

"Look," Jenson said, "I'm growing rather bored of this lecture, would you at least grant us the courtesy of a response? Let us know that you're not a totally thick-headed Grotesque."

"Don't call me that," John said, surprised at the surety of his voice, the booming quality in this room. He had never been used to hearing his voice come back at him as an echo.

Both Jenson and Frum flinched. Even the two guards glanced up at him as if he might be pre-empting a breakout. Jenson composed himself then said, "Well you'd better tell us what your name is, then."

"John."

"John?" Frum said, arching an eyebrow. "Hardly instils fear, does it?"

"I never wanted to 'instil fear,'" John said.

Frum turned his back to John and spoke with Jenson. John overheard him say, "No, that'll never do, we'll have to think of something better than that." Frum turned his attention back to John. "We'd like you to join the King's army. What do you say?"

It would beat execution, that was for sure. In fact it might well be the perfect way for him to escape the castle. He would only have to blag his way through in the Army and then, whenever they cut him a bit of freedom, he would take it and run as fast as he could.

John inspected the guards either side of him, then looked back to Frum. "Okay," he said.

Frum couldn't restrain a grin. "Good," he said.

Jenson bowed his head slightly. "There is one minor condition."

John exhaled, knowing that something like this might be coming. That they were hardly going to turn him loose right away, without having some assurance that he truly was fighting for their cause, and not his own.

"Go on," John said.

"You'd be fulfilling the role of King's Champion," Jenson said.

That sounded fine. To be honest, John quite liked the ring it had to it.

Jenson continued, "It's more than merely a ceremonial role. You would become a symbol of the might and force of the army, the Champion takes his place on the front line of any battle and leads his men onward to victory."

Now this was getting a little tenuous. "I've never fought in my life," John said.

"Oh," Frum said, "I'm sure you'd be fine. A gentleman of your physique could snap spines in his sleep"—he cracked a grin —"and what's more I'm sure you realise that."

Still, John didn't particularly like his chances in an actual battle, tens of men digging their swords into his flesh. There were limits to his abilities.

Frum continued, "You would be given all the training you'd require, so there's really nothing to worry about." He waved his hands up to show the room. "You would have any weapon you would require, and be granted every indulgence. Wine, women, music, it'll all be yours once you become Champion."

John strengthened his grip round the bars and thought that this was what he had always waited for, to have some tangible role in the human world. Was this his opportunity? He couldn't think that he would ever get a better one. Perhaps he could have his cake and eat it. If he took on this role he might have the opportunity to meet the King and to convince him that he didn't really want to destroy the Damned Forests. It seemed worth a shot.

Jenson waggled a finger. "There is just one tiny considera-tion, something which you'll have to take into account."

"What?" John said, already basking himself in the possibilities facing him in his new role.

Jenson twitched his nose. "You *would* need to beat other contenders in a competition."

John's heart sunk. "'A competition?'"

"Yes, there are several applicants to the post, a couple of hundred as I understand it."

Frum nodded in agreement.

John's eyes rounded. "'A couple of hundred?'"

Jenson waved his hand. "Oh, I'm sure they'll be no problem for you. For the most part they're nothing but hopped up peasant boys."

"And what about the other part?"

Jenson blinked the request away. "Really, there's nothing for you to worry about. I'm sure your strength shall see you through the competition."

John looked at Frum, who looked less convinced, and was toying with the hem of his undershirt. John felt a knot form in his throat. He swallowed it back. "And what happens if I fail in the competition?"

"Fail?" Jenson said, with a scowl.

"Yes."

"In this competition you fight to the death. The survivor shall be named the King's Champion."

John's blood cooled. Him against hundreds of other competitors, all armed to the teeth? The dream of being the Champion went *poof* in his head. Feeling cramp setting in, he shifted his weight from one leg to the other. "And what if I refuse to accept?"

Frum sneered. "Then I shall have you put to death."

John sunk back in his cage, looked up at the weapons bearing down on him and thought whether he really was a warrior. He supposed he had spent his entire life trying to convince himself that his deformity wouldn't define him. But he guessed that at some point he would have had to make this choice, whether to spend his life fighting the curse the witch had cast on him, the nature she had condemned him to, or to accept it, to make peace. Surely, if he really wished to save Witney Branches, he would need force?

A HERO IS BORN

TREVOR HAD to admit that, all things considered, the hospitality at Gotnot Town was really top notch. Every morning he was woken by the clanging bells, the laughter of children as they skipped through the streets on their way to church, and then the waft of his breakfast drifting in with the draught beneath his door. In short: paradise. The only hitch in the whole deal was this hero business. Try as he might, he really could think of no way of quietly stepping aside from it all—making the townspeople of Gotnot see that he had nothing distinguishing him for the role, and that they'd be better off looking for someone else.

After breakfast that morning, and once Trevor had squeezed himself into a pair of leather trousers—which were, apparently, the *official* hero's garb—and buttoned up his tight-fitting beige tunic, Gyt came to him brandishing a smile, like always. He clapped Trevor so hard on his back that he thought his breakfast might make a reappearance. "Today we work on archery!"

Trevor forced a grin.

He had to admit that thus far every skill Gyt had painstakingly attempted to teach him had been an unmitigated disaster—especially the wood run, which had basically been a natural obstacle course. He'd ended up about twenty feet in the air, with his ankle stuck in a tree branch, dangling. Nonetheless, Gyt's positive outlook remained unshakable.

Gyt tugged Trevor out into the street, the hairs of his moustache fluttering in the light breeze. As he yanked him up past the men and women, making their way to the market, or out into the fields, they all smiled at Trevor, wished him good luck in their language.

When they got to the outer limit of Gotnot, which Trevor remembered vaguely from the day of his arrival, as he had celebrated the fact that he would not have to return to the old man's shack, to be beaten over the head, Gyt led them down a dusty track which was partially obscured by thick hedgerows. As they left the town behind, Trevor noticed Gyt's usual happy-go-lucky composition fade somewhat, his smile dialling itself down to vague amusement. Trevor didn't think to ask what might be on his host's mind, not wanting to come across as rude, but that observation bothered him.

As they reached their destination, Trevor picked out the bow and quiver of arrows all laid out on the ground, ready for them. A little further up ahead there was a target, a scarecrow with a piece of paper pinned to its chest. Trevor could make out the coloured rings painted onto the paper and knew right then and there he would never, ever, in his life get an arrow anywhere near one of those.

Gyt went through the motions, showing Trevor how to fit the arrow to the bow, and then, after that, how to take aim, holding onto Trevor's arm as he did so, guiding him through the motions. After Trevor had sent a couple of arrows tumbling down onto the dusty ground, Gyt reached out and touched Trevor on the arm, meeting his eye. "You really don't have much aptitude for this, do you?"

"That's what I tried to tell you."

Gyt frowned. "But you are the hero, just as the prophesy is written. You would come to us speaking a strange dialect of the common tongue, and lead us to victory over the Rabbit King."

"Uh, who?"

"Our adversary. The one who has terrorised our town for years."

Glad to be getting a little more on the inside turn, in terms of what was going on with his being a hero—what he was actually supposed to be fighting against—he lowered the bow in his hands and said, "What does he do?"

"He steals our children."

"Really?" Trevor said, thinking that he had seen lots of children back at the town, that if Gotnot could afford one thing it was to exercise a bit more contraception amongst its population, not that losing kids was ideal. "What does he do to them?"

"We don't know, but you're the one appointed by our gods to bring them back to us. The message was transmitted through our wise man. He said you would come to slay the Rabbit King and return all our children to us."

"What if . . . what if he's already eaten them, or something?"

"Then we must seek revenge."

Trevor stared at the bow in his hands. "And where does this 'Rabbit King' live?"

"In the Damned Forests."

"That's not a particularly droll name."

"It's not a particularly droll place."

They remained in silence for a long time, neither saying anything or making any motion to continue the training with the bows and arrows. Finally, it was Trevor who broke the silence. "Um, so, what you're saying is that this hero training might be quite urgent, that you really need someone to head into these Damned Forests and sort out the Rabbit King as soon as possible?"

"Yes," Gyt said, raising his stare to meet Trevor's. "The situation is really quite perilous. More children go missing every day."

"But, how?"

"We don't know. The disappear from their beds, on their way back from school, even, sometimes, when they're out in the fields with their parents nearby. When the parents look for them, realise that they're missing, they're nowhere to be found."

"Have you thought of setting up a neighbourhood watch, that sort of thing?"

"Of course, but no one ever sees anything. We believe that the Rabbit King is using some form of dark magic."

That didn't sound especially droll either, in fact it sounded downright nasty. Trevor knew now, better than ever, that he really stood no hope of helping these poor people with their plight, and more than anything he had to be honest. He handed the bow over to Gyt. "I don't believe I'm the one you're looking for. I think you'd be better off finding someone else. Surely there's someone in the town who's young and strong or, failing that, not in their fifties and podgy."

Gyt took the bow without a word, nodding at Trevor's words.

It was better that Gyt admit Trevor wasn't the right fit as a hero because the sooner he realised it the sooner he could move on with a suitable replacement.

Trevor moved away from Gyt, heading out of the clearing. He planned on moving on, taking a diversion round the town, and never returning. If he just kept on with his onward journey perhaps he would come across another town before the sun set —one which didn't have unrealistic expectations of him.

"Trevor," Gyt said.

Trevor thought about walking on. He knew what Gyt had invested in him staying round, that he would look a fool in front of his people for having declared Trevor to be what he was not. But he would look even more of a fool in sending off Trevor only to find his well-picked bones a few days later, and no children. He had to be cruel to be kind.

And yet, he couldn't just leave Gyt in the lurch like this, after he had treated him so nicely, given him such wonderful hospitality. He turned back to look at the man, his moustache, somehow, looked wilted, and he wondered whether it might have some connection to his mood.

Gyt grasped the bow in his hands. "We still need you. I'm sure you are the hero we require. It's too much of a coincidence for you to arrive here, just as it was written, and for you not to be the one. While it's obvious that you lack many skills I'm sure that the gods have blessed you with other attributes, attributes that may only become apparent in circumstances of great danger." He looked up at Trevor and smiled—it was a shadow of his usual, boomerang grin. "I will put together a party for you, give you two of our strongest men, and together you shall go to slay the Rabbit King."

How could Trevor argue with that?

By evening all the arrangements were in place. Trevor hardly had time to gather his thoughts with the speed that Gyt made the preparations for his slaying of the Rabbit King. He had been outfitted with light armour, a heavy sword, with which he could barely walk, let alone swing, and a shield had been strapped over his shoulders, which was already sending tell-tale tweaks of pain through his lower back. When he'd asked whether there might be a chiropractor in Gotnot, the question had been met with blank looks.

And so Trevor had his two companions, Zend and Plont. As promised both were rugged young men. Zend had short brown hair and broad shoulders, with forearms which reminded Trevor of tightly-coiled ropes. Plont, on the other hand, was lean and tall, at least six foot six. He kept his hair in a business-like pony-tail and he looked quick on his feet. Zend carried a broad sword which seemed twice the length and weight of Trevor's, while Plont had a bow and a quiver of arrows—he also had a couple of daggers strapped to his belt. They both had bristling, healthy moustaches, of course.

Trevor could hardly believe that the time had come for them to leave—that he had been approved as ready to set off on what was certainly going to be a journey fraught with danger. But Gyt was certain, unshakable in his belief in his gods, that they had been correct in electing Trevor for this task. Trevor wished he shared Gyt's confidence.

Gyt had assured him that once he had completed his quest, got back home safely—the part which worried Trevor the most —he would help him to find his way back to his own world. To tell the truth, if Trevor did somehow manage to return to Gotnot alive then he might well consider staying. If he'd received the welcome he had merely for being hero-elect, he wondered what it might be like to return here as hero-proper. But that was all a long way off.

They paced off into the twilight, turning round to wave to the gathered crowd—the entire town—cheering them on their way along the path. Their cheers resounded in Trevor's ears even when they'd slipped from sight—they carried him forward, gifted him with confidence that he could do what was expected of him.

Plont took up the front of their expedition, while Zend took up the back.

Trevor felt somewhat protected having these two along with him, and he began to believe that he was in capable hands, hands which would protect him when they stumbled across danger.

They moved quickly through the night, but Trevor dared not complain about their pace, after all it was *their* children who were on the line, and they had already indulged him with their welcoming feast, and by proclaiming him their hero.

Around what Trevor presumed to be midnight, by the way his eyelids were drooping, Plont led them into a clearing, covered on three of its four sides by thick rock, and set his pack down, before helping Trevor disarm his sword and shield—the 'light' armour he wore across his chest. Then Plont slipped off into the tall grass to set about gathering firewood, while Trevor could just about summon the energy to slump down on the hard ground.

Zend sat himself down with somewhat more style, taking care with his broad sword, to lay it down on the earth rather than drop it. He rummaged in the grass behind Trevor and produced a pair of discarded logs, which he placed for them to sit.

Trevor just about managed to catch his breath to thank him.

Zend unsheathed his broad sword and laid it across his lap. He produced a dark stone which he used to sharpen the blade.

Despite his fatigue, Trevor felt the need to make conversation, and he decided to pick up on an issue which had been tumbling round his head for the hours-long hike. "Did you lose anyone to the Rabbit King?"

Zend scraped the rock along the blade. There was a shimmer of sparks and then he glanced at Trevor. "My younger brother." He retained the eye contact for a few beats and then returned his full concentration to the sharpening. "They took him weeks ago, right from his bed. I was on the look out, in the town, and when I returned he was gone. So we must go to rescue him, with *you*."

Trevor sensed a certain frostiness in Zend's tone. "Would you rather have come out looking for him alone?"

Zend paused his sharpening, looked Trevor up and down then snorted. "What do you think? Me and Plont are a team, we always have been, together we could single-handedly bring them back. But our mayor, in all his wisdom, wouldn't let us go until the 'chosen' hero had come."

"Me?"

Zend grunted in reply.

Trevor did his best to assess the situation, to work out how he might make some kind of peace with Zend. If they were going to work together in situations fraught with mortal danger, then they would need a good working relationship—as he had learnt from years and years of teambuilding courses, if there wasn't communication, then there wasn't anything.

He rolled his shoulders, trying to loosen the stiffness in his neck. "I understand that I'm probably not your first choice of hero, that you might see me as some kind of burden, that you might spend more time helping me out of danger than saving your children."

"Hmm."

"But I believe in Gyt, I think he knows what he's talking about, and I trust in his judgement. Maybe he's seen something in me that no one else can, perhaps he's seen something that not even I can see for myself."

Zend raked the rock along the blade of his broad sword, so that the scraping rebounded round the whole clearing, stiffened the hair on Trevor's arms. "Yeah, well," Zend said, "Gyt sees a lot of things, talks a lot of crap about the gods. What you've got to realise about me and Plont is that while we're loyal to our people, our village, our *mayor*, we're not taken in by any of that mystic rubbish." He grimaced as he dragged the stone back along the blade's edge. "And, between you and me now that Gotnot's a long way behind us, I live in hope of the day that the people come to their senses and throw Gyt out on his arse."

Trevor felt somewhat shocked, not least because Gyt had spent so much time with him over the last few days, and that he felt they had bonded in some way. It seemed like it would be a betrayal for him not to stick up for him now.

"You know," Trevor said, "before all this travelling, arriving here to Ethereal, when I had no concept that other worlds might exist, I have to admit that I too was sceptical about 'mystical rubbish,' but coming here, having hopped between worlds, I've found that my entire perception has change, that no longer can I take things at face value. And, with this new acknowledgement I feel that I should remain open-minded, at least long enough to take full stock of the situation."

Zend's eyes lingered on Trevor's, as if he had truly caught his attention, then he shook his head and let loose a cackle. "You're just as crazy as that old man." He gazed at his gleaming blade. "What has he got us into this time?"

MEETING THE KING

H ENRIETTA SPENT the best part of an hour listing things which Alexis shouldn't do in the presence of the King. Once she had got through with the various taboo subjects and actions, she flapped round her, picking at various bits of her frock, making sure that everything was straight and presentable. When she'd contented herself, she stood back as if assessing the arrangement of a bouquet of flowers.

A shudder passed through Alexis. For most of the time the idea that she would have to physically give her body to the King had never sunk home, but it had started to now. And only in this moment did she realise how much it repulsed her, turned her insides to hot worms and churned the food digesting in her stomach. She eyed Henrietta in the mirror. "I don't think I can go through with this."

Henrietta gave her a faint smile. "Don't be silly, dear, you'll be fine, I promise. You're just nervous, all the girls are like this before their first time with the King. It'll be over before you know it."

"No," Alexis said, "you don't understand. I really can't do this. I mean, physically. It feels that if he comes close to me that I'll slap him or fight him off. Act out of reflex."

"If you do that the King will have your head, Jenson will be sure of it."

Alexis's eyes filled with tears. "I know, so what am I supposed to do?"

Henrietta laid her manicured hand, so cold and rigid, on Alexis's bare shoulder. When she spoke, her voice was a husky whisper. "What I find helps is to think of something nice, perhaps something from your childhood. If you're somewhere else in your mind you can hardly absorb what's really happening."

Alexis stared into Henrietta's face, trying to read her expression. She kept her face powdered pale and her eyes seemed to be perpetually glazed over, as if she had been living in that fantasy world for a long time and become quite lost there. Would that happen to Alexis if she spent too long here in the castle as one of the King's maidens?

Henrietta parted her lips, drew a breath and then said, "Usually the King doesn't take his maidens on his first night, when he's just met them. He prefers to get to know them first, to speak with them, learn about their background." Her expression darkened. "But if he does wish to take you to his bed, you must oblige him, I make no bones about that."

Alexis thought of Sydney and Courtney down in the dungeons. Were they still hanging by their ankles in chains? This was all for them, and she hoped they appreciated the efforts and sacrifices she was making for their sake.

Henrietta accompanied her through the corridors, the guard following on their heels, still holding his spear, keeping his chin tilted upward, as if an unpleasant smell were coursing up his nostrils. They reached the King's chambers after passing a pair of guards, who checked Alexis for any kind of weapon on her person. She waited patiently, not daring to make a sound, as they patted down her thighs, buttocks and breasts. But inside she was already steaming, knowing that if the King tried the same she would break his arm, right there and then, who cared about the consequences?

Finally, the door covered in burgundy-patterned wallpaper swung open and the familiar figure of Jenson stood in the doorway. He had a smile plastered across his lips and delivered Alexis a mock bow and insincere smile as she passed by him. Alexis glanced back over her shoulder, just as Jenson brought the door shut, to get a final look at Henrietta's face—what she read there was really nothing like sympathy or fear on Alexis's behalf, but, impossibly, envy. Did she want to be in Alexis's position? The thought sickened her.

The King sat up at his desk, scrawling with a feathered quill. A golden crown perched on his forehead and his head bobbed as he wrote. He remained utterly absorbed in his note-taking as Jenson shepherded her onto the edge of the enormous bed, large enough for at least six people—and she wondered whether the King had ever filled it to capacity, after all he counted on five 'willing' maidens.

For another ten minutes the King made no sound other than the scratch of nib against parchment. His hand wobbled about the paper, producing his elegant handwriting, all loops and twists and curls. When he reached the end of the page he paused then scribbled a final note before sliding the parchment off the desk and thrusting it in the air for Jenson to collect.

Jenson took the parchment with a half bow, then rolled it up as he left the room.

The King wore a velvet night robe and a pair of sheepskin slippers. A candle burnt away on the desk, its flame illuminating his profile. He turned on his stool at his desk and looked over Alexis, almost bored. "And what might your name be, my dear?"

Alexis thought about lying, but recalled that she was effectively still his prisoner, only not in the dungeon. "It's Alexis."

He frowned. "And you have a strong accent. Where are you from?"

"The real world, I mean, Earth."

The King nodded his head solemnly, as if they were discussing some lifelong illness. "And that pretender brought you here, I suppose?"

She supposed he meant Courtney. "Yes, that's right."

"You do realise it's most irregular for me to pardon a prisoner in the dungeon—I have never before done it."

She examined the loose skin dangling from his neck, and thought that he reminded her of an iguana. She remembered herself, that she had to be dutiful. "I must offer my thanks. It really was a wonderful act of mercy."

"Yes," the King said, "I suppose it was."

From everything Courtney had told her about the King, the comments filled with barbs and poison, she had been expecting some sort of lecherous monster. But, being here with him, she felt more like she was in the company of a tired, old uncle who had had a tough day at work. Then again, it wouldn't be the first time Courtney had exaggerated something.

The King shifted closer, squinting in the half light. "You have beautiful skin," he said.

She flinched at this remark, but followed it up with a smile, hoping he wouldn't notice. "Thank you, my lord."

He reached out and touched his hand to her face. His skin was dry and flaky, rough like sandpaper. It seemed odd for a king, strange to think that he must've worked with his hands at some point. Then she recalled that he must be something of a swordsman, more active than kings and queens in her world. She considered whether, if he ever became King, Courtney's hands would take on a similar condition. Perhaps he would be killed in battle.

As he broke off contact, she caught a glance at the other side of his face. It was blackened, his eyeball raw and unshielded by its socket. His skin was rubbed down to the bone. A shudder passed through her and she couldn't help but stare.

The King brought his hand up to his cheek, as if in recognition of her attention. He grimaced. "Yes, a most unfortunate accident."

"What . . . what happened?" Alexis said.

The King breathed in deeply and then exhaled, wincing as he did so, holding the afflicted side of his face. "Black magic is a sore on the Land of Ethereal, a parasite eating away at its host."

"I see," Alexis said, still transfixed by the King's face, noticing that a strange purple glow emanated from the wound—as if it were infected with radiation. As far as she knew magic might well be a form of radiation here, in Ethereal, considering it didn't exist on Earth.

The King turned his face away from her, so she couldn't see the wound any longer. "I was moving with my army, through the swamps after retaking land stolen by a group of rebels. The battle had been long and arduous—my Champion was killed—so instead of skirting the Damned Forests, I took the decision to cut through them, to save a three-day journey."

"'The Damned Forests?'"

"An evil place, where magic festers. If I am to have my way, and by the gods I will, the whole place shall be destroyed within the week." He took a deep breath. "Anyway, I led us into the Forests, and we trudged through the trees, staying wary, alert the whole time. And then, out of nowhere, a witch appeared. Before I could raise my sword she hexed me, explained that the right side of my body would waste away so that the left would collapse of its own accord."

Now Alexis noticed the King's right hand poking out from his robe, frail and bony. She met his eye once more. "What happened to her?"

"She fled into the Forests, back to her home. We searched for hours but we were never going to find her. She could simply disappear into the evil of the place. The men were weary from the battle, we had no choice but to return to the castle." He jabbed his finger in the air. "However, now I have hundreds of men tearing the place apart, trying to find that witch, and when they do we shall force her to remedy the curse."

"How will you destroy the Forests?"

"I have a machine which digs the trees out by their roots, then churns them into dust. I would burn them down if it weren't for the witch. I need her alive long enough to fix what she's done, and then I shall oversee her painful death."

Alexis recoiled a little from the mention of pain, knowing that beyond this reasonable, though clearly ill, man, she knew that he had great power and was capable of inflicting great misery—as he was now doing with her friends down in the dungeon.

The King's eyeballs rolled upward in their sockets and he rubbed the pits either side of his nose. "Do you not yearn to return to your own land?"

Alexis was a little caught off guard by the question, that he was changing the subject so willingly, and now that as she had no prepared answer it would be easier to answer honestly. "Yes, my lord."

"We all yearn for our homes. I know that I do." He turned his head slowly to her. "This isn't my home, this *castle* doesn't belong to me, not really."

Alexis's surprise gained pace by the second.

The King continued, "It's my brother's castle, he was the King before me, until he was killed in the Battle of the Twin Rivers."

Alexis's throat felt parched. "Where's your real home?"

"Oh"—he waved his hand toward the curtained window —"somewhere out there, in the mountains, where I lived most of my youth in anonymity, until my brother called me here, told me that I had to accept responsibility."

"Why would he want to share?"

The King stroked his withered right hand with his strong left. "He told me that he needed someone he could rely on in his court, that he was surrounded by backstabbers." He sniffed at the air. "He was paranoid, my brother."

Alexis tried to absorb all she'd heard so far, to work out

whether she really could participate in this conversation. She thought back over everything Henrietta had warned her against saying to the King—but surely this was different, since he had raised the subject himself. She had to know what he really thought of Courtney and she needed to ask now, before the atmosphere changed. "So, your brother never did have a son?"

The King stared at her long and hard, flaring his nostrils. "No."

Alexis took that information on board.

The King continued, "It's okay, I don't blame you. I know that you've been locked up with that imposter for so long he's probably brainwashed you—gods know, I would probably start believing some of the tripe which sprouts from his mouth given the time."

"And you're quite sure that there's no possible way Courtney can be your brother's son, your nephew."

"Impossible."

Alexis got the impression, from the King's tone, that it was time for her to drop the topic. The way the King answered with such resilience, such surety, suggested that there was more to this than he was letting on. But now wasn't the time to pursue the matter.

She glanced round the room, looking for a conversation piece. In the end her attention settled on a large sword which hung from the wall. Every so often its blade caught flickers of candlelight. She did her best to inhabit the id of an Etherealean maiden. "How many men have you slayed with that blade?"

The King looked over at it, as if he needed to see it to answer. "I'd say a hundred or so."

Even if he were exaggerating, if he'd only killed half or

quarter that number, she was still terrified to be in his presence. Never, to her knowledge, had she met someone who had killed another human being.

"Does battle interest you?"

Alexis guessed that an answer along the lines of 'no, not particularly,' wouldn't be suitable in this case, so she said, "Oh, yes, a great deal."

The King gave her an approving nod. "That's good news. Whenever I talk about battle, killing, my other maidens go quite pale, attempt to change the subject. But I can see that you are quite different to them. I suppose your world is a bloodthirsty one?"

"Uh, yes, quite."

"Hmm," the King said, then, "I have a proposal for you, Alexis. In a few days time I'm planning on having a competition to appoint a new Champion. I'd thought of bringing another of my maidens to wait on my arm, but I think that I shall choose you instead. You seem to have the stomach for this kind of thing better than the others."

Alexis recognised the pause a second or two late, almost too late to give him an affirmative answer. But she did manage it in the end. "Yes, that would be lovely."

"I must warn you that it shall be quite bloody. Many men will lose their lives and only one shall be appointed the King's Champion. I would understand if you'd wish not to witness the competition."

Alexis supposed this to be another of those 'right answer, wrong answer' questions. "No, really, it'll be no problem at all."

"Excellent," the King said, stifling a yawn, "then I shall make the preparations, and inform Henrietta that you are to be my maiden at the event." He got to his feet and stooped over Alexis.

Again, she realised a few moments too late that he wanted her to get up too. So she did so. As she stood there confronting him, feeling his stale breath waft over her face—the after-stench of peppered steaks and vinegar—she trembled in expectation.

He bent over her and planted a swift kiss on her forehead, before turning away and getting into his bed. He pulled the sheet up to his chest. "Please don't be offended by the guard outside your bedroom, I promise that I shall relinquish him when it proves to be no longer necessary."

She lingered there, at the foot of the bed, before realising that he had dismissed her, that she could go back to her room— that it wouldn't be necessary for him to lay a finger on her. She skittered to the door, like a giddy dormouse. She tapped on the door, turned back and said, over her shoulder, "Good night, my lord."

"Good night, Alexis. I hope you sleep soundly and well. We shall be seeing much of one another, I am sure."

THE CONTINUED DESECRATION OF THE DAMNED FORESTS

H ORACE LAY on his side in bed, the only one awake in a room filled with sleeping bodies. He tossed off his sheet, tired of trying to drift into sleep. John had been gone for days now, and he knew, in his mind, that he wasn't coming back. He thought back to the day when he had scarpered off and how he had hung back, not gone with him. He had made a joke, hadn't he? Said that John would be back again once he got hungry. He had been so sure that John would return, and now he was almost certain that he was gone forever.

He headed into the kitchen where he smeared some honey onto a chunk of bread, and ate it in silence. His hands shook as he chewed, turning the mulch over in his mouth. They had been a team, him and John, but, more than that, John had been his best friend and he had left him on his own. What if he'd got himself into trouble because of something which Horace might've seen up ahead, coming for them? He would never live with the guilt.

After he'd finished his impromptu snack, he ventured out of Witney Branches and stood at the trunk, lingering at the entrance to their home. He stared out into the Forests, as if he might see John bounding his way back toward them. But of course there was nothing. Only the gentle buzzing of bugs as sunlight crept into the air round him.

He leant back against the trunk and withdrew his pipe from the inside pocket of his jacket. Next he pulled out a small cloth sack, in which he kept dried namtra leaves. He slipped them out and then crushed them in his hand, before depositing them in the end of his pipe. He glanced round to check no one was around.

Technically, at Witney Branches, the use of psychotropics was banned. Whenever Grotesque arrived at Witney Branches they were in a volatile emotional state—having left their families, their jobs, generally having had their lives turned upside down—and so, at the Branches, the administration did its best to protect its own, tried to encourage new members to open up, rather than dull their pain. But sometimes, Horace felt, he needed some namtra. And now was one of those times.

He lit his pipe with a pair of flints and then sucked hard, until the leaves glowed like embers. His mind mellowed as he sucked the smoke into his lungs. He held it inside for as long as he could before releasing, exhaling and then watching the purple-blue smoke rise up into the cool dawn air. He watched it disperse as it reached the first leaves of the trees. He returned the pipe to his lips for another go.

There was a stirring from within Witney Branches and,

before he had time to tuck his pipe out of sight, he saw Susan poking her head out through the door, her nose jutting through her hairy face, sniffing at the air. Her eyes came to rest on him. "Smells like namtra."

No point in hiding it now. He had been caught red-handed. "That's because it is."

Susan was one of the senior members of Witney Branches, only a handful of other Grotesque had been at Witney Branches longer than she. Perhaps now, just to cap off his disgrace and guilt at John having been lost to the Forests, he would be turned out. He would deserve it.

He held the pipe down at his side. Mind blurring from the namtra fumes, the soothing chemicals seeping into his muscles and relaxing his nerves, he found himself saying, "Would you like some?"

Susan wrinkled her nose and examined the pipe. "You shouldn't be smoking that so close by. One of the new recruits might smell it."

"Sorry," Horace said, feeling the crackle of the burning namtra pass through the pipe, into his hand. "I just needed something to take the edge off."

Again, she eyed the pipe. "We all do sometimes."

"You're not angry, then?"

She shook her head. "I'll have breakfast on soon, in about half an hour, so don't get yourself too far gone, will you?" Her voice hardened a touch and she pointed off into the distance. "And go over there a bit. I don't want anyone smelling that stuff near here."

Horace watched her retreat inside and then jabbed his pipe back between his lips and made off for the area of trees which she had indicated. When he reached the area, he sat down, resting his back against a thick tree trunk. From here he could stare upward, into the sky, see the birds flapping back and forth, chirping their little songs, weaving in and out of each other's flight paths.

And then a huge tremor broke off Horace's train of thought. It trembled through the ground, shaking his teeth as they bit down on the stem of his pipe. It held off for a few moments and then was back, more intense than ever.

When Horace tried to stand he fell back down, tripping over his own feet. The pipe slipped out of his mouth and fell, still smouldering, onto the dew-wet ground. He didn't pause to retrieve it, already filling his sight with the door to Witney Branches. He simply had to get back inside, to safety.

About halfway to the door, he halted. He recalled the day that John had disappeared, that there had been the same earthquakes. But they had been much fainter that day, and hadn't returned since his disappearance. This meant that, whatever or whoever it was, was coming closer. And he wondered if those vibrations had something to do with John's disappearance.

Mind still simmering from the namtra, he looked to the door. He could so easily rush back inside, go to breakfast, wait for it to pass as all the other Grotesque must be doing at that moment. These woods were thick with black magic and the solution was almost always to keep out of sight until the weird things passed. Even if it was black magic this might be Horace's chance to redeem himself, to find out what had happened to his best friend.

He lingered a further few seconds before shaking himself out of his indecision, making his mind up that he would follow the sounds of the vibrations, wherever they led him. If it was dangerous then all the better, he deserved some form of punishment for deserting his best friend.

And so he jogged through the woods, his breathing coming thick and hard as the remnants of the namtra smoke lurked in his lungs. He had to keep moving forward, not think about the consequences, or what horror might be awaiting him. That part should come easily, after all he was a Grotesque already, what could a witch or wizard do—hex an eye onto his arse?

As he passed through the trees, daylight flickered through the branches high above, adding to his drug-induced daze. He followed the sound, just keeping his body aimed in the direction of the vibrations, certain that he would reach the source, that he would get to the bottom of what had been going on.

Soon the sound was so thick in his mind that he felt his brain slip from side to side, slopping against the sides of his skull. He paused at a tree, balanced himself against its bark, tried to get his orientation back so that he wouldn't be coming across whatever this thing was blind. Feeling a little more clear-headed, he continued on his way, skirting bushes and keeping his eye peeled for anything odd.

Another few footsteps further on and he stopped dead to stare. Up ahead he made out a shape. It was enormous. There was no way that it could be a being, could it? He slunk closer, his eyes coming more fully into focus.

He made out the large, box-like shape of the object. It was a machine of some sort, all made of metal, glinting in the sunlight. Below, hidden behind the ground-level shrubs, he heard the shouts of encouragement coming from the operators as they lugged it forward. He watched the machine slide forward, on what he supposed to be wheels, and deal a hammer blow to its current target, a towering pine.

As Horace got himself closer to the scene of the destruction he realised, on the horizon, that the entire line of trees had been brought down by this machine. How had they been so naive, allowed this operation to go on for so long? He thought about all the witches and wizards, the enchanted creatures of the Forests. How had they allowed this to happen?

With a final, great big grunt of effort from the men, the machine bucked into the tree and, with a dying quiver of its leaves, the pine fell backward, landing with a brushing *thud*. The group gave a large cheer and the machine moved onto its next target.

And then Horace took his time to count all those involved. He recognised the blue and white of the King, and realised that the King must've sent his entire army to level the Forests. Sure magic was useful, but no way could it compete with manpower of that scale—not unless it were used together, and witches and wizards were solitary beings, if nothing else.

There was a cry from within the group cutting down the trees. Only several precious seconds later did Horace realise that someone had spotted him, that a solider was pointing toward him, and barking orders.

Only then did Horace's legs catch up with his brain, and he obeyed his instinct to run. He bolted through the trees, doing his best to ignore the shouts ringing through his mind. When he looked back over his shoulder he saw five men on horseback chasing after him. Their faces were mean and their swords drawn.

He weaved through the trees, doing his best to throw them

off the trail. After about twenty minutes of aimless sprinting he was sure that he had achieved his goal. When he took stock of the world round him, scanned the horizons, he was sure that he had lost them. Now he had to deliver the news to the hierarchy back at Witney Branches, to let them know that their home was being destroyed at a rate of knots, and that they had to call everyone within the Forests together to fight back against this onslaught. He took a moment to find his bearings and then set off at a run in the direction of Witney Branches, intent on warning the others.

Horace arrived back with barely any air left in his lungs. On top of the namtra the running had really done him in. It had been a long time since he'd had to run from anything—since he'd always had John around to take care of anything that required a physical response. He supposed he'd have to get used to standing up for himself from now on.

He found the door to Witney Branches shut and so he hammered his fists against it and called out to those inside. It seemed like an eternity passed before Susan came to the door. Although her thick hair hid her expression, Horace was sure she was scowling at him.

"Where've you been?" she said, in an unsympathetic tone. "Got yourself lost, did you?"

Horace continued to catch his breath. He waggled his arm back in the direction he had come, back to where the machine was tearing the Forests apart. "They . . . they're tearing it down."

She closed the door a fraction behind her, as if worried that someone inside might overhear them. "What did you say?"

"They have a machine. We have to gather everyone together, everyone in the Forests, and tell them what's going on."

She lingered on the doorstep and it took Horace a while to realise that she was no longer looking at him, wanting him to explain himself further, but she was looking back over his head to the three horsemen gathered there, smirks fixed on their faces, and swords drawn.

Horace felt every muscle in his body tense up as he grasped the gravity of the situation. He looked into their mean, dark eyes and examined the sharpness of their blades. He had led them right to their home. Once again it had been his fault, only this time he hadn't only betrayed one Grotesque, but put their entire community in peril.

A COMPETITOR SLUMBERS

W ITH NOTHING ELSE to do until the tournament, John accepted the offer of the quarters and took to slumbering in his bed during the day, as he wasn't permitted to leave. The first few hours he had spent outside of his cage he had tried his best to find someway to escape the castle, but it had proved impossible. He had faced down his guards and they had waved their spears in his face. Although he could've snapped either one like the proverbial twig, he had no intention of doing so. As he'd spent the time alone thinking the idea of becoming the King's Champion, actually being someone in Ethereal, had appealed to him more and more.

Sure there were the hundreds of other competitors to take care of, but he was steeled by the fact that Frum had shown faith in him. If the General of the King's army believed that John had potential, that he saw no obstacle stopping him from becoming the King's Champion, then who was John to argue. But still there were the nerves, creeping into his mind. And he would like to get an audience with the King so he could follow up the questions about the Damned Forests, perhaps he could make him see his side of things, get him to call off his men, to stop them cutting down trees.

A little later there was a knock at his door, and, so used as he was to the informality of Witney Branches—people coming and going as they pleased—it took John a long time to realise that he had to give whoever was waiting there permission. So he did.

A diminutive black-haired boy with laser blue eyes entered his quarters. He was fully-suited up in armour and had a sword at his belt.

John wondered whether this might be a kind of test, that they were checking to see whether he would knock the boy down, steal his sword and go on some sort of rampage.

Clearly nervous in John's presence, the boy's bottom lip quivered as he spoke. "John Stonefield, I have come to escort you down to the armoury, where you shall be given your first lessons in the arms for your coming participation in the tournament to determine the King's Champion."

Judging from the monotony of the boy's delivery, John assumed he had learnt those lines by heart, been instructed to pass on Frum's exact words. John rose from his bed and headed across the room. He smiled at the boy, who flinched by way of reply. "What's your name?"

"Arnold," he said, before adding, "my father's a knight," as if it were some sort of qualification.

"I see," John said. "And do you want to be a knight yourself one day?"

Arnold's eyes bulged in their sockets. "I *will* be a knight."

John thought about following up this affirmative attitude by explaining the kinds of things knights did within the world of Ethereal, how they crept into the habitats of innocent people and creatures and tore the place to pieces. But he held back. After all, Arnold was only a boy. "Shall we go, then?" John said.

Arnold nodded enthusiastically.

As they descended through the castle, Arnold's previous shyness all but evaporated as he detailed his father's various feats in Ethereal, how he had slain dragons, elves and, he said it with a little foreboding, giants. John took it upon himself to explain to Arnold that he wasn't in fact a giant, and that he was only suffering from a curse put on him by a witch, when he had not been much older than him.

Arnold stopped in the middle of the corridor and scowled up at John. "You mean like what's happened to the King?"

John frowned. "What's happened to the King?"

"As he was on his way back from a fight with some rebels a witch cursed him in the Damned Forests."

Arnold made to venture on, but John snatched him by the sleeve. "What did she do to him?" John said.

Arnold gazed round-eyed at John's enormous fingers gripping tight to his sleeve.

John realised how tightly he held the boy and loosened his grip, apologising.

Arnold's unshakable enthusiasm returned. "She cast a hex on him. It's wasting away the right side of his body."

"And is there no cure?"

"I overheard my father saying that the King's trying to find the witch so she can reverse the spell. But it's difficult because he says she's in the Damned Forests, and she could be hiding anywhere."

Now it all made sense. The King could hardly burn the Forests down, or he might kill the witch doing so, and thus destroy his chances of having her cure him. That explained why they were rooting out every tree, and why the King's army was involved. One single thought struck him and he obsessed on it. Again, he took hold of Arnold's sleeve. "Do you think you could get me a meeting with the King?"

Arnold shook his head, trembling at John's touch. "No."

"Do you know who can?"

This time Arnold wriggled himself out of John's grip, brushed the creases out of his tunic and said, "You know, my mother gets angry when she finds folds in my clothes. If you want to grab me, yank me by the hair or something, okay?" He gave himself another brush down. "If you want to speak to the King then you'll have to win the tournament. He doesn't speak to just anyone."

Yes, more and more that was seeming like it might well be the case.

The armoury remained much as it had been before. The place was empty except for Frum who awaited him, wearing his familiar armour with the purple sheen, his clumpy braids rattling slightly as he moved his head to glance at Arnold. "Thank you for bringing him to me, you may go and play with the other children."

Arnold stood firm. "Aw, can't I stay to watch? It's so boring playing with the kids, all the boys want to do is play with wooden swords and the girls are worse, they want me to play their husbands."

Frum gave a firm shake of the head. "You're not old enough yet. Next year maybe."

Reluctantly, Arnold traipsed out of the room, his hand resting on the hilt of his sword, head bowed as he went.

Once Arnold had left, Frum cracked a grin. "That boy will be an excellent knight someday, just like his father." He turned his attention to John, his smile easing up a little. "John Stonefield, it's time that you were given a different name. The one you have will not do for the tournament."

"What do you suggest?"

"Meat Smasher."

John thought that name over in his mind. "That name sounds a little, I don't know, direct?"

Frum crossed his arms. "Then what do you suggest?"

Over the years, when John had thought about how he might re-invent himself outside of the Forests, that he could go up to the mountains and work as hired muscle, he had always toyed with one name in particular. Now seemed as good a time as any to float it.

He glanced Frum over. "Mountain Crusher."

Frum stuck out his lower lip and tilted his head to either side as he considered. "Yes, that might work. It boasts of your size as well as your force." He broke into a wide grin. "I think it shall be quite appropriate."

Glad to have had his suggestion approved, John took to gazing over the many arms decorating the walls. "What do you suggest that I start with?"

Apparently with his mind still fixed on John's new name, Frum missed the change in subject, only recovering a second or so later. "Oh, uh, yes," he said, looking over the arms. "What you need is something basic, something which exploits your size and power." He strode over to the rack and fumbled a mace on a chain free from its catches. He handed it over to John. "Try this out."

Not really sure what exactly he was meant to do, John weighed the mace in his hand, then gave it a slow trial swing. He nodded. "This'd be okay, I think."

Frum rested his fingers on his chin and shook his head. "No, we can do better. It's too static, too predictable. You're main weakness will be your speed and manoeuvrability. You need a weapon which shall afford you time, a weapon which you can quickly manipulate into a position for a counter attack." He shifted along the row and reached for a large axe. Despite it being taller than him, he held it up without much trouble at all.

John took it off Frum and weighed it. Of course for him it was really no bother swinging it round his head, manipulating it however he wished. Once he'd swung it about a bit he really didn't have much of an idea what to do next. He looked to Frum for prompting.

Frum drew his sword. "Let's see how you spar."

John stood stunned, unable to move his feet, just staring at Frum. He grasped the handle of the axe tighter. "I . . . I don't want to hurt you."

"Don't be ridiculous, do you think I haven't fought with giants before?"

From Frum's stance, John didn't doubt his confidence, in fact he was actually afraid that he might get hurt himself. If he got ruled out of the King's tournament it might be the end of everything for him. He would no longer have the hope of a life outside of the Damned Forests, and no chance of saving them either.

"Come on! Strike me!" Frum said, dodging from side to side.

Seeing that he really wasn't going to get out of this situation other than by indulging Frum, John whipped the axe through the air, narrowly missing one of Frum's braids. He had to give it to him, that Frum really could move quickly when he wanted.

Frum countered, leapt to the side and thrust his sword upward, catching John on his arm.

John groaned in pain and clutched at where he'd been struck.

Frum cackled. "Don't be such a child! That barely nicked you."

John inspected the spot. Indeed, he really only had a light scrape from the sword. His thick skin warded off all but the sharpest cuts and blows—he'd learnt that from falling out of trees, hitting every branch on the way down.

Frum beckoned him forward.

This time John tried harder, actually attempting to make contact with Frum, albeit still only lightly. He swung the axe back and forth, hoping that he might catch the General at some point, but he always seemed to duck out of reach just at the final moment.

Frum stepped inside John's reach and flashed his sword upward, catching John's chest and knocking him back, stunned.

All the wind rushed out of John's lungs and he staggered about, trying to find his feet, to get himself upright again. His axe dropped from his hand and clattered to the floor.

Meanwhile Frum laughed away as he sheathed his axe. "You really have never fought before, have you?"

Still getting his breath back, staring at the axe lying useless a few feet from him, John said, "No. Just like I told you."

"I still think you'll be fine once you've had a bit of practice. We all started out as squires."

John ran his hand over his chest. It felt warm, sticky with blood. "Yeah, but I've got only a few days."

Frum stooped closer, holding his hand on one knee. "What you've got to remember is that, even before you start, you've got the advantage. Your competitor is going to be so focussed on your size, that you're somehow going to 'crush' him"—he grinned —"like so many mountains."

"And what happens when they realise I'm not up to much?"

Frum laughed again—it seemed like he was having a merry old time laughing at John's misfortune. "That's the part you're going to have to work on." He stood up straight, regained something of his general's air. "You'll have access to the armoury every day, I'll see to that, and I'll be on hand if you fancy some sparring. All you can do is practise and do your best."

John rubbed his chest, trying to put pressure on his wound. "Is it really true that there's only one winner—that the rest are all killed?"

"Only the most callow."

John thought that tag probably applied to him. Unlike his competition, he had spent his childhood gathering berries and, at most, killing animals to help feed his family. He had never, ever battled against other human beings, as he would be doing now. At some point he would be called upon to kill, and he had doubts in his mind he would be able to.

Frum sidled up beside him and slapped him on his lower back. "You've got to stay positive, eh? Attitude is half of everything. I'd never have thought to enter you if I didn't think you could win."

If Frum hadn't thought John could win the competition he surely would've just had him executed out in the Damned Forests, to avoid a whole dimension of hassle.

As Frum reached the exit to the armoury, he turned back. "I'm trusting you down here, you know, trusting that you won't run off, try and make a break through the castle."

"I promise I'll stay to go through with the competition."

"I hope you're good to your word, because you may be a large man but I have armed lords who will take you down just as easily as any other. Only difference is you might take more arrows." This time there was no smile from Frum and he proceeded out of the armoury, leaving John alone.

Over the next few days, John went down to the armoury every day where he would take up his axe and head outside to the barracks, where a series of scarecrows were set up for practice. At the end of his first morning session he had scythed every one of them down, and one of the soldiers, quite politely, had suggested that he might like to try something more substantial in future—he had brought him a sack of bricks. John had made noises about blunting the blade, but the soldier had just slipped away, a frightened smile playing out on his lips.

Arnold attended all of John's practice sessions without fail. It seemed that he had acquired a fan. He thought this to be a good thing, since he would need just about all the support he could get if he were to have a chance of winning the tournament. Arnold would shout tips from where he watched, perched on a bale of hay. At first John hadn't paid him any mind whatsoever, thinking it below a competitor to take on the advice of some ragamuffin son of a knight, but when he'd put some words of the advice into practice and seen that, actually, the boy might be onto something. And from that moment on he had appointed Arnold his personal trainer.

As John returned to the armoury after a hard morning's practice, the day before the competition, he noted Frum standing at the other end, bowed over with his head resting on the hilt of his sword. Frum arched an eyebrow at him. "Do you think you're ready to go for another round?"

John felt the sweat dampening his entire body.

Arnold appeared at his side—John had quite forgotten he was there at all. "Yeah! Course he will. He's more than ready."

"Hmm," Frum said, bringing his sword upright in his grip. "I see you've gained an extra head."

Arnold scowled at him. "I'm staying to watch this time."

Frum flashed his eyes. "I can see that much." He waved off to the side of the armoury, at the stone steps which led up into the castle. "Very well, go over there and spectate. You might learn something your father neglected to teach."

Arnold did as he was told.

John, however, really wasn't so sure about the fight. "I have to be careful. I don't want to get injured for the tournament tomorrow."

Frum shrugged. "You'll be fine. I'll go easy on you. I promise."

John still had serious doubts. He glanced up at the hooks for his axe on the wall and made for it. "No, I'd really rather not. It's better that I just get a good night's rest. I think I covered all the basics in training today."

A frostiness entered the air and Frum said, "If you turn me down then I can guarantee that I'll have every last member of your Grotesque bunch brought to this castle and tortured to death noisily below your chamber window."

Blood pumped to John's chest. He turned on Frum, anger seething through him. How dare he make such a threat against his family?

Frum maintained eye contact. "Don't think that you're merely a guest in this castle, another invitee. You're here because I've seen potential in you, seen that you might serve the King. If it appears that you're taking indulgences then I'll have to order for it to be stopped. Because there's one thing we cannot abide by and that's disloyal subjects."

John still lingered at his axe's place. He was fuming, and couldn't account for what he might be capable of with this rage coursing through his veins. He flexed his fingers round the grip, considered Frum and knew he had to face him—he had no doubt that Frum could have him murdered, he had that extra ruthless streak which allowed him to kill without discretion.

John was aware of Arnold's excitement, his rounded eyes, as he took his place ahead of Frum, marked out his patch to defend against the King's General. He squeezed the axe in his hands and stared into his eyes.

Frum bounced off his mark and swung his sword up at John's face.

John sidestepped round the blow and countered him with a

strike of the axe, which Frum stopped dead with his shield over his head.

Frum attempted to chop at John's shins, but John caught him with the hilt of the axe and knocked him back. As Frum regained his balance he shot John a sinister smile. "You've certainly improved since our last fight. But I'm not convinced it will be enough." He sprang forward, trying to cut one of John's arms, but all he caught was the material of his tunic—leaving a jagged tear in the sleeve. "Impressive," Frum said, gathering himself for another strike.

But John was ahead of Frum, thinking the battle through several steps at a time. If only he could back Frum up against the wall then he could force him to surrender. They could dispose of all this nonsense, and he could get round to forgiving Frum for what he'd said—he saw now that it had only been said out of anger. John would have to take more care in knowing his place.

John rolled his wrists and swung the axe at Frum's midriff.

This took Frum by surprise as he had to improvise a dodge backward, toward the wall.

John kept up his forward movements, pushing Frum back further with each swing of his axe. Although Frum had all the talent and technique, John had raw power, and he saw how it inspired fear in his opponent. He kept up his motions until he had Frum backed up against the wall.

John was on the point of asking Frum for his surrender, when Frum flashed his sword back and made for his throat. John brought his axe up to block the strike and then slashed out at Frum, catching him on his forearm.

Frum dropped his sword. It landed on the tiled floor with a metallic *chatter*. Frum's hardened expression, his icy stare, remained unmoving for a long moment, and John thought that he might try to fight him barehanded. And then Frum broke out in a smile and held up his hands. "You certainly have put the work in these past days."

"You're bleeding," John said.

Frum examined the deep cut on his forearm, like an infant's mouth yowling open, spewing crimson blood. He applied pressure to the wound with his other hand and then turned his attention to Arnold. "Boy? Call the surgeon, have him see to this."

Arnold, still transfixed by what he had just witnessed, scuttled back out of the armoury, his light feet skittering away up the stairs.

Frum turned to look at John. He removed his good hand from applying pressure to his cut, wiped it on the side of his tunic and then held it out to John. "No hard feelings about what I said, eh? I was trying to get you riled up. Wanted to see what you might be like with rage burning in your belly."

An echo of the anger racked John. He stared at the offered hand, but kept his hands gripping tight to the handle of his axe. "And did you like what you saw?"

STILL IN THE DUNGEON

S YDNEY TRIED to put his mind to rest, to stop himself
from wildly imagining all the horrible ways in which his life
might be snuffed out. He must've been hanging upside down like
this for days now. He had gone beyond the point of pain and
numbness, and started to feel like his body was changing on him,
that his organs were finding new places within him, perhaps his
lungs would be more at home in his shins, his eyeballs in his
ankles and his heart—well the least said about his heart the
better. He supposed it to be some by-product of his extreme
boredom. His mind was playing tricks on him, entertaining
itself.

Courtney sneezed and then coughed, three times, as always,
each louder than the last.

Sydney squeezed his eyes shut as he noted this piece of minu-
tiae—one of several which he had built up after being in close
proximity with this person for too long. In a way, if he was given

the choice between living out a miserable life down here in the dungeons or being killed, put out of his misery that afternoon in a particularly messy fashion, he was sure he would go with the latter. Life wasn't so much passing him by as slowly smothering him.

Courtney sniffed a little and then said, "Do you want to try and play checkers again?"

Sydney thought of the pitiful grabs Courtney had made for their checkers pebbles the last time he'd suggested they play. He seemed to have ignored the fact that, even if, by some miracle, he did manage to grasp a knuckle full of the pebbles, they were so far apart and immobile that they would have no chance of moving their pieces about an improvised board.

Sydney sighed. "No, I'd rather not."

"What do you think Alexis is up to right now?"

Every time Courtney asked him that question, Sydney had the urge to answer him with some answer along the lines of: 'spreading oil over the King's wrinkly navel' or 'picking lint from between the King's toes,' but there was just no point in winding Courtney up—Sydney would only have to put up with the reaction which followed. So Sydney just settled with an, "I don't know."

Courtney closed his mouth for a few seconds, clearly thinking hard to himself, then he said, "You *are* sure that she still love me?"

"They say that true love never dies."

"That's true, I suppose," Courtney said, then, mercifully, shut up for a while.

Sydney concentrated on breathing deeply and exhaling through his nose, trying to get his wits back. He had resolved that he couldn't stand another minute being with Courtney—being turned upside down and being forced to listen to every inane thought which slipped into his deluded brain. It was enough to turn anyone batty.

Footsteps sounded on the steps leading down into the dungeon.

A flicker of hope warmed Sydney's chest. He turned his attention to the approaching sound. It wasn't time for gruel—his stomach was still churning it over, as if trying to work out exactly which direction it was supposed to send the food.

Jenson, the King's aide, passed through the doorway and stood before them, clasping his hands at his waist. A pair of guards emerged behind him—the same two large guys who Sydney had told the limerick to. He looked over the prisoners, a slight smile curling the corners of his mouth. "How're we getting on down here, then?"

"Perfectly fine, thank you," Courtney said. "Has the pretender relinquished his throne yet?"

Jenson batted his eyelids as if Courtney had just cursed his mother. "I see that this punishment has done nothing to curb your treason."

Courtney's tone lowered a pitch. "The only treason is that I —the rightful King—am down here in the dungeons, while someone else is warming *my* throne with *their* buttocks."

Jenson whipped out a ring of keys and jangled it from his fingers. "So, what you're trying to tell me is that you wouldn't be interested in being turned right side up?"

"No," Courtney said, "in fact I—"

Sydney stirred from his silence. "Shut up, Courtney!" He turned his attention to Jenson and put on his best smile, aware that his yellowed teeth and dirtied face must've made for a real sight. "Yes, I'm ready to go the right side up. I think I've learnt my lesson quite thoroughly."

Jenson's smile widened. He minced toward the bars and toyed with one of the keys—the one which Sydney recognised as the key to their cell. "We never did quite see eye-to-eye in the court, did we, fool?"

"Poet," Sydney said, through gritted teeth.

Jenson waved his hand. "Let's not split hairs." He held his tongue between his lips, clearly enjoying this power, being able to make such a difference to their pitiful lives. "The King has taken quite a shine to your ex-cellmate, in fact he plans to take her to the tournament to determine the new Champion tomorrow."

Courtney writhed against his chains, sending them clanking dully. "If he so much as lays a hand on her then he will answer to my blade."

"What blade would that be?" Jenson said.

"Well, I don't have one right now. But I will! And when I do, I'll keep it sharp so I can slice through the King's neck as easily as scissors cut thread."

Sydney would've kicked Courtney if he could.

Jenson's smile faltered. "Yes, I can see you've still got the passion. That's a good thing, I suppose. At least you're not letting life get you down." His eyes lingered over them. "If it were up to me I would leave you two hanging by your ankles until the day of your deaths, but I've got orders from the King that you're to be made more comfortable. Then again, the King isn't likely to come down here on an impromptu visit so give me one reason why I should comply with his wishes."

Courtney opened his mouth to speak.

Sydney talked over him, knowing that any chance they had of getting themselves more comfortable rested entirely on himself. "Look," Sydney said, "I'm sorry for any misconstrued impression you have of our relationship when we were in the court together, but, please, I'd like to put it behind us and move on. We're not children, we shouldn't dwell on petty squabbles. All I'm asking is that you look into your heart, empathise with our situation, and do the right thing."

"Hmm," Jenson said, twirling the ring of keys round his thumb, then looked off to Courtney. "Does our pretender have anything to add?"

It was clear that Jenson was looking for any reason to not let them out of their current position, and he wanted Courtney to give him the perfect opening. But Sydney was determined that he would get them free—no matter how hard Courtney attempted to keep them in their same position.

Sydney put on his best 'pleading' eyes and said, "You know what they say about good deeds, that they come back to those who commit them. Perhaps it's not entirely the most logical thing to do—to have us made more comfortable—but it would be an act of mercy." He glanced off to Courtney, daring him to open his mouth, then he turned his attention back to Jenson. "We would be forever in your debt, for the rest of our lives."

Jenson narrowed his eyes and looked between them, clearly summing up the situation, trying to work out whether there was any substance to Sydney's words, or if he were just trying to pull the wool over his eyes. Finally, he said, to the guards behind him, "Very well, release the prisoners from their chains." He paused for a moment. "No, don't release them, but have them turned the right way up."

Sydney could've kissed Jenson's feet, but he settled for a piddly, "Thank you, sir, thank you so much."

Jenson gave them a parting sneer and then tossed the keys to one of the guards, who moved toward the cage to open their bindings and reposition them.

Sydney could hardly restrain his utter and total ecstasy at having been turned the right way up. He had never experienced this level of gratitude in his entire life, but, there still remained the nagging reminder that he had to direct his thankfulness to Jenson—that snide, sly old bastard.

The guards stood at their cage, chattering among themselves. There was no game of slapsies today.

Feeling pert, unusually upbeat, Sydney decided to push his luck in addressing the guards. They had struck up something of a rapport beforehand, hadn't they?

Sydney wriggled his toes and waggled his head, enjoying the freedom of movement he possessed in his upright position. "To what do we owe your company this fine afternoon?" he said.

One of the guards, the one who had claimed he was called Clive, glanced over at him. "We're not needed anymore, up in the castle."

"What were you doing up there?"

Clive wrinkled his nose and then stuck an especially thick index finger up his left nostril. "Guarding some giant they brought in from the Damned Forests."

'A giant?' That interested Sydney. "What's the King doing with a giant?"

"Tournament," Clive said, as if that explained everything.

Sydney scowled, putting together the pieces of what Jenson had told them just now. "You mean a tournament to appoint a new King's Champion?"

"Yup."

"But has the King changed the policy? I thought he only accepted humans to the post."

"Nah, he is human, apparently. Something about a witch's curse."

That twigged with Sydney. "You mean to say that he's one of the . . . the Grotesque?"

"Dunno."

Courtney snorted a laugh. "When *I* am King, I'll be damned before letting a Grotesque run about free in my court."

Clive shot Courtney a glare. "Like to see you tell it to this one's face. He's the size of five men, enormous guy. I've got six bits on him winning the whole thing."

For once Sydney considered that Courtney might have a point, the wisdom of letting a Grotesque—one on the scale of a giant at that—run about the castle unescorted smacked of an accident waiting to happen. There could only be one explanation, that the King had something on the Grotesque, was blackmailing him in some way, keeping him on his best behaviour. Come to think of it, it might be a good idea to have someone like that on his side.

"What's his name?" Sydney said.

"Mountain Crusher," Clive said, sniffling back some snot.

And with a name like that, it suggested that this Grotesque

was not one to be messed with. But, and Sydney knew it better than most, nomenclature was often misleading or thrown about willy-nilly without much thought to its consequence. At least it was in King Fredrick's court. No, this all stunk of intervention on the part of someone in the King's court, someone who was trying to build a profile for this character.

"You think he's got a chance of winning, then?" Sydney said.

Clive plucked out a bogey, rolled it between thumb and forefinger and flicked it into a dank corner of the dungeon. "I don't throw money about. You might not quite believe it but working in the King's Royal Guard doesn't make a man rich."

Sydney continued to turn the thought over in his mind, the idea that this Grotesque might be just like them—held as a prisoner. If only he could find a way to get to him, so that they could speak, so Sydney could ascertain whether or not they could strike some sort of a deal. For the first time in a long time, Sydney could see a clean possibility of escape. Sure they had Alexis on the outside, but if Jenson was to be believed, she had already forgotten all about them—thrown herself into her life as one of the King's maidens.

Even if Alexis were working on an escape plan, as he hung there, and she had simply done a marvellous job in convincing the King that she really had come over to his side, it wouldn't hurt to put his mind to a project, so that he didn't go insane from the drawl emanating from Courtney's mouth.

———

As Sydney plotted throughout the rest of the afternoon he noted that Courtney was taking a nap, going over his relentless hoping and dreaming, his own wild plans—gods help them—that he would put into place once he was on the throne. He heard the familiar scuffle of shoes coming down the stairs and, to his dismay, watched Jenson stride into the dungeons once again.

Jenson cast a glare over the sleeping Courtney and then bucked up to the bars, where he wrapped one of his claw-like fingers round the lock. He stared at Sydney with an expression halfway between delight and regret—regret that some especially droll period of his life might be nearing its end.

It all seemed horribly ominous to Sydney, but he did his best to force a smile, so that Jenson wouldn't feel the need to order them back into their upside down positions.

Jenson's eyes finally found Sydney's and when he spoke his words sounded dry and flaky, as if they might crack in the air before they reached his ears. "You're to be executed at the competition tomorrow as part of the centrepiece."

With his news delivered, Jenson gave each of the guards a nod and then pivoted on his heel and slunk back up the staircase and out of sight.

Sydney looked at the sleeping Courtney, his eyelids fluttering and a faint smile on his lips as he dreamt away. He wondered whether he should wake him to deliver the news or let him live on in his fantasy world for a little while longer.

HOT ON THE TRAIL OF THE RABBIT KING

A REAL MEAN CHILL crept its way down Trevor's collar around the early hours of the morning. When he opened an eye, he could make out the sun rising on the horizon, an array of pinks and purples. For a second he had himself utterly convinced that he was really still on Earth, that he had never witnessed the End of Time, and been subsequently sent on a mission to reclaim the children of Gotnot from the Rabbit King. And then he heard a loud snore emanate from Zend.

When the sun rose on them, Plont scrubbed together a fire and got their breakfast cooking—a collection of grains he had collected the night before, which he boiled up in a pan of water. He produced some porcelain bowls and served both Trevor and Zend a portion, before taking one for himself and crouching over it, protectively, half-turned away from them.

Trevor really hadn't been able to put his finger on Plont— unlike Zend he had more or less kept to himself, busying himself with the camp chores: cooking for them, washing out pans in nearby brooks and lighting fires. He hardly uttered a word as he did so. His quick eyes were the only aspect of his character which broke the impression that he was a statue. They scurried about in their sockets, scanning the terrain, sometimes lingering on a tree branch, a bird singing, or looking off into the tall grasses to where a rabbit sniffed about.

After the conversation with Zend, in which Zend had revealed his mistrust for his mayor, and already called into question Trevor's qualifications as hero, Trevor had tried his best to stay out of the matters—not participating in the mostly one-way conversations, on Zend's part of course, between the other two about their best route and what might lurk up ahead. In any case, Zend was totally right. Trevor had no qualifications to be a hero. He was a square peg in a round hole.

They broke camp after they had eaten, keeping up the same relentless pace from the day before. Trevor found that rather than sleep having cured his various aches and pains, it had actually exacerbated them, and a shrill tweak passed up his spine, threating to transform into a spasm. He had no intention of sharing this information with either Plont or Zend. He was enough of a burden as it was. He would just suck it up and get on with the task at hand.

The path wound its way into deeper and deeper grasses, until Trevor spotted the commencement of trees up ahead, which he supposed to be the start of the Damned Forests, where they were headed. As he'd eavesdropped on Plont and Zend's conversations—or, really, Zend's lectures—he had established the fact that Zend was somewhat hesitant about heading inside. For someone who was quick to deride his mayor for his belief in hocus pocus, he sounded apprehensive about the stories of witches and wizards: hexes and spells, flying about.

They paced on in silence until the trees towered over their heads and the leaves grew so thick that they blocked out the sun, throwing a—not unwelcome—shade over them. Trevor had no idea what Zend had been so worried about. To him these 'damned' forests looked just like any other nature walk he'd ever been on.

He noticed Plont slip his bow off his shoulder and fit an arrow, his watchful eyes already shimmying around their perimeter, ready to take anything down. Meanwhile, Zend unsheathed his enormous broad sword and held it in a double-handed grip out in front of him. They slowed down as they continued into the Forests, partially due to the undergrowth snatching at their boots and partially because of the eerie quiet. The only sound was the crunching of their footfalls over the dead leaves which carpeted the floor.

Against all odds, it was Trevor that spotted the first sign of life. He spotted a bearlike face staring at them through the leaves and almost called out in fright. It was enormous. Although he'd never in his life seen a bear up close, this one, he wagered, was at least four times the size of a normal one. He managed to get himself under control and give Zend a firm, but sure, tap on the shoulder to alert him to the danger.

Plont aimed his bow at the bushes. Zend readied his sword and widened his eyes, ready to strike. Trevor just watched on, caught between the reactions of his companions and this gigantic bear staring at them, looking mean and ready to attack at a moment's notice. So it was a little unnerving when Zend let out a long, smooth chuckle and lowered his sword.

At first Trevor thought Zend had gone mad, lost his mind in the face of such insurmountable danger. Trevor felt for his own sword, still snuggly strapped to his back, and knew that there was no way he could step in. The beast would make dog meat of him, of them all. His voice shook as he spoke. "Why don't you attack him?"

Zend sheathed his sword. "That's a blood bear."

"A blood bear?" Trevor said, feeling the remainder of blood leave his cheeks.

"Yes."

"Then why in hell's name aren't you taking care of it?"

Zend gestured to Plont, who had already lowered his bow.

Plont stalked through the bushy undergrowth, over to where the blood bear stared at them hungrily. He got within a few feet of the bear and then leapt forward, flailing his arms and shouting, "Boo!"

The blood bear groaned, dropped to all fours and then slunk off into the bushes at a trot.

As Plont returned to them, smiling away, Trevor could only gawp. He managed to summon the energy to speak. "How . . . how did you know—"

Like always, Zend stepped in, to answer in Plont's place. "Common knowledge round here. I know they look menacing, but blood bears are just harmless foragers: eat roots, mushrooms, that sort of thing."

"Then why do you call them blood bears?"

Zend shrugged. "I dunno, I don't make the rules."

Trevor glanced back at the bushes into which the blood bear had disappeared. He wasn't convinced that it wouldn't perform a U-turn and come back at them, teeth bared and claws swiping.

He tried to get his trembles under control. "Is there anything that I should be watching out for?" Trevor said.

"Honey boars," Zend said. "Those are the ones that'll get you killed." He headed on, into the trees, making a show of picking up his feet to avoid the undergrowth. "Let us know if you see any of those."

"What do they look like?"

Zend held his hand at about his shin. "This high, vicious little blighters. Pointy teeth. Once they get a bite of your leg that's the last thing you'll know."

Needless to say, for the rest of the day's trek, Trevor tripped over his own feet countless times, trying to stay alert to any sign of honey boars.

They only made camp once it was impossible to see their own hands in front of their faces. The pain worming its way over every crevice of Trevor's body was intolerable. He had a crick in his neck, back spasms around the base of his spine and, just to round off the set of maladies, blistered feet. He was impossibly glad when, from somewhere in his pack, Plont produced three hammocks, which he set about hanging from nearby trees. His body being in the state it was, though, he had to ask Zend for a leg up.

Trevor lay in his hammock, swinging gently from side to side, and staring up at the space in the forest canopy, at the twinkling stars in the wispy grey-black night sky. He thought about whether it was an entire other universe up there. If there were countless other planets, stars, galaxies, like in his own world. Or was Earth up there too? Were they part of the same plane of reality? He suspected that work-for-hire heroes Plont and Zend weren't quite the people to ask.

That night they ate some pork off a pig Plont shot as it came too close to their camp. Trevor had to admit that he was impressed with Plont and Zend's self-sufficiency. He thought they could teach young people back in his world a thing or two.

When they bedded down, Trevor struggled for a long time with his hammock, trying to get himself into a comfortable position. No matter how he orientated himself, he would find himself aching soon after and have to rethink. Sometime into the night Trevor drifted off, he guessed it was more down to his overwhelming fatigue than having found the hammock's sweet spot.

In the morning Plont treated them to another of his breakfast spectaculars and they headed out on the trail, looking for the Rabbit King.

After several hours of hiking, Zend brought them to a halt, holding up his hand and waggling his sword around. Trevor glanced back to Plont, looking to gauge the seriousness of whatever situation was about the befall them, but, like always, Plont's features gave nothing away—he remained stoic as he fitted an arrow into the notch of his bow.

From below his feet Trevor sensed what he supposed Zend had also sensed, and the reason that he had brought their procession to a stop. It was a faint vibration, a moving of the earth. It reminded Trevor of some kind of an earthquake. He looked to the other two for answers, but both of them only tilted their heads back, listening intently.

Trevor's heart rapped in his eardrums. He hated suspense,

always had, and this, being thoroughly out of his comfort zone, topped just about every suspenseful situation he had been involved in. He wanted Zend or Plont to break out into laughter, as they had with the blood bear, but they remained utterly still, focussed. This time it was serious.

Zend broke out of suspended animation first. He lurched forward, breaking into a trot, as he carried on, apparently in the direction of the noise. Only when Plont laid his hand on Trevor's shoulder, did he think to follow.

It was hard to keep up and, several times, Trevor thought he might slip and crack a hip, or, equally, that he might give himself a heart attack. He recalled going to a medical appointment recently when the doctor had advised him that he had high blood pressure, given him a new salt-free diet and generally instructed him to take up a healthier lifestyle, 'get into the Great Outdoors, perhaps.' He wondered if the doctor had bargained for the fact that the 'Great Outdoors' might kill him.

Zend finally came to a stop when he emerged into a clearing up ahead. Just in time too. Trevor had a prickling sensation up his left side, working its way over his chest. However, despite his ailing health, he tried his best not to make a spectacle of himself —not to double over huffing and puffing. It appeared that the situation demanded a certain degree of stealth, from the way Zend was hiding himself behind a tree and peaking out on the scene down below.

Trevor dared take a look himself after he'd observed Zend for several minutes, with frown lines sketched on his forehead. He held himself as well as he could, keeping his body concealed behind the thick tree trunk.

The valley below had been cleared. Overturned trees, yanked

up by their roots, dotted the landscape for miles and miles. A large, metal machine glinted in the sunlight which now beamed down on the naked earth. Several people crowded round the machine and seemed to be rolling it forward. They bucked it up to another tree, where it rocked back a few times before ploughing into the trunk, knocking it down in a single, smooth action. The tree fell with a wailing *creak*, its roots rustling out, sprinkling a veil of dirt as they came.

Trevor backed away then exchanged glances with Zend. "Gosh, what's happening here?"

"I don't know," Zend said, then looked back to Plont, who looked just as bereft of ideas.

"What do we do now?" Trevor said, half-hoping this might be a deal breaker, and they might turn right round and go back to Gotnot, where they'd be celebrated for their good, honest try at locating the Rabbit King. Alas that wasn't to be the case.

Zend scowled. "We will have to go round them."

Before Trevor got a chance to put in his own opinion, they were off and moving through the forest once more, and Trevor was back to raking in air only to puff it back out.

Zend remained focussed as he guided them round the perimeter of the tree-clearing area. A few times he had no choice but to bring them closer to blowing their cover, where the foliage got too thick to pass through. Trevor just felt the sweat drip down his forehead and his muscles screech in pain, and wished for them to come across somewhere they might make up a decent camp for the night.

The noise and vibrations emanating from the machine got quieter as they left the tree-choppers behind. Trevor allowed himself to relax somewhat, telling himself it was no good getting himself het up about whatever it was they were doing. After all, these forests belonged to the people of Ethereal, Trevor was nothing more than an inter-dimensional alien so he left it at that.

When the vibrations and shouts from the men totally slipped out of earshot, Trevor began to miss them, his mind already running wild with imaginings surrounding the various croaks and growls which came from all sides. He kept telling himself that he was being escorted by two very capable, very serious young men. But hadn't Zend intimated that they'd be better off without Trevor on this quest? What would happen if he got himself caught up in trouble? Were Plont and Zend likely to just let whatever took him carry him away, then declare him to be collateral damage when they returned to Gotnot? It really didn't bear thinking about but, all the same, he kept himself as close as possible to Zend's heels, basing his theory on the principle that whatever took him would take Zend too—that Plont would need to rescue the both of them.

As night set in, and Trevor assured himself that they would be stopping soon, Plont raised his hand and brought them all to a halt. Trevor sidled up beside him and followed his stare.

There was a single, white bunny rabbit gnawing away at a bright-green blade of grass. It had the pink eyes and the way it wrinkled up its nose would've brought out an 'aw' from Trevor if it weren't for his complete exhaustion. All he could muster was some bitter thought about how rabbits never had the sorts of problems he'd been having recently.

He turned his attention to Zend, wondering whether he was waiting for Plont to shoot it with his bow. Despite how cute this rabbit looked to Trevor he would have no qualms about seeing it on the sharp end of a pointed stick, roasting over the fire that night. He had built up a hefty appetite over the course of the day.

Rather than gesture for Plont to shoot the bunny, Zend held up his finger for silence—as if there weren't already total quiet around them—and he tiptoed toward the bunny, eyes fixed on it, as if it might be about to lay a golden egg.

Trevor leant into Plont and whispered, "Is he really going to take it with his bare hands?"

Plont gave him a muted grunt, which could've been read as either a 'no' or a 'yes.'

Trevor didn't press him any further.

Zend got within a matter of inches from the bunny and then, all of a sudden, snatched at it. He caught it by its ears and held it up for his own, Trevor thought, smug inspection. He dangled it in the direction of his spectators and managed a grin—the first Trevor could recall having seen on his face.

Zend brought the rabbit over to them, while it squirmed in his grip, squeezing its pink eyes shut and kicking frantically with its legs. He spoke with Plont in their local dialect. When Zend made to lead them on, still grasping the struggling rabbit, without offering an explanation, Trevor had to take exception.

"I don't know a lot about hunting," Trevor said. "But shouldn't you put the poor thing out of its misery rather than let it suffer like that, worried about what's going to happen in its immediate future. I mean, if I were going to end up in a boiling pot of water I'd rather be dead first."

Whatever trace of a smile that had marked Zend's lips disintegrated, and his familiar, sneering lips made a reappearance. "We're not going to eat the rabbit," he said, his tone akin to that of a bully mocking a weedy kid in a playground. "It's going to lead us right to Rabbit King's lair."

"Ah, right," Trevor said. "Obviously."

Preparing the rabbit for its leadership duties involved Plont stomping through the undergrowth and tearing off some branches and hard bark from a nearby tree. With extreme speed and skill, he fashioned a harness and lead, which he tied round the rabbit's skinny frame, before handing it over to Zend, who thanked him in their dialect.

Trevor watched the whole episode pass thinking to himself that they apparently weren't going to stop for the night, fry up some food and get some rest. Sometimes he wondered where young people got all their energy from.

They marched onward into the night, not bothering to stop for so much as a handful of berries. Trevor tried to gauge whether Plont might be tiring at all, that they might somehow be able to affect a change of heart in Zend—allow him to see that they should take a little break before so bravely tramping on into the Rabbit King's headquarters. But there was no chance of that. Plont remained as resolute and stoic as ever. He would've been an excellent bridge partner.

The rabbit made several bids for freedom early doors but calmed down after twenty minutes or so, after he'd tired himself out trying to bustle off into various hedgerows. To tell the truth, he became somewhat domesticated, hopping along in what seemed an organised and determined way. Perhaps they weren't the first he had led to the Rabbit King's den, and so he knew the drill.

They kept on padding through the Forests, out into a more exposed patch, with a large glade opening out before them, high grass towering above their heads, all set in stunning yellow moonlight. It was nice to get out into the open for a bit. Being underneath the trees the whole time bred a sense of claustrophobia. Out here, it felt that, if there were an attack coming, Trevor would spot it straight away—and be able to promptly inform either Plont or Zend.

The rabbit led them out into the glade.

Trevor had to take care avoiding, well, rabbit holes. It was easier said than done, considering that he couldn't see in front of him, let alone his feet. He tripped a fair few times, only prevented from landing flat on his face by the sure support of Plont. Maybe he had been too hasty in his judgement of them. Why would they go to all the trouble of bringing him this far when they might've slit his throat a mile from Gotnot, had they been that way inclined?

The rabbit bounded onward, slowing its pace until it came to a stop at a seemingly innocuous patch of land, at least it was just as hidden by the tall grasses as the rest of the glade. He looked on as Plont and Zend stared down at the rabbit, then Zend looked back at Trevor and said, "This is it, the entrance to Rabbit King's lair. You wait here."

Trevor considered the command, took one look round the quiet glade, thought a second about the honey boars, then said, "And get eaten?"

"Preferably," Zend said.

"I refuse."

Zend sighed then exchanged glances with Plont. He made no further comment to Trevor, but Trevor assumed that he was back in the advance party. Zend bent over and tugged at something unseen below their feet. With a masculine grumble, he pitched off a large rock, hurling it into the middle-distance.

Trevor supposed that, with muscles like that, Zend hardly needed a personality at all. He could get away with treating people however he wanted.

Zend disappeared from view and Plont followed.

Trevor glanced back over the glade, heard a howl in the distance and then bobbed down after them. He found a large hole in the grass and felt for its sides. It seemed just about big enough for him to pass through. He had some second thoughts before he felt a tug at his trouser leg and found himself slipping down a sheer, muddy slope.

He continued unchecked down the seemingly unending slide, until it ended. He landed with a soft *wallop* and scrabbled to his feet. It smelled very earthy and was pitch black, unsurprisingly considering it was a rabbit hole. He got the horrible feeling that something ominous was about to happen.

There was the faint *thump-thump* of the rabbit desperately beating its back legs, clearly trying to break free from wherever Zend clung onto its lead.

Just as Trevor was about to ask the other two what was going on exactly, he heard the unmistakable whisper of a flame creeping into life. As the light steadied itself a large thing stood over them, staring. It took Trevor a couple of moments to realise that it was a person, or it *had* been a person, for the man's whole body, everything except his face, was covered in white fur, and two felt ears sprouted from the top of his head.

Rabbit King, Trevor presumed.

And then he noted that both Zend and Plont had already passed out at the Rabbit King's feet, and then, a second later, noted the club in the Rabbit King's hand / paw. His final observation was the club swinging back and landing right on his noggin.

BLOOD, GUTS AND LIPSTICK

A LEXIS SPENT most of the time leading up to the competition doing her best to get medieval make up to stick to her face. It seemed that as soon as she applied some powder to her cheeks or applied some of the red-orange slime, that passed for lipstick, onto her lips it and her skin would go their separate ways in a matter of minutes. If this competition was anything as bloodthirsty and tense as the King insinuated, then she'd need all the support she could get from her cosmetics. Just to make matters worse there was a knock at the door.

She toyed with the idea of telling them to shove off but decided, in her role as the King's currently-preferred maiden, she should be doing her best to act civilly, lest he change his mind and decide to have her head after all. So she asked whoever was there in.

It was the well-endowed girl with the red hair and freckles. She shot Alexis a smile as she rounded the door, closing it behind her. She stared at her bare toes and paced her way up toward her, as if whatever she was doing in Alexis's bedroom had some taboo element to it—as if they were girls in a boarding school and the girl didn't want to get caught out of bed by the matron.

"Hello," Alexis said, trying not to transmit her frantic heartbeat, to let this girl know that she was truly terrified of what she might be about to experience with the King.

The girl uncurled her limbs, like a cat, and reached Alexis. She laid her hands on her shoulders and stared into her eyes. Alexis had no choice but to reflect on the girl's emerald-green irises. "How're you getting on? Henrietta sent me to give you some moral support. You must be quivering yourself to death, poor thing."

Hiding her fear, Alexis said, "Actually, I'm doing fine. It's this make up which is doing my head in, to be honest."

She batted her hand and flashed her eyebrows. "Oh, you're not using any of the tricks, are you?"

"Tricks?"

"Candlewax, love, it's all in the candlewax. Keeps everything together."

Before Alexis could make some sort of a challenge to this simple solution, the girl was skipping her way across the bedroom, her breasts jiggling against her tightly-wrapped bodice. When she returned she bore a burning candle and a metal dish. She poured the wax into the dish and then thrust it at Alexis. "Take it, then," she said.

Alexis did as she was told, accepting the metal dish. She stared down into the gloop of hot wax and then back at the girl. "Uh, what am I supposed to do with this?"

The girl rolled her eyes. "The lipstick. You've got to mix it up with the lipstick."

Alexis reconsidered the red-orange slime and then brought it down to the dish of wax. Under the girl's watchful gaze, she dunked it into the slime and then smoothed it along her lips. Finish, she put the lipstick down and looked at herself in the mirror. The candlewax went unnoticed, but the real test would be whether or not it stuck.

The girl drummed her fingers on Alexis's dressing table, making the mirror jiggle a little. "You haven't asked my name yet."

"What's your name?" Alexis said, pouting into the mirror, testing out the lipstick's resolve.

"Cherry."

Alexis took in the girl's physique once more, her flame-red hair. The name fit.

"You haven't been very sociable with us other girls since you got here."

"No, sorry," Alexis said. "It's all been a bit of a blur."

Cherry nodded in understanding. "Yes, it's always difficult when you first get here. King can't keep his hands off you, you think that you've been sent to heaven, gods be praised." Her look hardened. "But bear in mind that it won't last. Sooner or later you'll be just like the rest of us, until . . ."

Alexis took in the hollow silence and then found she could no longer manage the not knowing, equally realising, at the same time, that she was falling right into Cherry's trap. "Until what?"

"Until he gets bored," she said, grinning smugly.

Alexis studied Cherry's expression in the mirror, judging whether or not she truly meant real malice or she was simply stating the facts. This whole act, her coming into her room, her chirpy, friendly tone, put Alexis on edge. "What happened to the last girl who had this room?"

Cherry pursed her lips, forming an 'oh' shape. "Just got too old for all this. I suppose that you caught the King's eye and he decided enough was enough."

"Where did she go?"

Cherry jerked her thumb over her shoulder. "Down to the barracks. First she'll be passed round the officers, then the soldiers, finally, when she really hits rock-bottom, they'll turn her out to the stable boys and hired hands, let them have a go with her."

Alexis's stomach tightened. "That's the most revolting thing I've ever heard."

"That's life, my love."

Another question burnt through Alexis's mind and she felt it might effectively end Cherry's nice streak with her, show up her true colours and get her out of her hair so she could get on with preparing herself for the competition. "Aren't you worried that he'll turn you out, just like her, when your time comes?"

Cherry let loose a cackle and slapped Alexis's cheek lightly. Her birdlike eyes twitched over Alexis's features. "Oh no, I'm his favourite, see? Doesn't matter how many come and go, the latest trends, I always end up creeping back into his affections." She crushed her lips together so they were no more than a pale pink line of flesh. "He *loves* me, I know it. He'll be long dead before he ever gets an inkling to throw me out. And even then, when his successor arrives, I'm as good as lined up for Henrietta's job."

Now Alexis believed she was beginning to see the central

reason why Cherry had come to her bedchamber. She wanted to warn Alexis off her territory, to tell her to watch her back.

Cherry traced her finger along Alexis's collarbone. Her touch brought goose bumps to the surface of her skin. "It is a shame, though, that he's got himself so set on you for the moment. I do love a good Champion's competition. All that sweat and blood dampening those muscles, it's enough to raise the dead, I can tell you."

Alexis thought she might see the connection between the King and Cherry already—she wondered about what he'd said about his other maidens 'not having the stomach' for the competition, and presumed that he had taken Cherry's glassy-eyed stare for one of terror, rather one of enchantment.

Cherry picked out an especially smooth section of skin at Alexis's neck with her fingernail and dug it in.

Alexis was so taken off guard by the action, that she had hardly time to squeal in pain before it was over, and Cherry had whipped her hand back.

With a sly smile, she stepped back across the room, lingered at the door, and then, with a flick of her red locks, disappeared out into the corridor.

Alexis rushed to the bathroom to pour cold water over the wound at her collar.

Henrietta arrived to escort Alexis to the Royal Box about half an hour later. Alexis was burning to ask her about Cherry, to get some of her history, to try and understand exactly what she was in the middle of here, but she was so apprehensive both about

the spectacle she was about to witness and the King's expectations of her afterward in his bedchamber, that she neglected to
mention it. And Henrietta was hardly in the mood for listening
to her pour out anything and everything on her mind, her cheeks
were flushed and she made sudden movements, plucking off bits
of lint or fluff which had become stuck to her frock. It seemed
she had quite a stake in how Alexis turned herself out for this
competition.

The corridors, too, were bustling with activity, courtiers
rushing this way and that, some carried covered silver trays while
others bore casks of wine. A band of strings played down in the
courtyard, their upbeat melodies wafting up through the castle.
Alexis just clung onto Henrietta's hand and tried not to get lost
in the hurry.

Jenson waved them through into the King's day quarters, a
large and well-lit room, with windows surrounding it on all sides.
Alexis could make out the King's silhouette on the balcony as he
sat with his back to her, gazing downward at the entertainment.
He sensed her footsteps approaching and twirled on his seat,
giving her a wide smile from the good side of his face. She
observed that he wore a veil to hide the wasting right side.

"Wonderful to see you, my dear," he said, helping her down
onto the seat beside him. "You really become more lovely with
the days." He peered at her lips. "And that lipstick, most
unusual, wherever did you find it?"

Alexis felt her heart flutter in her chest. "Oh, I just amongst
the cosmetics in the drawer."

"Yes, it reminds me of . . . reminds me . . ."

She thought of asking him to follow up, but, she realised
that, in all likelihood, the lipstick, all the make up she was using,

had once belonged to the girl who had been cast out, thrown away like an unwanted cut of meat to the dogs.

The King seemed to have forgotten all at once, as his attention was now drawn to the line of people emerging from one of the many lower doors of the castle. When he leant into her, his breath smelled rotten, although he had obviously attempted to cover it with a lemony scent—and she knew it must be the witch's disease. How long did he have?

The King pointed out over the lip of the balcony. "Those are the competitors. All of them have come from all across the Kingdom of Ethereal to put their lives on the line for the honour of being called my Champion."

"How wonderful," Alexis said, hoping the King wouldn't pick up on her barely disguised sarcasm.

"For all the ill I've committed throughout the Kingdom, the blood spilled, the rebellions put down, I am content that I have brought great happiness to some people, and I believe that's all that is."

A smile twitched on Alexis's lips. "You can't please everyone all the time."

The King nodded. "How noble, said like a true monarch."

Alexis hooked her hands over the lip of the balcony and saw the wooden stalls, packed with people. She wondered whether they would ask questions as to who this woman was sitting beside the King in the Royal Box, but, she supposed, that was really something the King himself would have to worry about for himself.

She took in those passing below, the men, all dressed in blue and white, which, she'd established over her time in the castle, were the King's colours. They just kept on pouring out through the gate, into the courtyard, waving their banners as the crowd cheered away. All of them wore smiles and she knew that the King was right—that whatever she thought about monarchy, the people really did adore him.

As the competitors continued to file out, she picked out one of the figures among them. It was an enormous man, towering head and shoulders, and waist, over the rest. She turned to the King. "Who's that, down there?"

"Oh, he's a Grotesque we captured in the Damned Forests. One of my lords thought he might make a good fighter, so they brought him here to participate in the competition."

Alexis took in the man's enormous muscles and the giant shadow he cast on the competitors behind him. "Will it be fair him fighting against the others? Surely he'll just crush them all?"

The King chuckled. "Who said anything about fairness, here, eh? The whole point of this competition is for me to handpick the strongest of the strong. I'm not looking for a decent spectacle, I'm looking for a decent appointment."

Alexis took his point, but thought, if that were the case, why he couldn't just award the huge man the title of King's Champion and avoid the bloodshed. She supposed that here, in Ethereal, the ability to spill blood went a long way and so must be proven.

Under the orders of a mounted rider, the competitors lined up and held their flags aloft. When they were all in place, looking neat in their rows, the mounted man raised his hand upward and pointed off toward the Royal Box.

"That's the General, Frum, on the horse. Good man."

Alexis felt the weight of all those eyes on her. Not just of the competitors, but the spectators too.

The whole arena fell into a profound hush and the King rose from his seat and tilted his head back to address his people. "Thank you for gathering here today for this afternoon of sport. I hope the competition shall please you and bring me a ferocious and loyal warrior, of whom the entire Kingdom can be proud." His eyes wandered over the gathered people. "And we pray to the gods above us, that they may guide whoever is to be my future Champion and to keep him noble, and to see him through the battles on light wings."

The King returned to his seat and, almost instantly, the crowd roared in reply to his address, while the warriors broke apart and rushed to the edges of the arena to collect their waiting weapons.

Alexis remained captivated by the whole spectacle, her pulse rapping away with anticipation. She watched the competitors take their weapons, the large man seize hold of an axe.

Down below, General Frum stared up at the King. When the King nodded in reply, the rider brought a trumpet to his lips and blew a long, flat note. As if it held them by a string, the competitors rushed into action, bearing their weapons.

The King rose once more from his chair and brushed his fingertips along Alexis's shoulder. "Come, my dear, the preliminary rounds are never all that interesting. We must wait a few hours yet before the fight begins to reach any conclusion."

With one eye still firmly glued to the action unravelling below, she followed the King into his chamber, the scene outside only becoming obscured when Jenson—who had been standing silently by all this time—drew the netted curtain for their privacy.

Outside swords clanged and ravished cries burst out. It was strange to be in this placid room while so much violence went on a matter of feet beneath them. But it didn't seem to much affect the King, indeed he seemed almost bored by it.

The King winced as he sat himself down on the bed. He had to tug his right leg up onto the mattress.

Alexis told herself to forget about what was happening outside, the lives being lost, she could do nothing for them. She hovered at the King's side. "Have they had any luck in finding the witch?" she said.

The King slipped another few pillows beneath his back, to make himself comfortable. "No, nothing." He grimaced as he dragged himself back a few inches. "They've destroyed more than half the place and found nothing." He patted the mattress. "Lie with me, my dear. Please."

Alexis remembered her place, that she was meant to be a maiden. She took up the spot he had indicated, but stopped short of reclining completely. She felt too on edge to lie down.

The King gazed at her with his pale blue eyes. His lips on the left side of his face were cracked, on the right side of his face they were scar tissue. He reached out for her and stroked her forearm, skirting her fair downy hair. "You are quite different. You've come from another world entirely."

"Yes, sire."

"Remarkable, truly remarkable."

She followed his touch with her eyes. "Am I the first person you've ever met from Earth?"

He chortled, his throat rattling with phlegm. "Gods no!

You're not even the first *woman* I've met from Earth." He stared off toward his balcony, as if he had only just recalled the subjects destroying themselves so willingly in his name. "But there's certainly something about you. You are really quite *different*."

Alexis wasn't quite sure if she should take this as a compliment.

His hand wandered up her arm, to the delicate skin surrounding her armpit and then to her neck, where it rested and stroked away.

All this mild petting made her think she'd swapped bodies with a cat—not that she was complaining. Better to have all this stroking than to have to defile herself.

When he reached the cut Cherry had inflicted on her, he paused. "What have you done to yourself here, my sweet?"

Unconsciously, Alexis's hand met his at her neck. She passed her fingers over his, feeling the cut for herself. "Oh, that, nothing. I just . . . just caught myself with my fingernail, while I was bathing."

"Ah," the King said, his fingers still exploring the mark. "Then it wasn't Cherry who did this?"

Her mind spun. How could he possibly know that? And then she recalled that he was the King and she was a prisoner on parole. He had her bedroom monitored twenty-four hours a day.

The King's fingers left the mark and turned their attention to her hair. "Cherry gets so jealous when there's a new maiden around, feels that her position is threatened."

Alexis told herself to hold back, but she just couldn't. When she spoke she surprised even herself with her snappy tone. "So it's true, then?" she said. "That Cherry is your favourite?"

The King lopped his head back gently and snickered. "I don't play favourites, but I have had some of my maidens for many years and I've grown . . . attached to them."

Alexis attempted to reel herself in, tell herself that she was getting herself upset about a king's affections that she didn't even want. She was only using him as a means to an end, to free her friends from the dungeon and then, eventually, to free herself from the castle and get back to Earth. This time she managed to stay quiet.

The King drifted off into a doze.

Alexis thought of going over to the balcony, to look out over the arena and to see the blood and guts, but every time she cooked up the courage, she failed to rise at the final moment. In any case, the King still held her fingers intertwined with his.

Only when Jenson appeared out of thin air and summoned the King, did he stir.

The King blinked away the sleep, carrying that familiar expression of someone confused, trying to put themselves back together again, to work out what was dream and what was real. He allowed Jenson and Alexis to help him over to the balcony and back down into his chair.

Alexis got her first look of the carnage when she took up her own seat. She felt bile sting the back of her throat and her heart rattle in her ribcage.

THE HEAT OF BATTLE GETS A TOUCH TOO HOT

CRUMPLED BODIES drenched in blood. Faces contorted in agony. Limbs flailing out at odd angles, missing bits and pieces—fingers and thumbs dotted about amongst the dusty ground. John stood in the midst of it all, chest heaving, sweat soaking his entire body, clutching his axe.

He had avoided any actual fighting yet. Whenever a warrior would catch his eye, they would quickly move away, pretend not to have seen him at all. At one point, a competitor had backed into him, glanced up at him, and apologised as he bounded away to find a more levelled fight. So here he was, playing an odd sort of waiting game knowing that—logistically speaking—he would have to fight at some point.

He did his best to conserve energy, while casting his eyes round him to check no one would attempt to sneak up on him and jab him in the back. He watched on as the last dozen or so warriors fought among themselves, each of them dying in turn, until one prevailed. After looking round the arena, John established that only the two of them remained.

John picked out the crowd over the warrior's shoulder. Arnold sat on the front row, balling his fists, swept up in a mixture of excitement and fear, willing John to fulfil all those heroic expectations he'd laid out for him.

The remaining warrior was dressed all in black. He wore a shawl which covered his entire face, leaving only his eyes exposed. He grasped a sword which took on a green glint in the sunlight, at least where it wasn't covered in blood. His rugged complexion, diminutive posture and style of dress marked him out as one of the people of the Death Valleys: a Narbut.

Nerves jangled through John's arms and the axe slipped a little in his grip. He had to pull himself together and take down his adversary. If not, it would be him who would be killed. He breathed in and out profoundly and then readied his axe, bringing it up to his shoulder, prepared for the Narbut to rush at him. But the Narbut stayed back, apparently reluctant to be the first to attack.

John surveyed the Royal Box. He could make out the King sitting there, a young woman by his side. He was waiting for John to move in and make the kill—to confirm himself as his new Champion. Had he seen that John had been no more than an observer in the battle thus far, that he was just a coward after all?

Just as John thought about striking a deal with this Narbut, making an agreement for peace, the Narbut broke from his daze and rushed toward him, holding his sword above his head and screaming at the top of his lungs.

John side-stepped the Narbut, who tumbled into the dust.

He could see that the Narbut was exhausted following the battle, that he had got his hands bloody. John, on the other, hand was physically fresh. It was his mind which was causing him all the trouble.

The Narbut didn't stay down long. He flipped up onto his feet, still brandishing his sword and locked his eyes with John. He lurched forward, chattering away in his local dialect, and swiping his sword.

Each time John stepped back out of the Narbut's reach.

Finally the Narbut got himself tired, shook his head from side to side and then pulled his shawl down from his mouth. His accent was jagged and uneven, and his eyes shuddered in their sockets, as if struck by some fever. "Why do you not fight me?"

John heart rapped in his throat. "Uh, I am."

"No, you are not. You have not so much as lifted that axe to strike me. Look, you can finish me in a second, so why do you not do it? Please, put me out of my misery."

John stared into the Narbut's eyes, saw that he was at the end of his tether, that he was quivering from all the death he had dealt. Appreciating the fragile nature of life, John could only imagine what it must've been like for him to have extinguished several lives that day. He must've felt empty, like he'd been hollowed out from within.

The Narbut had no fight left in him. He dropped his sword to his feet and fell to his knees, bowing his head, ready for John's killing blow.

The crowd quietened in anticipation. John felt thousands of eyes burrowing into his skin, making him squirm. He knew he had to do this, had to kill this Narbut, or he would be killed himself. He eyed the General, Frum, seated on his horse on the edge of the arena, looking on with expectation. Worse, if John didn't do this, Frum would torture and kill his Grotesque brethren. But, all that aside, did he really want to join these people, the court of the King who would so willingly watch hundreds die, the same which was tearing apart the Damned Forests, the only home he had ever known?

General Frum glared at John, his body completely still, his hand resting on the hilt of the sword which hung from his waist. He was ready to kill this Narbut, even if John wasn't.

And then, gently, almost at a whisper, the crowd took up a chant. "Kill. Kill. Kill. Kill. Kill." It rose to a murmur. "Kill. Kill. Kill." And then into an all-out shout. "Kill! Kill! Kill! Kill! Kill! Kill!—"

John made his decision. He dropped the axe and ran for the entrance through which he had entered the arena. He heard the dull *thud* as the axe padded onto the dirt. When he reached the entrance to the castle, the two guards held their spears across the opening. One of them declared him under arrest for treason, but John grabbed hold of their weapons and snapped them in two. He tramped down the steps and into the castle, leaving the noises of confusion in the crowd and the unmistakable *plod* of horse hooves behind him.

Armed men watched him blaze past in confusion, obviously not yet having heard about what had taken place in the arena above. John had to take advantage of this moment to make his escape.

He dodged through servants and other members of the court, located another flight of steps and took them. They led him deeper into the castle. He thought about retreating, but he could hear the mounting bootfalls of the King's soldiers beating their way in pursuit. He was resolved that if they caught him they would have to kill him. No way would he go back there to finish off the job, even if they offered it to him. When he had seen into that Narbut's eyes, he had been staring into the abyss, and that was what killing would do to him, turn him empty from the inside.

He stamped down the staircase, sure that—like so many of the staircases in the castle—it would take an upward route at some point. But, if anything, its gradient became steeper until he ran out of stairs and skidded into a dug out room—the castle basement.

It was dank and dark down here. It stank of earth, reminding him of being in the Forests. He wished he could simply close his eyes and when he opened them he would be standing back amongst the familiar trees, ready to go out scouting with Horace, to have some bacon at the table while Susan verbally jibed at him. That was all gone now, in the past. Unless he could find some way to escape.

He moved forward through the darkness and pricked up his ears, listening for any sound of his pursuers. Nothing. He had managed to give them the slip. Nonetheless, he had to find a way out sooner rather than later, because he was sure they would scour the castle from top to bottom in search of him. For now, though, this place seemed as safe as anywhere else, off limits to the immediate search.

He felt the wall. It was cold and wet. When he brought his hand away, his palm was sticky with mud. That reassured him somewhat, since he had noted during his stay at the castle that the King did not tolerate any level of—what he construed to be

—uncleanliness. This place must be low down on the cleaning rota and on the list of places to search.

Finally, he located a torch hanging from the wall and, beside it, a pair of flints. He almost dropped them as he brought them into the palm of his hand. He managed to get them into position where he could hold them straight and he struck them together, holding them to the torch. It burst into light in a blaze of flame and the shadows scurried for the corners of the room.

It took a few moments for John's eyes to get used to the new level of light and when he did he realised that he was standing in, what seemed to be, a dungeon. He took a couple of steps forward and took in the cell standing before him. The bars were a little bent and the metalwork was flaky. Within there were two men chained up against the wall, both of them stirring from their respective slumbers.

John blinked at the two prisoners and they blinked back at him. His throat felt tight and his voice took on a floaty quality. "Um, would you be so kind as to tell me how to get out of here?"

One of the prisoners had wavy blond hair and a fragile face. If John had seen him under any other circumstance, he might've taken him for one of noble blood. The prisoner beamed at him. "If we knew that then we wouldn't be down here, would we? When I'm King I'll make sure that there's—"

The other prisoner, bald with a bit of a gut, cut him off. "Break us out of here and we'll show you the way!"

John considered the bars, seeing that they were fairly flimsy. If he exerted any lasting effort he was sure he could break through. The chains each prisoner wore might give him a little more trouble, but he would still back himself to get them off. He shifted toward the cell.

There was a *lurch* from above.

As he glanced upward, at the ceiling, it gave him pause for thought. These two men were locked up for a reason. How did he know he could trust them? What if they might be murderers or thieves or, worse, out of control members of the King's army just looking for a way to win their way back into the King's affections. Seeing that he was on the run, they might simply choose to bring the guard's attention to his whereabouts, and then trade their freedom for John's. This might be his last opportunity to run back the way he'd come, find his way through the castle before the guards got up their defences. He hesitated.

"What are you waiting for?" the bald one said. "Let us out of here!"

"How do I know I can trust you?" John said.

The blond one smirked. "Trust, I'll tell you something about trust. When I am King you shall be the first to be knighted, I shall give you—"

Once more, the bald one cut off his cellmate. "Please, we were locked up here for offending the King. Now, I'm certain from your demeanour, that frantic look in your eye that you're not exactly in the King's good books either. I served in the King's court for decades, I know this place like the back of my hand, so you'd be best served in springing me free, if not my companion."

The blond one's expression darkened. "You absolutely cannot leave me behind!"

"Shut up," the bald one said, then turned back to John,

returning to his reasoning tone. "We want out just as badly as you do, so why not help us, eh?"

It wasn't the most convincing argument John had ever heard, but, all things considered, he might as well let them out while he was down here. If the worst came to the worst and they were some kind of agents working for the King then he would throw them into the moat and make his bid for freedom.

He approached the bars, under the gaze of the hopeful prisoners, where he reached out, taking a bar in each of his ginormous fists, and bent them back as easily as a toddler might manipulate spaghetti. He stepped in through his newly-made hole and strode up to the prisoners, getting to work on their chains, pulling them apart in the same way he had done with the bars. In a matter of seconds, both prisoners stood free. Stood might well have been an overstatement because, in fact, both of them wobbled about, knees knocking together, scrabbling for something to hold onto. It seemed that they had spent quite some time in the cell, in those chains—so much that they had forgotten how to walk.

Knowing that he had no time to carry anyone in the course of his escape, he made for the stairs, assuming the two prisoners were following him. He was halfway up the stairs, when he heard their shaky steps drifting up behind.

He bounded up the staircase and emerged back into the corridor. It seemed like he had to wait an eternity for the bald and blond prisoner to join him. He thought about running off several times, but stopped short of doing so, telling himself that the bald one had promised to get them all out, and so he would be better served to exercise a bit of patience.

When the bald one did get up, stumbling into the corridor

and squinting in the bright daylight, he grabbed hold of John's sleeve and steered him off in a direction opposite to the arena. "Come on, this way!"

At least the prisoners weren't taking John directly back to the King as quickly as possible. All he could do now was hope that they would lead him right, that they wouldn't betray him.

The blond one took up the rear of their group, in between long-drawn breaths of one who hadn't done any form of exercise in quite some time, declaring that he was the truthful King of the castle and that he would take control from the foundations to the turrets one day, and he would never again find himself a prisoner in his own home.

John wished he would shut up.

When they arrived in a large hall, unguarded—presumably because the entire force of the guards were searching the castle —the blond prisoner pivoted and made a break for one of the double-helix spiral staircases which lead up into the castle. "Onward to rescue Alexis!" he said, thrusting his arm in the air dramatically, as if he were brandishing a sword.

"Not bloody likely," the bald one said, dragging John onward, toward the exit.

The blond one paused on the first stair, stared upward, as if thinking it over in his mind, and then made the decision to come with John and the bald prisoner after all. As he followed on their heels, he kept on talking. "I shall be back for you, Alexis, my sweet! Do not worry!"

"Keep your voice down!" the bald prisoner said. "You'll have the whole damn army after us!"

However, as they ran out into the courtyard which prefaced the drawbridge, John saw that the whole army was already there, crossbowmen pointing their weapons down on them, spearmen standing round the edges, ready to move in at a moment's notice. To John's abject horror, General Frum stood up on the battlements, somehow still on his horse—which must've negotiated several narrow stairways and corridors. He sneered at them. "Stand down and I shall spare your lives. For the time being."

John's pulse rippled through his body. He eyed the drawbridge up ahead. It was down, the green grass of freedom awaiting them just outside. If only they could negotiate the courtyard they could get away. That was rather a large 'if,' though.

He sensed the bald and blond prisoners closing in behind him, using him as a sort of human shield. He was still dressed in his armour from the King's competition, so he fancied his own chances of getting through the groups of soldiers. His companions, on the other hand, would need some luck to avoid getting themselves shot apart.

John had very little time to think things over because, by the second, the spearmen were closing in on them, their faces half-hidden by their snug-fitting iron caps. He glanced back up at the battlements. It would take just one of those crossbow bolts to find his bare face or neck and he would go down. Then he caught General Frum's eye once more, saw the unchecked ire and fury, the cruelty there, and John knew he had to attempt an escape from the castle, otherwise Frum might take out his anger on his family in the Damned Forests, just because he could.

The bald prisoner was nattering away about something in John's ear, while the blond prisoner was making yet another case for his claim on the castle and the throne. John cuffed his arms round the two prisoners and clutched them, squirming in fright, to his chest, as he sprinted his way through the spearmen, who were a fraction late in employing their weapons—so sure had they been of the escapees' predicament.

Crossbow bolts whizzed past John's ears and rattled off his armour. A few of them skimmed his skin and sent searing pain through his body. Some of them pierced his armour and sank into his flesh. But he kept himself fixated on the green grass beyond the moat and told himself that soon they would all be there—away from the castle. And then he heard the clanking of the chains, the sound of the drawbridge being raised.

John bustled through another group of spearmen, blocking their way. One of the spears opened a gash in his thigh. He ploughed on then leapt at the drawbridge which was being brought in at a steady speed. His weight kept it from moving on any further and he scaled the slowly inclining surface feeling the crossbow bolts rattle all round him. He ducked his head and prayed to the gods that they would keep him safe. It was a surprise when he reached the top, so much so that he almost lost his balance and fell into the moat. He regained his balance, glanced back over his shoulder, catching sight of General Frum's austere expression, and then jumped off, into freedom.

THOSE DAMNED FORESTS

IN THE RABBIT KING'S BURROW

T REVOR'S FIRST THOUGHT on waking was that his
hands and feet were bound, next that his chest felt tight,
so tight that it was difficult to breathe. He opened his eyes and
then realised that they were already open. His surroundings were
set in pitch black. He recalled something about rabbits being
able to see in the dark—something about all those carrots—so
he supposed this was to be expected.

Somewhere off to his side there was a groan.

Trevor was sure it would be Zend, Plont wouldn't make such
a spectacle as that. He wriggled his way into a more comfortable
position, propping himself up against the wall of the burrow, or
wherever they were. "Where are we?" Trevor said.

"Are you stupid, or what?" Zend replied.

Trevor decided that now might not be the best time for him
to try and get his bearings, via Zend. Since Zend had confided in
him before this quest that he had never been into the Damned

Forests before, and that the townspeople of Gotnot actively avoided entering, he assumed that they were pretty much on a level-pegging as far as their predicament was concerned.

There was a shuffling and then Zend said something in his language to Plont.

Trevor thought it to be something along the lines of, 'Can you reach my bindings?' but it might equally have been, 'Let's get out of here without that idiot human noticing.'

Their conversation, however, was curtailed by the sound of thudding footsteps heading along the corridor, coming toward them. A light accompanied the sound and soon a torch shone, revealing the tight space they had all been squeezed into, the bodies of Zend and Plont huddled up on the floor, while, at the same time, obscuring the shiner of the torch.

Trevor wanted to hold up his arm to shield his eyes from the sudden, bright light, but, his hands being bound, that was nigh on impossible. So he had to shut them altogether.

Rabbit King shuffled further into the room, the light getting brighter on the backs of Trevor's eyelids. He stationed himself, Trevor guessed, a few feet away from him. "Quite rude, you know, going barging into someone else's home like that."

Zend and Plont remained quiet, so Trevor supposed it might be up to him to make some sort of an explanation. At work he'd had four employees under him, so he was used to accountability. "We're terribly sorry for encroaching," Trevor said, "that we've come here uninvited, but it's just that we've been sent here on a quest, you see?"

"Open your eyes," Rabbit King said.

Trevor hesitated a moment, still seeing the bright red on the back of his eyelids, and then he risked it. The torch was still bright but his eyes were beginning to adjust. He took in Rabbit King's face, the fur covering his body and, most of all, those flappy ears protruding from his head.

Rabbit King sneered. "That's right, just stare away, won't you? Do you think I set up home out here in the sticks so that I'd get a procession of tourists passing through to gape at the monster?"

Zend, apparently not having seen Rabbit King before he had been knocked out, did gape, and then, his voice gruff, suggesting that he might still be nursing a migraine following the encounter, he said, "You're a Grotesque."

Rabbit King narrowed his eyes. "I've absolutely nothing to do with the Grotesque and I resent the association."

Trevor wished to butt in at this point, to inquire as to what were these or *the* 'Grotesque' but he noted the tone of the conversation, his slighted host, and decided this might be a good time to keep schtum.

"But," Zend said, "you were cursed by a witch?"

Rabbit King crossed his arms over his chest. "None of your business, that."

"Then how did you turn out . . . as you are?"

Rabbit King ignored the question and turned his attention to Trevor. "Don't know what you're looking at either. Fancy you coming down here. An older man like yourself, would've thought you'd know better."

Trevor did his best apologetic grin.

Rabbit King sighed and leant back against the wall of his burrow. "So, what is it you've come here for? What lies have they cooked up about me this time?"

Zend's tone hardened. "You have taken the children of our village."

"Rubbish," Rabbit King said.

"We have come to reclaim them."

Rabbit King turned his paw over and examined his claws. "What use would I ever have for *your* children?"

This seemed to stump Zend momentarily, but he cast off his doubts and regained his previous, resolute expression. "Because we're sure of it."

"Oh right," Rabbit King said. "My apologies, sir." He gave a mock bow. "I completely misjudged your scientific process of investigation. I'll go and get your children right away."

Zend remained stiff, apparently not appreciating the sarcasm.

Trevor thought about stepping in to diffuse this rather tense encounter, but before he got the chance, Rabbit King was speaking again.

"The question now is, what am I going to do with you all?"

This time Trevor couldn't resist speaking up. "You could let us all go and write this off as a bit of a misunderstanding."

A smirk crossed Rabbit King's face. "Yes, and I suppose that if I were to do that, you'd all come plodding back over here, pitchforks and torches in hand ready to burn the 'evil' Rabbit King out of his lair so that he returns your children."

Trevor glanced over at Zend and Plont's faces and realised that Rabbit King hadn't been far off with his assertion. This might be Trevor's chance to play his trump card. "Well, I'm from Earth, I'm not from Ethereal at all. You'll find that I have quite different morals from those two, and I can assure you that I'd be more than happy to let bygones be bygones, and go our separate ways."

Rabbit King examined Trevor. "You look pretty much the same as us, and you speak a bit funny, but what makes you think that I believe your little story?"

"Because it's true," Trevor said, feeling desperate."

"Sounds like these two's reasoning skills have rubbed off on you."

A bunny hopped in and sniffed round Rabbit King's feet.

Rabbit King stooped down and lifted it up into his arms. "While we're all busy making promises, I can promise you that I've had nothing whatsoever to do with your children. My life's complicated as it is without needing a bunch of screaming brats in it." His claws scratched at the rabbits neck, causing the rabbit to close its eyes in pleasure. "No, I made peace with the curse they cast on me long ago, and I sought out a home in which I'd feel comfortable, animals with whom I have an affinity. Those *Grotesque* are only concerned with celebrating their curses, joining together as one as if that might make them a *family*, or some such rubbish." He scoffed. "Putting together a freak show more like."

It sounded like Rabbit King had a bit of a chip on his shoulder concerning these 'Grotesque' people, but at least Trevor was getting something of a lowdown of who they were— people who had been cursed by witches and exiled. If he had ever once in his life thought it remotely possible that witches and wizards existed then it might've sounded quite reasonable. Then again, he'd never thought he would travel to Ethereal, or any other world for that matter.

Rabbit King slunk his way toward the exit, still stroking the bunny in his clutches. "When it gets light I'll be tying you each to a stake and leaving you to the honey boars." He yawned. "So if you've got any escape plan among you, you might be advised to put it into action as soon as is convenient."

Before Trevor got another opportunity at appealing to Rabbit King's reason, he had already slipped down the corridor and away—bunny and all.

Trevor exchanged glances with Zend and Plont, looking for some sign of a plan. Worryingly, they looked just as out of ideas as he was.

They sat about in the darkness, no one saying anything. And they stayed that way, silent, in the dark, until Rabbit King returned. He looked them over and then let out a long sigh. "I don't like leading people to their deaths, you know? But sometimes it's unavoidable." He traipsed up to Plont and grabbed him by his bindings, then dragged him toward the exit.

Zend struggled to help his friend, but Rabbit King had tied him up tight, and he could do no more than a passable impression of an overgrown worm.

Trevor was more resigned, just watching Plont's head disappear round the corner, and off into the burrow.

Once Rabbit King's torch had gone out with him, the room returned to its familiar gloom.

"Any ideas?" Zend said.

"Nothing."

"Thought as much."

Trevor would've liked to take up his frustration at Zend's

constant berating of him, as if it were Trevor's fault that the mayor of *Zend's* town had selected him to be *his* hero. All Trevor had ever wanted was to return to Earth, preferably in one piece —although this latest turn in the road looked like it might prove touch and go.

Rabbit King returned for Zend a few minutes later. He cast Trevor a thoroughly fed up look and then dragged Zend out by his ankles. Zend did more of his useless wriggling as he went. Rabbit King struck him over the head with his club and that stopped him.

Trevor sat in the room, alone with his thoughts, desperately thinking of a way that they might all escape this perilous situation. He had never been an outside-the-box thinker, his boss had always praised him for 'doing the basics well' or being 'strong and steady.' That conservatism might well get him killed right now.

Not only did he want to save his own life, and those of Zend and Plont, but he wanted to show them that he was worth respecting—that he wasn't as purposeless as they imagined. He wanted to surprise them with some ingenuity or stroke of flawless logic. But, like always with needing a good idea on demand, nothing came to him that was remotely worth considering. And before he had even realised that he was going to come up with nothing, that they were all going to be munched to death by honey boars, he heard the familiar footsteps of Rabbit King coming for him.

He said a little prayer to himself and then took in Rabbit King's furry, mutated face. Out of the blue an ingenious idea struck him, so ingenious that he could hardly believe he hadn't thought of it before. With Rabbit King looming over him, ready to—unceremoniously—yank him after Zend and Plont, he managed to spit it out. "There're destroying the Forests."

Rabbit King cocked his head to one side, actually looking interested for the first time in their brief relationship. "Say what?"

"Yeah," Trevor said. "We saw some men tearing the place down, on our way here."

Rabbit King furrowed his brow. "What do you mean, 'tearing the place down?'"

"They're uprooting the trees, moving their way deeper and deeper. You'll have to get out of the way before they reach here."

Rabbit King appeared to think this matter over. He twitched his mouth and nose, as if he had caught a whiff of something in the air and then he broke into a wry smile. "Nice try, earthling, but it's not going to work. I'd do the same thing in your situation, try to save my own neck."

"No," Trevor said. "I swear I'm telling the truth, ask the other two if you don't believe me."

"Yes, that'd make sense, wouldn't it? I'm sure they'd be wont to tell me the truth if you weren't."

Trevor did realise that logic had somewhat deserted him, but he *was* fighting for his life, that much was true.

Without any further messing round, Rabbit King seized hold of his ankles and dragged him out through the tunnels, up and down uneven ground, and then, finally, up a long slope. They emerged into the morning air. All things considered, Trevor's impending death at the tusks and teeth of honey boars, the air smelled quite fresh and sweet. Trevor had always thought of living in the countryside, rather fallen in love with the idea, but he'd always found himself chained to his desk in the city. Now, in retrospect, having suffered quite a bit at the hands of the Damned Forests, he was reconsidering his dream, thinking that, perhaps, he might've been fine all along, living his city dweller's life.

Rabbit King dragged him through the tall grass, the dew wetting Trevor's face as they went. As he was lying on his back, he could stare upward at the cerulean sky stretching above him, the bright sun just rising above the forest canopy. All things considered this was quite a beautiful day to die. And then he turned his thoughts to other morbid matters, he thought back to the graveyard, the End of Time, and wondered which one he would end up in—the one for Earth or the one for Ethereal. He supposed it really didn't much matter one way or the other.

Rabbit King flipped him over and then yanked him up onto his feet.

Trevor took in the other two, Plont and Zend, both of them tied up to their respective stakes, hands bound behind their backs and gags stuffed into their mouths. Both of them worked to avoid Trevor's gaze, which he found wholly telling.

Rabbit King swaggered his way along, keeping Trevor by his side effortlessly. A couple of bunnies emerged from nowhere and bounced round his feet, either unaware of or celebrating the men being put to the slaughter. Being a positive-minded individual, Trevor preferred to believe the former.

Rabbit King busied himself at Trevor's designated stake, tying up his hands and legs, fitting his gag, then he stood back, hands on hips, looking over the whole group of them, as if admiring a good job, well done. "Got any last words?"

Since they'd all been gagged, there was a cacophony of moans and groans.

Rabbit King nodded to himself as if he empathised with their predicaments, then stretched his arms and yawned, as if this were just any other day. He gave them all a final look and then turned on his heel and made his way back over the glade, to the hole he had dragged them out of.

Rabbit King was on the fringe of Trevor's vision when a hefty tremor leapt through the earth, its vibrations burrowing their way through Trevor's arms and legs. Rabbit King paused, looked back at them, and then continued on his way. There was another tremor and, this time, it knocked Rabbit King off his feet. He got back up, brushed himself off and then proceeded back down the hole leading to his burrow.

Much to Trevor's delight, he noted that the tremors had loosened the foundations of his stake. He looked over at Plont and Zend, seeing that the tremor hadn't had the same effect on their own stakes. It was his time to shine. He shook his whole body, feeling the stake bob about in its hole and then, with an almighty tug, he knocked it back. It flattened the tall grass with a wet *smush*. He worked quickly to slip the knot tying his hands up over the end of the stake. Now able to move his hands freely, he tugged at the knot and, a few seconds later, got some slack to work with. He slipped the bindings off and turned to Plont and Zend.

Maybe it was some sort of semi-subconscious punishment for how Zend had treated him thus far on their quest, but Trevor first turned his attention to Plont, to work at the rope tying his hands. However, he had hardly got started when, over his shoulder, he heard stirring in the bushes. He looked back to see what looked, to all intents and purposes, like a honey boar.

At first Trevor's breath stuck in his throat and he thought he had been rendered immobile by the sight. He was only brought round by the combined moans of Plont and Zend.

The honey boar was tiny, barely reaching up to knee-height. Trevor wondered what all the fuss had been about. Nonetheless, his companions' muted screams suggested he should be scared.

As the honey boar sniffed about in the tall grass, its snout half-burrowed in the damp ground, Trevor took his opportunity to free Plont. Staying true to his character, Plont kept his lips pursed and his voice silent. Together, they worked on the knot tying Zend to his stake with Plont maintaining the honey boar in the corner of his eye while Zend groaned out his impatience.

Just as they got some slack into Zend's ropes, Trevor felt the rough skin—all bristle-like hair and caked on mud—brush against his calf. He looked down in time to see the honey boar lunge at Zend's leg, fangs bared and eyes wild. Without thinking any further, Trevor jacked back his leg and let loose a hard kick, catching the honey boar in its belly and sending it off into the bushes, several feet away. He heard it squealing away, no doubt furious at having been treated so rudely on its own patch, before scuttling off back amongst the trees.

When they got the rope and gag free, Zend looked over at Trevor, eye lolling about in their sockets. He laid his hands on Trevor's shoulders, tears gleaming in his eyes. "You . . . you saved my life."

Trevor was rendered speechless. What was he supposed to say to that? So he just enjoyed the sensation of basking in Zend's gratitude rather than being the target for his shame.

But there wasn't much time for a tearful strengthening of manly relationships, though, as, through the trees, the vibrations increased in ferocity and then, almost out of nowhere at all, one of the trees bordering the glade shimmied, bucked then tumbled down, falling in a whisper of leaves and a wince-inducing crack of branches.

All three of them exchanged glances and then quickly got to their feet and bolted across the glade, stumbling as they went. Trevor dared a few looks back, where he caught sight of the machine ploughing its way through the Forests. As they crossed the threshold of Rabbit King's burrow, Trevor paused and looked down at his feet.

"What're you doing?" Zend said, still struck with gratitude.

"We can't leave him here," Trevor said.

Zend widened his eyes. "Of course we can. Don't you remember that he put us to death not five minutes ago?"

Trevor surveyed the fallen tree on the other side of the glade. He could already see men swarming their way round the downed trunk. Soon they would swamp the glade. He could only imagine what they might do when they uncovered Rabbit King's lair. These were the types more likely to smoke monsters out than reason with them, try to see the world through their eyes.

Decision made, Trevor pulled at the loose earth, just about covering the opening to the lair and then, still under the disbelieving dual-gaze of Plont and Zend, he dropped down into the darkness once more.

When he reached the bottom of the slope, he was already having second thoughts. What in hell's name was he doing? For all Zend's malice he had warned Trevor off doing what he had just done, and he knew that he had unnecessarily put himself into danger. But his choice was made now. He would stick with his gut.

Since it was pitch black, he had to guide his way along with the earthy wall. He took another couple of steps before calling out. "Rabbit King? Rabbit King?"

No response.

Trevor felt his throat tighten and he glanced off up at the slope leading up out of the burrow. If he scrabbled his way up that slope right now he might have a hope of outrunning the men who were destroying the Forests. But he would have to live with the fact that he'd left Rabbit King behind to suffer his fate. If there was one thing he grasped about regret, it was that it would follow him back to Earth—if he ever did manage to return.

"Rabbit King?"

There was a scuffle off down the burrow.

A tingle ran up Trevor's spine and he tried to peel back the darkness with his eyes.

There was a gigantic vibration which passed through the entire burrow.

Trevor rocked against the sides of the burrow, involuntarily letting out a small cry.

And then, out of the gloom, the large form emerged. Rabbit King stooped forward, reached out and snatched Trevor by the collar of his tunic. "What is this? Some kind of joke? You should be dead right now."

Feeling Rabbit King's grip tightened about his throat, Trevor managed to get the words out. "They're . . . here."

Rabbit King loosened his hold a fraction and glanced up to the roof of his burrow.

As if in reply, there was yet another tremor, this time accompanied by distant cheers.

"They'll root you out," Trevor said. "Come with us. We have to escape this place."

Rabbit King held onto Trevor as he breathed deep and long, clearly thinking over the situation. He glared into Trevor's eyes. "I'm keeping you close by. That way, if this is a trap, if you've somehow brought out reinforcements from your poxy little village then I'll crush your windpipe."

Trevor didn't doubt Rabbit King's sincerity, so he just nodded manically, hoping that Rabbit King would agree to his offer and drag them both out of the burrow.

Rabbit King called out into the darkness. "Lulu! Frankie!"

A few moments later a pair of bunnies, maybe they had been the same ones as before, hopped up to Rabbit King's heels. And then they were going up, very quickly. They burst out into the daylight and Trevor felt Rabbit King's anxiety in his strengthening grasp.

Rabbit King looked round, saw the men dressed in blue and white making their way across the glade, no more than a hundred yards away now. "The King's men. My gods," he said. And then, without warning, he took up running, lugging Trevor along with him.

Rabbit King swung Trevor up onto his shoulders and then they were bouncing, taking six foot high leaps over the glade until they reached the fringe of the forest, out of range of the onrushing men, who now chucked spears and shot arrows in their direction.

They picked their way through the trees until they came to a clearing where they met with Plont and Zend, both of whom wore darkened expressions, clearly not at all in favour of the decision to liberate Rabbit King from his burrow. But Trevor knew he'd done the right thing—his conscience was clean.

"Believe me now?" Trevor said, feeling breathless.

Rabbit King gazed round the clearing, at Plont and Zend's face, then back to Trevor. "Yes, yes I do."

HOUSE ARREST

HORACE SKIRTED the edges of Witney Branches
trying to work out any sort of frailty in the King's men's
line of defence. There were about twenty of them, all working a
perimeter round their home, camps set up, fires smoking away.
They might've been anywhere else, judging from their cackling
laughter and the quantity of cider and fruit liqueurs being
knocked back. And all this, the Grotesque hideout being discovered, was his fault. He had brought them here and he would be
responsible for anything that happened.

One of the King's men gaped at him from over his fire. Even
when he noticed Horace looking back at him, he didn't turn
away. It was like they were using the discovery of Witney
Branches as an opportunity for some light mid-forest-destruc-
tion entertainment. The Grotesque had been reduced to some
kind of sideshow—the reason most of them had left the residen-
cies of man in first place.

The day the men had arrived, they had thrown Horace aside and scrounged through Witney Branches, turning the whole place upside down, looking for anything valuable. They had been wasting their time, of course, because there was nothing of value in their home—why would there be? Out in the Forests there really was no use for anything of monetary worth. They *had* taken his namtra, though—a banned substance under the King's law.

When the leader of the men, some lord, had come up empty handed he had knocked Horace about, demanding to know about some witch they were searching for. Like the rest of the Grotesque, witches were something of a taboo subject, seeing that witches' curses had led them to flee into the Forests in the first place. And when the lord had encountered that reluctance to talk, he had automatically taken it as a sign that they were, indeed, hiding something. They had been staked out ever since.

Horace let out a long sigh and thought about John. If only he were here with them then they might have a chance of fighting back against the King's men, really taking the fight to them and driving them out. But he knew, deep down, that it was hopeless. John wasn't coming back anymore than the King's men would just up camp and leave them in peace to live out the rest of the their cursed lives. That meant that it all fell on him. He had to take responsibility for freeing his people.

One of the men at a nearby campfire called out to Horace. "Oi! Cyclops!"

Horace toyed with the idea of returning to Witney Branches, where he could have some tranquillity. But he was resolved not to become a prisoner in his own home, to feel uncomfortable going about his daily business. So he met the man's eye dead on and said, "I'm not a Cyclops. I'm a human, just like you."

The man chuckled. "Then how comes you've only got one eye!"

Horace thought about some witty come back, but none appealed to him. He hated wasting energy on these halfwits and their half-baked taunts.

"What you gonna do?" the man said. "Fry me with magic?"

There would've been a time when humans would fear speaking that way in the Damned Forests, so enchanted and steeped in magical awe as they were. However, he saw that the King's men had become accustomed to the spectacle, learnt to live with the myths and come to see, well, that mostly they were myths. Their machine had crunched its way through a sizeable chunk of the Forests searching for gods knew whatever it was they were searching for. Now there were no more mysteries. They would map the place and move on.

"Oi!" the man said. "You deaf or what?"

"What do you think?" Horace said, tilting his head to one side.

The man burrowed his little finger into the inner recesses of his ear. He gave it a good wiggle and then withdrew it, caked in yellow wax. "I don't think you're all that. You hide away in the Forests, frightening our children and making our old folks sprout off with tales, but you aren't really scary at all. You're just a bunch of freaks hiding away out here."

Horace thought about shaking the man by the hand, congratulating him on his genius piece of deduction. But he supposed that he was already revered amongst his fellow men as something of a wit, so he didn't want to make the guy big-headed.

Reluctantly resigned to not getting any peace out here on the porch of Witney Branches, Horace turned and headed back through the door.

"That's it!" the man said. "You run away. Just like the coward you are."

Horace did, however, take exception to that comment. He glanced back at the man, maintaining the steel in his eye. "You have no idea what you're got yourself in for. You and your men, you shall be cursed for the rest of your lives. Your children shall be born with two noses, closed eyelids and hairy ears. You shall rue the day that you encroached on the Damned Forests. You shall pray that you can somehow undo your mistake. But the gods shan't listen."

The man's jovial grin disintegrated in record time and he tapped his neighbour, who was in the middle of knocking back what, by the state of his roaming eyeballs and flushed cheeks, looked to be his ninth or tenth fruit liqueur. The neighbour joined his friend in staring at Horace.

"You hear what he said?" the man said.

"Wha?" his neighbour replied.

"Just about cursed the entire blooming Kingdom of Ethereal, he did."

The neighbour squinted at Horace. "Why's he only got one eye?"

"Like I told you, Nigel, these are them Grotesque we've been searching for—cursed by witches. Maybe you should give those liqueurs a rest for an hour or two, get your wits back about you. Lord Eversham explained it all days ago, don't you remember?"

Apparently his neighbour didn't.

"Point is," the man continued, "this blighter here's just about poxed our children's generation. Says they're going to be born all funny, like them, and that."

The neighbour was obviously having trouble fully comprehending the implications of what Horace had said, but he was getting riled all the same, scrunching his hands into fists and puffing out his cheeks. "Wanna teach him a lesson?"

The man rose and flexed his muscles.

A voice sounded from off across the camp. "What's going on over there?"

The man flinched at the voice and turned to look.

Another man, who Horace recognised as the lord who had confiscated his namtra, strutted onto the scene. From the men's conversation, Horace established that this must be Lord Eversham. Lord Eversham brought himself between Horace and the two men. He looked over Horace with a sneer fixed on his lips. "Whatever do you think you're doing speaking to my men, Grotesque?"

Horace really had no answer. Speaking to any of the King's men was a hiding to nothing, like pressing his eyeball to a hot stove. "Nothing, my lord," he said, having learnt that was how he should address this man, after he'd been struck several times over for leaving the correct address out of his replies.

"Then you'd best stay away," Eversham said. "Else we might have no choice but to relieve you of your remaining eye."

Anger writhed within Horace. These people had no right to come here, turn up on their land, imprison them in their own home and, to top it all off, insult them. He had a burst of courage and said, "What is it that you're looking for, sire?"

Eversham scowled. "That's none of your business, Grotesque."

Much to his displeasure, Horace winced. He hated letting the King's men know that they had got to him on some level. He reeled himself in and tried to steel himself beneath their gaze. "Then what do you hope to achieve by keeping us here?"

"It simply means that you're not going to be bothersome to our plans. We can keep a close *eye* on you."

The two men burst into a fit of giggles behind him.

Eversham, too, cracked a grin. "You'd be better off trotting back inside your nasty little home and going about whatever it is you Grotesque do with your days."

But Horace wasn't finished yet. He hadn't stood here, been insulted and laughed at, not to get some information out of them. "What did you do with John?"

"John?" Eversham said, arching an eyebrow.

"I know you took him. There's no one else who would be capable."

Eversham stepped closer. "What makes you think that the Forests didn't simply gobble him up?"

"Because you're the most dangerous entity here. Nothing in the Forests is as evil as you."

The men behind Eversham oohed and exchanged glances, expecting Horace to really get it now.

Eversham squeezed his lips together. "Both you and I know that, simply, that's not the case. This place"—he waved his hands round him—"is rampant with black magic and wicked creatures, like yourself—"

"I'm human, just like you," Horace said.

"Nonsense," Eversham said. "You lost all status as a human when you allowed that witch or wizard to curse you."

The two men behind Eversham muttered between themselves.

Eversham glanced back. "What is it, you two? Go on, spit it out."

Neither man looked likely to speak up.

Eversham's snappy reaction caught Horace's attention. What did he possibly have to worry about? All he was doing was spinning all the usual human attitudes to the Grotesque, things that Horace had heard millions of times before. There had to be something sensitive in what Eversham had said, but what might it be?

Eversham turned his attention back to Horace. "Get back into your dishevelled, rotten tree trunk and you'd be best advised not to poke your dirty eye out of it for some time."

Horace gave the two men a parting look, and then disappeared back into Witney Branches, already speculating as to what had got Eversham so riled.

Back in the kitchen, he took up a place on the rickety wooden bench. He planted his elbows chest-width apart and rested his head in his hands.

Susan was frying up lunch at the stove. "What's it like out there?" she said.

Horace relayed the exchange he had just had with Eversham and the men.

Susan looked up from the pan she stirred with a wooden spoon. "There's a lord out here?"

"That's right, at least was how he introduced himself to me."

"What would a lord be doing out here, in the Forests?"

Horace shrugged. "Whatever it is that lords do."

"That's precisely it," she said, wagging the wooden spoon in mid-air as she spoke. "For the most part lords spend their time at the castle, getting drunk, entertaining the King. They're supposed to stay there to provide some sort of guard at the castle. The King would only assign a lord to a task in the Forests if there were truly something monumentally important at stake."

"Like what?"

"No idea," she said, returning to her cooking.

Horace puzzled it out, staring at the wood grain, following its loops and curls with his eye. "Well, we can establish that they want to tear the place apart, uproot all the trees. Do you think that's really just down to the King deciding that he wants no magic in his kingdom?"

Susan shook her head. "There'll be more to it than that, there's bound to be."

"When Lord Eversham started speaking about us being sub-human, that ever since we'd been cursed we'd lost our status as humans—"

Susan held up her hand. "Don't mention that here. That's the reason we all take shelter out here, remember. Witney Branches is a refuge from all that ill-informed abuse."

"No, but, it was the reaction of the two men behind him. They seemed unsure about how he spoke that information, like it was fact."

"So what can we establish from it?" she said.

"I think someone in the King's court has been cursed by a witch or wizard, someone who the King holds dear. I believe that he's searching the place to dig up the perpetrator and have them brought back to the castle to reverse the spell. That's why they hassled me about a witch when they finished searching Witney Branches."

Susan shook her head and stirred on. "It must be someone important if he's sent a lord out here, that's all I can say about it."

Horace managed a slight smile for the first time in days, because he felt that—finally—he was beginning to get a grasp on what it was that the King's men wanted. And the more he knew about his enemy, the better he could plan on how he would overthrow them.

Susan shovelled the pan off the stove. "Call the others, will you? It's time for brunch."

Horace left the table and skirted his way down the corridor, toward the sleeping quarters, resolved to get all the Grotesque together so they might plot.

DEALING WITH THE FALLOUT OF AN ESCAPED CHAMPION

A LEXIS PACED her bedroom, writhing her hands, unsure what was going to happen next. She had heard the news —her guard had passed along the latest gossip, that the Champion-elect had not only escaped, but broken Sydney and Courtney out too. Although she had had nothing to do with the escape—for goodness's sake she had been sitting beside the King, stifling the urge to vomit at the spectacle—she feared that some sort of recompense might be headed her way. Her thoughts had been so far away from any prospect of escape that she knew she was innocent herself. But still, she had been responsible for those two. The King had used them as leverage to keep her in line. What would happen now that the leverage had gone?

She was glad when Henrietta arrived, pleased that she would no longer be condemned to be alone with her thoughts.

Today Henrietta was wearing thick blue eye shadow and wore a crinkled shirt which rose just above her well-preserved kneecaps. She pressed on a smile, but Alexis could see, a little beyond, that there was a weariness in her eyes, that she might have to be party to some unpleasantness before long. "Alexis, dear, how have you been holding up?"

A shudder passed over her skin. "When . . . when the Champion broke loose, that was when Jenson escorted me back here, he had several guards put on me, to prevent my escape. And I've been here ever since. I've hardly slept over the last few nights. I'm too frightened that they're going to take me away. One of the other girls, Cherry, told me that—"

Henrietta's smile widened. "Don't worry yourself about, Cherry. She's always aggressive when she feels her position with the King is threatened. As far as I'm concerned you had nothing at all to do with the escape, how could you have done? Like you say you were sitting beside the King. And what use would their escape be if they didn't attempt to rescue you along with them?"

Alexis had felt bitter about that fact, that, as far as she was aware, neither Courtney or Sydney had even tried to break her out. She supposed she had been right all along about Courtney's posturing, all his claims about his kingly virtue. He had only led her astray. And, above all, it justified her decision to save her own neck—to spring herself from the dungeon. Then a horrible thought struck her that, perhaps, Sydney and Courtney had believed that she had forgotten them completely, lost herself in her new life as one of the King's maidens, abandoned her promise to free them. The worst part of it all was that Alexis thought there might be some truth to it.

Henrietta had been speaking, but Alexis hadn't taken in the words. ". . . and so, I thought I'd come here to tell you, to let you know that you should be wary."

Alexis blinked away her daze. "Wary? About what?"

"Oh, dear, I can see that this whole episode has really taken a toll on you. I wanted to warn you that there will be an investigation. I expect that General Frum, among others, will want to speak with you."

"Am I in trouble?"

Henrietta shook her head vigorously. "Oh goodness, no, my dear, it's just . . . protocols must be followed. I mean this is the King's castle we're talking about. And a pair of prisoners have escaped. Everything must be followed up, lessons must be learnt and the escapees must be brought to justice."

Alexis's throat dried up at her thoughts of what might be about to unfurl. She sucked up the courage to confront Henrietta with her concerns. "They're not going to send me back down to the dungeons, are they?"

"I shouldn't think so, dear, just as long as you can prove that you had nothing to do with the escape."

Alexis looked out the window, down into the courtyard which had hosted the competition. She could hardly believe that General Frum had executed the remaining competitor—the one who had slumped to his knees and waited for the giant to finish him off. When Frum had sliced off his head, the King had leant into her with a gentle smile and said, "It was only a Narbut. I would never have accepted him as my Champion in any case. Nasty, dishonest people. Cannot be trusted."

Afterward, among the panic and feeling herself numb all over, she'd asked one of the guards escorting her back to her bedroom what a Narbut was. He had spoken in a similarly disparaging tone to the King, claiming that they were only good enough to spit on. She supposed it had been that point, when she had returned to her bedroom, with the thought of the Narbut's decapitated corpse blazoned on her mind, that she had decided she must escape from the castle, as soon as possible. At whatever cost.

Just as Henrietta had warned, later in the evening a representative summoned her down to meet with General Frum. Alexis felt like she was pacing out a death march. It seemed like the whole castle was draped in a sombre tone, the guards look quick-eyed and nervous, knowing that they had failed in their duty.

She tried her best to keep her eyes fixed to the floor for the remainder of her journey, and soon her escort brought her to a large oaken door with a large brass knocker and led her inside.

General Frum reclined in his chair, his feet up on an enormous table which occupied most of the expansive room. The table was covered in maps, tens of them, their paper yellowed and corners turned up. They were covered in scrawled notes in a notation Alexis had no hope of understanding.

He puffed away on a pipe while he considered the map he held in his hand. When the escort officially announced Alexis's presence in his quarters, Frum merely gave a wave of his hand to dismiss the man, and went on reading.

Not quite knowing what to do and although there were several, very comfortable-looking, chairs dotted out round the room, Alexis hovered at the door, feeling thoroughly awkward.

About ten minutes later, Frum slapped the map down on the table and dumped his pipe down on top of it, seeming not to care about the ash which spilled out. He strutted over to the window and clasped his hands behind his back, taking in the view of the landscape which rolled away from the castle. On a hill, right on the horizon, there was the beginning of a forest. He glanced back at her, meeting her eye for the first time in their meeting. "Do you know why I called you here today?"

There seemed little point in glossing over it. The sooner they got this meeting over with, let him know that she knew nothing about this whole escape business, then the sooner she could go back to being the best King's maiden she could possibly be— while nursing her secret thoughts on how she might bust out of the castle herself.

Frum chewed on his lower lip. From the dark pit of skin there, she supposed it must've been a nervous habit of his. "You were allowed out of the dungeons on the condition that your friends would be harmed if you dared not fulfil your duty to the King appropriately."

Was this why he had brought her here? That she had somehow failed in her role as one of the King's maidens? If that were the case she was certain that Cherry had been behind it, that she had somehow contrived to convince the King and the General that she had had something to do with the escape, known about it.

Frum continued, "Now that they're no longer among us, that they've escaped," he said, with slight snarl, "we must reconsider how we might ensure your complete loyalty to the King."

Alexis would be damned if she'd let his guy simply decide her fate for her. She glared at him. "I've been nothing but loyal to the King. You're seen that. You can ask him yourself."

Against all odds, Frum gave her a boyish look, as if he might've been a tad harsh with her. He nodded to her, in acknowledgement. "Granted, the King, so far, has been quite satisfied with your loyalty." He paused. "However, others among us cannot be quite so bold. You see, following this breakout we really cannot afford any more lapses of judgement. We must be quite sure of where the members of the court stand."

Alexis held her hand to her breast. "I swear to you on my life that I'm totally loyal to the King, that I would never do anything to harm him or the Kingdom." As she said it she felt that she almost believed her words. "May the gods strike me down."

"May they indeed," Frum replied.

She studied his face, sure that she had done a good job in convincing him. If only he would take her word for it she could allow herself to relax, to give herself a chance to enjoy something of her time in the castle, to taste the fresh cow's milk, the duck eggs and the honey liqueur. But if she were in a constant panic, always looking over her shoulder, lest someone be about to chop off her head, life would be a misery.

Frum caught her eye once more then looked away. He called out to someone outside the room.

This was it, the time that they dragged her away, back to the dungeons, to be hung upside down. Or perhaps she wouldn't be so lucky. Maybe the King would deign to have her head lopped off then and there. She squeezed her eyes shut and waited for the familiar rugged touch of a soldier's hands. But it never came.

When she opened her eyes she saw that a soldier *had* entered the room, but, instead of seizing her, he held a boy in his clutches.

The boy had black hair and clean, blue eyes. He was wearing a tiny set of armour.

"What's this about?" Alexis said, her heart doing a jig in her chest.

Frum remained serious. "This boy here, Arnold. He was a great friend of our escaped, would-be Champion."

"And what's he got to do with all this?"

Frum approached Arnold and reached out for his chin. He grasped hold of it and tilted his face upward, as if he were inspecting a horse he was looking to purchase. "I believe that Arnold here might well have had some inside knowledge about the escape and chose not to divulge that information." He stared into the boy's eyes. "Eh? Is that right, boy?"

Arnold's eyes widened. "No, sir, I didn't know anything about it. All's I did was watch him practise everyday, give him some tips. He never said anything to me about any escape."

"But how can I tell if you're telling the truth or not?" Frum said.

"I promise, sir, on my father's honour."

"Your father's honour?"

"Yes, he's a knight."

"Oh, I know that. In fact your father is under my command. It's a pity he's not here right now to deal with you himself, isn't it? Whatever might he say if he were to find out you'd been fraternising with a traitor?"

A panic entered Arnold's eyes. "Please, sir, I didn't know anything."

Frum turned back to Alexis. "Do you believe him?"

Alexis's voice was hardly a whisper in her throat. "Yes," she said.

Frum released Arnold. "Shame we can never be completely sure, isn't it? Sometimes I wonder whether we might invite some witch or wizard into the castle just so they could brew up a truth serum." He unsheathed his sword and held it to Arnold's supple throat. "But we have other methods that are just as effective, if a little more direct."

Alexis wanted to lurch forward, to knock the sword from Frum's grip, but she knew that it would be utterly useless. He would overpower her. If he hurt the boy because of her she would never forgive herself. "Please, don't touch him. What do you want to know?"

When Frum spoke, his voice took on a snarl, like a dog backed into a corner. "I want to know where they've escaped to."

"I don't know, I'm sorry."

Frum nicked Arnold's throat. A bead of black blood rolled down his Adam's apple, leaving a brown-red trail, and soaked into the collar of his tunic.

Arnold gasped.

Alexis's muscles tautened and she felt her voice go shrill. "No!" she said. "Leave him alone."

Frum kept the blade in its place. "I'll leave him alone when you start telling the truth."

"But I am! I promise I am! How could I have known about the escape? I've been up in my bedroom the whole time. I was with the King when they broke out of the dungeon."

"Perhaps there's someone else, in the castle. Another traitor."

Alexis noticed that there was a paranoid tone in Frum's voice now. And, as she knew from experience, there was really no reasoning with a paranoid person. All she could hope to do was limit the damage, to keep that boy from harm.

Alexis shook her head. "No, there's no one." A tear streaked down her cheek. "They left me behind, they didn't even try to rescue me. Surely that tells you all that you need to know about them?"

Frum's eyes wandered over her, in consideration. He hesitated a further second and then, without breaking eye contact, he released Arnold, shoving him in the direction of the soldier, who took hold of him once more.

Frum approached his desk, stooped over his maps, as if he had forgotten that he had anyone in his room, that Alexis was sobbing her eyes out in his quarters. As if he had just remembered, just been struck by an afterthought, he raised his head and addressed the soldier holding Arnold. "Take him to the dungeon until further notice."

"No!" Alexis said, her lungs billowing with the screech.

Frum looked up at her stunned.

She rushed at him, her arms flailing and her brain boiling inside her skull. When she got up to him she lashed at him with her nails, catching him on the cheek before he could block her, bring her under control. As he knocked her to the floor and held her down, she observed the blood pooling in the three marks she'd indented in his cheek, and she felt a moment of absolute, unadulterated pleasure. And then she felt the guards' hands on her, their collective hold bringing her back to her feet and escorting her to the door of Frum's quarters.

If they took her down to the dungeons now then at least she would be able to comfort the small boy. She would rather that than keep some dying, half-mad tyrant happy. But, she supposed, she really had no choice in the matter.

RECOVERING IN THE DAMNED FORESTS

S YDNEY BENT DOWN at the stream, clutching the bucket he had stolen from a nearby house, on their way into the Damned Forests. The water ran into the bucket with a trickle. Once it was full he straightened up, looked about—still not quite used to the idea of being here in the Forests, and expecting a witch or wizard to sneak up from behind at any moment—then shifted off back toward the camp.

They had set up camp below a large elm tree with low-hanging branches. They'd made their beds using a few cast off sacks, which they'd swiped from the same house they'd stolen the bucket. All in all, it was fairly cosy. When it rained they had shelter, when they needed water they went down to the stream. The only real problem was John—he was still in a real state following their daring escape, and could hardly muster the effort to wake up and drink.

Right now John lay on his side, eyes shut and body twitching, a droplet of drool clinging to the corner of his mouth.

Sydney crouched down beside him , placing the bucket down too, and then he scooped up some water with his hand and, gently, dripped it onto John's lips.

John stirred in his sleep, his mouth responding to the water by opening up a little and his tongue lolling out to dab at the liquid.

Sydney surveyed John's wounds. He was no doctor but he was sure that John was in a bad way. They'd done their best to patch up the wounds on his arms and legs, to yank out all the odd pieces of crossbow bolts and arrows from his skin. His neck and face, however, were a different matter entirely.

Fresh cuts collected up his neck and marked his cheeks. They had a green tinge to them which Sydney didn't like the look of. Since they had nothing to treat the wounds with then there was really nothing else they could do, except pray to the gods. In fact, Sydney was worried that they might wake up one day to discover that John had slipped away in the night.

Since they'd escaped the castle, Sydney had had no chance to thank the giant for having got them out of there, and it nagged at him. John had seized both him and Courtney in his arms and, with no regard to his own body, rushed them free of the drawbridge. This stranger, whoever he was, had a good heart and he wished to know him personally.

Courtney's footsteps sounded over the dried leaves and twigs, then he appeared from round the side of the elm tree. He jerked his thumb over his shoulder. "There's some of the"—he made quotation marks with his fingers—"'King's' men back there. Got some sort of machine with them that's knocking down trees."

Sydney startled slightly. He couldn't go back to the dungeon. Not now he had sampled freedom. He looked up at Courtney. "Are they coming this way?"

Courtney dropped onto his makeshift sack-and-leaf bed and reclined. "Nah, they're going off deeper. Shouldn't think they'll bother us."

Sydney was of half a mind to go and look himself. All things considered Courtney wasn't really the perfect scout, the man to keep them safe from danger—he seemed to lack the capacity to sense it or, at least, judge it as threatening. Maybe someone had dropped him on his head as a baby. But Sydney fancied he would make an even worse nurse.

"What're we going to do?" Sydney said, half to himself.

Courtney clucked his tongue. "I'm going back to save Alexis and reclaim my throne, that's my destiny."

"No," Sydney said. "What're we going to do with *him*."

"Sure he'll wake up sooner or later."

That tickled Sydney the wrong way. "Look, how can you be so carefree about the whole thing? This guy here saved our lives. If it weren't for him we'd still be down in that dungeon, in those chains. He could've escaped if he'd wanted, left us behind, but he didn't."

"And why should I care?"

Anger flushed through Sydney. "'Care?' 'Care?' Are you absolutely insane?"

Courtney examined his nails. "I would've got us out of there eventually. When I'm King—"

"Just shut up, Courtney, please."

"That's no way to speak to your future king."

"Gods help us if you ever do become King."

Courtney beamed. "Yes, I'm sure they will."

There was a scrabbling off in the bushes close by.

It could have been anything: honey boars, one of the King's men, some other foul creature that they had no capacity to even imagine. Sydney jerked round.

From behind a bush an elderly lady with leathery skin and long tangled white hair emerged. She had a crooked nose and a hooked chin. She grimaced at them. "Do you two realise the racket you're making out here?"

Both Sydney and Courtney's faces reflected the fact that they did not.

The elderly lady sighed, then nodded at John. "What's the matter with him?"

Still feeling a little numb at finding another person out here in the Forests, Sydney said, "Uh, he had a nasty run in with some arrows."

She screwed up her eyes. "Not at the hands of King Fredrick's men, was it?"

Sydney exchanged glances with Courtney, trying to judge what might be the right answer here. Since he really couldn't think the situation through all that logically, he decided to just go with the simple truth. "Yes."

She burst into a grin, said, "In that case, follow me," and then waddled off back the way she'd come.

Sydney remained by John's side, not sure whether or not he should follow her. He examined John's sleeping body. Even between him and Courtney, they would struggle to shift him after the elderly woman. And then, as if someone had accessed his mind, read his thoughts, John floated upward gently. He hung there, motionless for a second or so—as if to give both him and Courtney a chance to marvel at the spectacle—and then his body floated off in the direction in which the woman had disappeared.

Now it was quite obvious who they had stumbled upon. The elderly woman was a witch.

Sydney felt a touch apprehensive as he followed John's body as it sped through the air, along an invisible trail. He had heard all sorts of stories about witches as a young boy—as a man too—and without exception they always ended badly for those who trusted them, and especially so for those who followed them to their houses. But what was it they said about an enemy's enemy being a friend? Then again, they also said that there was no honesty amongst thieves, and although the witch wasn't a thief, he supposed the saying held true in essence for all outlaws.

Courtney, usually so ready to leap head first into anything with even a hint of risk, held back and rested his hand on Sydney's shoulder—a gesture which Sydney hated since he was a good foot shorter. It made him feel like a human armrest. "Hey, Syd? What do you think about this character? Do we trust her?"

Watching John's feet disappear behind a thick tree trunk, he said, "I don't think we have much choice."

Courtney closed one eye. "Hmm, we could run off, you know, while we still can."

"No," Sydney said, marching onward after John. "This man saved our lives and so we must protect him with ours."

Forget the part about there being no honour amongst thieves—there wasn't any honour amongst noblemen either, at least not where Courtney's bloodline was concerned.

They hiked onward through the Forests, getting a glimpse of the soles of John's feet every so often. The witch seemed to have judged the speed with which John moved just so he floated quickly enough to keep them on their toes—moving on after him and not dawdling back on the trail, having should-we / shouldn't-we debates.

When they came upon the witch's house, it was a sight more hospitable than Sydney would've expected. It was a solid brick structure, washed in white, with a tiled roof covered in moss. The windows were, for the most part, clean and it was obvious that some effort had gone into the upkeep of the front garden and the pebble path which ran up to a racing green front door—already propped open, inviting them inside.

"Last chance, Syd," Courtney said, with a raised tone.

Sydney gripped a handful of Courtney's tunic and dragged him up the pebble path and onto the threshold. Not wanting to intrude, Sydney rapped a couple of times on the door and then stepped in.

From somewhere within the house there was the cheery tone of the elderly woman. "Come on in, dearie, tea's on the stove. Get yourselves warm by the fire."

Feeling a little more confident, Sydney stepped into the house, instantly feeling the warmth settle into his cheeks. After years down in the dungeon, and several nights under the stars, he had just about forgotten the pleasure of that sensation, and recalled that he quite liked it.

Sydney followed the source of the voice and arrived in a cosy kitchen. It had a wood burning stove, on top of which water was boiling away, tea leaves floating on the surface. He looked off onto the other side of the kitchen, where the witch perched beside John, who lay on a table, his feet, from the knees down, dangling over the edge.

The witch produced a bottle from within her robe, uncorked it and then dribbled the liquid onto John's lips. Finish, she returned the bottle and then stood straight on to Courtney and Sydney, taking them in. "Well, you two don't look like you've bathed for days."

"Years actually," Sydney said.

The witch cackled then prodded Sydney in the chest. "You've got a sense of humour, I like that. Character."

"Thanks," Sydney said, his voice hardly rising above a murmur.

The witch hobbled over to the stove, put on a glove and then took the boiling tea off. She poured out three cups and handed one each to Courtney and Sydney. As she led them off, out of the kitchen, into a sitting room filled with well-upholstered furniture, Sydney glanced back at John. "Will he be all right on his own?"

The witch waved her hand. "Yes, dearie, he'll be fine. He needs rest. His healing will take time."

Courtney looked alarmed at this comment, but Sydney ignored him—knowing that he was wont to start a fight trapped alone in a paper bag.

The armchair was just about the most comfortable thing Sydney had experienced ever—that or he had a slight penchant for exaggeration following his incarceration. It was true what they said about the world smelling sweeter after having been inside a long time, and Sydney was determined that he was going to do some serious smelling.

He examined the artwork on her walls, blurry paintings done with materials from the forest, pastes made from berries, canvases weaved from tree bark, he wagered. He felt a little awkward in the silence, as they all sipped at their cups of tea, so Sydney attempted to make conversation. "Your painting are very nice," he said.

The witch turned in her seat, as if she had never seen them before. "Oh yes," she said. "I do that quite a bit, in my spare time. Good to get my mind off witchcraft sometimes."

Courtney's eyes looked as if they might bulge from their sockets. Sydney noticed that he hadn't as much as taken a sip from the mug of tea, obviously afraid that she must've poisoned it in some way. He motioned for him to drink, not to be the completely rude, anti-social cannonball, just for once. Courtney refused to take the hint and, inevitably, the witch noticed the awkwardness passing between them.

She perched forward in her chair. "What is it? What's the matter?"

Courtney stayed silent, obviously terrified that she might hex him if he so much as talked out of turn.

There seemed little point in beating about the bush. They were already in the witch's house and, if she wanted, she could easily destroy them in a dozen different ways, so, once again, Sydney went with that old friend: honesty.

"I think what the problem is," Sydney said, "is that we're a little uneasy about being around a witch. I don't mean any offence, of course. It's just, you know, throughout our lives we've been bombarded with propaganda, people telling us that your kind are basically the root of all evil."

"I know what propaganda is," the witch said, blowing on her tea, and sending up a curl of steam. "Don't think that just because I've spent the best part of my life out in these damned forests, I'm some kind of hermit."

"No, of course," Sydney said, already feeling like he'd committed a social faux pas—he'd really lost his practice at avoiding those since he'd been chained to a wall for so long, had so much blood go to his brain. "It's just, well, I think I've made myself fairly clear."

The witch nodded her head and gave a solemn smile. She slurped up some tea. "First off all, dearie, you've nothing at all to worry about with me. I'm what's known as a white witch. It's my cousins, those black witches and wizards you've got to keep your eye out for."

"Ah," Sydney said, frowning. "Right."

She jerked her head to indicate the kitchen. "Your friend, back there, he ran into a black witch some time ago, didn't he?"

"I . . . I really don't know," Sydney said. "To be honest we barely know him. We were prisoners in the King's dungeon, you see, and he, well, broke us out of there." His throat tightened. "He rescued us."

"Yes," the witch said. "I read his aura. He seems a good sort. Shame that he didn't think to come and see me a little sooner after that witch cast her hex on him." She slurped more tea. "Nothing I can do for him now, of course, it's too late. The magic's taken hold in his blood, in his bones."

"If that witch hadn't cast her hex on him then me and my companion might well still be down in the dungeon. Without his strength we never would've broken through the castle defences."

The witch stared into her mug, perhaps reading the tea leaves. "It's funny how often even the most evil of acts can produce something positive. I suppose it's just the way of the world—the way of the gods."

"Yes," Sydney said. "I suppose it is."

The witch, whose name, it turned out, was Francesca, introduced them to their *separate* bedrooms, which Sydney was most glad about—given that he had spent every waking and sleeping moment at Courtney's side. If Courtney ever did make it to become King of Ethereal, he hoped to be granted the much-promised knighthood in recognition of this feat.

Courtney seemed to get over his fear of Francesca and, quite happily, took up residence in his bedroom, slipping between the sheets and falling asleep with more ease than a six year old after a bumper Christmas.

When Sydney reached his own room and had got himself comfortable when he noticed Francesca standing on the hearth, smiling at him. Sydney smiled back, not quite knowing what else he could possibly do. He wished he had something to give her for all the kindness she had shown. He supposed that something worthwhile would present itself in time.

Francesca pressed her hands together. "You know that the Forests are in disarray. We are being driven out, one-by-one."

"What do you mean?"

"The King's men, they are knocking down trees, tearing

them up by their roots. They are disturbing magic that is better left alone. Already they have caused irreparable damage. The Forests will never be the same."

"But why?" Sydney said.

"Why what?"

"Why're they digging up the Forests?"

Francesca sighed. "I hear that the King was cursed by one of my cousins, a black witch. The story I've heard details that he and his men traipsed through the Forests and came upon her—and, of course, as they entered her territory, she believed them to be a threat and acted quickly. I have to say her actions may be justified, considering the reaction of the King. I understand he will stop at nothing to tear the Forests apart in search of the witch, so that she might turn his curse around."

"But could you fix his condition, neutralise the curse?"

"Perhaps," she said. "But why would I want to do that? During his rule all the King has ever shown is hatred and intolerance for the mystical, for anything he doesn't understand. Why should I help him now that he needs help?"

"You're helping my friend."

"Yes, but that's different. Your friend was a victim. Another victim of King Fredrick."

Despite all those years that Sydney had spent down in the dungeons, he still had a strange voice, right at the back of his mind, which stopped him short of coming out and declaring the King to be nothing more than a sadistic, idiotic autocrat. For some reason he felt like he had deserved his punishment, against everything else. Then, on the other hand, he knew that he was ridiculous to be thinking that way—that the King had stolen years of his life for something so petty as Sydney having humiliated him in front of a lord. He supposed he still held onto a shred of sympathy because the King had spared his life.

"It's no good for you to dwell on how the King treated you in the past. He was cruel, merciless. Do not try to put any other spin on those facts."

Sydney gripped the sides of his head. "Are you reading my mind?"

Francesca gave him a slight smile. "I'm sorry, that was quite impolite of me. Next time I'll ask, I promise." She gripped the door handle then said, "Goodnight, I'll let you know if your friend wakes during the night and calls for you."

Sydney watched the door whisper shut and slumped back on his pillows, allowed himself to sink into the soft mattress, and he thought about how his life had completely changed—for the better—ever since he had been sprung from the dungeon.

RABBIT KING JOINS FORCES

TREVOR SAT ABOUT staring into the crackling fire. They had marched for hours to reach this point, where Zend had decided was a relative point of safety, far enough away from the King's men making inroads into the Forests. It was strange what a difference a matter of hours could make. Only this morning Rabbit King had been tying them to stakes and leaving them for the honey boars and now they were sitting round, everyone quite pleasant—at least Zend was being as pleasant as he could be—toasting some vegetables Plont had foraged from a nearby patch of earth. No one had brought up the subject of eating meat, not wanting to get on Rabbit King's nerves, but Trevor had to admit he would've killed for a bit of Lulu or Frankie, who both lay sleeping, snug against Rabbit King's thigh.

They agreed on the sensible option of taking turns to watch over the camp. It fell to Plont for the first watch, while Zend would take the second, and in the early hours of the morning it would be Trevor's turn. Once more Rabbit King was overlooked in the form of another diplomatic pirouette to keep him onside.

Trevor bedded down on a fairly comfortable pile of leaves and some clods of soil. He was well past the point of caring what state his clothes were in, considering he did look like he had been dragged backward through a rabbit burrow twice, and he cared even less where his odour was concerned.

With Plont watching over them, Trevor felt secure, that nothing would befall them with his watchful eyes twitching through the darkness. And if anything did stir them he was certain that Rabbit King would have something to say about it. It was quite comforting for Trevor to have two hefty guys around, and another who was handy with making whatever he could with the resources at his disposal.

At first Trevor believe it had been an owl's hoot which had disturbed his slumber. Then, when he took stock of the scene, the camp fire now burning down to embers, he realised that Plont was standing over him, shaking him awake. Zend and Rabbit King were already up and about, their eyes wary for any motion in the gloom. Even Lulu and Frankie were up and about, their ears pricked up and their noses twitching.

They all stood there, in silence, listening for whatever it was that had alerted Plont. Soon Trevor saw what it had been. Out there, in a clearing not far from them, he saw a group of men trudging their way through the undergrowth. As they drew closer, he could overhear their conversation. They sounded . . . drunk.

One piled into the other and there was the swing of a fist, followed by another of the men seizing the one who had swung his fist from behind and preventing him from striking out again. There was a lot of, what Trevor presumed to be, swearing and cursing among them, and the one of the men called for quiet, telling his companions that they had to take care that Lord Eversham wouldn't hear them arriving at the camp in that state.

Trevor exchanged glances with Zend and they watched on as the men bundled their way through the woods, looking to pass right by their camp. And then, right at the last moment, as they were just about to stumble on out of sight, one of the men near the back of the group turned his head, held his hand at his forehead to better see and then called to the others.

Trevor clenched his stomach in anticipation. He wished for them to go away, to return to wherever they'd come from, but the other men were returning to where the last man stood pointing, right at them.

Plont grasped his bow and notched an arrow.

Zend picked up a nearby rock and clutched it in his fist.

Rabbit King scowled.

The men snuck closer, one of them, comically, holding his finger to his lips, motioning for them to be very quiet.

Trevor took this for a sign of Dutch courage, he was unconvinced they would've acted like this at home in the Forests had they been stone sober.

As they got closer and closer, Trevor felt the tension build up among his companions. When the first man drew into range, only twenty feet or so from them, Plont let fly with his bow, catching the man in the chest, sending him down, gargling, to the floor of the forest.

The other men barked among them, drew their swords from their waists and formed a circle, backing into one another.

Although Trevor had little to no experience of military tactics, this struck him as an especially bad one, because it presented Plont with a large target to aim at. Plont swiftly fitted arrows and shot each of the men, one-by-one. Each of them dropped to their knees, more surprised than the first to see another man hit. When they all lay on the ground, gargling and writhing about, the group slipped from cover, with Zend—as always—leading them forward.

Zend towered over one of the men, squeezing the rock in his fist. "What are you doing out here?"

As the man spoke, blood dribbled down his chin. "You . . . have . . . killed . . . us."

"Not quite," Zend said, frown lines appearing on his forehead, "my friend here has just given you a few flesh wounds. When your patrol comes round in the morning I'm sure they'll pick you up and patch you up fine." He rested his hand on his hip. "But if you don't give us any information soon then I'll take medical help out of the equation."

"No!" the man said, holding up his arm, as if it might help him ward off any attack. "We're . . . we're stationed . . . not far from here."

"And what're you doing here, so deep in the Forests? Why aren't you with the rest of your group chopping down the trees?"

The man grimaced and then, a moment later, Trevor realised that he was doing his best to smile. "We were . . . put in charge of . . . guarding the . . . Grotesque," he said the last word with spittle in his throat, as if it physically hurt him to say it.

There was that word again.

Rabbit King stooped forward and got right up in the man's face. "You mean, like me?"

The man's eyes widened and his lips parted. His breath slipped out as if it were a whisper. "Yes."

"And where might they be?" Rabbit King said.

The man shook his head and clamped his eyes shut.

Zend sighed and bent down so that he could grab the man by his throat. "Listen, if you don't cooperate with us fully then I'll let my furry friend here have a private word with you. And I don't think you've made the best impression on him thus far."

The man glanced about, caught the eye of one of his silent companions and then jerked his head off to the right. "That way. Along that path." His whole body shook as he drew a breath. "But . . . you'll have no . . . chance. It's guarded by . . . dozens of us."

"Dozens?" Zend said, with a slight laugh. "Oh no, looks like my friend will need a few more arrows then. Tell me, do they all back up into a circle when under attack, or is it just your select group?"

Even through his intense pain, the man glowered at Zend. "You caught us off guard, it wasn't a fair fight."

Zend snorted. "You mean to say that you don't know how to fight in the woods, you never went on that particular training course."

"We . . . don't need to . . . we've had no . . . resistance. Soon the . . . Forests will be ours."

Zend patted the man on his shoulder then rose. "That's positive thinking, always good to look on the bright side." He looked over the rest of the men, apparently judging whether any might be a threat from now on, then he turned back to Plont. "Better get a move on, if we strike on now we should be able to find the camp before morning. Can't imagine it can be far off if this lot managed to get away from it in this state. If they've taken apart as much of the Forests as they claim they might have seen our kids."

Rabbit King gave the man who had said the 'G' word a final menacing stare and then followed Zend and Plont's lead. Trevor hung back for a second looking over the men. He thought about saying that he was sorry, but supposed that wouldn't really help much—that it might come across as a touch pathetic, so he went on his way without another word.

They tramped on through the undergrowth, this time Rabbit King leading, since he had a superior sense of smell. He guided them along the path, telling the whole time he smelled man strong in the air. And his sense proved to be correct because, with the sun rising on the outer fringes of the Forests, they came across the first guard outpost—where the guard was sound asleep.

Plont and Zend despatched him quickly, tying him up and gagging him before leaving him in a bush out of sight of the main track. Up ahead there were several tents pitched and a few fires still smouldering away in the rising dawn. They stalked closer.

Rabbit King brought them off to the side of the trail and

briefed them on the Grotesque's home, which he informed them was known as Witney Branches. He told them that it was one of the trees among the tents and that it was semi-hidden normally. He only speculated about how the, largely incompetent, King's men had stumbled across Witney Branches, and then made some comment about the Grotesque lacking ingenuity such as his, not having the courage to hide themselves away better, individually in the Forests.

Trevor considered pointing out that Rabbit King's home had been discovered by the King's men too and, as they spoke, it was being torn apart, piece-by-piece, scrutinised by the men. But this was neither the time nor place, and he had no intention of getting himself on the wrong end of Rabbit King's ire again.

Trevor hung back as Zend and Plont slipped into the tents, one-by-one, and did their same trick of tying the men up and gagging them. Meanwhile, Rabbit King kept watch over the camp for any early risers. About half an hour later, with the sun peeping over the treetops, Zend and Plont had managed to tie up the entire camp—now reduced to several fuming, but immobilised, King's men.

After a quick double check, and leaving Plont and Rabbit King to keep an eye on the prisoners, Trevor accompanied Zend to the door of Witney Branches, where Zend knocked twice and waited, as if he were paying a normal call to someone in his village.

There was a pregnant pause before the sound of footsteps broke the silence within, and the door, tentatively, creaked open. A woman—her face completely covered in hair—peered out. She looked them up and down. "Who are you?"

Zend puffed out his chest. "We've rescued you from the King's men."

She looked beyond them, over at the camps, then turned back to them. "Have you now?" she said, still with a wary tone in her voice.

"Yes."

"Then where are they?"

"In their tents. We tied them all up."

"What? All of them?"

"Yes," Zend said, already getting noticeably frustrated by her neglect to acknowledge a heroic task well done.

At this confirmation she seemed to brighten considerably. "But there are only four of you. How ever did you take down their entire camp."

Now Zend managed a smile. "Really, it was nothing. We live lives fraught with danger, and we're used to it."

"I should say so," the woman said, extending her hand to welcome them inside the tree trunk. "Please, come inside. My name's Susan, thank you for liberating us."

Zend patted Trevor on the back and then followed Susan. Trevor hung back a moment, taking another glance back over the camp, at the silent camp with each tent containing the King's men thoroughly tied up.

Trevor was still getting over the fact of there being a woman with her face completely covered in hair, when he emerged into a kitchen to be confronted with all manner of deformed humans. He traced the faces, the man with flaps of skin covering every crevice, hiding his eyes, nose and mouth, then he took in the young girl with eyelashes curling up and out, over her forehead, her fingernails wrapping round her hands several times. And then, finally, he absorbed the man with a single eye, occupying his entire head.

Susan stood at the head of the table, wiped her hands on the sides of her apron then said, "These men have taken care of the entire camp, tied them all up and everything."

"Impossible," the man with the eye said.

"Nope," Zend said. "It just took a bit of initiative. Took them off guard at dawn."

The man with the eye shook his head. "I just can't believe it."

Susan leant into Zend and Trevor, hand covering her mouth, but neglected to drop the volume of her voice so it was still obvious to the rest of room exactly what she was saying. "That's Horace. He might be a bit bitter because he was determined that he should be the one to save us all from the King's men."

Horace grasped his head in his hands. "I brought them here after all."

"Oh well," Zend said. "The end justifies the means, or so they say. At least you won't have to put yourself in any danger."

Horace looked up at him with a glum expression written all over his eye. "I suppose you're right."

Trevor stood about at the stove, not quite sure what he was supposed to do. They had come here and liberated this lot and all they'd really got was a muted celebration. He decided that now was his time to speak. "I don't mean to sound rude or anything, but I'm a little surprised that you're not cranking out the wine or beer, or whatever it is you have here. Aren't you ecstatic to be free?"

Susan gave him a half-smile, while the others shot him blank looks. "The problem is that they're destroying the Forests. You may have taken down those men outside, but there will be more on their way, every day. The King's dedicated his entire army to the eradication of the Damned Forests and so, you see, we really cannot afford to get our hopes up too much."

Strangely, at this comment, Horace stirred from his melancholy, and looked round the kitchen. His eyelids shrivelled back so that he lost his droopy-eyed expression. "I've been putting together the ground work for an underground movement, a way to fight back against the King's army."

Trevor glanced at Zend, who seemed to get the message he was trying to transmit.

Zend gave them an easy smile. "Yes, well, that seems a bit beyond our brief, to be fair. You see, we've been sent by our village to search for our missing children—they've been snatched from us by forces unknown. We believed it to have been Rabbit King for a long time, but, as it turns out, he really had nothing at all to do with it."

Horace slammed his fist into the table, sending dirty plates and cutlery rattling. "Then you've wasted your time coming here. You might as well have just left us here to be kept prisoner. Now when they return with reinforcements, they'll only treat us harsher."

Trevor tried to catch Zend's eye, to communicate the message that, maybe, they might be better served making a sly exit at some point, to leave these people with whatever bad feelings they'd so deeply etched upon themselves. But Zend remained resilient.

"Look here, now," Zend said. "Do you think it was easy to tie up all those guards with just four men? Would you rather that we would've just kept on walking through the Forests, not bothering to help you out?"

Horace glared back at him. "If you've got no interest in saving the Forests, then yes."

"Right then," Zend said flashing his eyebrows, then beating a hasty exit. "We know where we're not required. We'll leave you in peace to your enslavement and future life as prisoners of the King. You do realise that he'll put you all in sideshows, use you as common entertainment? The man has no morals."

Horace said, "Not if our uprising has anything to do with it, he won't."

Zend gave them another moment to change their minds, to fall about his feet with gratitude then, seeing it wasn't forthcoming, headed out the door.

Trevor stood there for several seconds before coming to the realisation that this too was his cue to leave Witney Branches. He, after all, really had no commitment to this uprising either. If he started accepting every side quest which crossed his path he would never get back home—this missing kids one was enough to fill anybody's plate.

He shifted from his position, feeling the heat of the Grotesque's collective glare, and beat a hasty retreat back along the winding, corridors which sloped upward, until he could see daylight pouring in from outside, through the door.

As he emerged outside, he felt that the atmosphere wasn't quite right. All the birds in the trees had stopped singing. He noticed that the outside of Witney Branches was steeped in shadow, and then he saw it was because several men, armed with swords and bows were standing round the clearing, aiming at him and Zend.

One of the men stepped forward—apparently the leader. He

wore a self-satisfied smirk and had a thin moustache. "What exactly do you think you've been doing round here?"

Zend was smouldering away, pressing his lips tight together.

A little further along, in the centre of the clearing, several of the King's men had Rabbit King and Plont surrounded.

The leader wore a sword at his waist. He gripped the hilt and unsheathed it, holding it down by his side. "I am Lord Eversham, and I shall not be messed with." He brought the blade of the sword level with the line of his nose. "So, will you be so kind as to inform me as to what in the world you thought you were doing with my men?"

Zend found his voice. "We incapacitated them."

Eversham chuckled. "Yes," he said, drawing out the 's' into a hiss, "I can see that. But how did you think you could get away with it? Didn't you do a proper headcount? Realise that we keep at least half of our men out in the Forests patrolling at any one time? Have you got no brains about you?"

Zend remained silent.

"You Grotesque have been trapped inside there for many days and nights, and this was the best you could come up with?"

Trevor caught up with the line of Eversham's logic, and realised that he had taken them for inhabitants of Witney Branches, rather than some outside invaders. That gave him hope. At least they shouldn't be put to death right away.

Eversham continued, "I would like to think up some suitable punishment, but, to be honest, your attempt at escape was so pitiful, so lacking in any kind of guile, that I would feel terrible taking advantage. My orders are to finish with the Damned Forests, not slaughter Grotesque. As a lord I have a conscience, which is less than can be said for you people." He thrust his sword in the direction of Witney Branches. "So, back into your home, all of you, and try to behave yourselves."

Hardly able to believe their luck, Trevor stooped off back toward Witney Branches. After a brief eyeballing with Lord Eversham, Zend followed. Rabbit King and Plont came after. As they headed back along the crooked corridor, back to beg their hospitality from Susan, Trevor turned to the others and said, "Do you think they found that party of men you injured back in the clearing yet?"

Zend visibly stiffened at the reminder.

Plont, too, looked faintly vexed.

Rabbit King, however, held up his hand. "If they want to get some revenge then I'll be ready for them. They can answer to my back legs."

Trevor supposed that Rabbit King might well be first in line to sign up for the uprising. He thought that now they were trapped, with King's men on all sides, they might well consider getting themselves involved, if it had the possibility of nudging themselves closer to achieving their own goals.

A TENSE DINNER

A LEXIS GOT HERSELF ready for dinner with the rest of the maidens, plastering on more powder to eliminate the redness in her cheeks which had appeared following her bouts of tears. She couldn't take her mind off that boy, Arnold, down in the dungeons. She hoped that he would at least be given free roam of his cell—the thought of him hanging upside down, or in chains at all, was too much for her to bear.

She tottered down the steps to the kitchens, already smelling the gorgeous odours of the cooking roast—the herbs mingling with one another, the succulent scent of simmering meat—wafting along the corridor. But today all thought of food turned her bowels to water. She had only to think about Arnold, all alone in that cell in the dungeon.

Cherry glared at her from her position at the table as Alexis walked in to take her seat near the door. The other girls hadn't yet arrived, and neither had Henrietta. So the two of them were alone, much to Alexis's dismay.

Cherry unfolded her napkin and laid it on her lap, lips puckered, just as Alexis supposed she had been taught to do. She then stared over the table at Alexis. "I hear your friends managed to escape the castle."

Alexis would've rather talked about anything else—had Cherry hurl barely-concealed insults at her or had her make threats—but she really had no desire to bring up anything to do with the escape.

"Yes, they did," Alexis said.

"I hear that half the garrison couldn't stop them, that the great, big lump who should've been appointed the King's Champion burst through them all."

"That's what I heard, too."

"Still," Cherry said, "you must be pleased for them. You know, that they've managed to get out."

Alexis probed her tone, focussing on the subtext. She knew that Cherry was searching for a chink in her armour, some means of catching her out—have her reported to General Frum and thrown back in the dungeons. But wasn't that just what she deserved?

"I really have no opinion about it."

Cherry eyes lolled from side-to-side, as if some spy might be hiding themselves behind one of the curtains and she leant over the table, in intrigue. Alexis got an eyeful of her sizable bosom. No wonder she was the King's favourite. "You know," Cherry said, "I've often thought about escape myself, thought there might be a way for me to escape the castle, find a better life for myself."

If this was really the best that Cherry could do then Alexis was deeply disappointed. She had expected much more in her rival—had hoped she wouldn't so hopelessly underestimate Alexis's intellect. Then again, she supposed that schooling wasn't high on an Etherealean girl's list of priorities.

"Have you really?" Alexis said, taking care to keep her tone to one of polite interest.

"Oh yes. In fact I've done more than think, I've made inquiries. You see, I've always fancied myself as a dancer, there're several travelling pleasure shows and I'm sure I could find one and realise my dream. You don't think I'm too old, do you?"

"Oh no," Alexis said, tugging at her napkin and folding it into various shapes.

Cherry beamed. "It is wonderful to have someone to confide in," she said it with a lingering suggestion that Alexis should add some kind of a revelation herself, so that the rapport would flow both ways.

Alexis, however, was not in the mood of obliging. This conversation had all the makings of a trap. As far as she knew, General Frum and a dozen men were waiting behind the kitchen door, ready to jump her at a moment's notice, at some signal from Cherry.

They spent the rest of their waiting in silence, with Cherry keeping her mouth shut for a change, while Alexis lost herself in thoughts of despair for the boy down in the dungeon. She had resolved that she needed to take more proactive measures to get him out. Perhaps the King would listen to her the next time he called her into his chambers—if he ever called her again into his chambers. Maybe, as she sat there at the table, he was conspiring to have her thrown back into the dungeons, had decided she wasn't worth the risk of keeping around.

When Henrietta arrived she sensed the tone and tried to raise the humour round the dinner table, as the brewing tension between Alexis and Cherry dampened the mood of the other three maidens, but all she managed was a few nervous titters and, after the main course, she gave up trying to entertain altogether.

Alexis rose from her seat at the earliest opportunity and returned to her bedroom, glad that Henrietta hadn't tried to keep her behind 'for a chat.' She had no intention of throwing a damp rag over the tumultuous relationship between herself and Cherry—at least not for the time being—she had more weighty matters on her mind than schoolgirl tiffs.

She was surprised to see a representative from the King's court waiting at her bedroom door, informing her that the King would like to meet with her. She asked him for a few minutes, at least to freshen up her mouth following her robust dinner. When she was ready, she accompanied him to the King's chamber, not knowing quite what to expect. Might this be her last night as one of his maidens?

Jenson was there, as always, to shepherd her inside. He closed the door behind her and lingered in a shadowy corner.

The King was lying on his bed. He looked more frail than when Alexis had previously seen him. As she drew closer she took in his pale complexion, the way his exposed arm and leg, on his right side, appeared no thicker than toothpicks.

The King managed a smile through his quite obvious pain. Creases ingrained the corners of his eyes and lips. There was a yellowness to his complexion. The overall effect was that he looked a decade older than he had been at the competition to appoint his new Champion.

Feeling nervous, trembling slightly, she took his offered hand. She felt like she had to be pre-emptive, to get out the reason which she believed he'd summoned her here, so she said, "About the escape, my lord, I promise I knew nothing about their plans."

The King gave a weak nod. His lips were pale and cracked.

Alexis continued, "And I just want to swear my complete loyalty and allegiance to you, and—"

He raised his hand, apparently for her to stop speaking. His voice was low and gravelly, she had to lean into him, bring her ear almost right up to his lips for her to distinguish the words. "Alexis, my sweet," he said. "I am dying—"

Feeling a faint burst of hope, Alexis did her best to conceal it. "Oh no, my lord. Please don't speak like that. You must be—"

He feebly waved away her protests once more. "Please listen to me." He tried to straighten himself up in bed, to prop himself up on the pillows, but he gave up, clearly not having the strength. "I have no heirs, so when I die the Kingdom of Ethereal shall enter a period of anarchy."

That would open huge opportunities for her. Maybe she could sneak away during all the madness. Alexis could hardly hide her jubilation at the news. Of course no death of a human being was a time for celebration, but the facts were as they were. Perhaps she would be allowed out of her prison without much of a fight—permitted to walk over the drawbridge herself.

The King reached out for her hand and took it in his fragile hold. His eyeballs lolled about, as if free-spinning gyros.

"Sire?" Jenson said, from his position in the shadows. "Do you wish for rest?"

The King shook his head and concentrated on Alexis—although his arthritic movements hardly let him keep still for any length of time. "As King I have one great regret. I never married, and I would like you to do me the pleasure, to fulfil my dying wish of marrying me, of becoming my queen."

The breath deserted Alexis's lungs. She simply had no response to his request. She had come here believing she would be turfed out and now she had ended up on the pointy end of a marriage proposal. She turned over the idea in her mind: Queen Alexis.

The light seemed to be fading in the King's eyes—he was growing tired, and his hold on her fingers was growing limp. "It shall be your duty to oversee the transition of the Kingdom from my mantle to the next—while the true heir is sought."

What could she say to that? When she'd been back on Earth, she recalled that once while working at her local corner shop her boss had left her in charge for an afternoon. In the course of that time she'd managed to screw up half the invoicing system and some whip-smart middle-aged man had offered to help her and ended up nicking several hundred pounds from the till. There was no telling what she might get up to if all the responsibility for Ethereal fell into her hands, albeit temporarily.

"Tell me your answer," the King said.

She glanced back over her shoulder, to Jenson, who continued to lurk, his expression was hard to read because of the shadow falling over his face, but she was sure that this offer from the King had come across as unexpected—that he would've much rather have put his oar in before the King had made such a rash offer.

And then she thought about all the good she might be able to do in provisional power. Should the King die, she could order for Arnold to be released from the dungeons and, it went without saying, that she should be able to wander freely throughout the Kingdom—perhaps even lose her escorts and slip off back home, back to Earth, if that was what she wanted.

The King's dim eyes fixed onto her.

Alexis straightened herself up on the bed, pulled back her lips in a smile, and said, "I accept."

A twitch took hold of the corners of the King's mouth, and Alexis looked back to Jenson, worried that something might be coming over the King, and then she realised that he was only attempting to smile. Once again, he reached for her hand, brushed his flaking skin against her flawless skin.

It was the middle of the night when Alexis heard the unmistakable patter of footsteps outside her door. She rose onto her elbows and attempted to penetrate the gloom. She watched as her bedroom door slowly creaked open, just a crack, enough to allow someone to slide inside, before closing again.

Alexis's muscles tensed and she got herself caught in a panic, thinking about how she might protect herself. She kept no weapons in her bedroom, of course, the best she had was a razor in the bathroom which she used to shave her legs—but she wouldn't have a chance of crossing the room before the invader would be upon her so, paralysed in terror, she watched on.

The invader snuck through the shadows, keeping to the walls, as if it might make them invisible. They drew closer to Alexis's bed, holding something down by their thigh.

"Who's there?" Alexis said, her voice feeling strange, alien in her throat.

The invader halted.

"If you don't identify yourself, I'll scream, wake up the whole castle."

The invader stayed silent for a long while, so long that Alexis prepared herself to call out—already worried that when she attempted to do so she might not have the ability to get out any sound. What if this intruder just acted quickly, killed her where she lay?

Alexis loosened her throat.

"It's me," the intruder said, in a gravely tone. "Cherry."

Alexis made out her form now. Cherry was all dressed in black, even with a matching netted, charcoal-coloured veil drawn down to hide her face. Alexis turned her attention to Cherry's hand and tried to work out the object there. "What're you doing here?" Alexis said.

Cherry bowed her head. "I heard about the news. That the King has proposed to you."

"This seems a pretty strange time to come round congratulating her."

"You do understand that it's most irregular? That for the King to marry a commoner, let alone a maiden, such as you, is simply unheard of, it will cause all manner of scandal throughout the Kingdom."

"He took me off guard, I really had no idea what to say."

"There will be an outcry, a rebellion throughout the land. If you do actually go through with the wedding, and the King happens to die, the court shall turn on you, tear you off the throne."

Did Cherry really believe that Alexis hadn't already considered all of these factors, that, as she'd pointed out, she'd had no choice in the matter, been backed into a corner? In any case, what did Cherry's opinion have to do with anything?

Cherry stole closer.

Alexis kept her eyes alert to that object in her hand.

"He made a mistake," Cherry said. "He never meant to ask you to marry him. He must've been delirious. He must've believed that it was me there with him, holding his hand."

Now this was just moving into delusional territory and, having had many years of experience with Courtney, Alexis had a very low tolerance for it. "Cherry, I think you'd better go now. We can talk more about this tomorrow."

Cherry drew closer still.

"I'm not joking," Alexis said. "I'll call out to the guards and they'll take you away. Just think how they'll handle you're being in the bedroom of the King's fiancé, uninvited. If you're lucky they'll turf you out, send you into the barracks, just like they did with the last maiden, or maybe they'll throw you down into the dungeons."

This seemed to give Cherry pause for thought, but she still made no sign of retreating from the bedroom. She met Alexis with a steely gaze. "You will never be Queen of Ethereal. I shall never bow down to you."

"Fine," Alexis said, "but just go, won't you?"

Cherry lingered for another moment or so before rising from the bed, making her way back across the bedroom. As she reached the door, Alexis caught sight of the object in her hand. A knife blade glinted in the moonlight. Cherry had come here to kill her. That was how far her hatred extended, how much she resented Alexis's place in the King's affections. No longer could Alexis afford to fob off Cherry as just a dizzy girl—she was dangerous a threat to her life.

Just as she made to round the door, and leave the bedroom, she sent Alexis a frosty glare. "You will never be his. He shall always be my king, and I will be there to meet with him when he comes to his senses."

WAKING UP IN A WITCH'S HOUSE

JOHN'S CHEST tightened and his breaths came hard and fast. His heart took on all the qualities of a rabbit foot, pounding up and down against his ribs. He tried to steady himself but all round him was black. He was somewhere unfamiliar and his whole body, but, in particular, his legs ached. He strained his neck to get a look at them and saw that they dangled off the edge of the table.

When he tried to sit his strength deserted him. He felt like a little child again, weak as a kitten. Ever since that final fight, where he had faced off with that Narbut, he had the recollection of running. Had he killed the Narbut? He couldn't remember. He considered what he could recall beyond that, going down to the dungeons, stumbling across those prisoners who he'd freed. Had they betrayed him? Captured him and brought him here? Was he still in the castle, just in some kind of house inside the grounds? Perhaps he was being prepared for execution.

His muscles knotted together and a migraine seeped into his skull. He analysed his situation. He had no chains, nothing tying him to the spot, so they must've given him some kind of potion, something to keep him still. His eyes trembled in their sockets as he absorbed his surroundings.

Although it was still dark, he could make out the form of the room with the moonlight which dribbled in through one of the windows. He made out a stove, a fireplace replete with chalky ash and on the other side of the room he saw a collection of pots and pans.

His mind skimmed back through his memories. Everything about this place, the kitchen, the smells but especially those pots and pans: cauldrons, pointed to one fact—that he was in a witch or wizard's house.

At first panic seized control of his system and he told himself that he had to get the hell out of there as soon as possible, but just as he had realised already, he had lost the capacity to manipulate his body, so he was stuck with wondering. Was this a plan of the King's? To let one of his witches or wizards loose on him? Somehow, in John's mind, it just didn't add up that the King would allow any association with magic, let alone allow it practised within his castle grounds. So perhaps he was mistaken about the King having him under control. But, if that were the case, then where was he and how had he got here?

A tentative answer presented itself shortly after, in the form of a voice in the gloom. "How do you feel?" it said, a female voice, an older woman.

With magic on his mind, John felt his whole body stiffen, but still he couldn't move his limbs—only the feeling of cramp clawing its way through his muscles and nerves.

"I noticed that you have a history with witches and wizards, this . . . condition you find yourself in, the gigantism, I know that only magic could have had such a dramatic effect, so that's why I've sedated you."

John tried to move his lips to speak, but found them just as useless as the rest of his body. He was resigned to merely following the voice, wherever it might be coming from, with his eyes.

The voice continued, "If your friends hadn't brought you here, you might well be dead by now. They brought you to me and I saved your life."

What 'friends' was she talking about? He supposed she must've meant those prisoners who he had freed from the dungeons. He wasn't sure how much of this witch's story he should believe—whether she might not have done away with his 'friends' and then brought him back here to salvage his organs or harvest his blood for some ritual.

The witch said, "I'm sorry to have had to give you a sedation potion, but I really had no other choice. I wanted the chance to speak with you, to explain what had happened and to assure myself that you wouldn't try to strike me in any way."

She trod closer to him so that he could make her shape out in the half-light. Her face came into view just about: a bent nose, tousled white hair, that was enough for John to know she was who she said she was. She produced a vial from inside her cloak. "But, I think now that I'm satisfied that you've heard me out and that you'll make an informed decision on whether or not to kill me. Your friends tell me that you're a hero, that you led their escape from the King's castle. I suppose now will be a nice test of your powers of forgiveness and gratitude." She stooped over him, uncorked the vial and fed the liquid into John's lips.

If he had been able, John would've spat it out, but his body betrayed him, his throat forced him to take it down. He felt the liquid trickle down through his system, like a match being held along a series of firecrackers, lighting them all, one-by-one. Touch returned to him slowly with little prickles moving their way along his skin—his hair stood on end. As the potion took hold of him more completely, he found he could flex his fingers and then his toes. Soon he had regained control of his arms and legs, had enough strength to lift himself up into a sitting position and dangle his legs over the edge of the table so that he faced the witch.

The witch rested her hand on his knee. "How're you doing, dearie? Are all your senses back?"

John rolled his shoulders. It felt like he had been sleeping in a poor position and, he supposed, that was because he had. He eyed the witch and, he had to admit, the thought of tearing her apart with his bare hands crossed his mind. But his logical brain kicked in, told him that this witch had in fact saved him from whatever mess he had got himself involved in.

He rubbed his head and squinted. "You said I was a hero? That I led my . . . friends out of the King's castle. It's just . . . just that I don't remember."

The witch nodded. "When you came to me you were at death's door. It looked like you'd fought off the King's garrison to get out of there—and from what your friends say, that doesn't sound far from the truth."

"I don't remember any of it."

"The memories might come back or they might not. All you'll need to know is written on their faces or, well, that bald one's face in particular."

"About my friends, where are they?"

She jerked her thumb upward. "Sleeping away. Anyone might've thought that they'd never seen a bed the way their faces lit up on seeing them."

"Can I see them now?"

She shook her head. "It's better to let them rest. You should rest, too. Get yourself back fighting fit. I shouldn't wonder that you'll feel a whole heap better by morning."

So John did as the witch instructed and lay back down on the table. He didn't really notice the various splinters or the hard surface so much—feeling totally exhausted by whatever it was that he had done.

Breakfast was solid: a stack of pancakes plastered in syrup with a fresh pot of tea made from guar leaves, which Susan would often make for them back at Witney Branches. During the course of breakfast, the witch told him her name was Francesca and he found his gratitude toward her grow as she recounted the various wounds she'd fixed up, shown him the arrow heads and crossbow bolts she'd magicked out of him. He was sure that she hadn't been exaggerating when she'd said that she'd saved his life—that without her he would've died. Now, as far as he was concerned, that levelled up the score. While one witch had thoroughly ruined his life another had saved it.

He was in the middle of his third stack of pancakes, feeling that his familiar appetite had been fully restored along with his wounds, when he noticed the sound of footsteps coming down the stairs. He turned his attention to the doorway to see one of the prisoners, or ex-prisoners, wander on in—the bald one.

For a second or so, the prisoner just stood there and stared, as if he were watching an ape in a zoo having lunch, and then, all at once, he cast off his catatonia and burst forward, arms outstretched and rushed to throw his arms round John's neck.

Not having ever really been one for physical contact, John was a touch taken aback. A piece of pancake stuck in his throat and the whole jubilatory scene was rather turned on its head as John half-choked on his mouthful.

The bald prisoner backed up, displaying reverence for John's condition, but he continued to look on him with an idiotic grin parting his cheeks. "You saved our lives."

Just about having himself composed following his near death by pancake, John straightened himself up in his chair and took a large glug of guar tea. "Please, don't mention it."

"Don't mention it!" the bald prisoner said. "How can I not mention it. Do you know how long we were down there in the dungeon? How we'd got to thinking that we'd never get out? Not in our lifetimes anyway."

Francesca cooked away a fresh batch of pancakes at the stove, clearly enjoying eavesdropping on this moment of melo-drama—John guessed that moments of melodrama were spread fairly thin out here in this neck of the Forests.

John felt a trifle foolish to ask, but he had to, otherwise this awkwardness would grate at him forever more. "Uh, what's your name?"

The bald prisoner's glittering smile faltered. "Sydney," he said. "Don't you remember?"

John shook his head and finished off the last pancake on his plate, only for it to be replenished seconds later by Francesca. He smiled at her politely and then turned back to the bald prisoner. "Look, I'm really glad that I was able to help you out, not that I can recall any of it, but I've really got to be shoving off after breakfast. You see, I need to get back to Witney Branches, where my family is."

Sydney looked over at Francesca, then back at John. "Sure, you can do whatever you want. I mean, you're the hero."

"I might be a hero but I'm not a champion, not the King's Champion in any case."

"That's nothing to feel ashamed of. I mean, I'm a poet, not the King's poet anymore—I found all that did was get me locked up in dungeons."

"How *did* you get locked up?"

Sydney scratched the back of his neck and took sudden interest in the flowery patterned tiles lining the stove. "Oh, just some silly little thing. A story for another time, perhaps."

John decided to let the matter drop—they all had their secrets after all.

Francesca pulled a jar down off the shelf and peered inside. "Looks like we're running low on flour." She glanced at John. "Are you going to be all right with that serving? If you want another batch there's not going to be any left for the other two."

Already feeling his stomach bulge against his belt buckle, John said, "I think I'll be just fine after this, thanks."

"Good," she said, laying the jar down and resuming her pancake cooking. She caught the corner of John's eye as she stirred away. "You know," she said, "I just wanted to check that you've kept up with the latest gossip in the Forests, you do realise that the King's men have seized Witney Branches? They're keeping the Grotesque hidden inside."

John held up his hand and responded, out of reflex, "Please, don't use that word." And then the implications of what she'd just said sunk in. He dropped his fork onto his plate with a clatter and his stomach churned. "They've taken control of Witney Branches?"

"Keeping it captive," she said.

"Since when?"

Francesca rolled her eyes up at the ceiling, in thought. "Oh, I don't know, maybe a week, two weeks ago."

"Gods," John said, staring down at his empty plate, his thoughts going off—recalling images of Horace, his single-eyed mate, and then to Susan, his de facto mother.

"Sorry to break bad news," she said.

Sydney approached John, laid his hand on his arm. "Whatever you need, if you want us to help you win back your home, then count us in."

Through the penetrating numbness which had accompanied the unwelcome revelation, John felt a brief glimmer of warmth. "Thanks," he said, at the same time a little wary at Sydney's apparent hero worship.

"What you need," Francesca said, returning to her pancakes, "is a plan. You need to work out how you're going to overcome all the King's men and send them packing from the Forests once and for all."

John crunched his teeth together. "How many of them are there?"

"Oh, I should think a few hundred," she said.

John bashed his fist against the table. "Damn! That's too many."

"Even for you?" Sydney said, starry-eyed gaze still etched on. "But you got us through the King's garrison with hardly a scratch. Granted you took most of it, though."

"That was different, an escape, this will be a battle. How else are we to get them out?"

A wily smile crossed Francesca's lips. "I might have a suggestion."

The other prisoner, who John had also apparently saved, was called Courtney and he went on and on about being the true King of Ethereal. John was tired of him almost immediately— and beginning to regret having saved him in the first place. Unlike Sydney, he showed no obvious gratitude toward John, which, to be honest, made John feel somewhat more relaxed about the whole thing.

Courtney pranced his way over to the kitchen window and peered out, turning up his nose slightly at what he saw. "So, what you're saying is that you'd like *us* to help you liberate the Grotesque from the King's men?"

"Your help would be appreciated," John said, through gritted teeth—thinking the exact opposite.

Courtney pouted. "And what's in it for me, exactly?"

"Well, you'd be fighting back against the"—John recalled up the phrase Courtney had used to describe the King—"the 'imposter.' Can't you see that this might well be a wonderful opportunity, that you've got the chance to take out the best part of his army while they're in the Forests? Once we've got them out of the way, it'd only be a case of taking the castle garrison."

John looked to Francesca and Sydney for encouragement that he was working along the right sort of line here—both of them gave him faint grins in reply.

Courtney rested his finger in the pit of his chin and hummed to himself, then, apparently with his mind made up, he said, "I am looking, first and foremost, to reclaim my throne, and then, second on the list, is to reclaim my queen-to-be, Alexis. And I do suppose, for better or worse, the landscape is looking more and more likely to be set up for war—and perhaps you're right that it would do my ambitions well to weaken the King's army. But . . ."

John stooped forward, absorbed by the towering silence. "But what?"

"It would involve teaming up with some rather unbecoming creatures, all this talk about getting our hands dirty with magic, that's never really been what my family's been about."

John felt like palm slapping his forehead. All they were doing here was dragging up Courtney's old prejudices and bringing them out of parade.

"Look," Francesca said, stepping forward, "I'm going to level with you. We do not need you to accomplish our task. The mere fact that we're asking for you to join us is because you owe John your life and this might well be your opportunity to repay him, to save the necks of his family as he saved yours. So don't get on your high horse and start making excuses about having to work with 'unbecoming' individuals. I'll have you know that you and your family are quite 'unbecoming' people in some circles of the Damned Forests—which is to say all of them."

Courtney's mouth flapped open and shut, like a banked fish. Every time he seemed to formulate a reply it seemed that his own realisation of how unreasonable he was being came back to him and extinguished any argument he could think up. In the end he admitted defeat, looked down at his shoes and said, "All right. I'm in."

Francesca ran her hands through her long white hair, pushing it back from her fringe. "Finally, I thought we were going to be here all day." She stooped over, glanced from side-to-side, as if there might be someone peeking in through the window, and then plucked up a few of the bricks in her kitchen floor. A few minutes later, a layer of sweat lining her forehead, and blood reddening her cheeks, she had the bricks taken up and had revealed a hole. She turned to the others. "This'll take us right through to the Coven."

"'The Coven?'" John said. "What's that?"

Francesca produced a thin smile. "Fancy that, growing up in the Forests, living here all your life and you've never heard of the Coven." She batted a hand. "Still, I suppose they keep you all cooped up there in Witney Branches, suppose it's somewhat of a bubble."

"Just because we're Grotesque doesn't mean we're backwards."

"Oh, dearie, I know, I know. But you have to admit that your kind haven't exactly taken pains to reach out into your elected habitat."

John was rendered speechless, but he didn't have anything with which to reply because, he knew, she was telling some element of the truth. One of the central ideas of the Grotesque was to hide themselves away, ideally to never go outside.

Francesca hopped into the hole with remarkable nimbleness for someone of her age. She looked up at them with her large, glassy eyes. "You lot coming in with me, or what?"

PLOTTING AND UNWELCOME GUESTS

HORACE KEPT TO HIMSELF as much as he could. He actively tried to keep away from the newcomers. Whenever they would enter a room, he would leave right away, whether he was in the middle of eating, or a conversation, it didn't matter—he had no intention of associating with these pretenders, riding in on their white horses thinking they were coming to save the day, when really they were out for their own ends. Things had got tougher since they had arrived, just as he had predicted. Now they had no permission to leave Witney Branches, and the King's men had orders to shoot on sight if anyone so much as poked their nose out the front door.

Meanwhile, when he wasn't busy avoiding the newcomers, he was putting his plan together, drawing up a map of the area and working out how he might be able to defeat the King's men, take their camp down for good and drive them out of the Forests. So far he really had nothing. From what he'd established so far he could declare that the King's men not only had a numerical advantage but they had better training, equipment, organisation and they had the tactical upper hand, given that they surrounded Witney Branches on all sides.

One evening Horace was scrawling away in the bedroom, since there wasn't anyone there at this time, all of them being in the kitchen having dinner—and since the newcomers were eating there too, Horace had decided to drop into the kitchen only once they'd left. He worked with his tongue jutting out of the corner of his mouth, drawing thick lines to represent where they might find gaps in the enemy's lines. After half an hour he had decided that they really had no chance of finding anyway through—not without heavy losses, in fact, more realistically, probably total losses. Despite what he had overheard Lord Eversham declare—that he hadn't come here to slaughter Grotesque —Horace was certain that, if provoked, the King's men wouldn't hesitate to pick them off one-by-one. From a logistical point of view it would make the job for them much easier, not having to expend so much manpower in watching over Witney Branches.

"Knock, knock."

Horace turned his head to see one of the newcomers standing in the doorway. It was the one that they called Zend. Upon recognising who it was, Horace ducked back down and continued to plot his map.

"Can I come in?" Zend said.

Horace remained silent, pretending that Zend wasn't even there, going over the thick lines showing their projected paths through the enemy's lines, hoping that Zend would get the message and bob out, go back to indulging himself on their hospitality.

Permission not forthcoming, Zend took it upon himself to step into the room. "What're you working on there?"

Horace sighed. "It's a plan."

"Plan for what?"

"To get us out of here, to fight back against the King's men."

"Ah, right."

They remained in silence, Zend glancing over Horace's shoulder, Horace scrawling away at the map, trying his best to look determined and busy.

"Do you mind?" Horace said. "You're standing in my light."

"Sorry," Zend said, bobbing out of the way. However, instead of getting the hint, ducking out of the bedroom and going back to the kitchen, he crouched down and ran his eyes over the map. He pointed to one of the lines. "You want to plough right through, just like that?"

Horace squeezed his eyes shut, massaged his temples with his fingers. "*No*, these are just ideas. When you're coming up with a plan you have to look at all the angles, think about all the theories. Something you wouldn't know a lot about considering the way you went about attempting to 'liberate' us."

Zend continued to examine the map, continuing not to get the hint. He pointed at another line. "This won't work either. You'll be spotted on either side, from across the camp."

Horace threw down his piece of chalk. It broke into two on the floor, further infuriating him. He got to his feet. "What do you want? Can't you see that I want to be left alone? I've had it with you people, marching in here with your own problems, burdening us with them. If you've got such a great idea for an escape plan then why don't you put it into action and leave?"

Zend remained calm, catching Horace's eye before looking

back down at the map. "I was about to say, before you blew up, that this line just here"—he indicated with his thumb, the nail of which was thoroughly chewed—"might well be what we're looking for. If we can get one of us out the front door without the King's men noticing, then it would be a clear passage out into the trees."

Horace scoffed. "Yeah, but it's all very well getting just one of us out, but there're more than thirty of us here. We're going to need a more robust plan than that. The chances are that the King's men will spot us at some point sneaking everyone out."

"Hey," Zend said, throwing up his hands, "I'm just trying to help you out. It's as much in your interests as ours to get out, you know."

"Wrong," Horace said. "It's in our interests to defeat the King's men, not just merely get outside. They're destroying the Damned Forests, not that I suppose any of you people care. For you I'm sure it's this dark and mysterious place, where all the evil comes from."

"What can I say? That's what we've been brought up to believe and it's proving pretty difficult to shake, especially considering bolshie specimens such as yourself about the place. And it's not like I see much magic round here, although we could sure do with some."

Horace sneered. "In case you'd forgotten we're humans. At the end of the day we're just as unwelcome in the Forests as you and the King's men, the difference being that we respect the place—we're here to hide ourselves away, not to damage something we have no capacity to comprehend."

The argument settled to a simmer. Susan called out along the corridor, wanting to know what all the raised voices had been about. Horace told her not to worry and turned his attention back to Zend. "Go on, back to your dinner, gods know you deserve it for all those acts of valour you've clocked up in your time."

Zend glared at Horace and—just for a moment—Horace was sure he was going to strike him, teach him who was the physical superior of the two. But Zend turned away and headed off up the corridor, back to his complementary dinner.

Horace sat back down, cross-legged, and continued to work away at his map, examining the route out which Zend had highlighted and, begrudgingly, realising that he might well be right— that this way through the tents might well signal a terrific opportunity to get one or two of them out of Witney Branches.

———

While Horace chomped on his food, the leftovers of the large meal which Susan had prepared—horse radishes and mushrooms mingled in rice, no meat, yet again, as the King's men refused to bring them any of the spoils of their hunting expeditions—he thought over the plan, fixing it in his mind. It made sense that one or two of them would have to get out of Witney Branches, to bring help for the rest of them. At present he had no idea where he might look, who they might turn to in the Damned Forests, but he hoped that opportunity would present itself once they had escaped.

As he swallowed back his Luke-warm rice, he thought about who he would bring with him. If John had been there—if he was still alive—Horace would've had no second-thought as to who would be the perfect companion, but now he was thoroughly stumped. From among the other Grotesque, he could really think of no one who would be satisfactory—they were either too young or too old, or too slow-moving. In any case, if he managed to convince one of the other Grotesque to come with him, he could only imagine the disapproving look and, soon to follow, the persuasion Susan would exact on his elected individual, convincing them not to go. No, what he needed was someone with a hardened physical condition who wouldn't be afraid to take the risk, which meant one of the newcomers.

Plont was too tall, perhaps nimble and quick moving, but he would be awkward on a mission such as this, easy to spot. The old man, Trevor, was an earthling, and so would be mere baggage on such a quest. And Rabbit King didn't bear thinking about, considering his enormous height and white fur. And after over an hour of puzzling it out, there was only one person he could think of who would be appropriate. It had to be short, stout, broad, and heroically- idiotic Zend.

If having picked Zend for this tentative mission wasn't enough, he would have to keep the fact of its existence away from Susan's knowledge because her protectiveness of the Grotesque extended to Horace too. She would be unwilling to let him go on such a life-threatening quest. And so he would have to get it done quickly, to avoid the prospect of their plan being discovered. In fact it would be best for him to do it tonight, while he still had his courage, and a full stomach.

Horace waited for the rest of Witney Branches to be snoring away before he dared deposit his plate in the washing bowl and slink his way along the corridor to their sleeping quarters. As luck would have it, Zend slept on the fringes of the others, doubled up on his side. Horace took a quick glance round the sleepers to establish that they were all asleep and then he crouched down beside Zend and gave him a light shake.

Zend snored on.

Horace shook him a little harder.

Zend muttered something about a girl called Emily and then opened an eye. "What? What is it?"

Horace bent low over him and dropped his voice to a whisper. "I've been thinking about what you said."

Eyes half-open, Zend grunted.

"You know, about the escape, through the camp. I think . . . I think if a couple of us can get free, we can go for help."

"What's it got to do with me?"

"I want you to come with."

Zend blinked the sleep from his eyes, peered round at the other sleepers. "What time is it?"

"Doesn't matter. Are you coming or not?"

Zend looked like he had more questions to ask, to probe over the details of the plan, but instead of raising them he just said, "All right," and got to his feet to follow Horace out of the sleeping quarters, down the corridor and out to the front door of Witney Branches.

Horace could hardly believe how easy it had been to convince Zend to go along with him—he supposed that he had got the upper hand right from the start by catching in a moment when he'd just woken up. Hopefully Zend wouldn't start to analyse the details of his choice until much later and they were, hopefully, many miles away from Witney Branches.

"So," Zend said, "what do we do now?"

Horace shrugged. "I guess we just shove the door open and go out, taking that route you showed me on the map."

"You, you don't have anything to bring with you."

"Like what?"

"Oh, I don't know, a sword, shield, anything like that would be useful—you see I lost my sword back in a rabbit burrow. Long story, but the point is, do you have anything?"

Horace shook his head.

"Damn," Zend said.

"Does it really matter?"

"Well, if we come up against a honey boar it probably will. But I suppose we have to get past the King's men first, and it wouldn't do much good with them since they've got a significant numerical advantage."

"Fine, then we'll just go, shall we?"

"This is your whim, not mine. I'm just a passenger."

Horace sighed and then reached out for the door. He listened for any sound within Witney Branches. As he had imagined it, Susan would come along the corridor at the final moment and ask them what they were doing before stopping them just before they acted. As it played out, however, they got away scot-free.

He grasped the round handle, paused a second just to consider what he was about to do—risking not one, but two lives—and then he turned it. The door swung open and the white canvas tents were revealed to them. Smoke curled up into the air as fires burnt out. He could hear faint sounds of snoring coming from various tents and he guessed the men had been at the liqueur again.

He gestured for Zend to follow, and Zend did as he was asked. Together they skirted the trunk of Witney Branches and got themselves round to the back of the tree, where the line of tents would, according to the plan, offer them shelter from any watchmen.

In Horace's head he expected the cry of a watchman at any second, but none came. He had to keep telling his feet to keep moving, despite their constant shaking, and before he knew it they had rounded the trunk and they stood on the cusp of the line of cover which would guide them out into the rest of the Forests.

Zend leant in close to Horace. "You're totally sure about this? I mean, this is our last chance to turn back, to forget all about this."

Horace clenched his fists, eyed the line of tents, seeing the dense forest ahead. He knew that he was going to save his people, all of Witney Branches and he was prepared to die doing so. He grasped hold of the front of Zend's tunic and tugged him after him, along the line of tents.

Just as they got halfway along, with the trees that were their target growing larger in Horace's sight by the second, there was a cry out from within the camp. Stupidly, Horace stopped to look round. He caught sight of an archer, high up in one of the trees. He must've stirred from his sleep because from where he perched he had a perfect view of the front door of Witney Branches. He gave no more warning before fitting an arrow to his bow and letting fly.

The arrow zipped through the air, skimmed the top of Horace's head and pierced through the fabric of a tent behind him. There was the sound of stirring in the tent, a few swear-words uttered and then a light blinked on.

Another arrow soared past them and another.

This time it was Zend who rushed them into action, grabbing hold of Horace's tunic and dragging him along, toward their target.

More and more men rose from their slumbers and called out to each other in the night air. When Horace looked back over his shoulder he saw that most of the tents were now illuminated by the orange light of lanterns. They had to escape quickly, slip away into the deep forests before daylight, because there would be an expansive search party sent after them.

But, as Horace traced the thoughts in his mind, Zend acted them out, pushing their pace forward, determined to reach the trees ahead, apparently unaware of the arrows missing them by impossibly narrow margins.

They reached the trees just as the shouts back at the camp were reaching fever pitch. Zend dragged Horace on before he could stop them for too long and get them shot at. He brought them into a clearing, the camp now a speck of orange light far away and he doubled over, panting. Hands on knees, he glanced up at Horace. "That was a close one, eh?"

"Yeah," Horace said, still captivated by the camp stirring into action.

"You think there'll be any consequences of our escape?"

A tremble passed through Horace's bones and he felt the trace of a tear dampen the lower lid of his eye. In all the quick action he had hardly had time to think through that aspect, what might happen to his family, the rest of the Grotesque. But it had been a choice of either staying there, being completely useless deadweight or doing something about their situation, as he was now, going for help. For the first time since he had brought the King's men right up to the door of Witney Branches he felt like he was actively doing something to put his mistake right, and that was better than kicking his heels back home. Now he knew that all the responsibility for his family's reprieve fell on him. Only he could save Witney Branches.

THE CONSEQUENCES OF AN ESCAPEE

T REVOR WOKE to alarm and chaos. He had hardly stumbled out of bed before someone barged into him, muttering something about Horace, and how the King's men had taken him away. He made it to the kitchen, where Susan sat slouched at the table, head in hands, tears forming rivulets down her cheeks.

She peered up at him as he entered. "I suppose you've heard?"

"Just a word or two. Horace? He's gone?"

She swallowed and then nodded with brisk strokes.

"When?"

"This morning."

Trevor thought he'd heard something, some muttering going on, but he'd been so conked out after the slap-up dinner, had filled himself so completely with that rice, that he'd not had the energy to so much as crack an eyelid.

"Oh dear," Trevor said, thinking that those words matched his sentiment.

Susan's shoulders shook as she sobbed into her hands.

Trevor had never been very good at consoling crying women, not even his wife. He recalled one such instance when he had been working late and he'd heard one of the women from the accountancy department crying her eyes out at her workspace. He had been desperate for the toilet and so snuck past her on tiptoes—he was pretty sure she hadn't noticed him, and if she had done she was probably glad that he'd left her to her weeping, or so he liked to imagine it.

This time, however, there wasn't such an easy getaway, so he sidled up behind Susan, laid a hand on her shoulder, brushing against her lush brown hair. As he gave her shoulder a squeeze, he tried his best to forget the hair covering her entire body—something which he just hadn't managed to get himself over since he'd arrived at Witney Branches, but, to be fair, he hadn't really got over the man with the wrinkly face either.

"Um," Trevor said, after a few minutes, feeling intensely awkward, "would you like me to prepare something." He paused. "Some tea, perhaps?"

She shook her head.

"Ah, right."

She cried on.

Trevor tried to calculate an exit strategy, but none occurred to him. Whatever way he tried to excuse himself from this situation it would come across as wildly insensitive, so he just maintained his posture, hand still gripping her shoulder, and looked for fate to intervene.

As luck would have it fate did just that. Rabbit King

bumbled in through the door, took one look at Susan and Trevor then said, "What's happened, then?"

Susan explained the situation for Rabbit King's benefit.

Rabbit King sighed. "Ah well, he'll be dead now. I'm sure of it."

Susan let loose a wail.

Trevor shot him a 'thanks very much' look. That was the thing with living in solitude—it did nothing for one's manners.

Rabbit King withered a touch and then excused himself from the kitchen, hurrying out as quickly as he'd come.

Trevor turned his attention back to Susan. "Say, have you seen Zend this morning?"

"No," Susan said, through her sniffles.

"Do you think . . . would it be . . . I mean, could it be possible that Horace left with Zend, that they've gone to get some help, you know, all that jazz?"

Susan collected herself, reeling in her emotions—much to Trevor's relief. "I suppose that could be what happened."

"It's just it seems odd, you know, considering Horace spent most of his time trying to keep from breathing the same air as any of us. Do you think he might've had a change of heart?"

Susan straightened herself up in her chair then blew her nose on a frayed, tartan-green rag which served as a handkerchief. "That must be right. Horace was the one that brought them here."

"Who?"

"The King's men."

"Ah, yes," Trevor said, feeling like an idiot.

Susan continued, "He's been feeling guilty about it ever since.

Maybe he sees this as the way he can pay us all back, by bringing help, saving us."

Although well-aware that he had worked hard to reach this point, to get Susan's emotions under control, he knew that he had to ask a question which had a chance of upsetting her all over again. "Does he have an idea of who he might ask?"

Susan turned face on to Trevor and said, "There are strange and mysterious things in the Forests. I'm sure that something will present itself." She shook her head. "To think that all these years I've been preaching to everyone here, warning them off integrating with our surroundings. I was afraid, you see? There's magic out there: black and white, good and evil."

"And," Trevor said, feeling that he was getting a handle on this, finally, "you think that he's gone to get the good or evil kind?"

"'Good,'" Susan said, with a glimmer of a smile. "My, you really are the stereotypical earthling, aren't you? Do they teach you nothing in your world?"

Trevor flushed a little at the slight on Earth. "No, I suppose they don't. Not really."

After Susan's crying fit had passed, Trevor found himself, strangely, feeling restless—bored even. There was nothing at all to do in Witney Branches except lurk round the corridors or open up a conversation with one of the residents, which would lead to the telling of the tragic story of how they got cursed and ended up here. So he preferred to keep to himself. At his wit's end, he decided to explore Witney Branches further and, with no one to tell him not to, he embarked on a journey up a spiral staircase.

He shifted his way up the narrow steps, taking care not to fall—whatever else the residents of Ethereal boasted, he wasn't convinced they would have the standard of medical care to see to any grave injury. The stairs went on and on, up and up. When he reached the top step, he took in a panoramic window, which looked out across the woods and, of course, the King's men's camp down below.

The King's men were just about rousing from their night-long slumber. At the fringe of the clearing he made out a group of men, lead by Lord Eversham—as he had introduced himself before—who was barking orders at them and gesticulating wildly. It seemed that Horace's disappearance had made quite a splash.

Once he'd tired of the view, Trevor slumped down to rest his aching back against the wall. All this trekking, the endless marching and the floor which had served as his mattress for the past few nights, had taken its toll on his fifty-year-old body. He was looking forward to a time when he could put his feet up for an extended period of time—let alone getting back to his own world.

Just as Trevor was thinking about letting out a long sigh and going down to the kitchen to check what was cooking for lunch —presuming that Susan had pulled herself together—he observed, out the window, the King's men shuffling toward the front door of Witney Branches, looking determined.

He watched on for another few seconds before realising that this might well be one of those times when it would be a good idea to give other forewarning of what was about to happen. He lurched to his feet and trotted back down the spiral stairs. When he got to the kitchen, almost filled with the lunchtime crowd, everyone seemed quite tranquil, if a little downhearted at the absence of Horace, however, when Trevor delivered his news, that the King's men would be bursting through the door at any moment, the whole room descended into bedlam.

Grotesque rushed by him. A skinny boy, no older than eight, wiggled past him, seemingly built of rubber limbs. The man with the face full of wrinkles stumbled by, while one woman, who had no eyeballs, bumped into his chest. She apologised and then moved off down the corridor and out of sight.

Where they were running to Trevor had no idea. If the King's men's intentions were anything along the lines of their previous searches then there'd be nowhere worth hiding in Witney Branches.

There was a wooden *slap* as the front door crashed open and Lord Eversham bobbed his way along the corridor, his eyebrows like a pair of sable lightning bolts. A pair of his men hovered at his heels, dark circles beneath their eyes. Eversham swept past Trevor and into the kitchen, where he confronted Susan. "One of you Grotesque got out this morning."

Susan couldn't speak for a couple of moments, obviously surprised at the sudden entrance of the King's men, despite Trevor's warning. Then she collected herself. "I . . . I have no idea what you're talking about."

Eversham frowned. "What do you mean? I'm sure you've noticed that one of your lot snuck out last night—two of them according to some of my men's reports." He glanced her up and down. "You must know something about it. Go on, tell me where they're headed."

Susan looked over at Trevor then back to Eversham, the whites of her eyes growing and her shoulders slumping. "Really, I have no idea where they've gone."

Eversham raised an eyebrow. "So there *are* two of them?"

"Yes, no, I really don't know anything about it."

"They've gone for help, haven't they?"

"I don't know."

"Yes," Eversham said, raising his tone. "Yes, you do."

Tears gathered in Susan's eyes and Trevor anticipated being called into action again. He needn't have worried, however, because Eversham snatched her by the arm and yanked her to her feet.

"You'd better come with me," Eversham said.

Through her screwed up, bawling face Susan beat her fists against Eversham's chest. "No! No! Leave me alone! I don't know anything!"

Eversham shoved her into the arms of his awaiting men. "Tie her up and keep an eye on her."

Trevor looked about for any sign of help, but everyone else had made themselves scarce—even Plont and Rabbit King had hidden themselves away. It would all fall to him to do something. Without thinking about it too much, he lurched into action, arms thrashing and making some warbling battle cry. He caught one of the men on the chin and the other just below the eye. His resistance extended to another strike, catching the first man in the stomach, before he was put out of action by Eversham—who merely grabbed hold of the back of his tunic and dangled him.

When Eversham spoke the stench of pork carried on his breath—no doubt his breakfast that morning. "You want to come too?" he said.

Trevor writhed in his grip, tried another of his swipes, but failed, only catching air.

"Yes," Eversham said. "It looks like you might be trouble."

Still being held by the other two men, Susan gazed at Trevor. "No, not you too. One of us has to stay behind, to keep an eye on things here."

A smile crossed Eversham's lips. "I'm sure you'd like that, wouldn't you? Let's see just how well things go when the two leaders are kept away from their sheep." He nodded for the guards to take Susan away while he, himself, took care of Trevor. "If those two escapees do try some trick to spring the Grotesque they'll find themselves shorthanded and have to come to me for the remainder—if they ever do come back."

Just as she disappeared round the corner, Susan said, "Horace will be back, I know he will, and you'll regret ever having laid a hand on me or Trevor."

Eversham snorted a laugh. "That's what they always say. You'd be quite surprised to hear how infrequently that threat is actually carried through."

Trevor sat with his back to Susan's in one of the tents which surrounded Witney Branches. Susan had been crying again and, like before, he'd felt pretty useless with his choice of words and attempts at consoling life examples, so he thought it best just to stay quiet. As they sat with their bodies touching he couldn't avoid feeling the tremors moving through her body with each sob. He would've thought, with the amount of tents about Witney Branches, that they might've given them one each. But then, he supposed, that might mean complicating the guard rota, not that he had any plans or capacity to escape from this, his latest perilous situation.

Trevor flexed his toes, trying to regain feeling in them. He decided that he wanted to know more about what was going on —whether he'd been left out of the loop on anything big—so he said, "Do you know anything about Horace, where he's headed?"

"No," Susan said.

"But you do expect he's gone for help, as Eversham said?"

"Yes."

"Well, I've been thinking about what you were saying, you know, about white and black magic." He paused, thinking this through a little more, actually trying to get a grip on the fact that the word 'magic' had passed his lips in something less than jest—he was, apparently, speaking about a living, breathing facet of the world, well, of the world of Ethereal. "What's the difference between them?"

"Like I said before, good and evil."

"Right," Trevor said, "but what does that mean, you know, tangibly speaking?"

"It's intangible."

"Yes, I see that, perhaps what I'm trying to get at is, what kind of effect does it have on the world? I mean, is there a real chance that magic can save the day, as far as clearing out the Forests of the King's men goes?"

"Yes."

"Ah," Trevor said, feeling like he was getting somewhere, at last. "Like what? What kinds of effects?"

"White or black magic?"

Feeling like he was being led in circles, and beginning to

doubt Susan's in-depth knowledge of magic—since she had professed herself that she'd actively kept her brood clear of such matters, he said, "'White.'"

"Ah," she said, "white magic."

"Yes," he said, growing increasingly impatient. "White magic. What does it do?"

Susan took a profound intake of breath. "White magic," she said, as if it were some memory far off in the past—one which she cherished most fondly, "would take care of the King's men by turning the very essence of the Forests against them. The intense beauty, the scent of flowers would prove overwhelming. The air would take on a frosty, fresh quality and the men would be compelled to cease their activities because they'd be so trans-fixed with wonder, so captivated by nature."

"And what if that doesn't work?" Trevor said.

Susan shook her head. "It's hard to communicate the power of white magic, but when you witness it first-hand, see it and feel it around you, only then can you be a true believer."

This was all getting to feel a touch familiar to Trevor—all those men who would approach him on high streets, either dressed exceedingly smartly or exceedingly oddly, they all pushed the same general idea, they just had differently coloured pamphlets.

Trevor tried to loosen his hands, tied behind his back, not to get himself free, but to have a go at an annoying itch behind his left ear which was slowly driving him crazy. Having failed, he decided to make another foray into his ever-expanding knowl-edge of magic. "And it's fairly easy to get your hands on white magic, then?"

"Oh, no," Susan said. "In fact it's just about the rarest essence there is."

"But you trust that Horace will be able to uncover some?"

Susan paused, gathering her thoughts. "I'm sure he will do his best."

Trevor managed to tilt his head down toward his shoulder and rub up against his itch, giving himself some kind of relief. Once he came back up, he said, "And what about black magic?"

"That's a different story altogether."

"Why?"

"Well, to take that example you asked for, how it would treat our captors. There would be none of the intense essence of nature, that would be foregone completely. Instead, shoots would sprout from beneath their feet and clasp round their ankles, branches would beat down on their brows, breaking their skulls like horse chestnut shells, honey boars driven wild with hunger would bear down on them."

"In short, some fairly evil things."

"The best way of thinking about it is like this, whereas white magic gently persuades, black magic bludgeons."

Trevor turned his attention to the canvas roof of the tent, examining the off-white coloured cloth and wondering whether there might be mould growing on the other side. He only had so much daily tolerance for this wistful, new age crap, and his meter was just about full. "And I suppose there's some sort of a battle going on between this 'white'"—if his hands had been free he would've made quotation marks with his fingers—"and 'black' magic?"

"Perhaps you're not quite as stupid as I first took you to be."

"Thanks."

"As you say, black magic battles to consume everything, chaos reigns. It's by far the most common of the two types and threatens to completely extinguish the white."

"So, what you're saying is that it's most likely that Horace is going to run into black magic on his search for help?"

"In so many words, yes."

"But that'd do the trick?"

Susan quietened. "Of course it's powerful, deeply effective, but it also destroys everything, without discretion—black magic is what has infected the Grotesque, we are all victims. For Horace to get himself involved with black magic would be extremely difficult for him. He would be afraid that it would choose to finish him off before aiding with his own ends."

"Better than nothing, though?"

"Yes, I suppose it would be."

A ROYAL WEDDING

A WHIRLWIND swept in through Alexis's bedroom in the days leading up to the wedding. A group of seven lean men wearing sable cloaks turned up to outfit her. They had tangerine-coloured skin and blond hair, and they bobbed about her muttering to each other in their own language, obviously making stylistic decisions between themselves. When Alexis had asked about their presence there, Henrietta had explained that these men had come from the Darguk Mountains, and they were known throughout the Kingdom of Ethereal for being the best designers of clothing. After a week of trying on exquisite wedding dresses, all pearl white with elements of blue—the King's colour—dabbed about here and there, she found herself believing Henrietta's claim.

Not only did the men deal with her dress, they also took control of her make up, every so often dabbing powder onto her cheeks or experimenting with lipsticks. There seemed to be no leader, the seven of them worked together as a single organism. She might've thought they shared the same brain if they hadn't so obviously been chattering amongst themselves.

On the evening of the wedding she noted the finality with which the men were acting—the fact that they were standing back more, considering her from several steps away, rather than fussing over details. And, sure enough, after a little adjustment to a few petals of the blue rose pinned to her corset, they looked to one another and let out a proud cackle, clapping their hands together.

Before she had any opportunity to thank them for their assistance, the men were making for the door, their long cloaks sweeping at their feet. Not one of them looked back over their shoulder as they slipped out of sight.

Alexis stood before the full-length mirror and considered herself. Although she had a healthy distaste for cliché she couldn't avoid describing herself as 'stunning.' Her dress swathed down over her legs, which she'd always considered one of her better features, and plumed outward at just the right moment to expose a bit of ankle. Then the corset sat snuggly against her bust so as not to show off cleavage, but not to give the impression that she was flat-chested either. The make up job they'd done on her brought out the pale tones of her skin, emphasised the rosiness in her cheeks. Her hair had been pinned up onto the top of her scalp in ringlets. And, again worried about slipping into cliché, she caught a tear glistening in the corner of her eye. She had never, ever in her life, ever, been this beautiful.

Heels clacked along the hallway behind her.

Alexis turned away from the mirror.

Henrietta poked her head inside and then entered. She was

wearing a scarlet dress with a black necklace at her throat and a black pair of high heels on her feet. Her smile widened as she took Alexis in and stepped closer. "You . . . you look, well, just marvellous!"

A knot caught in Alexis's throat. Although she knew it herself, it was completely different to hear a point of view expressed out loud.

Shaking her head in disbelief, Henrietta threw her arms round Alexis and drew her to her chest. And, before she knew it, Alexis was sobbing away into her chest, her tears splashing onto Henrietta's well-lotioned skin. She made to apologise, but Henrietta waved her concerns away. As Henrietta drew back, Alexis saw that she was crying too. "This, all this," Henrietta said, her voice croaking in her throat, "it's just all that I've ever dreamt about for one of my maidens. I never believed this would happen, could happen, but here you are, real as the night sky."

Alexis could only beam back at her, feeling like she was actually glowing, and not even thinking too hard about Henrietta's trite metaphor.

"Tomorrow will be the most wonderful day," Henrietta said. "I just know that you'll be so happy in your new position, actually privy to the King's company throughout the entire day."

Alexis had to admit that was the part she wasn't looking forward to so much, having to be at the side of a dying tyrant, to stroke his hand and whisper sweet nothings into his ear. The only consolation was that, in his condition, at least she wouldn't have to sully herself for his benefit. Then the question that had been bugging her throughout the day made a reappearance in her mind.

"How am I supposed to sleep?" Alexis said. "I mean, this all looks wonderful and everything, but do I have to stay like this until the wedding tomorrow?"

Henrietta squealed with laughter.

The sound caused Alexis to flinch.

"My dear, of course you can sleep," Henrietta said. "You can get out of those clothes right now if you so wish. The Darguk will be by in the morning to fix everything up all again. They just wanted to get it right this evening."

"No one needs to"—she thought of saying 'take a picture' but decided that might well be lost on Henrietta—"paint a picture?"

"Oh goodness no. They live for this sort of thing, outfitting us. They'll have an impression of just how to turn you out in their minds."

Alexis examined herself in the mirror again, noting her wondrous appearance. It seemed such a waste for her just to scrub all this make up off, to ruffle her hair and strip off her dress.

Henrietta clacked up behind Alexis and rested her hand on Alexis's shoulder. "I did come here to have a word with you about everything that's going to happen."

"Like what?"

"Well, you know what kind of a state the King's in at the moment, that he's knocking on death's door, and I suppose he's seen fit to tell you that there's some confusion about the succession of the throne."

"Yes, he told me all that."

"It's just . . ."

If Alexis hadn't been already worried about her impending rise to the throne then she most certainly was now. She knew it would be a heap of responsibility and she would find herself somewhat cut adrift, culturally speaking—as even during the years, in Ethereal time, which she had spent down in the dungeons she had hardly had much of an opportunity to immerse herself in the culture here, only Sydney and Courtney had been her gateways, so that really hadn't helped much.

"What is it?" Alexis said, getting annoyed at Henrietta's continued silence.

Henrietta tilted her head back and gazed into her eyes. "There will be certain people round the castle who will resent your power should the King pass away."

"And so what? They'd have to respect me, wouldn't they?"

Henrietta smiled weakly. "What I'm trying to say is that all should go fine if the true heir to the throne is uncovered quickly, but if it proves a challenge I'm afraid that unrest might rise round the castle and you could find your throne coming under threat."

"You mean they'll enact a coup?"

"All I'm saying is that it's been known, I'm just giving you some warning so that you may make an informed choice."

"An informed choice about what?" Alexis said, creasing her forehead.

"About who you choose to hand your power to in the event of the King's death." Henrietta held up her hand, to block any attempt Alexis might make to cut her off. "There're several suitable candidates, right here, at the castle, but I believe that—under the circumstances—the best option would be to select General Frum to take control of the castle in the meantime. He has experience of leading men and he—"

Alexis's blood throttled through her veins. The image of

Frum holding the sword to Arnold's skin rocked back into her mind's eye. She clenched her fists. "No!"

Henrietta held her hand to the pit of her throat. "But, Alexis, please allow me to finish. You need to hear my arguments before making an informed decision."

"You mean before making *your* decision. I refuse to give up the throne to that madman. He would tear down half of Ethereal in a fortnight."

"Now, Alexis, let's be reasonable about this, you see—"

Alexis turned on her, eyes blazing, her tongue felt like a hot slice of meat. "Did he send you here, to try and convince me? Don't you see what he's trying to do? He wants to become King of Ethereal, and he thinks he can do it by taking my throne, if it does come to me." She shook her head, now completely resolved. "If that's the case then he'll have to kill me first."

Henrietta stayed seeped in silence for a few moments, then said, "I never believed you would be the one he would choose to marry, I mean I had an idea, I heard through Jenson that he had been talking about marrying one of his maidens before his death, but I thought, we *all* thought, it would be Cherry." Her hands trembled slightly as she held them at her waist. "In fact, Cherry had gone as far as drawing up the agreement with Frum, that she would happily pass him power once the King passed on, and take her hand in marriage for good measure. But when he proposed to you it ruined everything."

Alexis looked herself over in the mirror once again, taking in her incredible appearance and thinking that, from now on, she would have to look this way everyday—use every facet of herself to intimidate the other members of the court. Before she'd seen this whole arrangement as her chance to get back to Earth, but to what? She would go back to her normal, ordinary life, applying for universities, going out with boys, having a career, having a family. Could she ever really change anything back on Earth, or was this, her position here in Ethereal, her real chance to make something of her life? Why was she in such a hurry anyway? It wasn't like she was aging at all in Earth time, she could just as easily slip back into her old, mundane life after she was done playing queen here.

"I'll leave it with you," Henrietta said, brushing away a stray curl at the nape of Alexis's neck. "The option remains open, perhaps you shall snap back to your senses at some time, and then you will recognise that there are good people round you who wish to help."

As Henrietta trotted out of her bedroom, Alexis glanced out the window at the full moon in the clear night sky. Its faintly blue light beamed down on the land which unfurled beyond the castle. She looked further away, to the rolling foothills and then the snow-capped mountains in the far distance. After tomorrow, and if the King had died of his curse, all this would be hers.

A light shudder passed over her bare arms and she resolved to undress and get into bed, beneath the blankets warmed by a brass pan of hot water, and try to get some rest before her life, as she knew it, changed forever.

The next day a chorus of trumpets, down in the corridor, blared Alexis awake. She stumbled out of bed, her sheets coiling themselves at her feet, and she bounded into the bathroom to go through her morning toilet. Her stomach was already boiling with anticipation at the day stretched out before her: Queen Alexis, would be her name before its end.

When she emerged from the bathroom with a towel wrapped round her, feeling fresh, if not a little dragged down by sleepiness—she had hardly been able to sleep last night—she was shocked to find the seven Darguk all standing before her, in a V-shaped formation. So much so that she let out a little shriek.

The Darguk, however, seemed utterly impassive to her extreme reaction and, before Alexis could quite get her bearings, they bobbed round her, one of them managing to unravel her towel, leaving her naked.

Alexis held up her hands to cover her bare breasts and crossed her legs. She watched them picking at her skin with their tools: something that felt like sandpaper, going to work on her as if she were some unruly block of wood in a carpenter's workshop. They kept up this act for the next half an hour, leaving no patch of skin unattended. Then, she was pleased to note, they turned their attentions to refitting her dress and doing her hair once again.

Alexis only really felt comfortable again when she was fully-dressed, appearing just as she had the night before. The Darguk had done their job from memory, as Henrietta had told her they would. And, as they had the night before, they all scarpered before she had any chance of attempting conversation.

She strutted up to the window and glanced out, down into the courtyard. The trumpeters continued to warble away, while the area was abuzz with members of the castle propping up wooden tables, throwing spotless, white tablecloths over the rustic frames. Guards stood up along the turrets, eyes watchful on what was passing below, their white and blue tunics looked like they had been washed and pressed especially for the wedding.

Jenson arrived around midmorning, his fakest of fake smiles emblazoned on his lips. He gave her a mock bow. "Queen Alexis, if you are quite ready."

Alexis remained straight-faced as she walked past him. "I'm not Queen yet."

"I thought I should give you the pleasure of your title . . . while it lasts."

Alexis paused halfway down the staircase then glanced back over her shoulder. She took in the man-boy's well-sculpted features and thought about making some retaliatory threat—to have him thrown down into the dungeon when the King popped his clogs, and she was in charge. But she caught herself. That would be exactly the sort of scummy thing that General Frum would do.

Jenson showed her the way through the castle, though a dozen halls which Alexis had never entered before. Then he led her down a narrow corridor, a velvet carpet beneath their feet, and into a small side chamber, a cold room, its walls comprising of grey stones. Alexis actually shuddered as she crossed over the hearth. The only bright note inside the room were the blue and white banners which unfurled beside the slender windows looking out on the courtyard. Jenson bowed once more, again muttering, "Queen Alexis," under his breath, and then took his leave.

"You must be out of your skin."

Alexis startled at the voice and turned to look.

Over, in the corner of the room, there were a couple of padded chairs on which sat all of the King's maidens. Cherry sat perched on one of them, hands piled onto her knee, head cocked to one side, wearing a gravel-blue frock—only a shade or two off white. She beamed at Alexis, as if nothing had passed between them, as if she had never snuck into her bedroom during the night. "Unbelievable what those Darguk can do, isn't it?"

Feeling wretchedly uncomfortable, Alexis stepped toward the maidens. She cast her gaze over the others, their faces. Each, in turn, became too uncomfortable to meet her eye and, Alexis realised, that they all—to a certain extent—shared Cherry's insane jealousy.

Cherry plucked an invisible piece of lint from her dress then said, "It's an awful amount of responsibility you're taking on marrying the King. Have you stopped to think about it? I mean, *really* stopped to think?"

The other maidens all concentrated their mournful looks onto Alexis, and she felt her cheeks blushing, words drying up in her throat. But she told herself that if she really was going to survive in this role, that she was willing to take on the responsibility of being Queen of Ethereal, then she needed to stick up for herself in front of a bunch of whores. She might be counted among them but she had never, technically, slept with the King. "I think I'll be more than up to the task and, anyway, what makes you think that I will have to take on any responsibility? How can you be so sure that the King's going to die."

As Cherry's smile crumbled Alexis was certain that she had struck just the right tone—kept the conversation just open enough to suggest that Cherry might well be treading on some very delicate eggshells as far as treason was concerned. Then Cherry exchanged glances with the maidens and seemed to catch her second wind. "You do realise that there has never been a Queen of Ethereal?"

Although she had been previously unaware of it, that face didn't do much to subvert Alexis's expectations of the Kingdom, just another case of feminism going missing—but she was set to change all that.

Alexis shrugged, quite enjoying the sensation of showing off the sparkling bare skin on her shoulders. "If it comes to that, I'm sure that I'll be up to it."

Cherry glared. "There will be uprisings in the Kingdom, they shall never accept you." She got to her feet, smirking, obviously having something up her sleeve. She kept her eyes set on Alexis until she was only a matter of inches away, and she dropped her voice to a whisper. "You know, there's an easy route out of the castle from here. I could show you if you like."

Alexis's heart gave a loud *thud*. Although she knew that she'd be better off not trusting Cherry, keeping her at arm's length, she also knew that Cherry would stop at nothing to get rid of her from the castle so that she might return to her 'rightful' place in the King's affections, maybe even have a royal wedding herself. This might be the last chance Alexis would get at a clean escape, of getting out of this whole mess and making her escape back home. However, she also knew there was a boy down in the dungeons who was there because of her—who was her responsibility. If she were to leave right now she would be deserting him, perhaps even leaving him to his death should Frum get his wish to become King of Ethereal.

"Well?" Cherry said, her eyes darting all over Alexis's.

"No," Alexis said, stunning herself with her firmness.

Cherry held her gaze a little longer. "Are you sure?"

"Yes."

"Very well," Cherry said, with a sigh, then headed back over to the other maidens and then returned to her seat.

Not wanting to go over and sit with the rest of them, Alexis stood over at the window and watched the presentation kicking into high gear. There seemed to be a greater note of panic dominating now, an extra urge from the members of the court to cap off the preparations. She stayed there for a long time watching, until all the members of the court had scuttled off to the sides and the guests streamed their way into the courtyard, all wearing their very best outfits: men with well-polished boots, women with their bosoms almost bursting from their corsets. A line of children, all holding hands, and dressed in tunics which went down below their knees, wormed their way round to the side of the seats. Some were so overcome with the occasion that they were crying.

Once all the invited were in their places, every seat in the courtyard filled, with members of the court and soldiers standing alert round the periphery, the trumpets blew and sustained a chord.

Alexis observed as the King, helped by Jenson and a cane, limped his way up the aisle. He wore a loose-fitting charcoal-coloured cloak which hid his afflicted right side. A couple of times he stumbled and Jenson had to help him along, that snide smile never leaving Jenson's face.

When they reached the alter, where a vicar stood with his hands folded over his large gut, she watched Jenson leave the King's side, helping him balance his weight onto the cane, and then make for the chamber in which Alexis waited watching.

This was it. She had made her choice and there was no going back on it. Not now.

Alexis took a deep breath and then straightened her back. She watched Jenson appear in the doorway, his snide smile—as always—present.

"It's time, my lady."

THE COVEN

FUNNILY ENOUGH, the underground tunnel which Francesca led them along, lived up to just how John had imagined life to be like underground—that was, damp, dark and cold. At least it wasn't *pitch* black, however, as Francesca had clapped her hands together, muttered a few words and then a spark of light had appeared at her shoulder, giving off a faint green glow. The tunnel itself was dug out in a circular shape and when John had remarked on this geometrical perfection and asked how Francesca had done it, how many workers she'd employed, she'd merely tapped her nose and winked. He supposed things were much easier when you could just magic up solutions all over the place.

John found himself at the back of their group, as often happened when he travelled with others. They seemed to think that if anything tried to sneak up behind it would have John to contend with. He supposed that neither Sydney or Courtney had seen him bottling the chance to cut off that Narbut's head.

They carried on along the tunnel for what seemed like hours. Underground it felt like time stood still, that it held its breath while they stomped about beneath the girth of the land. John was less enthusiastic about this reflection, though, being that he was much taller than the others and he would knock his head on the ceiling of the otherwise roomy tunnel.

Francesca brought them to a halt when they reached a wall.

John's palms got sweaty. Despite everything, his interactions with her, he just didn't trust anyone involved with magic—not yet anyway. How did they know she wouldn't just turn round and throw hexes in their faces?

Francesca felt up the wall, her crooked, bony fingers feeling out the cracks in the mud, pausing occasionally to retrace a space she'd already checked over.

"What's the matter?" Courtney said.

Francesca glanced back at him. "Just looking for the way in. It's been a while since I've been down here, had to come for a meeting. I'm not usually much up for Neighbourhood Watch gatherings, but I thought that enough was enough with the King's men bobbing round, tearing apart our woods." She grimaced and then hooked her finger into a crack. She smiled, revealing a mouth of crooked, but quite white, teeth. "There we go!"

There was an earthy *shudder* which passed through the entire tunnel, shaking the ground beneath their feet. John didn't dare blink, his mind still overflowing with imaginings of what Francesca might be about to cast on them.

The apparently solid wall groaned in its place and then, with an ominous *creak*, it drew back into itself, into the darkness, revealing a path much like the one they had just passed along. John observed that it had a good amount of head clearance. And so they went on their way.

John thought his mind was playing tricks on him when he noticed the roof rising above his head, the walls retreating away from his arms—so much so that he no longer grazed his forearms against the muddy banks either side. But, as he took in the phenomenon, he realised it was actually happening. It all had that medicine-like stench of magic to it, so he remained wary, clear that he might need to leap in to protect his companions, and himself, at any moment.

They emerged into a large circular chamber with steps carved into the ground. There were several lights, similar to Francesca's, hovering about in the air—hanging nearby to their owners. And John came to realise that this was nothing less than a gathering of all the witches and wizards in the Forests.

The lights hanging above the wizards and witches were of differing colours. The tones ranged from bright white, almost-too-painful-to-look-at lights, to brooding dark glows of red or purple, some were so dark that they hardly lit up their conjurers at all.

Once he'd got over his initial timidity of being round so many wizards and witches, John approached Francesca, who was busy chatting away with a nearby witch who had a thin, creamy light. He waited for her to round off the conversation before stepping in. "Those lights, what're they about?"

Francesca looked off round the chamber. "Those lights are no less than a reflection of the witch or wizard's anima, their 'soul' for want of a better word."

"Right," John said, then, feeling a touch naive, said, "And what've the colours got to do with it?"

"Oh, that's such a silly thing, not worth thinking about."

John thought about accepting this remark but decided that, since he had come this far into a magical lair, and that he might not have the opportunity of being able to talk the ear off a witch or wizard any time soon, said, "I'd really like to know."

Francesca flushed a little, and John realised she was blushing, that she was embarrassed about answering his question. But, just as John was on the point of issuing a retraction, she said, "As I said, the lights show you what type of a witch or wizard you're dealing with. And just as there is white and black magic, the anima reflects that."

When she stopped, John felt like he was getting short changed somewhat. "So how do you read the colours?"

Her cheeks turned a shade of puce. "Well, it's really quite simple, there's no mystery to it."

John continued to stare at her, not quite catching her drift.

Finally, after looking round to check no one was in earshot, she stalked up to John and said, "If you have a white anima, then that shows you're entirely harnessing white magic, however, if you have a black anima then it suggests you are more at home with black. The shades in between are a measure of how far you are along the scale."

John considered Francesca's light green glow then said, "So you're a fairly good witch?"

Francesca puffed up her cheeks. "Yes, well, we all have our little secrets, don't we? We're all curious when we're younger. I suppose you stole some honey liqueur from a cupboard back in Witney Branches—it's nothing more than that in my case, but with magic. The only thing is that magic never forgets the choices you make, while, in your situation, memories fade over the good and evil deeds you do."

Now that he'd had it explained to him so thoroughly, John was prepared to drop the subject. He could see how it had got Francesca riled—she was constantly jabbing her tongue into the side of her cheek, as if someone might be listening in.

"Okay, okay," she said, holding up her hands, while her anima bobbed round her head. "I'll tell you what happened. I was a young girl and I was in love with a boy." She rolled her eyes. "And he took me aside one day and told me that we should try hexing a branch, nothing bad, just to make it dance around, for our entertainment more than anything. Anyway, so this boy does the branch thing, gets it twitching away like it's been possessed by some kind of tiny animal, and then, all at once, it breaks out and starts lashing out at our faces." Her tongue flicked out of her mouth, moistening her lips. "There was nothing else to do. I had to fight back, so I uttered a curse to make it stop. And it did." She sighed. "Ever since then I've been stuck with this less-than-perfect anima, but we all have our skeletons."

"Then what happened?"

Francesca's manner changed from one of embarrassment to frantic looks from side-to-side, clearly extremely worried about what she was about to impart. "That boy fought back against my curse, brought the branch back up, and I realised that, all along, he had been trying to attack me with it." She swallowed back a knot in her throat. "Well, I had no intention of sullying my anima any more than that, so I just ran off into the Forests, back to my mother."

John felt like he could empathise with Francesca's experience

—she, like him, had been a victim of black magic, and, as such, could understand how it had the power to terrorise and cause real damage.

"I never saw that boy again," she said.

"And what happened to him?"

She pointed her chin off down the chamber to man wearing a pair of black and green plaid trousers and a patched up tweed jacket. He had shoulder-length grey hair. Although he looked innocuous enough, his anima was almost jet black, the colour of tar, and his face remained in shadow because of it.

The meeting was called to order by a wizard standing on the stage. He wore blue robes and had an, almost, white anima hovering about his head. He took his time, waiting for everyone to shush down, like a headmaster. Once he did have silence he started. "We are all here today to discuss the threat posed to the Forests as concerns the influx of King Fredrick's men."

Much muttering broke out.

The wizard continued, "What I must stress, before anything else, is that if we are to come up with a solution we must come up with it together, there shall be no vigilante action, that helps nobody and only serves to give the Forests a bad name. Whatever we choose to do it must be agreed upon so that we may all respond and take responsibility."

"Get on with it!" someone called from the front row.

The wizard obliged the heckler. "Right, any ideas?"

A younger witch, with blond hair and light green eyes,

wearing a purple cape and with a matching headband, stood. Her anima was a light orange colour.

John wondered whether that made her a bad or good witch.

The witch said, "We should create a earthquake to drive them out to the fringes and then inspire them with such awe that they shan't return."

The wizard standing on stage shook his head. "No, there's a flaw in that plan. They would be running screaming out of the Forests before they'd have a chance to be struck with awe." The wizard gyrated his head round the chamber. "Anyone else?"

With a scowl, the witch took her seat.

The witch who Francesca had been talking with at the start got up and waved her hand at the wizard—the one with the cream-coloured anima. The wizard acknowledged her and she spoke. "I suggest that we just strike them with awe right now, stop them in their tracks and have them realise the very beauty of the place they are so intent on destroying."

The wizard nodded along with this suggestion, smiling to himself. "My thoughts exactly. Yes, that sounds like quite a wonderful idea."

There was a scoff from the front row, the wizard who Francesca had claimed had attacked her with black magic in her youth—with the almost black anima.

"Yes, Maxeth?" the wizard on the stage said, his eyes not looking at all comfortable looking at him.

Maxeth cracked his knuckles and remained seated, his head tilted to one side.

John felt Francesca tense up beside him. He reached over and squeezed her hand.

"That's an indirect way," Maxeth said. "I mean, we *could* do that if we really believe that we'll manage to convince them. But, I can't help thinking, that's a very optimistic viewpoint. I say that these men have trespassed on our lands and worse, they've taken liberties in our home. They need something to bring them back to ground. Something that will inspire fear in them."

There were murmurings of approval throughout the chamber.

John observed the various animas around him and noted that most of them were down the scale, closer toward darkness than toward light. He supposed it followed that there would be more black witches and wizards than white since it was easier to stamp on an ant in his path than to take pains to avoid it—just human nature.

The wizard on stage squirmed at the suggestion. "Uh, uh, I really think we'd do better not to provoke the King—he is, after all, the ruler of the land."

Maxeth did stand now. "And I say that it's time that magic took over. Why should we live like common moles when we could take the whole land for ourselves? These men have taken too many chances with us. We've tried living in peace and what happens? They get complacent and decide they can do whatever they please. Make no mistake about it, these men are destroying the Forests because they fear magic. The time is ripe for a counter-attack."

There was a mixed reaction to this suggestion, some moaning of disapproval among the roars of encouragement. John noted that Francesca didn't seem to react either way. He wondered whether her feelings for Maxeth, even after all these years, had not yet abated.

A wizard with a light-blue anima got up. "The only reason

the King's tearing the place apart is because *someone* cast a hex on him, and his body's wasting away."

"Only the right side, I heard," someone added.

"Point is," the same wizard continued, "he's coming after us because we struck the first blow, we attacked him. Why, if I were in his position I might feel a similar way. Guy gets told his whole life that magic's evil and then, indeed, it jumps up and bites him."

The blonde witch, who had made the first suggestion, entered the conversation. "From what I heard he came into the Forests first, he got what was coming to him."

The debate broke down into an all-out argument and, despite the wizard on the stage's attempts to cool things down, it only grew more and more heated on either side. There were only a dozen or so white magic witches and wizards compared to the, what seemed like, hundreds of those leaning toward black. He wondered whether the witches and wizards had noticed this. And then, all of a sudden, his question was answered.

John saw exactly who it was who threw the first hex. It was Maxeth. He hurled a purple bolt toward the wizard on the stage who, failing to duck, was struck in the chest and sent tumbling backward, dead or unconscious, John couldn't be sure.

And then the blonde witch threw a green cloud at the witch with the cream anima, sending her into the wall with a muddy *thump*. She turned on Francesca and, without thinking, John threw himself in front of her, but, somehow, the cloud bent round him and smacked into Francesca, sending her, breathless, onto her back.

The blonde witch bared her teeth at John. "What do you think you're doing down here, Grotesque? Haven't seen enough black magic?" She raised her hand and her lips motioned as she rapped out another hex.

But, before she could released it from her fingertips, Sydney leapt up from his seat and head butted her in the stomach. She doubled over and Courtney gave her a shove which caused her to trip over her seat and fall backward, with her legs waggling in the air.

There was a loud roar from the black magic witches and wizards, as it appeared that they had defeated all of the white magic practitioners. Then Maxeth called them all together. "Friends! Let us retreat to my house where we shall think on our plans to drive out the *real* evil from our forests and to take control of the Kingdom."

Another roar, and then the witches and wizards filed out after him, apparently heading off down the corridor which led to Maxeth's house, sending up bursts of colour and clouds as they went.

The three of them knelt down at Francesca's side. John observed a rivulet of blood trickling down from the corner of her mouth. When she opened her eyes, they seemed to be looking some way in the distance, as she spoke her voice was a low drawl. "You must find . . . Yvonne."

"Yvonne?" John said, taking hold of her flailing hand which felt as if it consisted of only bird bones.

Francesca nodded.

"But you'll be fine," Sydney said, at John's shoulder.

Francesca smiled at him vaguely. "No. She hit me with a killing curse. I'll be dead in seconds."

Courtney, against all odds, chirped up. "Don't say that. I'm sure you've got something back at your shack we can cook up to save you."

John wanted to give Courtney a smack, right in the nose, but when he looked at his expression—saw the genuine wrinkles etched in his forehead—he saw that the suggestion had come out of the right place, if it had been spoken with little, or any, thought to tact.

Francesca screwed up her eyes and her grip lost all its strength. As her body shrank back from them, becoming dead weight, her lips seemed to shrivel up. "Yvonne," she said, then went still.

Courtney frowned. "Yvonne? Whatever was she talking about? Mad old bat."

This time John did give Courtney a light punch on the upper arm.

Courtney squealed out in pain and scowled at him. "You bloody brute, you've broken my arm."

"Shut up," Sydney said, nodding at Francesca's body.

Courtney glanced down at her, still wincing and rubbing his afflicted arm.

John stroked her silky hair and then got up. He looked over Sydney and Courtney. "Looks like we have to find this Yvonne character."

"But how?" Sydney said.

"Guess we'll have to ask round."

IN SEARCH OF WHITE MAGIC

HORACE EXAMINED the path ahead. Tangled branches and thick bushes. He looked back in the direction they had come. Not much different: sprawling roots and trees noodled close together. He paused to think, trying to work out where he might go.

"Where next, then?" Zend said, wiping perspiration from his brow.

"I . . . I don't know."

"Don't know?" Zend said. "You mean you've dragged me all this way, had us walking for days and nights, and only just now, this second, you admit that you don't actually know where we're going?"

"Sorry."

Zend exhaled through his nose and kicked at a tree root. "Please tell me that you at least know *what* we're supposed to be looking for?"

"White magic."

"And what's that when it's at home?"

"We'll know it when we sense it."

"Is that so?"

"Yes."

Zend placed his hands on his hips and glared into the trees, as if they were looking for a fight. He drew the stick which hung from his waist, and served as a makeshift sword, and thrashed at a few leaves.

"Don't do that!" Horace said.

"Why not?"

"You've got to respect the Forests. Don't you realise that power of the magic stored here? If we turn to defacing the place we'll be no better than the King's men."

Zend gave a tree branch and almighty, final *thwack*. "Listen, I didn't come into these forests to be all respectful. I came here because something here stole our kids from our village."

"And how are you so sure something from the Forests took them?"

"Well, what else is big, evil and near to our village?"

Horace sniffed. "There are lots of people who say the Grotesque are evil, but what do you think after taking advantage of our hospitality these last few days?"

"We're getting off topic," Zend said. "What this all boils down to is that you have no idea where we're going, do you?"

Horace glanced off up at the trees ahead.

"*Do* you?" Zend said.

"I have the feeling that we're getting close to something."

Zend flared his eyes. "'Something?'"

"Yeah, just bear with me, okay? I promise that we'll find the white magic. Remember that it's my family on the line here. If you didn't want to come with me you had the choice not to, and you chose to come, so now you're stuck with it, you've got to see this through."

Zend hung his head in disbelief. "This is where charity gets you, always. Should've listened to my old man, always telling me not to get tangled up in charity. Everything should work like a business—"

There was a tittering in the trees and Horace held up his hand for Zend to be quiet. "You hear that?"

"Just some damn birds. What've they got to be so happy about?"

"No, you're not listening hard enough. Really listen to the sound."

Zend rolled his eyes, but made no more comments.

Both of them stood, heads tilted, trying to pick out the strange sound which Horace had just heard. There it was again, the tittering accompanied by an eerie hum. "There," Horace said. "Did you hear that?"

"Nope."

"It came from this way," Horace said, pointing, his eyeball aching from the intensity with which he gazed off into the distance, trying catch sight of a further clue.

"I don't hear anything."

Horace grabbed Zend's wrist and steered him through the trees, catching their feet in rabbit holes and stray roots as they went. Horace ignored Zend's various swearwords which tumbled out of his mouth as they navigated each obstacle. He dragged him along, realising that they were coming upon a beaten track —he could tell by the way the tall grasses were bent back, crushed against the ground. Someone had been along this way recently.

Through the trees, Horace spotted a shape shift from one tree to the next. Blood drumming in his ears, he pointed. "There! Over there! Did you see?"

Maintaining his monotonous, sceptical tone, Zend said, "No, not all of us have got binocular vision, you know?"

"Monocular."

"Whatever."

The shape shifted through the trees again, slipping quickly behind a bush before Horace could get a decent look at it. He tugged Zend on, taking no note of his quibbles as they ploughed forward.

Several times Horace was sure that he had lost the shape and he began to think back to those stories which Susan would tell them in the evenings, about how there were wisps in the Forests which would draw people into swamps or sinking sands. These all returned to him now and he considered his position, but decided, on balance, that they were doing the right thing, and that the Forests would recognise that.

The shape was drawing closer with each of their bounds forward, almost close enough for Horace to break into a sprint and trap whatever it was. And then, all at once, the shape was gone.

Horace brought them to a stop and spun round, desperate to locate what they had been following, but he had no luck. Whatever it had been had disappeared into thin air. He continued searching, not wanting to admit to Zend that he might've dragged them into grave peril.

"Well?" Zend said, smoothing out the sleeve of his tunic, still creased from Horace's tight hold.

"I know there was something. We were following it. But, just at the last moment, it got away from us."

"You're joking."

Horace cast off Zend's complaints and continued to scour for the shape. He searched high and low for many minutes before resigning himself to the fact that he would never find it again, whatever it had been had eluded them. He just hoped there was no malicious intent behind the wild goose chase. If they stumbled upon some black magic he would never forgive himself—already being a Grotesque there was a limit to the damage which a black witch or wizard could inflict on him, so he was more concerned for his fresh, limber-limbed companion.

Something tickled the back of his neck. Horace pivoted, but couldn't find the source of the sensation. He was sure that it had something to do with the shape they'd just followed. "Did you see anything?"

"What?" Zend said, scowling. "I haven't seen anything since we set off on your crazy little adventure."

Something brushed along Horace's fingertips. He glanced down. Again, nothing. "There's something going on here."

"Like what?"

"Something just touched me. On the neck, now on the fingers."

"Maybe your body's about to fall apart from scurvy."

And then, right ahead of him, Horace saw the thing. It was formless, like a cloud, but solid. When he had first seen it, off in the distance, he'd believed it to have been a smoky-grey, but now, up close, he saw that it was impossibly white. He reached out to touch, but it escaped his fingers.

Now even Zend was watching on. "What is that?" he said.

"Dunno," Horace said, trying to get closer.

The cloud jerked away from him, matching his distance each time. It reminded him of a fisherman trying to tempt a fish onto his line. And, ignoring what should've seemed obvious from that comparison, he kept on pursuing.

The cloud brought them to a tree trunk and then, promptly and without warning, it shot off upward, disappearing into the leaves above their head.

"What now?" Zend said.

Horace sized up the tree. There were no kind low-lying branches and no other trees in jumping distance. The lowest branch of the tree was at least twenty feet above them. "We've got to go up it."

They made little to no progress on getting up the tree. Horace half hoped that the cloud would return from within the leaves and lead them off in some other direction, hopefully to a destination, if not at ground level then easily attainable for his fairly unagile frame. After they'd spent the best part of the afternoon with Zend down below, shoving Horace up the tree by the soles of his feet, Horace decided that they might have more luck if they exchanged roles. This soon turned out to be infeasible when it transpired that Horace could not support Zend's weight.

Zend, unperturbed, said, "Guess I'll have to get up this myself, then," and he scrabbled his way up the trunk, slipping a few times, but generally staying in the tree—one of the key components of tree-climbing.

Horace looked up at Zend, shielding his eyes from the

setting sun, blinking through the leaves. "That's it," he said, unable to think of anything more encouraging to say.

Zend got his grip on the lowest branch just as twilight was setting in. He swung himself up, through the leaves and out of sight.

Horace, now standing at the base of the trunk and starting to think about stray honey boars strolling round, foraging for a pre-sleep snack, cupped his hands round his mouth and called upward. "Do you think I can get up?"

There was no reply.

After about a minute of silence, Horace's worries got the better of him and he glanced round wondering what he might do if he ended up being alone in the Forests. He would have to continue on his mission to locate white magic, since he could hardly return to Witney Branches—if the King's men didn't deal with him first, Susan would.

A vine dangled down from above. As it lowered itself down to the ground, Horace observed the various places where one vine had been tied to another. That was what Zend had been doing all this time.

Horace grabbed hold of the vine, wrapping it round his waist and then round his fist. He gave it a sharp tug and then waited. The unseen hands reeled him upward. He watched the ground judder below him with each of the thrusts Zend exerted on the vines and, before too long, he was moving up past the branch, feeling the leaves caress his cheeks. He spared his companion the last few feet by seizing hold of the branch and lugging himself up.

When he stood up on the mighty branch he caught sight of the house standing before him. It was built of twigs glued together with mud. It reminded him of a bird's nest in the way it had been constructed. He inched his way along the branch, almost neglecting to notice Zend, who was now puffing his lungs out on his hands and knees.

Horace patted him on the back. "Good work, thanks for pulling me up. Couldn't have got up here without you."

"You're welcome," Zend said, between inhalations.

Horace trod along the broad branch, marvelling briefly at its strength. He wondered whether magic might've had something to do with it. He reached the front door of the shack and noticed the bell hanging beside it, a rope dangling down. Without any other indication of what he should do next, he gave the rope a tug and waited.

In the meantime, Zend sidled up beside him, still making a scene over his exertion with the rope pulling. Horace stood by what he'd said about Zend being brought along for his muscle, and so he could have no complaints about having his skill put into action.

There was no answer from within the house.

"Guess we'd better go back down," Horace said.

Zend balked at the remark.

"Just a joke," Horace said.

"What do we do now, then?"

Horace sized up the door then gave it a shove.

It opened with a toe-curling *squeak* to reveal a dim interior.

"Isn't this trespassing?" Zend said.

"We've come this far so we might as well take a look round."

The shack carried a weighty aroma of damp wood and moss. This was hardly surprising considering the material the place was made from. The inside was quite simple: a clumsily-cobbled together wooden table, a bed make of twigs and lined with dead leaves and a bucket over in the corner, which Horace didn't think too hard about.

Gloom infested the place, smothering the light out of everything. Horace would've had second thoughts about being here, that it might be black magic he'd stumbled upon, if only he hadn't followed that white cloud all the way here.

"Not exactly up to Witney Branches' standards, is it?" Zend said.

Horace eyed a snail which was sliming its way across the table. "No," he said.

"And you're sure this is the home of white magic?"

"Absolutely," Horace said, still having grave doubts about it.

They shuffled round the room, going through the various nooks and crannies looking for something which might give a clue as to the resident. But, aside from a battered book of poetry, its pages half-rotten, they found nothing to enlighten them. Horace was about to call off the investigation, to instruct Zend to get them back down to ground level, when a figure darkened the doorway.

Stunned at their sudden appearance, and not being able to make out more than a silhouette, Horace said, "Terribly sorry to intrude like this. It's just that we're looking for some white magic."

The figure remained silent.

Horace felt Zend creep up beside him, as if it might make the two of them less conspicuous. Horace decided he needed to give further information. "We've come from Witney Branches, you probably know it, where the Grotesque make their home. It's all related to the King's men, you see? They've been destroying the Forests, as I'm sure you're aware, and they're keeping us held prisoner in our own home. If there's—"

"Why did you come to me?" the figure said, with a slightly shrill, feminine voice.

Horace managed a smile. "Actually, we were sort of going round the place aimlessly, looking for someone who might be able to help." He sank his teeth into his lower lip. "We saw the white cloud, down below, and it led us here."

The figure nodded her head and then stepped forward, into the shack. She had long white hair, so long, in fact, that it ended up down at her ankles. Her face was a mass of wrinkled skin but she had young, perky grey—or were they white?—eyes. Her limbs were nimble and spindly—she looked like she filled her days with quite a bit of tree-climbing.

She strutted up to within only a few inches of both Horace and Zend and then said, "The vapour only appears to those with noble intentions."

Finally, they were getting somewhere.

She continued, "But I never really had much respect for 'noble' intentions. Why else do you think I closed myself off up here for?"

The woman stooped down below her table and produced a corked glass jar from beneath. The jar was filled with a lime-green water which slopped back and forth. She held it to her chest and tried to loosen the cork, but it appeared that it was stuck fast.

Seeing an opportunity to make a good impression, or to

improve on the poor one he had already made, Horace stepped forward and offered his help.

The woman's eyes wandered over him then relinquished the jar. "You've only got one eye," she said.

"Yes," Horace said, gripping the cork and twisting it, "lots of people notice that."

The jar held onto the cork for several seconds before there was a satisfying *plop* to signal that cork and jar were separated. Triumphant, he offered the jar to the woman, turning up his nose a little at the stench of sour milk and pepper which emanated from the liquid inside.

The woman sniffed the liquid, peered into it and then knocked it back. Some of the liquid dribbled down her chin and onto the front of her robes, although this didn't appear anything of an event considering the dried on dark patches already there.

Apparently satisfied, she brought the jar down from her mouth and smacked her lips. "Nothing like oragnuck."

Having been party to the same sensory detail as Horace, Zend said, "No, I don't suppose there is."

The woman slammed the jar down on the table so hard it was a wonder it didn't shatter. Then she slunk over to her bed and slumped down, back against the wall and hands clasped together. "You said something about the destruction of the Damned Forests."

Horace took this as his cue. He took a step forward. "Yes, we've come to ask for the help of white magic, so that it might help us to drive back the King's men, rid the Forests of them. It's really in everyone's benefit to pull together."

She scowled. "Spoken like a truly desperate man, that. What makes you think that I care about the Damned Forests?"

"Oh, well, they're your home, aren't they?"

"Yes and no," the woman said.

"Um, what do you mean by that?"

She sighed. "I only moved here when I was a little girl and never saw sense to move out. But that doesn't mean that I might not be open to a change, might do me good, some new scenery. Maybe some mountains, a fresh stream burbling along."

"Right," Horace said, looking to Zend for some sort of back up and, finding none, turned back to the woman. "But you must have some sort of sentimental attachment to the place. That's to say, you don't want to see it turned into kindling?"

"What do I care? If those men try to knock down this tree they'll be in for a rather pleasant surprise. They'll be so struck by the very magnificence of my home that they'll have no choice but to back off and bow down."

Horace decided that it was time to alter tactics. From the strategy the woman had hinted at just now, the having the men struck by awe rather than branches, not only suggested that she *was* a witch, but also that she was a practitioner of white magic. They had found their pony now and all they had to do was tempt it out of the stable.

"And don't compare me to a horse!" the woman said.

Horace glanced round in alarm. "Uh, did you just read my thoughts?"

"You can bet anything I did. What else did you think I was going to do? Just listen to the tripe spewing out of your mouth?"

"Well, no, I don't suppose so."

She eyed them up, eyebrows twitching. "Look, if you really want my help, then you're going to have to try better to sell it to me. Why should I lower myself to getting mixed up with blithering men when I could be just as happy sat here in my house enjoying the rest of my, not so long, life?"

"It's . . . it's good versus evil."

"That's the best you've got, eh?"

Zend, who throughout the exchange had kept himself in a kind of silent daze, now took the opportunity to stick his oar into the matter. "Why're you being so selfish, sitting here on your backside while the Damned Forests are destroyed? I mean, what kind of pleasure do you get from that? If you're really allied to white magic as you suggest then you'll put it to some good use, actually do something other than moping about in this gods-awful shack all day long."

Horace covered his eye with his hand and rubbed, resigned to the onslaught which was about to fall on them, maybe the flowers would smell so sweet as to sting their nostrils or the tree branches cuddle them so tight as to bring on asphyxiation. Fortunately none of the above came to pass. Not right away, in any case.

The woman let loose a long and almost girly laugh. She slapped her thighs and rocked back, knocking her head against the wall of her shack.

Horace exchanged glances with Zend who looked just as surprised at her reaction as Horace was.

When the woman composed herself, wiping away the tears and shaking her head, she looked up at them, a fresh rosiness in her cheeks. "You've got a lot of nerve coming here and telling me that, but, I have to say, it is nice, once in a while, to get a kick up the bum, to be reminded of the moping wretch that I really am."

"Glad to hear it," Zend said, under his breath.

"But I really can't see the two of you overcoming the King's army, even with some of my magic on your side."

"Why not?" Horace said.

"Look, you two seem like nice boys, so I'll level with you. I am the whitest of white witch in the Forests."

Horace thought that if she were the whitest of the white witches, what must the blackest witch look like?

She narrowed her eyes at him. "I'd take more care with such careless thoughts, if I were you. Anyway, all it takes to be the whitest of the white witches is a will to steer clear of black magic, in all its forms, all the time. That's why I keep myself cooped up, away from the others. I'm not prepared to defile my flawless anima for some chance encounter."

"But, but—"

She clapped her hands together and smiled. "Good bye, boys."

A strange and intense happiness dawned over Horace. His mouth was moulded into a smile, the corners being drawn back into his cheeks. A strange tingle reverberated down through his legs, making them shake—no, *jig*.

He jigged his way toward the door, managing to steal a glance at Zend—who had been caught up in the same dance frenzy—as he went. He jigged his way right along the tree branch and then, with a curt flick of the heels, leapt off, Zend following soon after.

SO CLOSE, YET SO FAR

TREVOR WOULD'VE KILLED to get into a separate tent. He had been tied up here back-to-back with Susan for what seemed like an ice age. They had exhausted every possible polite topic: their favourite foods, what they liked to do in their spare time, and of course, that old reliable: the weather. Trevor decided that, if they weren't going to sit there in silence, if Susan couldn't help but open her mouth, then he might as well garnish some useful information, something that might turn out to be useful later on.

He straightened his back and flexed his fingers, trying to get some sort of blood flow going, and then he said, "So, how did you get into this predicament?"

"Which predicament?"

"You know, out here, in the woods."

"How I came to the Damned Forests, you mean?"

"Yeah."

Susan sniffed a little and Trevor was worried that he might've set her off again—that she might start off bawling her eyes out—but, instead, she sucked it all up and said, "I was quite young, sixteen or seventeen years old. I . . . I had a young daughter, a year old or so and was married to a charming farmer from my village—he was about five years older and taught me so much.

"We lived in a beautiful little cottage, not far from the Forests, where my husband would tend to the fields, look after the cows and sheep, the hens. There was a river which flowed at the bottom of the garden. It was a perfect life in many ways and I suppose I should've realised it right then and there, that I should've been on the look out for danger—but I was so carefree and happy. And then, one day, when my husband had gone off to market to sell some wool, I was hanging the washing out the back of the cottage when I caught sight of an elderly woman sitting on the opposite bank of the river.

"At first I just ignored her, assuming that she was a wandering beggar looking for some food or water—about four or five passed by our house every day, so we had tired of them. I went back inside the house, saw to my baby girl and spent the afternoon darning my husband's socks. That evening, when I went to collect the washing, she was still there, stooped over, face hidden by the hood of her robe, on the other side of the river. Again, I thought nothing of it and swept back into the house—deciding that she would be gone by the morning.

"My husband returned home that night quite happy. He had managed to sell the wool for a good price. Even though I did my best to summon the enthusiasm for this news, I found it impossible—with my mind still concentrating on that old woman out back. My husband noticed something about my expression, but said nothing, and we went to bed that night without speaking of her."

For a few minutes, Susan remained quiet. Trevor thought of prompting her to continue, but decided that he had to leave her to spin her story in peace. He had no concept for what sort of emotional toll it was taking on her to tell him—and, after all, he had been the one to ask her to tell it, so he must let her speak in her own good time.

Susan did continue. "I had a dream, a terrible dream. A group of men bore down on me, their hands grasping sacks, and they were smothering me with the rough cloth. When I tried to fight back, to flap my arms at them, it really had no effect. Their strength only seemed to increase. Behind them I saw a shadowy figure watching on, staring at me from beneath a black hood. And then I woke up beside my husband, the bed sheets drenched in my sweat.

"Having had a hard day's journey, to the market and back, my husband slept on soundly. My first impulse was to check on my little girl, and I did so, looking into her basket to see her with her eyes firmly clasped shut, fists curled up and lips suckling gently on thin air. The dream stayed with me, haunting me while I was awake, and I knew that I had to go round the back of the house, to check on the beggar woman. So, I skittered through the house, my mind telling me to go back to bed, to try and get some sleep before the next day, but I simply had to know. For, I think I knew then, that the source of that dream had been the beggar woman.

"When I padded outside the house, looked out over our

garden, I could make out the shape huddled up on the opposite bank of the river, and I felt myself drawn forward, by some invisible force, to meet with her. With my arms wrapped round my chest, I asked the woman what she wanted, and she asked me whether I had some bread, any water drawn from a well. Surprised at this woman's persistence but, at the same time, furious that she refused to leave me and my family alone, I told her to go away, to go off into the night. That was the greatest mistake of my life."

"Why?" Trevor said. "What happened?"

"I . . . I backed up, headed back toward the house. And, before I knew it, I was running, running as fast as I could back toward the back door. But, before I could get so much as onto the porch, an almighty surge blasted through the air and caught me on my lower spine. I dropped to the ground, writhing in pain, feeling my skin quivering to my touch. When I managed to flip myself onto my back, to see what it was that had hit me so hard, I saw the woman, risen now, arm outstretched, and, no doubt, a smile beneath that hood. She told me that I had denied her, a dying witch, mere bread and water, and that now I would suffer just as she had throughout her life—that I would be an outcast just like her."

Trevor considered that, if he'd been listening to this story, without the evidence of a woman wholly-covered in hair sitting with her back to him, then he might well have laughed it off long ago or, if he'd been in a more benevolent mood, he might've suggested Susan look up a psychiatrist with a respectably-high hourly rate. But, as the facts would have it, he was sitting with his back to a woman covered in hair and he wasn't in his world any longer—did psychiatrists even exist here?

"I watched as the witch trembled and then fell forwards, into the river, with a light *splash*, and she was gone—starved to death, I guess, or maybe she was just old. All I know is that when I stood back and observed my arms I saw that they were covered in hair. I felt my face and I had the same sensation. For a long time I thought about going back into the house, getting back into bed with my husband, waking up the next day and finding that it had all been just a terrible nightmare. But . . . but I just couldn't. I knew that it was as she'd said, that from now on I would be alone, never accepted."

"Couldn't you have tried to speak with your husband about it?"

"People in my village would kill any children born with any kind of deformity: eleven toes, an extra eye, one ear bigger than the other—it was well-known that witchcraft had touched them, manipulated some aspect of them, and the people would not have anything like that walking among them."

"Why not?"

When Susan spoke again, her voice distant. "Because they're different. We're different."

"And so you came to the Forests?"

"Yes, like so many others, I found myself drawn here, to Witney Branches. They took me in, treated me as if I were their daughter. And, when I grew up, I returned the favour, taking in the new Grotesque, helping them to feel at home." She took a shaky breath. "It's given me reason to live, I guess."

"What about your husband and child?"

"I used to stalk through the Forests and sit at the edge of the trees, as close as I would dare go, to watch them. They seemed to get on okay without me. I watched as my husband would strap my daughter to his chest or back as he worked among the animals. Some days I thought about going down there, admitting to him what had happened—that a witch had cursed me. My husband was a reasonable man and not so swept up in the fanaticism of the rest of the village."

Trevor's mouth felt dry and, he had to admit, he was moved by Susan's story—he had never experienced anything so sad in his own life, everything had gone so well from him, until he had been transported to Ethereal, that was. He needed closure from her story. "So why didn't you go down there? Surely he would've understood. Maybe he would've taken you in, loved you for who you are."

"No," Susan said. "It really wouldn't have done any good. You're right, maybe my husband would've taken me in, but it wouldn't have been fair. Our whole family would've been living in fear, for that group of villagers brandishing torches in their fists wanting to smoke the monster out. My daughter deserved a normal life, not to be condemned just because of who her mother was."

From outside the tent there was the muttering of voices. Trevor could make out the shadows of the men, their silhouettes in the late-evening sunlight. He identified the first man right away, from the sword hanging off his belt and the way he stood with his hand always at its hilt. Eversham. The other he either hadn't seen or could've just been one of the countless other King's men.

"What is it?" Eversham said.

The other man had a feeble voice and, if Trevor had had to guess, he might've supposed that he was not totally at home out here, in the Forests. "Forgive me, sir, but I thought that I should come here to see you personally."

"Who sent you? Frum?"

"No, sir, I decided to come of my own accord."

"What? Without orders?" Eversham said, drawing his sword. "I'll have you court martialled at dawn. How dare you leave the King's garrison without permission."

The pitch of the other man's voice shot up an octave. "Please, if you'd only let me explain—"

"Get it out boy!"

"It's your son."

Eversham lowered his sword to his side and the tone of his voice softened considerably. "My son?"

"Yes, sir."

Eversham lurched forward and seized the man by the collar of his tunic. He brought his face within inches of his. "What's happened to him?"

"He's been put in the dungeon."

"What?"

Trevor's muscles tightened at the thought. He had thought it brutal to put deformed babies to death, so although this should've come as little surprise after that nugget of knowledge it still shocked him.

"On whose orders?" Eversham said, gripping the man tighter.

The man couldn't reply, since Eversham was strangling him with the material of his own tunic. When Eversham let off his grip just enough for the man to breathe, he said, "General Frum's."

Eversham let go of the man and sheathed his sword. His hands flew up to his scalp and he ran his fingers through his hair. Although Trevor had no way of seeing the expression etched on his face, he was sure that it was one of anguish. Now, when Eversham spoke, his voice was soft, wobbling slightly, ready to give way at any moment. "Whatever has he put him in the dungeon for? What has he done that's so terrible?"

"Sir, I believe it has something to do with the King's bride, his new queen."

"And what of her?"

The man spoke quickly, as if worried that his life might be snuffed out at an opportunity of Eversham's choosing. "She was down in the dungeons, with a group of friends. She made a deal to become one of the King's maidens, which he accepted, and they kept her friends down their as sort of an insurance that she wouldn't attempt to escape. Then, during the competition to determined the King's Champion, they escaped with the champion-elect, so they needed some leverage over her."

Eversham pressed his hand to his forehead.

For once Trevor actually felt sorry for him. Being a parent himself, Trevor fully-understood the peril which Eversham's mind must be floating through right now. He would be tearing himself apart, trying to work out where he'd gone wrong, if he could've done something, anything, to protect his son further.

"Sir? Sir?" the man said, a quiver in his voice.

"What?"

"I'll need to be getting back to the castle. Like I said, I came here of my own volition, I thought that you should know."

Eversham craned his neck upward, reached out and touched the man on his shoulder. "Yes, yes you must. Thank you for coming, for bringing me this news. Please know that if I am ever to find better position within the King's court then you shall be right at my side."

"Thank you, sir."

"Take care on the road back, you are armed I trust?"

"Yes."

"Then good luck."

The man lingered, another question clearly on his mind, another purpose for his visit. "Sir?"

"Yes?"

"How does the search for the witch go?"

"I've nothing to report. When I do I shall send a messenger. How is the King?"

"Quite frankly, sir, he's at death's door. Some believe that he might not last the night."

Eversham snorted and then spat. "Between you and me, I don't believe it would be the worst of situations were he to croak it. The man who allowed my son to be put in the dungeons shall never have my respect."

The man inched away. "Very well, sir."

"Gods speed."

The man's silhouette slipped away round the tent.

Eversham stood alone, muttering to himself and then he looked back at the tent, to where Trevor and, he supposed, Susan watched on. At first Trevor was sure that Eversham was going to bark some order at them, if he could really see them through the canvas, but then, after so seriously staring, he shifted off to some other part of the camp.

Trevor believed that this might be a wonderful opportunity for them, if only they could think how they might play it. They had Eversham, the leader of the King's men in the Damned

Forests, and the one keeping the Grotesque under house arrest, making it known that he resented the King's treatment. If only Trevor could find a way to engage him in conversation perhaps he could make him see that their interests might well be mutually beneficial. Maybe they wouldn't need any magic after all.

AT THE KING'S DEATHBED

A LEXIS HAD JUST completed a week of being Queen of
Ethereal when Jenson, hair aflutter and cheeks puffed up,
rushed into her new—Queen-sized—bedroom. For the first time
in their relationship, Alexis noted that he actually looked
emotionally affected, that he had something that truly bothered
him and he either couldn't find way to hide it or just didn't care
about his official facade any longer.

"Come quickly!" he said, between snatched breaths.

Alexis laid down her book of poetry—one of several which
she had pilfered from Sydney's room. Now that she had free rein
of the castle she'd taken every advantage to poke her nose into
every cranny of the place. The poetry, of course, was written in
languages, or notation, she had no hope of understanding—one
of the covers featured a beaver-like man striking a heroic pose.
Who wouldn't go barmy with that sort of material lying round?

"What's wrong?" Alexis said.

"The King!" Jenson said, nearly fainting. "The King is dying!"

Alexis hurriedly jabbed her feet into a pair of sheepskin slippers and followed Jenson through the labyrinthine corridors. She reached the King's chamber with her heart rapping away at her tonsils. She turned her attention to the glazed looks of the courtiers standing in the hallway to the King's chambers, the mauves and powder-blues of their clothing reflecting the sombre mood. She slipped past all of them, with Jenson skittering along behind her, and threw open the doors to the King's bedroom.

The air was thick with moisture and she noted that steam clung to the closed windows. She wanted to ask someone to open them up, to let in some of the outside air, but she realised it had been at the King's request, that he was shivering beneath his layers and layers of blankets. The slap of her slippers on the tiles of the chamber rang hollow throughout the bedroom, as she drew up beside his bed and perched on the edge of the mattress.

The King looked shrunken and grey as he lay on his back looking up at her. His entire right side was kept hidden by the familiar veil, although she caught a glimpse of the shrivelled white hair poking out beneath. He smiled at her, a faint warmth in his eyes. His hand shook as he reached for her hand. "You came quickly," he said.

Alexis's throat felt withered, parched of any liquid. Although she wanted to ask Jenson to bring her a drink, partly to have him out of the room, she just couldn't bring herself to do it—she recalled the expression on Jenson's face and knew that, despite all his faults, he deeply and truly cared for the King, which was more than she could say for herself. Nonetheless, she did feel overcome with the occasion. Blood was rushing to her cheeks. She had never witnessed anyone dying before.

"I came as soon as Jenson informed me," she said.

The lines in the King's face creased as he nodded. His hand found hers and he brushed his fingertips against the smooth ridges of her knuckles. "It was nice . . . to have a wife, for a while."

"It was nice to be a queen."

The King smiled briefly, but it seemed to pain him, so he stopped. He cast a glance across his bedchamber to Jenson, who, Alexis observed, was shaking with sobs. "Jenson, please, come over to my side."

"Sire?" Jenson said, his voice wavering.

"Don't be shy. You've been like an older brother to me my whole life. Please, allow me this final pleasure of having you at my side, of us being equals just for a while."

Alexis registered the pure fear on Jenson's face, followed by the terrified acceptance—he had never disobeyed an order from the King and he had no intention of starting to now. Still, it was with resignation and tentativeness that he sat at that the King's side, almost daring not to look him in the eye.

The King's eyes lolled back toward Alexis. "This curse is nearly done with me. I cannot survive it."

A burst of emotion shot through Alexis. "But, surely, there's still a chance of finding the witch, if only—"

The King pressed his lips together. "No, it is my time now. It was with a heavy heart that I took this throne, and it's with an even heavier one that I hand it over to you, Alexis, while my true heir is located. I have failed my people. I leave Ethereal in greater danger than ever before."

"But you've almost destroyed the Forests," Alexis said. "You've almost ridded Ethereal of magic, all the evil you talked about."

The King jerked his head in Jenson's direction.

Jenson, seeming to understand the mere thoughts which passed through King Fredrick's head, leant forward and, with a delicate touch, took hold of the veil. He peeled it away from the King's face and from his hidden right side.

As he brought it away, it revealed the King's face, on the right side reduced to no more than a skeletal outline, the skin no more than tracing paper covering a skull.

Alexis gasped.

Jenson continued unabated to remove the veil. When he had finished the King lay there in his bed, wearing his pyjamas, his right side almost less substantial than the sheets collected round his form.

Alexis had never believed that the King's condition had become this bad. She supposed that he had kept it hidden from her well, that he had sacrificed knowing her body so that she might remain an enigma, perhaps he had been holding out for Alexis being his reward once he had been cured of the wasting disease—something to look forward to. And she was somewhat distracted from this lecherous thought by the spectacle of the King's soon-to-fail body.

A tremor passed through the King. It started at his toes, passed up through his skins, into his knees—which knocked together—and then proceeded on up to his head, which shook back and forth clasped in a fit. Alexis thought that he was going to slip away from them then and there, but by some deeply held inner strength he kept hold of himself, enough so that he might face up to them one final time, his voice barely a wheeze now. He could scarcely hold up his neck to eye each of them, but he just about managed to keep himself steady to address Alexis. "You shall be a good queen, a noble Queen of Ethereal. And I wish for you to promise to step aside from the throne when the true heir emerges. And . . . and . . ." he broke out into a series of splutters, and Jenson reached forward to aid him, but the King shook his head, determined to continue, ". . . I want you to oversee the destruction of those *damned* forests, if it's the last thing you ever do. The whole magical realm shall suffer for what it has done to a rightful King. It shall no longer be tolerated in the Kingdom. Is that understood?"

Feeling tears well in her eyes, Alexis nodded.

The King tilted his head to face Jenson. "And I should like you to honour your new queen. You who are my dearest friend must oversee the transition and help her with any trouble she might have." His gaze intensified—the old intensity, when Alexis had first met the King, returned. "Do I have your word?"

Jenson looked lost for a few seconds, his eyes roamed over Alexis, as if he were wary of making a promise which he might not be able to keep. And then, just at the final moment, he nodded vigorously.

A smile lined the King's lips and a croak resounded in his throat. His trembling hand reached up to his face, but, before he could reach it, it fell down by his side and the King breathed his final breath.

Cold blood dripped through Alexis's veins and centred in her heart. For a terrible second she thought her whole body might split apart under the intensity of the sensation.

Jenson muffled a sob and then reached over to shut the King's eyelids. He grasped the sheets at the King's feet, and then dragged the sheet over the King's body. He stood up, back straight, tears flowing down his cheeks and then looked over at Alexis. In a low moan, he said, "The King is dead, long live the Queen."

Alexis passed her coronation in mourning dress. Those same Darguks took responsibility for her outfitting. She wondered where they kept their quarters in the castle, or whether they might come from their homeland every time she was in need of a dress for an occasion. As she set about the motions, accepting the flowers which several members of the court held out for her, she noticed General Frum, standing in full uniform at the side of the priest who barked through the appropriate oaths. Although Frum bowed to her as he should when she confronted him, she noticed a lingering anger in his eye, and she knew that he would be after her, looking for any means to get his hands on her throne. In choosing not to run that day of the wedding, as Cherry had suggested, she had committed herself to this battle. But, despite everything, his command of the army and respect about the court, she backed herself to fight her corner—she would not be backed into submission by a bully.

The second after her coronation was finished she instructed Jenson to free the boy being held down in the dungeons and to have him brought up to the royal bedroom—what had been

King Fredrick's bedroom. As she paced through the large quarters: the velvet curtains which tumbled down onto the porcelain
tiles, the oak four-poster bed with silk fastenings, and, of course,
the goose feather mattress which—as she had found out last
night—provided the most comfortable bed she had ever experienced. Then again, as Queen of Ethereal, didn't she deserve only
the very best?

Jenson returned several minutes later with the boy, Arnold.
He looked absolutely pitiful. His skin was caked in dust and his
eyes were like a pair of egg whites peering out from within his
gloomy skin. His clothes, the tunic he had worn, were reduced
to rags and he wore no shoes on his feet. Jenson hung back, at
the door, awaiting her orders.

Alexis gestured for Arnold to enter.

Arnold's eyes flickered about their sockets, as if anticipating
some new form of punishment for whatever it was that he
had done.

"Are you hungry?" Alexis said.

Arnold nodded.

"I don't blame you. I remember that when I came back up
from the dungeons I was absolutely famished. Gruel doesn't
provide much in the way of nourishment, does it?"

Arnold shook his head.

Jenson broke from his stupor. "Speak when you're spoken
to, boy!"

Arnold flinched then said, "No, no it doesn't."

"Remember you're speaking to your queen."

"No, it doesn't, ma'am."

"Better," Jenson said, with a sigh.

Alexis thought of asking Jenson to be more laidback about

the whole affair but, she supposed, she needed to truly earn his respect too, and the only way she was going to do that was by conforming to his expectations of a true Queen of Ethereal. Then again, there was something that she might be able to do without losing face. "Jenson, you are relieved."

"Ma'am?" Jenson said, arching an eyebrow. "Do you believe that wise considering the company you are keeping? Wouldn't you rather I call a guard in addition to my presence?"

"No," she said, firmly. "Please, feel free to relax, I shan't be needing you for the time being."

Jenson glanced at Arnold, frown lines appearing on his forehead, and then, remembering himself, he bowed to Alexis and took his leave. Just as he was about to head out the door, he said, "Just for care's sake, Your Majesty, I shall leave a guard at your door. You've only to shout for him to attend to you."

"Thank you, Jenson."

"Ma'am," Jenson said, inclining his head once more before leaving.

Arnold scratched his dirty arm while he stared at the tiled floor.

"Do you understand why you were sent down to the dungeons?"

"No, ma'am."

"Really? No idea at all?"

"No, ma'am."

Alexis considered whether she should level with the boy. He was young, no more than twelve or thirteen. He reminded her of her younger brother who was the same age. They had the same oil-slick hair. She decided that she had to. "You were put in the dungeons because the King thought that I might try and escape from the castle. He believed that by putting you down there he could have an assurance that I wouldn't escape—on the basis that he would harm you if I were to attempt to leave."

She stepped over to the window which looked out on the courtyard. From where she stood she had a much superior view compared to either of her previous bedrooms. The window occupied an entire side of the courtyard, looking down on the fountain and well-trimmed bushes below, giving a view right down to the drawbridge, which was currently laid down across the moat as the day's traffic passed over it—mainly merchants and knights, either on their way to or from the Damned Forests.

She turned away, back to Arnold. "But I can promise you now that you are safe. Now that you are under my power I can assure you that you shall never return to the dungeons."

Arnold visibly brightened at this news. "Thank you!"

She gave him a smile.

Arnold twitched and looked away from her gaze. "I mean, thank you, ma'am."

"You mentioned that your father was a knight?"

Arnold's nerves seemed to desert him now, as the prospect that he wouldn't be returning to the dungeons dawned on him. He licked his lips—perhaps already considering a hearty meal following his liberation, Alexis would see to that. "Yes, ma'am, a knight."

"And he's serving out in the Damned Forests?"

"Yes, ma'am."

"What's his name?"

"Lord Eversham," Arnold said.

That name was familiar to Alexis. She had heard it banded

about during discussions between Frum and the deceased King Fredrick. "Is he important?"

"Oh yes, ma'am, in fact he's in charge of the siege on the Forests."

Alexis considered that Frum must've been playing some sort of political game. He had surely not just had Arnold locked up to keep Alexis honest—not if he would be risking the ire of such a high-ranking member of his army. She got the idea that, maybe, things out in the Damned Forests might not be quite as straight forward as she had believed. Perhaps Frum wanted to keep Lord Eversham in line just as he kept her in line. And if Eversham had something against Frum then he might well be an ally.

She looked Arnold up and down. "Tell me, I heard that you enjoyed hanging round with that escaped competitor, the large man, that you taught him several useful techniques. Are you good with a sword?"

"Oh yes, ma'am."

She thought over the idea again, wondering whether she might face some resistance throughout the court. Then she caught herself, reminding herself that she must think like a queen: act decisively and without hesitation, not be afraid to make mistakes.

"I'd like to make you my personal guard," she said.

Arnold's eyes bulged. "Ma'am?"

"That's right, first of all I'd like you to go down to the kitchens, ask the cooks to prepare you a feast befitting a knight and then, immediately after having had a good wash and having put on some fresh clothes, I want you to go down to the armoury to be fitted for the best armour and sword we have among our stock."

Arnold looked like he might faint at any second.

"Is that clear?"

"Yes, ma'am."

"Then hop along, down to the kitchens, and have a banquet."

Arnold stepped backward, toward the door, as if were he to turn his back to her, she might take it all back. He slipped out without another word.

Alexis stood upright and managed a smile, feeling that she had accomplished the first worthwhile action of her reign.

ASKING ROUND

J OHN LED SYDNEY and Courtney on through the thick
Forests, desperate to have something to show for all his
determination. He hadn't really known what to expect
following that meeting in the Coven—he supposed he had
expected the Forests to leap to life: branches snatching at them,
birds to peck at their eyes, roots to wrap round their ankles, but
it remained pretty peaceful: branches remaining steady, only
moved by a light breeze, birds chirping away happily enough and
the roots remaining, well, grounded. Either Maxeth was a
massive blagger or he was biding his time, deciding to work in a
more subtle way than he had suggested in the course of the
meeting. Whoever this Yvonne was, he was sure they needed to
track her down fairly sharpish, before Maxeth got a chance to
spring whatever plans he had into action.

Courtney whined on behind them, like a child being dragged
round a nature reserve by his parents: "My feet are aching right

off!" "Can't we just stop, for five minutes, just so I can catch my breath?" and "What're we doing all this trekking nonsense for anyway? We're going the completely wrong direction. The castle's that way, you should all be accompanying me to reclaim my throne. Don't think I'll remember that you've delayed my true claim when the time comes for me to elect my nobility."

John picked up on what Sydney must've been doing for years —namely tuning Courtney out, reducing him to mere background noise. Now that John had employed this method he found he was no more of a bother than a splinter between the toes or a nagging bit of phlegm at the back of a throat.

They reached a clearing where John decided to call them to a break, as Courtney had been nagging them to do ever since they'd started. He was a little anxious that, after hours and hours of hiking, they had yet to run into anyone who they might ask about Yvonne—only rabbits and other small rodents scarpering about the tall grass, thankfully no honey boars, yet.

They'd scrounged some bread and a little jam from Francesca's house, and John brought these out as he crouched down onto a nearby log. He recalled his sorrow at having to leave her little cottage behind, that it would be left uninhabited from then on. He only hoped that some young witch or wizard might come upon it and put it to use—it was sad to think it might just crumble away, although, if the King's men had their way, it would perish with the rest of the Forests.

Sydney bucked up beside John and took up a place on the log. "Where to next, then?"

John chewed on the bread. He had to be careful not to chew his way through their entire supplies—as he was wont to do if he left his hunger pangs unchecked. So he slowed his chewing down, trying to do his best impression of a cow chewing on some cud. "Don't know. I guess we've just got to keep walking till we run into someone." He checked Sydney over. "Don't feel like you have to come along, okay? It's not like you owe me anything because I sprang you from the dungeons."

Sydney seemed to consider this fact and then he broke out into his familiar smile. "No, we're right with you, all the way." He glanced back at Courtney. "Isn't that right, Your Royal Highness?"

Courtney had his boot off and he was jabbing at what looked like a blister on his toe. He glanced up at Sydney eventually. "Whatever. As long as it gets my throne back."

John offered Courtney some of the bread and jam. At first Courtney rejected it outright, claiming that it was hardly suitable for the heir to the throne of Ethereal, but then he saw sense, when his stomach started grumbling, and scoffed far more than his fair share.

With their impromptu meal done with, John heaved himself up and brushed the crumbs off his trousers. He peered off in various directions, looking for something which would lead him onto the right track. And then, off at about a hundred yards, he saw a man walking through the trees—away from them.

He thought of yelling out and then told himself that it might well be a member of the King's men. He checked the man out further. His eyesight had never been terrific and he'd relied on it less and less, ever since he'd begun hanging out with Horace, but he was certain that the man didn't wear the blue and white colours of the King. And so, he let loose his loudest yell.

The man kept on walking.

John yelled again.

Still the man continued on his way, unperturbed.

Sydney stalked up beside John. "What's going on?"

A jolt pulsed through John's chest. "Over there, do you see? There's someone. We have to ask him about Yvonne."

"Oh yeah," Sydney said, holding his hand over his eyes. "Sure it's not one of the King's men?"

"Ninety-nine per cent."

"What's he carrying over his shoulder?"

John examined the man further and saw that, indeed, he lugged something over his shoulder. If he hadn't known better he might've said it was a pike. But the man wasn't dressed for military service. Then again, he supposed that it was wise to take whatever weapon you could into the Damned Forests.

John shouted again.

The man still didn't acknowledge him.

"Come on," John said, breaking into a trot.

He heard Courtney's whiny protest followed by Sydney reproach, and then their soft footsteps sounded over the leaves.

John ran faster, quite forgetting that his companions were not as athletically able, even if they hadn't spent the best part of the last few years in a dungeon they still would've struggled to match his giant steps. He drew closer to the man and called out again.

No response.

As he got closer he picked out more of the detail. He saw that the man was bare-backed, that he had thick hair all over his torso. He wore a pair of trousers rolled up to his knees. Now he saw that it wasn't a pike that he carried over his shoulder, but several branches.

John kept on calling to the man but no matter how loud he

yelled he failed to get any response. Finally, he was so close that he could touch the man, and so he reached out to him.

He was expecting, at the very least, a slight flinch or a surprised look, but the man, quite calmly, turned round then looked John up and down, his whole manner expectant, waiting for what it was that John thought so important to interrupt his stroll through the woods for.

John, on the other hand, was taking in the hairiness of the man. He had never seen such a hairy person—other than Susan, of course. Unlike Susan, his hair stopped at his neck, leaving his face bare, just like any other man. "Hey!" John said. "We're looking for someone called Yvonne, can you help?"

The man gave a half-shrug and then made to continue on his way.

"Will you at least answer me?" John said.

The man broke into a whistle and a bounce entered his step.

Sydney and Courtney arrived at John's side, both breathless. Sydney had something useful to say. "That's a Beaverman."

"A Beaverman?" John said, stunned that Sydney had actually trumped his knowledge of the Damned Forests.

"Yeah," Sydney said. "I leant all about them back at the castle. Got some really cracking poetry."

"And I suppose they're not the most social of creatures?"

"What do you mean?"

"I've been trying to get an answer out of him for the past five minutes, but he's just ignoring me. When I mentioned Yvonne he just gave me a blank look and well"—he gestured at the Beaverman, who was continuing on his way along the path, unaffected by any of these people intruding on whatever it was he was doing—"he just keeps on going. How rude is that?"

Sydney sighed. "Beavermen don't speak."

"What're you talking about? You said that they write poetry."

"Who says you have to be able to speak to write poetry?"

Finding himself on the cusp of a discussion about the intricacies of rhythm and verse which, as John held, were vocal properties put to paper, he stopped himself and said, "Do you know how to speak to the Beaverman?"

"Well of course I do! How else could I read their poetry?"

"And could you do it right now?"

Sydney looked off to the Beaverman. "I don't know, he looks a bit busy, you know, wrapped up in his own world." He cast a glance back at John and realised this wasn't one of these 'yes' or 'no' questions, so he took off after the Beaverman and tapped him on the shoulder.

The Beaverman reacted with just about the same level of emotion as he had to John's attempt at an introduction, which was to say not at all.

Enthusiasm undiminished, Sydney proceeded to waggle his arms about, contort his mouth into all sorts of strange shapes and, a couple of times, leap up and down.

John got ready to step in, in case this Beaverman reacted adversely to this bizarre display and then, to his utter and complete shock, the Beaverman took up the same manner in his reply—with more gusto if anything.

So, Sydney and the Beaverman waved their arms and made faces at one another for a long time. Meanwhile Courtney actually stopped talking for the duration of their exchange, apparently just as absorbed by their interaction as John was.

Sydney wrapped up whatever it was that he was communicating and then shook the Beaverman by the hand and headed over to where Courtney and John stood. He had a smug grin impressed over his cheeks. "He's invited us back to his house to take tea."

"Did you ask him about Yvonne?" John said.

"Ah," Sydney said, flushing a touch. "No, that kind of slipped my mind, rather. You see, I've never had the opportunity of conversing with a native Beaverman so I got a little carried away. Sort of forgot about that."

"Why not ask him now?" John said, eyeing the Beaverman, who now smiled at them as he waited patiently for them to conclude their own conversation.

Sydney pouted. "Nah, I'll leave it for a bit. I don't want to seem pushy."

"'Pushy?' The whole reason you're here in the Damned Forests is to help me liberate my family, which, at present, involves finding information as to Yvonne's whereabouts."

"Aw, come on, can't I at least see their homes? I studied their language for so long to read their poems, I never actually thought I'd ever have the opportunity to see one of their homes. It won't take too long, I promise. We'll take the tea, be polite and then be on our way. Chances are that the Beavermen might well know exactly where to go looking if we put ourselves across as decent folk."

John studied Sydney. He could see from the slight skip in his step and the tone of his voice—a fraction higher than normal— that he was about as excited as a kid on Christmas Day. Who was he not to indulge him this tiny thing?

"Oh, okay," John said. "We'll go to their village but just to have tea, then we have to get a move on, all right?"

Sydney nodded back, his smile looking more and more likely

to split his skull by the second. He then relayed the acceptance of the offer onto the Beaverman and they were off, traipsing through the Forests, all at the Beaverman's leisurely pace.

John supposed he should've thought more carefully when he'd heard that this man they were following was called a 'Beaverman,' because when they reached his village, in a clearing of the forest where a river thrashed onward, he was surprised to see the dams replete with Beavermen, women and children, all pottering about. What he had expected, he really wasn't sure.

Sydney was stuck in a state of opened-mouth excitement. His eyeballs hardly able to control themselves as they rolled about, taking in every detail of the village. John, himself, had to admit that it was impressive too. When he looked back at Courtney, however, he caught him filing at his nails—where had he even got a nail file? Back at Francesca's cottage, John supposed.

The Beaverman, who turned out to be called Rick—or open mouth, sigh, arm flap, tongue to top lip, as Sydney translated— and he led them on along a tight line of earth, over to the dam that seemed to belong to him. To be honest, it was much like all the other dams in the neighbourhood, although John guessed it was all relative—where Witney Branches might've looked like any other tree to the Beavermen, these dams looked like any other to him and, if he'd bothered to look, to Courtney as well.

They had to stoop to get in through the entrance. John especially so. In fact he could only get himself under the hearth by getting down on his hands and knees. He wondered why, considering Rick was the same height as an average man, they didn't think to construct their dams any larger.

Rick and Sydney chatted along silently, the rustle of their clothing and the occasional slap of a tongue the only sounds in the dam. It appeared that Sydney was quite content with the state of things.

When there seemed to be a natural pause in conversation, John spoke in a hushed tone to Sydney, while Rick tended to a teapot at the stove. "Have you asked him about Yvonne yet?"

Sydney held up his hands. "All right, all right, I'm going to, don't worry. Don't bite my ear off or anything."

Courtney sniffed. "Smells of faeces in here."

"Thanks for that contribution," John said, making no remark on it himself because it pained him slightly that, for once, he agreed with Courtney's assessment.

When the tea was poured, they all sat about, John and Courtney peering into their cups, while Rick and Sydney continued their mute, but animated, discussion. John studied Sydney's gestures, his motions and watched Rick's stunned reaction—the first reaction he had noticed from Rick—as he clearly reeled through their story thus far, hopefully getting round to where they needed to be headed right now.

Rick took a sip of tea and then placed the cup down, thoroughly absorbed by whatever it was that Sydney was communicating at that moment. He shot a glance at Courtney and then at John.

"Well?" John said, to Sydney.

There was now no trace of Sydney's smile. "He says he can take us there."

John's chest warmed. "That's great."

"He says it might be dangerous that Yvonne, well, she can be . . . unpredictable."

John looked over Courtney who, as far as he could tell, had let this entire conversation breeze over him, then he took in Rick's facial expression—he looked a little uneasy. He wondered what exactly was meant by 'unpredictable.' Was that just a euphemism for 'dangerous?'

BACK TO SQUARE ONE

HORACE SHUFFLED ALONG the forest floor, shovelling leaves with the toe of his boot. They really had nowhere to turn now. He had brought them all the way out here, knowing that he might be able to bring white magic to bear on the King's men and he had failed—been turned away by the self-proclaimed best practitioner in the Forests.

"Where to now, eh?" Zend said.

"Don't know."

Zend stayed quiet a beat, then said, "How about we go searching for the kids for a while, you know, have a crack at my quest for a bit?"

"Your kids aren't in the Forests."

"What?"

"I don't think your kids are in the Forests."

Zend tilted his head back and gazed upward, at the canopy above them. "Why're all you forest dwellers so sure that you don't have our kids?" He sighed. "Anyway, even if you're right, it might be a good distraction. Sometimes the most obvious solutions happen when you're concentrating on something else entirely."

"What would you know about concentrating?"

"Eh?" Zend said.

Horace flashed his eyebrow at him. "You know what I mean."

Zend stepped into Horace's path and prodded him in the chest. "Not quite sure I do. Why don't you explain it to me?"

Horace looked into Zend's eyes—he wore an expression that said he could break him in two, one-handed. This bickering wouldn't get them anywhere. They had a million different things to think about and not much time. If he couldn't get the white witch on their side then they would have to find another solution. Should they look at a different option? Could they? Would it be sensible to search out black magic?

"What's that?" Zend said, giving Horace another prod.

Horace knocked Zend's pointing finger away. "I've got another idea how to liberate Witney Branches."

"Oh yeah? And does this involve some of your famous *concentration* or is it more aimless wandering, hoping to bump into something useful?"

That comment burnt Horace a little because he knew it was true. He thought about how he had just 'happened' upon the white witch, but, on the other hand, from what he understood from his childhood at Witney Branches, he knew that black magic was everywhere, much easier to locate than white. And it would just take one black magic witch or wizard to sort everything out.

Not wanting to indulge Zend, to let him know that he'd been

right about something, Horace stomped onward, scuffing his feet against the ground below. As he continued on his way he felt his foot come into contact with something hard.

Below him, on the ground, someone said, "Ow!"

Horace's heart fluttered in his chest. "Sorry!" he said. "I didn't see you there. What're you doing down there?"

A head popped up from within a pile of leaves—an elderly man. "Why don't you watch where you're going? Can't a man dig himself a hole and take a nap anymore? Why, I should cast a hex so bad that you'll pray that they'll make you a Grotesque again."

Zend brought his stick down on the man's head with a *thwack*.

The man swore several times over.

Zend was just readying his stick for a second blow when it stopped in mid-air, seemingly stopped by invisible hands. Zend struggled against the invisible hands for a long time before realising that it was futile and dropped the stick.

The old man scowled up at them both. "Just go away, okay? You're lucky I'm in a good mood or you two would've been so hexed by now."

Horace remained in awe of what he had just observed the man do. "Was that . . . I mean are you? . . . You know, a wizard?"

The man rolled his eyes. "If you want to split hairs."

"A . . . a black magic wizard?"

"That would seem to follow, wouldn't it?"

Horace bucked himself up, told himself that he had no reason to be afraid, that if this wizard had wanted to hex them he would've done it by now. He doubted whether this wizard really had that much strength left in him—that defence against

Zend had probably knackered him—but he probably would know other witches and wizards who *were* strong.

Once Horace got himself involved with black magic that would be the end, there would be no backing out, he would have to commit himself one hundred per cent. He really had nowhere else to go because, as bad as black magic was, it would be worse to return to Witney Branches empty-handed. He steeled himself and then said, "I suppose you've heard about the King's men in the Forests?"

"Who hasn't? Make an awful bloody racket, don't they?" He looked them over. "Say, you're not with them, are you? Because if you are I'll turn you both to stone right here and now."

Zend, who seemed much more affected by the display of black magic, since it had been performed on him, gave the man a glare.

"We're not with them," Horace said.

The wizard sneered. "And how do I know you're telling the truth, that there's not a group of King's men, armed with bows and arrows ready to leap out and kill an old wizard?"

"Well, for a start," Horace said, "I'm a Grotesque, and you know that the King would never associate with one of my kind—"

"Not what I heard."

"What do you mean?"

The wizard widened his eyes. "Goodness, I thought I was out of the loop, but looks like—compared to you—I'm a gossiping Mary. Didn't you hear about the Grotesque who won the King's competition, the one to appoint a new Champion?"

"No."

"He escaped the castle."

And then it suddenly struck Horace, out of the blue. "John!"

"John?" the wizard said. "No, the name I heard was Mountain Crusher."

"Where is he now?"

"How am I supposed to know?" the wizard said.

"Is he . . . I mean, has he come back to the Forests to fight the King's men?"

"I *said* I don't know!" the wizard said. "Now will you leave me alone to get on with my afternoon nap, or is your mate going to stamp all over my cerebral cortex too?"

The fact that John was free—it had to be John, didn't it?—lifted Horace. No longer did he feel alone out here, trying to save Witney Branches alone. If only he could track him down, get a message to him, then they could work forward together. But, he knew the impossibility of the task, because even if John were in the Damned Forests he would never find him with just aimless wandering—no way could he strike lucky three times. He had to be proactive, ignore the fact that there might be a possibility that John was out here and work to save Witney Branches *as if* he were going it alone.

Horace crouched down to the wizard's eye level. "Can you take us to meet other black magicians?"

"Why should I do that?"

"Because we want to fight back against the King's men, and we need your help."

The wizard looked them over and then broke out into a grin. "It just so happens that there's a meeting tonight on just the subject." His grin faltered slightly. "And if you are with the King's men then you'll be in for it with all that black magic in the air—

we'll have the real answer out of you, find out who you really are."

Zend exchanged glances with Horace, looking thoroughly alarmed.

Horace nodded to the wizard. "Okay. Take us there with you, please."

Horace's expectations for the dark magic meeting were somewhat associated with lots of people dressed in black cloaks, so it was something of a surprise to discover that most of the witches and wizards looked fairly normal—at least there didn't seem to be much evil about them.

He and Zend kept to the shadows, trying to remain inconspicuous, while the wizard—who was called Anthony—stood beside them, fully-excavated from the ground, but with bits of soil still clinging to his clothing.

The setting for the meeting was by a small pool with trees clustered round it. The witches and wizards each had that light shining above their heads—their animas, like the white witch had had, although, Horace noted, they were much darker colours, not much of a surprise seeing as Anthony had set this up as a black magic meeting.

A wizard stepped up onto a collapsed log, which would act as a platform for the purposes of the meeting. He had shoulder-length grey hair and a tweed jacket, and a anima that was almost black. Anthony pointed out that this wizard was known as Maxeth, the leader of the uprising against the King's men.

The muttering ceased and Maxeth spoke, his eyes shimmering over the crowd as if they were prey he was sizing up. "Brothers and sisters, we are gathered here tonight to discuss our plan of action to remove the King's men from the Damned Forests."

Horace could feel excitement creeping up on him. He could imagine the scene, his arriving at Witney Branches at the helm of a group of witches and wizards, sending all of the King's men packing.

Maxeth continued, "And then we shall march on Ethereal and seize the castle! We shall bring about a new sunrise on the land, where magic shall rule over all!"

Horace wasn't so sure about that part and he shot Zend a worried glance—Zend seemed to share his sentiment. Anthony, however, was clapping his hands, stomping his feet and hollering out in encouragement. Perhaps it was just exaggeration: the energy, the crowd, because Horace knew that, in reality, magic couldn't conquer an army as large as that of the King. Could it?

Maxeth punched his fist into the air. "All that we lack is the location of the camp of the King's men, then we shall march on them and drive them from the Forests."

This was the point where Horace could make himself useful. He waved his hand in the air, attempting to attract the attention of Maxeth.

When Maxeth cast a look over the crowd, saw Horace waving his hand in the air, he squinted and then said, "Yes, you over there?"

"I know where the King's men are."

"You are a Grotesque!"

"Well, yes, but, first and foremost, I don't hold any grudges.

In fact, I think that black magic might well be able to save our home, Witney Branches."

Maxeth glared at him.

"I can lead you there," Horace said, getting a little hot under the collar at all the witches and wizards staring at him, who were no doubt admiring the hex the witch had cast on him—the one that had turned his head into a large eye.

"Can you now?" Maxeth said.

"Yes."

Maxeth interlocked his fingers and continued to stare at Horace. "And what makes you so sure that we won't turn our ire onto the Grotesque, finish off what was started?"

A nervous quiver passed through Horace. "Because we're the same, you and us, why does a witch or wizard create a Grotesque? So that a human might feel the same pain of being an outcast—that which a witch or wizard feels."

At this Maxeth grinned. "Interesting. So you really have learnt your lesson?"

Not wanting to sound disingenuous, but, at the same time, not wanting to sound unconvincing he settled with, "Absolutely, yes. Now I know what the pain is like."

The witches and wizards surrounding Horace all stared at him.

Maxeth looked beyond Horace, to Zend. "And what about him? That one there, your friend. He's not a Grotesque at all, in fact he has the face of a villager of Gotnot, is that correct?"

This time Zend would have to speak up for himself. Along with the rest of the witches and wizards, Horace turned his attention to his companion.

Zend's lips moved but no sound came out.

"Well?" Maxeth said, then broke into a smile. "Perhaps I should turn you into a Grotesque right here and now, so that you might experience a similar enlightenment to your cyclopic friend here."

Horace heard Zend gulp beside him.

Maxeth raised his hands, ready to hurl a hex.

"No!" Zend said, grabbing hold of Horace's arm.

Maxeth let loose a roar of laughter which was echoed throughout the assembled witches and wizards. He lowered his hands and said, "No, I wouldn't do that. It would be too cruel. Even I have limits. I'm not one who's interested in turning humans into Grotesque. When I am King of Ethereal that will be no way to command power and respect—it would make me too like the men I wish to depose." He turned back to addressing the crowd. "Brothers and sisters, we must get rest tonight, for tomorrow we shall rise at first light and follow this Grotesque to where the King's men are located, and we shall drive them out!"

Huge cheers.

A wizard standing near to Horace slapped him on the back. "Good on you, boy! Good on you!"

Maxeth left the stage and the festival atmosphere simmered down to a mild buzz.

Horace looked to Zend. "What should we do now?"

"My vote is that we run."

"He was only joking about turning you into a Grotesque."

"I don't care, I'm worried about this whole thing. It just doesn't feel right. Can't you see that they're going to use you for their own ends before discarding you once they come across the

King's men? They might destroy Witney Branches, burn it to the ground."

Through the crowd of witches and wizards, the animas in various shades along the grey scale, Horace caught Maxeth's eye. They exchanged a long stare throughout which Horace was sure that he felt a connection—some common ground between them. When a witch tapped Maxeth on the shoulder the stare was broken, but Horace was sure of what he'd felt.

He turned back to Zend. "No, I believe that the Grotesque share more with black magic than they do with mankind. If you want to run you can go. I wouldn't blame you. But if you wish to stay and fight we shall accept you all the same."

Zend gave him a sidelong glance. "You're speaking as if you're one of them."

"That's because I am."

LEADERSHIP CRISIS

T REVOR GOT his opportunity late at night. As he had been for the last few days, he was slumped up against the wooden beam, still tied up. He could hear Susan's gentle snores, the occasional word she mumbled in her sleep. He would wake up several times during the night, finding it difficult to sleep in his position—what with his bad back and everything. Outside he could hear the steady snap of boot heels He remained alert.

Sure enough, Lord Eversham appeared in the entrance to the tent, his brow wrinkled up in thought and his eyes dragged down by purple-blue circles. He looked over them then caught Trevor's eye. He managed to summon a smirk. "Can't sleep?"

"No," Trevor said. "I don't suppose you have a spare mattress handy?"

Eversham's smirk widened.

Trevor considered his next move. It was probably best to come right out and say it—speak right to Eversham plainly, to lay out what he knew and to give him the proposal. So he rolled his shoulders, attempting to straighten out a particular ache in the pit of his back, and then said, "I heard you speaking, the other day. To that messenger from the castle."

Eversham's smirk disappeared.

"It must hurt that the King has such little respect for you that he puts your own son—"

Eversham glared. "Shut up!"

Trevor allowed the facts to settle between them. Now that Eversham knew that Trevor knew, the ball was in his court—he knew that Eversham must be consumed all night and day with thoughts for his son, whoever might be doing him harm back at the castle. He had already heard him deride his loyalty to the King, so it would only take a little, tiny shove to send him toppling off the edge, or so Trevor hoped.

"You know," Trevor said. "You should just sneak off from the camp right now. Go to the castle and confront the King over what he's done to your son. A lord, such as yourself, really shouldn't have to put up with such treatment."

Eversham eyeballed Trevor, but said nothing this time. He kept up his stare for several seconds and then blew out a long exhale, turning his attention to his dusty boots. "It's more complicated than it appears."

Trevor had supposed he would've had to suffer through some sort of outpouring of Eversham's reflections on the situation if his plan were to work. He had to stay patient, listen to the story, and keep giving Eversham gentle nudges in the direction of leaving the camp—marching on the castle for his answers.

Eversham continued, "Frum, General of the King's army, has had it in for me forever. We came through the ranks in the army together, always in competition—we both used the sword, you see, and, although he would never admit it out loud, I was much better in that regard. Indeed, even when it came to tactics, leading men, I proved myself superior, too."

"So why's he a general and you're out here in the Forests?"

"Because he has one thing that I don't."

"What's that?"

"Ruthlessness."

Trevor could already see the line of argument opening up before him, and he was almost certain that he was going to be able to make Eversham see sense, to manipulate him to his own whim.

"Yes," Eversham said, "when we went to study in the academy, in the time of the previous King, Frum would constantly be looking over my shoulder, trying to copy my work, always, *always*, asking me for clarification, getting me to explain the simplest of simple concepts to him over and over again. And I indulged him, because I was so confident in my own ability— that I would be able to beat him on whatever assessment the King deigned to select in choosing leaders for his army." He slipped his sword a few inches from its sheath and gazed at the grey-blue metal. "How wrong I was."

Trevor thought of breaking in with one of his gentle nudges, but it seemed that Eversham was in full raconteureal flow, and it was never polite to stop a gentleman in one of those, as he'd discovered during countless business dinners, trying to close deals.

Eversham continued, "And so we worked our way through the King's army, both of us were knighted within a fortnight of the other, me first, of course," he said, with a sly grin. "Well, just after the new King was crowned, the big opportunity arrived when we were putting down a sizeable rebel revolution on the Big River. The General, General Bloom, was struck dead by a stray arrow to the heart. And as I rested there, with General Bloom's head in my lap, blood splattering his lips, through all the horror of his death I consoled myself with the fact that, surely, I would be lined up to take his place when the decision arrived.

"We strapped the General's body to a pony near the back of our procession and I rode alongside him, keeping my head bowed in respect, but, all the time, with a vague smile on my lips knowing that my time was drawing near. Meanwhile, Frum led the procession along the mountainous passes, along stomach-lurching drops. On the third day in the mountains a blizzard set in and we were forced into making camp. I just about kept sight of the rest of the men, up ahead, and decided, against Frum's plans, to make my own camp away from the others in a nearby cave, just about large enough for myself, my horse and the pony carrying General Bloom's body where I got a fire going and went about making myself cosy. I informed Frum of my position and instructed him to wake me at first light. I can't believe I was so stupid, had underestimated him so greatly, because, of course, when morning arrived I left my cave only to find that the camp had broken up and Frum had moved the men on.

"Despite this setback, I was sure that I could catch them up that day. I rode hard, as hard as the pony carrying Bloom's body would allow me, but my efforts came to nothing and night fell again, with no chance of finding the army. As I found out later, Frum had been making a special effort to drive the men on, keeping up a relentless pace in order to leave me, and the fallen General, behind. When I reached the castle I was greeted with surprised glances and was informed that Frum had arrived more than a day before, and that he had declared Blood dead in the battle and myself lost in the midst of a blizzard, perhaps having wandered off a high ledge and having tumbled down into a ravine. In my absence, the King had acted quickly to appoint Frum as Bloom's successor. When I came across the King, asked for an audience and a chance to explain what had happened, he was sympathetic and quick to declare my virtues, but it was obvious that he had made his mind up—and now that it was he had no intention of changing it. And so I slunk off, like an obedient pup with its tail coiled between its legs, and took whatever scraps were tossed my way."

Trevor broke the silence which descended following the telling of Eversham's story. "Well, now's your chance to get back at him. You can surely reason with the King, if it truly was Frum who was behind this, and you can inform him that he's had your son thrown into the dungeons."

"I'm sure the King knows," Eversham said, but didn't sound like he was convinced.

"There's only one way to find out," Trevor said. "If you really want to impress the King then you must stand up for what's yours. He respects you and your opinions, perhaps he even has his own suspicions over Frum's methods. The worst that can happen is that he sends you packing, back to the Damned Forests."

Eversham remained still, but Trevor could see that he was making inroads. Perhaps the best thing to do now was just to leave Eversham alone, let him puzzle out the thing for himself. Finally, Eversham crunched his fingers into a fist then shot a look over at him. "You're completely right. I have to stand up for myself against them. It's no good that I just accept whatever they do to me—allow Frum to humiliate me at every opportunity."

"That's the spirit!" Trevor said.

In all the excitement, rather melodramatically, Eversham withdrew his sword and slashed it through the air a couple of times. "More than that, I shall challenge Frum to a duel, he's betrayed me for the last time, this time he shall pay and I will have my true position at the King's side."

Not totally convinced by this show of machismo, or in his encouragement of one individual attempting to kill another, Trevor opted to keep his counsel.

Eversham's eyes were now ablaze with passion, glinting like the blade of his sword in the ever-shifting candlelight. "I will go to the castle, right now. It's what must be done." He stooped forward and examined Trevor. "Thank you. It is with much regret that I cannot let you free, not yet, but I promise that once I am in charge everything will be different—there will be no more of this desecration of the Forests, nor will there be any more of this holding peaceful people in captivity. 'Grotesque,' or whatever despicable name we give them, it's not right that this should go on."

A little annoyed that this wasn't going to lead to his immediate release, but pleased all the same to have an iron in the fire, Trevor said, "I wish you all the luck in the world."

"Thank you," Eversham said, then, with a final, vengeful look round, he slipped from the tent and his boots pounded on the ground outside, speeding away from the camp.

Trevor remained where he was, still tied to the beam, when he heard Susan stirring behind him. He told her about what had just happened with Eversham. Although he felt quite pleased with himself, Susan remained more cautious.

"And how's that going to help us exactly?"

"Well," Trevor said, "I suppose it's going to throw the management round here into a bit of disarray."

"But even if Eversham does manage to get what he wants—get himself promoted to General of the King's army—what makes you certain he's going to do what he promised? After all the order to desecrate the Forests comes right from the King. What makes you think it wouldn't be much easier for him to just put someone else down here to watch over the Grotesque?"

Trevor had to admit that these were all very logical concerns. "I . . . well, you should've heard him, he sounded quite convinced about what he was saying. I trust him, I think."

Susan sighed. "All right, I guess it's better than nothing. Now all we have to do is find out how we're going to get ourselves untied."

"Oh, that's fine, he promised that'll all be taken care of when he's General."

Susan paused, obviously taking a moment to structure her thoughts so that she might deliver them in the most efficient manner possible, so that there would be zero chance of her being misunderstood. "All right, say that Eversham does go to the castle and challenges Frum to a duel. But what happens supposing that Eversham loses?"

"Don't be so negative," Trevor said. "I've got every faith in him. I'm sure that he'll win."

"Great," Susan said.

"Anyway, I stand by what I said before, the main thing is that Eversham's no longer round the camp, the King's men won't know what to do."

"Or, because they've got no supervisor, they might start chopping off heads."

Trevor's stomach clenched. "Oh, I'm sure they wouldn't do something as rash as that."

There was a series of hurried footsteps outside the tent. Trevor thought that it might be Eversham, that he might've reconsidered his quest—not that Trevor would've felt too badly about it, considering what Susan had just reasoned with him. However, when the footsteps sounded loud outside their tent and the soldier poked his head through the flap, Trevor saw conclusively that it wasn't Eversham.

"Have you seen the boss?" the man said, and Trevor recognised the voice as belonging to the man from the castle who had informed Eversham of his son's imprisonment.

"He just left," Susan said.

"Oh, right," the man said, his eyes flickering about their sockets. "Uh, did he say where he was going exactly?"

"No," Trevor said, before Susan could get herself tangled up in this.

The man stood there umming and ahing.

"Is there something we can help with?" Susan said.

"It's just some news."

"What news?" Susan said.

"I should really tell Lord Eversham first."

"Like we said, he's not here," Susan said.

Trevor caught his eye. "Go on, spit it out."

The man still seemed reluctant but almost despite himself

his lips started moving and once they'd started there looked to be no stopping them. "The King's dead."

"'Dead?'" Susan and Trevor said at the same time.

"Yes," the man said.

Although, as a tourist in Ethereal, Trevor had no real conception of what the King did, other than cut down forests and try to extinguish 'magic,' this seemed to him to be a catastrophic turn of events all the same.

Susan immediately brightened. "Does that mean the army's going to withdraw, that he's going to pull out from the Damned Forests?"

"No, definitely not. In fact the King's dying words were that we should do everything in our power to continue our good work here."

Trevor, who had just about caught up with the implications, said, "Who's the new King?"

"*Queen* Alexis," the man said. "A *woman*." The way he said the word made it seem like poison, that if he allowed it to linger too long on his tongue it would kill him.

"How modern," Susan said, dryly.

The man leant back on his heels. "So Lord Eversham isn't coming back?"

"Not tonight, no," Trevor said.

"Well, I guess I'd better try to catch up with him then."

"You'd better," Susan said.

The man hesitated another moment or so and then turned on his heel and rushed out, the *pitter-patter* of his boots sounding on the forest floor.

"Any luck with your bindings?" Susan said.

Trevor shook his head. "Nope."

"Then it looks like we're stuck here till events catch up with us."

Always having been one unafraid to sit back and wait for Fate to deal him a hand, Trevor was satisfied. He allowed himself to relax, closed his eyes and attempted to get a wink of sleep.

DUELLING

A LEXIS WAS WOKEN EARLY in the morning by the
sounds of shrieking at the drawbridge. She was used to
these occasional outbursts of glee at this time, usually one of the
men got loose from the barracks after a heavy night on the
mead, then somehow locked himself out of the castle. Normally
she turned onto her side and went off back to sleep, knowing
that the man's head would appear on one of the pikes in the
courtyard by morning—never a pleasant sight to wake up to. In
her mind she often compared this act of barbarity to a cat
bringing home a mouse to impress its master. Whenever they
put the heads on the pikes she did her best to force a smile and
nod gratefully, but, almost always, she found herself having to
rush for the toilet to be sick quite soon after. This man was
unusually persistent. There was no whistle of an arrow followed
by sudden silence. He kept on battering at the wooden
drawbridge.

Knowing that she wouldn't be able to sleep with this racket, she got up and crossed her room where she peeked through the curtains, down into the courtyard then out to the drawbridge. She saw several members of the garrison speaking through the wood to the person on the other side. Some sort of emergency, she was sure.

As she might be called into action at any moment, she dressed quickly, berating the absence of hot water at this time of the morning—she was beginning to become somewhat disillusioned by the role of Queen of Ethereal, since it really had nothing on the 'luxury' of a three-star hotel.

When she checked out the window once more she saw that the men from the garrison were cranking the drawbridge open, welcoming in whoever it was on the other side. She watched on as the man, still dressed in armour, stepped over and into the castle. The way that he bobbed about, hand clutching the hilt of his sword, she saw that he was pretty riled. She could make out his shouts. He was shouting, "Frum! Frum! I've come for Frum!"

Several different scenarios flashed through Alexis's head. She amused herself with each. Perhaps this man was a long-lost son of Frum or, maybe, he was a wronged husband of one of the many wives Frum had surely violated in the course of his crusades, it could be that Frum had simply cheated at some gambling game a few nights before and the man had taken this long to work out what had happened.

The garrison kept the man under control, stopped him gallivanting off into the castle in his hopped up state. That was one thing which a three-star hotel didn't offer—a private army. Over her shoulder she heard footsteps clapping their way up the corridor and then a knock, followed by the *creak* of her bedroom door.

"Your Majesty?"

Alexis turned to see Jenson there. During her time as Queen their relationship had thawed somewhat, she supposed that King Fredrick's words on his deathbed had done the trick.

"Oh," he said, "you're awake."

"That ruckus outside woke me."

"Yes, Your Highness, about that. It seems that Lord Eversham has taken it upon himself to leave his men out in the Damned Forests and return to the castle. What shall you have done with him?"

Lord Eversham, that was Arnold's father, she recalled. "What do you mean?"

Jenson's cheeks gleamed. He'd obviously applied make up. She wondered whether Jenson ever slept or if he just propped himself up, waiting for orders twenty-four hours a day. He dabbed at the corner of his mouth with his little finger, as if he might've left some morsel there. "He has disobeyed orders, ma'am, he must be punished."

"Why?"

"Well, far be it from me to lecture on the principles of an army, that's really General Frum's field, but as I understand it soldiers must be kept in line, prevented from simply wandering off, otherwise there would be serious consequences for its cohesion."

Alexis supposed him to be correct, like always. "And what's the usual protocol with a case such as this?"

Jenson's mouth shrank to resemble a corked bottle. "A leader just leaving his men? Why, ma'am, I should suppose that it should be matched with the harshest penalty available."

"And what's that?" Alexis said, already feeling that she knew the answer.

"Death."

She looked back out the window, where the garrison kept Eversham prisoner, circling him with their spears, all pointing at his throat. She wanted to know more about Eversham, why he had chosen to disobey orders. Had news reached him about his son? If that was the case then it was surely resolved now. Before she got the chance to make the request to Jenson, she heard approaching boots, hurtling toward her room. She turned to see Arnold rush into the bedroom, cheeks flushed and hair sticking up all over. He wore his armour and held his hand at the hilt of his sword—she saw also that he had a dagger strapped to his thigh.

"My dad!" he said. "They've got my dad!"

Jenson sucked himself up into a fury, his cheeks bulging with hold air. "How dare you run in here without—"

"It's okay, Jenson," Alexis said.

Jenson held his breath and then exhaled all at once, in a frenzy of frustration. He stomped to the corner and said no more.

Arnold's eyes were streaming. "Why're they holding him? They won't let me down into the courtyard. You have to do something. What's he done wrong?"

"Jenson?" Alexis said.

"Yes, ma'am."

"Bring me to see the prisoner, if you would."

Jenson blinked a couple of times. "But, ma'am, really, he's in a terrible state, there's really no accounting for how he might—"

"Just bring me to him, please."

Jenson nodded reluctantly and then trudged out of the bedroom. He returned a minute or so later with a pair of guards. Alexis filed out behind them, with Arnold on her shoulder worked up into a rage.

The guards unsheathed their swords when they reached the courtyard and kept their eyes fixed on Eversham—who was down on his knees, head bowed, as the garrison held their blades only inches from his skin. At the sound of their approach, Eversham glanced up.

"Dad!" Arnold said, but stopped short of lurching forward, obviously wary of the garrison men.

A look of alarm passed over Eversham's eyes. "Son, you're free."

"They let me go," Arnold said, then pointed back at Alexis. "She let me go, when she became Queen and now I'm her personal guard."

A slight smile appeared on Eversham's lips and he turned to look at Alexis. "Your Highness," he said. "I have only just caught up with current events."

She flushed a little, then said, "Stand down," addressing the men of the garrison.

They didn't oblige her right away, but, after a cold look from Jenson, they did.

Eversham stayed in his place, eyes still fixed on Alexis. "The crown fits you well, ma'am."

"Thank you," Alexis said, trying to detect any trace of irony in his words. "Why don't you tell me why you've come here."

Eversham nodded to Arnold. "My boy, they told me in the Forests that my boy had been taken down to the dungeons, but I see now that he's free. Still," he said, his smile fading, "I would like to know what he was doing down there in the first place."

Alexis explained about the escaped prisoners, her former cellmates, and how Arnold had been put down there as an insurance policy, a way to keep her from attempting to escape herself.

Despite this explanation, Eversham remained serious. "Then I owe you everything, My Queen."

"Please, think nothing of it. If you are to return to your duty you may consider this entire episode an anomaly and we shall say nothing more about it."

She felt Jenson stiffen beside her.

Eversham did manage to crack a smile at this. "That's really too kind, Your Majesty, and I really have no place to argue with your judgement—I know that your predecessor would not have hesitated in having my head. I shall not forget." He glanced round at the men of the garrison. "However, I would like to ask you something else, a favour before I return to the Forests. You see, I have unfinished business, if I may speak frankly, I really believe that I should confront the one who put my son down in the dungeons. May I speak with Frum?"

Alexis considered this request. There was a strong chance that any meeting between the men would end in violence, then again, as they were both soldiers in the army wouldn't they have to work together in any case? Wouldn't it be better to have whatever problems they had put on the table and got over with before they went back to more professional terms?

As it happened, Alexis had no need to make any decision on the matter because, in his distinctive, gruff tone she heard

General Frum, standing on a balcony looking out onto the courtyard, address them. Frum's voice sent cold shimmers across Alexis's skin. "You want to speak to me, Eversham? I am here."

Eversham tilted his head back and gazed up at him. He gritted his teeth, like a dog snarling at an intruder and got to his feet. "*You*. What were you thinking to lock my son up like you did?"

"We needed leverage, it was a matter of circumstance and your son just happened to be the most convenient way to achieve that." Frum raised his hand to indicate Arnold, stood at Alexis's shoulder. "Look at the boy, no harm's come to him, has it?"

"I don't know, I haven't had the chance to look."

Frum grasped the railing of the balcony. "So, what're we going to do about this, Eversham? I acted as I thought I needed to, nothing more, nothing less. I'm sure, in my position, you would've done the same."

Eversham's tone of voice lowered to the level of a growl. "I *never* would've put a child in a dungeon, I *never* would've done something so evil."

"'Evil?'" Frum said, with a guffaw. "Come, let's not talk in abstracts. There're situations and results, everything else is just window-dressing."

"You took everything from me and you wanted to take my son too!"

Frum held up his hand. "Please, let's not be melodramatic, remember that the Queen is in audience."

Eversham glanced at Alexis and made a silent apology.

There had been no need to do so, in fact, Alexis was quite

enjoying watching Eversham reprimand Frum, although Frum seemed to take it all so easily in his stride.

"I have a proposal," Eversham said, "with the blessing of Her Majesty, of course. I wish to challenge General Frum to a duel, whoever survives the fight shall be appointed the undisputed General."

Jenson leant into Alexis's ear, giving her a potted history of the relationship between Frum and Eversham—that Eversham was, objectively speaking, superior in every way and that Frum had been appointed as a consequence of circumstance, more than anything else. On that basis, and in the interests of continuity at the castle, it would be favourable to avoid any duel between the two them, since it would be almost certain that Frum would lose. Jenson didn't seem to consider that this might well be in Alexis's interests, to see Frum taken out of the way.

Decision made, Alexis faced up to the expectant Eversham. "Very well," she said. "There shall be a duel between General Frum and Lord Eversham. The winner shall be declared the new General of the army."

Jenson muttered some protest in her ear.

Alexis continued, "The duel shall take place in an hour, in the courtyard, weapons at the discretion of the competitors."

From his balcony, Frum scoffed then said, "Swords, obviously."

Alexis caught Frum's eye, that arrogant swagger, the wink he slyly gave her when he thought no one else was looking. Would she be 'evil' to wish for Eversham to take care of Frum in the duel?

Alexis took her seat up in the Royal Box, overlooking the court-yard. She had a horrible recollection of the competition to find the King's Champion. It sent a shudder down her spine. By endorsing this duel was she any better than King Fredrick? She told herself that the reason she was doing this was because the two men wanted to fight one another, it wasn't purely for her own benefit, was it?

The garrison lined the courtyard, now holding their spears so they pointed up into the air. They had orders not to move in unless ordered by Alexis. For the duration of the duel, Frum would be stripped of his command of the army, and they were to defer to her. If she wanted to, she could stop the duel at any time. At least that was the theory.

Frum already had his sword and was waiting impatiently at one end of the courtyard as Eversham selected his from the various swords which had been brought up from the armoury.

Arnold sat at Alexis's side, his sword lying across his lap. Alexis had been thinking about asking him to put the sword away for the duration of the duel, in case he got the urge to step in, she had settled on leaving him as he was—the poor kid would be wound up enough already, having to watch his father fight to the death.

One of the men from the garrison stood between Frum and Eversham, keeping them apart and explaining something to them—perhaps the rules of the contest. As he did so, both of the men continued to stare at one another. The hate flowing between them was almost palpable. Alexis was left in no doubt that either man would kill the other given the chance, and do so with great relish.

Under the man from the garrison's orders, both men took up

their stances, taking their swords in both hands and facing each other down. The garrison man counted and then stepped away, running to join the rest of the men at the edge of the courtyard.

Alexis's heart rapped in her throat.

The battle was underway. It was Eversham who swung first, the arc of his sword swiping at Frum's stomach. Frum sidestepped the blow and struck a counter volley. Eversham held up his sword to block it, sending the sound of tinkling metal all round the courtyard. As Eversham pushed Frum's blade away he let out a huge groan and thrust forward. Again, Frum dodged the strike.

Alexis wanted to look away but she found herself hooked to the visual. It was nothing like the King's tournament, when she had had no connection to any of the competitors—not that it had made the spectacle any less gruesome. But here she knew that a victory for Eversham would buy her an ally for life, whereas, if Frum conquered him, it would mean she would be stuck with him—because she feared any attempt to replace him would lead to a coup and, ultimately, her death. This would be the only means of getting Frum out of the castle.

As if the fight were catching up with her thoughts, Eversham flew forward and his blade bit at Frum's neck. Blood welled in the wound and sparkled in the direct sunlight. Eversham knocked Frum back. Frum stumbled, his sword dangled from his fingertips. He could only just keep his grip on the handle as he tumbled backward and fell onto his bottom. It was clear in which direction to duel was heading.

Eversham strode closer, raising his sword upward, readying the killing stroke. His eyes were wide and his lips parted. He had obviously been waiting for this moment ever since their rivalry had begun.

Alexis remained transfixed by the spectacle before returning to her senses, realising that she was doing nothing less than sponsoring, overseeing, this killing. If Frum were to die in front of her eyes, his blood would be on her hands. She could preserve his life if she chose to. And before she had thought the whole matter through, she found herself rising out of her seat and calling for them to stop.

Eversham faltered, the sword trembling in his grip, and then he slowly turned his head up to the Royal Box.

"Please," Alexis said, calling down to them. "No more. I think it's obvious who the winner is." She turned her attention to Frum cowering on the ground. "Do you admit defeat?"

Frum's chest rose and fall with his steep breathing. He could barely lift his sword now and the blood was trickling down onto his tunic at a steady rate. Even from her place on the balcony, Alexis could observe the sweat twinkling on his brow. He looked a spent force, and it was all she could do not to react in any way, not to shoot him a little smile.

Eversham lowered his sword and turned his back to Frum. As he ventured toward the garrison man who overlooked the proceedings, Alexis watched Frum struggle to his feet. Frum held one hand to his neck while he lugged his sword along behind him. It should've been obvious to her then, she should've warned him, but, before she knew it, it was too late.

Frum crept up behind Eversham, just as he was handing his sword back to the garrison man, and thrust his sword through his back. With iced blood numbing her veins, Alexis watched the tip of the sword come out the other side, damp with Eversham's blood.

Beside her, Arnold lurched to his feet and cried out.

Everything seemed to happen at once down in the courtyard. The garrison men leapt from their posts, some of them to Eversham's aid, others to force Frum to slip the sword out of his victim, but they were too late—Alexis could see that. Eversham could no longer hold himself up and so the garrison men laid him down on the grass of the courtyard. Blood stained his tunic, a dark patch seeping out of him, growing larger by the second.

Jenson arrived at her side and, between them, they restrained Arnold, kept him from rushing down the stairs, all the way down to the courtyard to have his revenge on Frum—who would surely not shirk from taking Arnold's life too, child or not.

As she looked over the balcony, holding Arnold in her arms, attempting to calm his sprawling limbs, she saw Eversham close his eyes and his shoulders relax with his final breath. The second man she had seen die. She turned her attention to Frum and the garrison men surrounding him, there was only one thing she could do now. "Take him to the dungeon."

She expected Frum to put up some kind of protest, at the very least to turn and shout some obscenity at her, but he remained calm as the garrison men yanked the sword from his grasp and slapped cuffs onto his wrists. Under her glare, they led him off through the courtyard and out of sight. She turned back to Arnold, to comfort him. "I won't have anything to do with a man like that. Nothing at all to do with him."

Arnold just sobbed on, inconsolable. He had lost everyone now.

SECOND TIME'S A CHARM

A S TWILIGHT SET IN on the Forests, John kept himself aware of his feet. Whenever he went out at night in the Forests he always managed to catch a cumbersome foot in some root or branch imbedded in mud. It was getting tricky to see Rick the Beaverman up ahead now, they had no torch with them because Rick had claimed that it would be deleterious to what they'd set out to achieve. Not being much of an expert in the Damned Forests—in fact a little repentant at how much of his life he had spent being afraid of Susan's stories—John was happy to take Rick's word for it. And it became apparent quite soon after that he had made the right choice.

There was a wispy cloud-like shape up ahead, in fact, yes, it was a cloud. A tiny cloud. John wanted to yammer in Rick's ear, ask him what it was all about, but, since the light was failing them and Sydney couldn't communicate a message to him, they had to make do with just following. John was sure that soon all would become clear.

They crept closer, Rick defining their cautious pace. The cloud made no attempt to evade them, but why should it have done? After all, it was a cloud.

John held his breath, worried that he might ruin everything if he made any sudden movements. He noted Sydney doing the same. Courtney, on the other hand, looked so bored that he had simply no interest in what they were doing or attempting to achieve.

The cloud shifted in the air, moving ahead of them. Rick pursued it patiently, the others following in his wake. They proceeded through thick forest branches scratching at their arms and leaves rustling beside their ears. As they continued up the path, the cloud picked up its pace a little, but not to much faster than a steady march.

It led them all the way to a tree where it promptly shot upward, into the branches above their heads. Moonlight now streamed down on them in the clearing. Rick turned to Sydney and made a series of gestures, with Sydney nodding along at each of them. When Rick had concluded his communication, Sydney turned to the others and said, "This is it. This is the place."

John gazed upward, unsure of what they had actually stumbled across. "Yvonne? She lives up there?"

Sydney shrugged. "Yeah, I guess so."

John considered the tree. If he took one of them on his shoulders he was sure that they would be able to reach the lowest branch. Getting himself up, however, might be a struggle. He looked to Courtney then said, "Look sharp," before grabbing him and thrusting him onto his shoulders.

Courtney had no time to issue a comprehensive complaint and a stream of obscenities—mainly Grotesque bashing—accompanied his ascension.

While John kept Courtney on his shoulders he took in the expressions of Sydney and Rick, both of them looked quite glad that John had chosen Courtney first, got him out of their sight for a while—and Rick didn't even speak the common tongue.

John stood on tiptoes, jolting Courtney upward. "Grab it!" he said.

"Grab what?" Courtney said.

"The branch!"

Above him, John felt Courtney sway as he attempted to get hold of the branch. It seemed to take an age before he felt the load on his shoulders steady, obviously having taken hold of the support.

"What do you see?" John said.

"Nothing much," Courtney said.

Rick and Sydney watched on.

"You must be able to see something!" John said.

Courtney twisted his body, trying to haul himself up onto the branch. "You do realise that it's pitch black up here, don't you? What you're asking me to do is physically impossible!"

Maybe he should've shoved Sydney or even Rick up there first—at least then they would've had someone up there with two brain cells to rub together. John rolled his eyes and then released Courtney's ankles. He stepped back to watch Courtney dangling from the branch, several feet off the ground.

"Hey!" Courtney said. "I demand you help me down right now."

"'Demand' doesn't get," John said.

"Whatever, you imbecile, when I'm King I'll have you hanging from the nearest tree in two clicks of my fingers."

Enjoying this now, John summoned a chortle. "I'll bear that in mind."

Courtney now had no choice but to drag himself up onto the branch, the only other option was a drop back down to the forest floor where he would surely break a leg if he failed to bend his knees. For John and the rest it was a win-win situation: Courtney would either find what they were looking for or he would have physical pain inflicted on him.

Unfortunately for their amusement, but fortunately for their quest, Courtney did manage to scramble up onto the branch, and just as he looked about to slip right off and fall, he got a better grip and clambered up, leaving their sight.

A silence settled over them as they listened in on the breaking of twigs and rustle of leaves as Courtney performed his tree-climbing antics. At one point he seemed to find his feet because the sounds of destruction subsided.

They waited in awe until a vine swung down and dangled in the air before their eyes. At first John thought that it was Courtney's attempt to harm them in some way, but, he realised after a second or so, that it was intended as their way up the tree, to follow him.

Sydney tugged on the vine, testing its strength. "Who goes first?"

"Well," John said, "I guess I should. It's the only way I'll ever be able to get up, and if it snaps I can still help you two up there."

Sydney passed the vine over to John, who took hold of it. He noted that it consisted of several vines tied together, quite impressive if Courtney had managed to produce it so quickly. Perhaps he was good for something after all.

Now that John clutched it in his fist it seemed quite flimsy, certainly not substantial enough to hold his weight. He glanced upward at his supposed destination on the branch above. Whatever secret held itself up there he was certain that it was the savour of Witney Branches—Francesca had known his goal and he trusted in her judgement in sending him to Yvonne.

Just as he wrapped the vine round his fist in preparation to scale it, he felt the ground beneath his feet shake. He looked about him for the source. It seemed too late for the King's men to be pulling down trees—they never used the machine after dark. And then he looked up in front of him and saw a cross-looking woman glowering at them. When he observed the light above her head, the anima—which they'd mistaken for a cloud a little earlier—he saw that it was almost blindingly-white.

"What in the gods' name do you want?" the woman said.

John stepped forward. "Are you Yvonne?"

"Depends."

"We've come to solicit your help to save the Forests from destruction."

She rolled her eyes. "Not another one."

"Another what?"

"More of you Grotesque coming about wanting to act the hero, wanting to snatch all the glory while I do all the legwork."

"That's just not true," John said. "All that matters to me is saving my home, Witney Branches."

"'Witney Branches,' 'Witney Branches,' 'Witney Branches,' that's all the other one went on about too."

John scoured his brain. Who would've come out here in search of Yvonne, what other Grotesque?

Just as he was about to ask the question, Yvonne answered it for him. "Old one eye, that was him, he came past here with his Gotnot villager and barged into my house, demanding that I help him to rid the King's men from the Forests."

"And what did you say?"

"'No!'" she said, with full force.

John collected his thoughts. "Francesca told us to come here, to seek you out."

She cocked her head. "Francesca? Really?"

"Yes," John said, glancing to his side, giving Sydney a chance to confirm this information.

From above their heads, Courtney called down. "Hey? What's going on down there? All I've found up here is some grotty little shack. Can I come back down now? Mission accomplished?"

Everyone, including Yvonne—who obviously caught onto things rather quickly—ignored him. Yvonne looked John up and down. "How is Francesca doing?"

John thought about a calm way to break the news, but his own emotions were still raw, and he couldn't help but just blurt it out. "She's dead."

"'Dead?'" she said.

"Yes."

Yvonne stalked closer, squinting. "How did she die?" Her cheeks went puce. "Did you kill here, Grotesque?"

John backed up. "No, I didn't. In fact she was our friend."

"Then how *did* she die?"

John relayed their experience of the Coven, what had happened with the black magicians, who had gone crazy and slaughtered all the white witches and wizards.

Yvonne listened with surprising indifference, and when John had got through the story she shook her head. "That's terrible, awful news."

"So you'll help us?"

Yvonne considered John for a while and then, pressing her lips together tightly, said, "I can't help you, not now. This has been coming for a long, long time. The dark forces have been threatening to rise up. Who would've thought a witch or wizard would dare hex a King of Ethereal? In what other time would that have occurred? No, perhaps if the King had not thought to come into the Damned Forests, to dig the whole place up then maybe that would've bought a few years, but no more than that."

"Won't you at least try?"

"It would be futile. I may be the whitest witch in the Forests but the opposition is much stronger, the darkest wizard, Maxeth, has a much great following and if it is as you have just described, then only a few of my allies remain, and they'll be scattered far and wide now, afraid that Maxeth might be coming for them."

John was now feeling incredibly small, that—probably as he'd always imagined it to be—Witney Branches was a tiny, insignificant nook of the world that would be nothing more than a scratch in this fully-fledged war. But he managed to hold onto his sense of perspective, it was just about all he had left. "There must be some chance for diplomacy. You can't think that the whole situation is utterly hopeless?"

"I'm sorry," she said. "But I speak plainly. There's nothing to be done."

John glanced back at Sydney, who had been translating the entire conversation for Rick's benefit. Both of them looked blank, about as empty as John felt.

Yvonne continued, "When those dark witches and wizards are done with the King's men, torturing each of them in the most painful way possible, then they shall destroy the Damned Forests, because what else have they offered us except a place to hide in hard times? For magic they represent the dimmest period, a period in which mankind's reason almost triumphed over our mysticism. But they failed to land the killing blow, and now they shall pay for it. In the new world order they shall be the slaves and magic shall be the master."

Again, Courtney announced his protest from above. "I'm not missing anything important down there, am I? I heard something about a revolution. I have to say I'd be interested if it brings back my throne—puts the rightful King of Ethereal back where he belongs."

John whirled his finger at his temple.

Yvonne seemed to have already clocked that she was dealing with a deluded individual without John's visual clues. She returned to her sombre expression. "My advice to you all is to make yourselves scarce, find somewhere you can hide away and stay there. *Capish?*"

John thought this over. Perhaps she was right, that they would have to find somewhere to hide while this whole black magic phase blew over, but, then again, he would have to track down the other Grotesque first, because he wouldn't go into hiding knowing that he had left them behind to suffer at the hands on the black magic rulers. And then, a thought struck him, a way for them to keep Yvonne with them, a member of their party.

"Won't you come with us, into hiding?" he said.

Yvonne stared at him. "I've always been a lonely woman, always travelling alone."

"So you must be ready for some company?"

"I don't know."

"If only you'll come with us to rescue my family then I promise, right after, that we'll run away, all of us together. If things are as dangerous as you say, you might be able to save our lives. What do you say?"

BLACK MAGIC AT DAWN

ORACE TRAIPSED ALONG at the front of the group of black magic witches and wizards. He was surprised at the mundaneness of their strolling—far from the blood and thunder he had expected the day before. But he supposed that they hadn't yet arrived on the battlefield. Then he would see the true power of black magic. It would be his first conscious brush with black magic since the witch who had cursed him.

He looked to his side where Zend slouched along, his face half-hidden in the shadow of the dawn. Although Zend had made several noises of protest against the proposed scheme he had failed to take any action, and he would be part of their force which would fall upon the King's men.

The sun was just nipping the tops of the trees when they arrived on the familiar path, the one which Horace had strolled along so many times with John on their morning patrols. That brought on some horrible possibilities, that, perhaps, they would arrive at Witney Branches only to find the camp packed away, the King's men nowhere to be seen—and that John had already stormed his way through everything and freed the Grotesque. Then the black magicians would be unpredictable, there would be no telling if Maxeth would see to their destruction just as a matter of course—to save himself the trouble of returning later.

Horace shook away the thought. He was just being paranoid. He had done his very best to save his family, he was sure of that, and all logic pointed to the simple probability that the King's men would still be there, occupying the same stolen ground as before.

Maxeth was never far away from Horace and, he realised, that it must've been because he didn't entirely trust him. In Maxeth's place, Horace knew that he would've felt the same. From where Maxeth was coming from, bringing about unsubtle death and destruction, he would've been suspicious of anyone who might have an ulterior motive—notably a wish to preserve life and save creatures.

Horace led them round a corner and then he spotted the first guard post—a ramshackle construction, several cut off pieces of wood nailed up into a tree. The guard himself was slumbering where he stood, his arm leaning up against the trunk, his nostrils flapping slightly with each of his breaths.

He thought of notifying Maxeth to the guard, but he was far ahead of Horace, already stalking his way along the path, hands down by his sides. When Maxeth reached the base of the trunk, he flapped his hands upward and launched a hex at the unsuspecting guard. A flare of purples and oranges streamed out from his fingertips and caught the guard in one massive, bleed of colour. The guard stirred just in time to see the flare consume his body and melt him down to nothing. Maxeth glanced back over his shoulder and grinned at Horace.

A chill ran round the collar of Horace's tunic and he reconsidered what he had done in leading the black magicians here. But if he called off the raid now they would turn on him—and he couldn't help the Grotesque if he were dead.

So they carried on, this time with Horace content to hold back. Maxeth and his group of black magicians had spotted the camp now. It would just be a matter of watching on as they brought the camp to its knees.

Zend leant into Horace, his complexion drained of colour and now a kind of light-yellow. "Do you think, if we wanted to, there might be a way to stop them?"

Horace watched on as Maxeth rushed up to the first tent and then, with a waggle of his hands, sent it up in a plume of black smoke. He trotted onto the next and this time made it disappear in a haze of green, all the time with a smile peeling back his lips.

Horace turned back to Zend and shook his head. "No, I don't think so."

―――――――――――

Screams seared the crisp dawn air. The King's men ran back and forth, most of them only wearing their undershirts, some without so much as socks on their feet. Fires broke out all over the place. Black magicians whooped round their targets, throwing hexes and curses as they went, at the petrified men. Some of the braver men grabbed their swords or spears and fought back against the magicians, but they were brought down quickly by a few well-thrown spells. Whenever the men attempted to flee the campsite, to rush out through the trees and escape the Forests, the branches would snag hold of them and fling them back, onto the slaughter pile.

Half an hour later the battle, if it could be called that, was over. Scorch marks bruised the previously-green grass. Remnants of the tents: poles reduced to mere piles of ash and canvases burnt into scraps of threads, were all that marked the presence of the King's men.

Horace now turned to observe Maxeth, who had gathered the witches and wizards together, and was explaining something to them, waggling his hands as he went about it. What was he planning next? Had he been truly serious when he'd outlined his plans for world domination? Surely that was the refuge of tyrants and fiends. But, if Maxeth wasn't a tyrant or fiend, considering the acts he and his people had just committed, then what was he? There was one thing that consumed Horace's mind right now, and that was getting all the Grotesque out of Witney Branches and to take them far away, somewhere they would be safe.

Horace grabbed hold of Zend's shirt sleeve and dragged him off in the direction of Witney Branches, ensuring that at no second he took his eyes off the Coven, so patiently awaiting their master's next orders. They skipped over the exposed roots and dodged the bleached bones and cast off limbs. Several times Horace felt bile snap at the back of his throat, but he forced it down, knowing that there was a cause much greater than himself, than he or Zend, that needed to be attended to. He had brought this horror down on these men, and it would weigh down his conscience forever, but it would all have been for nothing if he couldn't accomplish his goal now.

When he reached the door of Witney Branches, he balled his fists and thumped away.

No one arrived at the door.

He glanced upward and saw, out of one of the windows in the upper branches, a collection of faces there. He picked through the individuals, trying to locate Susan, but she wasn't there. He tried the door again and then, when he had almost lost his nerve, he tried to door handle and found that it wasn't locked. He pulled Zend in after him.

His brain slopped against the sides of his skull as he navigated the winding corridors, shouting out all the time for the Grotesque to prepare to leave. He had no wonder that they'd stayed where they were, had no thought of escape, having witnessed the massacre which had taken place right on their doorstep. Every second was precious because Maxeth could turn his ire onto Witney Branches at any time.

He collected them together, watched on as they streamed past him, down the stairs, doing a mental headcount. The very last of them, the ones at the end of the queue, were Rabbit King and Plont. Through his panic and the blood rushing to his head, Horace recalled how he had felt about them when they'd first entered Witney Branches, that he had resented their coming here, trying to be the heroes, but now that he was seeing them again, he could hardly believe the relief which overwhelmed him, and he realised that he had truly thought that he would never see them again. He gave each of them a smile and a pat on the back as they passed by. Zend and Plont embraced briefly before skedaddling out after the others.

Horace conducted a top-to-bottom search of Witney Branches, in an attempt to locate Susan, or that other 'rescuer'—

Trevor had been his name, he seemed to recall. But his search came to nothing and he could hear the sound of voices, outside, getting louder and, reluctantly, was forced to call it off.

With a heavy heart he sprinted for the front door of Witney Branches, only to come nose-to-nose with Maxeth.

"And where exactly do you think you're going?" Maxeth said, his voice like a bumpy road.

"I . . . I, please. Just let us go. We're nothing to you. It wouldn't be a fair fight, you know that."

Maxeth arched an eyebrow. "Who said anything about a fair fight?"

Horace looked beyond him. All he could see were those hundreds of pairs of beady eyes, the bare outlines of their animas at their shoulders, all sable-black. There was no sign of the Grotesque, and he hoped they had all managed to reach safety before Maxeth had noticed the evacuation.

"Tell me," Maxeth said. "Now you've led us here, had us destroy the King's men, why should we let you live?"

Horace's vision blurred. He knew he was staring death in the face. If he wished to cling to his life he would have to think quickly and act bravely. But, try as he might, he just couldn't come up with a reason—not a single one.

"Well?" Maxeth said, his breath wandering up into Horace's nostrils, the rusty stench of blood thick on his tongue.

All Horace could do was shake his head and avert Maxeth's gaze.

"Okay then," Maxeth said, taking a profound breath and then rocking back on his heels.

As Maxeth launched himself forward, Horace observed the crackling colours webbing their way along his hands, the glow they gave off, as they sprang up and ripped through the air. He felt a large, invisible cocoon spiral round him. All sound was lost to its barrier, the same sensation he got when he cupped his hands over his ears. Maxeth's magic bounced off and jetted off upward, into the sky.

Frown lines etched themselves in Maxeth's forehead and he widened his eyes. He cast a glare over his shoulder. Through the strange barrier surrounding him, his voice came to Horace like music through water. "Who's doing this? I know it's one of you. Come on! Own up to it, and we shall have it out right here."

None of the black witches or wizards admitted to the protective spell.

Maxeth turned his glare back to Horace. He bit into his lower lip and scowled at him. "If no one's going to tell me who's behind it then I shall have no choice but to bring this protective shell down, as a common builder brings down a house." He raised his hands into the air and wiggled his fingers again, his face frozen in anger. "You shall rue the day you came to me asking for my help, all the way to hell!"

Horace shut his eyes. He knew that this shield, whoever had cast it, would not last forever, that he would succumb to Maxeth's brute strength eventually. All that rested with him now was making peace with himself and making a noble exit off the face of Ethereal.

Magic crackled all round him. And then he felt it enter. It tickled his spine, sent a fire bolt up his spine where it addled his brain. He opened his eyes at the last moment to see Maxeth with his teeth gritted and magic, in all the colours of the rainbow, spraying from his fingertips. Sweat pooled in his temples and dribbled down the sides of his face, and Horace was in no doubt that he was stuck into a hefty battle indeed. And then a voice, as if carried on the wind, whispered in his ear.

"Walk through them," it said, a female voice—familiar. "I can only hold him off for so long. You must go now."

Horace was so stunned to hear the voice, that someone was actually interested in protecting him, that he had to remind his feet to move under him. When he took a step forward he was certain that Maxeth would knock into him, shove him back into Witney Branches and allow him to burn along with the tree, but, instead, when he moved he felt an infinite power swell within him. He strode up to Maxeth and just rebounded off him, thudding off into the crowd of the gawping, black magic onlookers. The other black magicians parted for him, repelled by the protective shield which covered him. Some of them hurled hexes after and he listened to them *plink* off the shell of the shield. Soon he had got past the group of witches and wizards, and then the voice said, "Run!"

And he did.

STORMING THE CASTLE

RUNNING, QUITE FAST

T REVOR HAD HARDLY BEEN ABLE to keep up with
the relentless flow of new information. Sure, he had
watched the whole scene unfold, the black magic witches and
wizards closing in on the Grotesque with the large, eyeball face:
Horace. When the giant, John, a new member of the group, and
—apparently—a fellow Grotesque, and others had come to
rescue him and Susan a few hours earlier, just before dawn had
broken, he had imagined that they were going to cut free and
escape into the woods. Not so, instead they lingered about in
earshot of the camp. There had been no big alarm over their
escape and Trevor put this down to the lack of leadership—he
was convinced that he must've done something right, for once.

At first it had been difficult to understand his companions'
apprehension at the arrival of the black magic practitioners,
considering all he had heard, they seemed the sort who were set
right against the King's men. However, when he'd been forced to

watch their atrocities taking place before his eyes—the multi-coloured spells pinging through the air and ending their victims in quite horrible, albeit varied, ways—he had come to understand it completely.

He recalled the blood throbbing in his ears as he had watched on as Horace and Zend had sprung the hostages at Witney Branches, and observed each of them run toward their hiding place in the bushes. He had felt a pang of joy as each of them had joined them, and then his concern had turned to Horace, who had stayed behind for some reason.

He had wanted to scream out to him when he had noticed the dark wizard—Maxeth—break up his group and lead them off to investigate Witney Branches. The only reason he hadn't was because he would've given their hiding place away, and then Maxeth would surely have ended all of them.

Just as things were looking particularly grim, when Horace had emerged onto the doorstep to confront Maxeth—he had believed he would be witness to a painful death. And then, the white witch among them—Yvonne—had cast her protective spell over Horace, so that he could walk through the crowd of black magic witches and wizards, sending them tumbling as he went.

Trevor had expected there to be a recess before they headed on again, but, they hitched off into the Forests sharpish before the witches and wizards got their second wind.

And so, here they were now, continuing on their frantic pace, not daring stop to get a lungful of air. Trevor could feel all the muscles in his back knot and his calves seize up, but fear drove him on. He thought that if someone might be able to bottle the sensation it would make an extremely popular exercise enhancer.

He hadn't once had the urge to rest his aching limbs for fear that a hex might cut right through his flabby chest.

It was several hours before the voices on their heels ceased, and someone—probably Yvonne, the witch witch—took the executive decision to take a rest. They arrived into a clearing, with many conveniently placed logs, and they all slumped over to catch their breath.

There were a lot of new faces for Trevor and, to be honest, he was rather losing track of them all. Some were easy enough, the giant John, and the one-eyed Horace, of course he had no problem in identifying his companions Plont and Zend, or, indeed, Rabbit King. However, those others, the ones who had been introduced to him as Prince Something-or-other and Simon —or had it been Snidely?—had been totally lost on him. In the midst of all this he was quite glad that the Rick—a 'Beaverman,' easy to remember since he looked like a beaver combined with a man—slipped off, declaring in translation, through a sequence of flailing arms aimed squarely at Simon, or Snidely—the bald one —that he was going off to warn his village, and attempt to save them. One less face.

There was only one thing that really mattered to him, however, and so he decided to put the question out there for the group's consideration.

"Does anyone know how I might get back to Earth? You know, go back through the End of Time?"

There was a long, uninspiring silence and then Yvonne said, "Only way I know is in the King's castle, in the graveyard on the north side."

Sitting beside Trevor, Zend nudged him in the ribs. "Hey! What about the kids? You know, the simple matter of the previous quest you signed up for? You might've saved me a while back from Rabbit King, but don't think you can get off your hero duties so lightly. We'd look like idiots going back to Gotnot without you."

To be honest, the kids had totally slipped his mind, amid all the flying spells and spat hexes. He straightened himself up. "Well, where do you think they are?"

"I still think they're here somewhere, in the Forests."

Yvonne scoffed. "Silly little man. You're nothing more than a hopped up boy, are you?"

Plont looked up dolefully.

Zend puffed himself up. "How do we know that you're not seeing all this through rose-tinted spectacles? How do you know that those black magic friends of your don't have our kids?"

"I'm sorry," Yvonne said, "would you like to go back and ask them?"

Zend fumed to himself.

"Anyway," Yvonne said. "I keep myself abreast of the latest gossip in the Forests and I can tell you, beyond doubt, that there are no children from Gotnot village here."

Trevor wondered whether Zend might follow up the question, asking how they could trust her, but he supposed that— even to Zend—her putting Horace in an invisible, protective sphere and guiding him back to them was enough to dash that argument.

Zend collected himself and then said, to Yvonne, "If you're so sure that our kids aren't in the Forests then where are they?"

Yvonne pouted. "What makes you interested in my opinion all of a sudden?"

Zend sighed and threw up his hands. "Who's the one acting like a 'hopped up' child now, eh?"

"You certainly have a way with people."

"Just tell us what you know, will you?"

Yvonne stretched her arms and gave a wide yawn, like a cat. She glanced upward, to the sun towering over their heads, coming into its highest position. "Well, there was something I overheard from a pair of the King's men."

"What?" Zend said, eyes sunken in their sockets.

"I heard them discussing a new programme, brought in by General Frum—"

"Who's he?" Zend said.

"Really, you are out in the sticks, aren't you?"

"When we're done with social slights, can we get on with the facts?"

Yvonne did get on with the facts. "Frum is the General of the King's army, of course." She clucked her tongue. "Anyhow, while I was having breakfast, sat up on my branch, quite happy and content, my anima floated up to inform me that I had company. Thinking that this might be even *more* wannabe heroes, I prepared myself to hurl a couple of enchantments, so that they'd rush away in awe. However, when I got a look at them, through the thickly-leaved branches, I saw that they were dressed in blue and white."

"The King's colours," Zend said.

"That's right, Mr Cosmopolitan, 'the King's colours.'"

Trevor observed the biting look Zend shot her.

Yvonne continued, "Anyway, they were strolling along, paying no notice to anything, probably didn't even notice my anima if their observation skills were anything in keeping with the average soldier in the King's army's attributes. So, just as they passed below me they started to talking about a scheme which has been up and running over the past few years and they commented that they'd managed to snatch several children from out-of-the-way villages and take them back to the castle."

"Monsters!" Zend said, flashing his eyes.

"Quite," Yvonne said, eyeing him with indifference. "They claimed that they'd been doing it on General Frum's orders, that he wishes to have a large pool of children in his barracks and to cherry pick the best among them as they grow older—I established all this because they were complaining about how difficult it was to slip them out of their beds without their parents knowing, that they'd both got several bites and scratches from doing so."

Trevor felt the need to butt into the conversation. "And what happens to the ones that fail?"

Yvonne shrugged. "I don't know. Probably just toss them back to their villages. It's not like the villagers are going to argue anyway, not against the King's entire army, especially when some of their own children are counted among its ranks."

Zend snatched up a twig and snapped it. "I'll show them what a 'villager' can do."

"That's the spirit," Yvonne said. "I'm sure they'll have a good time hacking you up into tiny pieces."

"I'm as strong as ten men."

Yvonne snorted a laugh. "Ten men against the garrison, I'd pay good money to see that."

This time Zend didn't take the bait, perhaps getting used to this whole teasing business, realising that, as with all bullies, it was better not to rise to the challenge.

Zend stared down at his manky boots, probably wishing he had some polish to give them a shine. "Then we must go to the castle."

This turn of events thoroughly suited Trevor. On balance he supposed that, in Ethereal, there was danger all over the place, so he might as well push himself in the right direction, head for the portal leading back to Earth in the graveyard. That way he'd be putting himself in risk for something worthwhile.

Prince Something-or-other paraded over. "Did you say something about the castle?"

Zend glanced up at him. "They're keeping the children from our village there."

The prince scowled a touch, an expression that, Trevor guessed, was meant to convey a degree of sympathy—if that were the case then he had half a mind to suggest he practise it a little more. The prince struck a pose, holding a hand on his hip, while he gazed off into the middle distance. "I am the true King of Ethereal, and I must venture forth to reclaim my throne from the imposter who uses my title. Will you accompany me on this quest?"

Trevor realised that he was in the know here—he'd sat here quietly long enough, listening to the wrong assumptions flying all over. "You do realise that the King is dead, don't you?"

"Do I . . . what?" the prince said.

"The King's dead."

"Really? You're quite sure?"

Trevor looked about him, realising that Susan was the only one who could confirm his story, and she was off with some of the other Grotesque, doing God knew what. "Well, one of the

King's men told me and Susan, while we were tied up in the tent."

The prince's gurn transformed into a grin. "Then the time is right to reclaim what is mine!"

"Actually," Trevor said, already having second thoughts about flagging up obstacles which might stand in this fanatic's path, "the way I understood the news was that a successor has already been named. That there's now a Queen of Ethereal."

"A *Queen?*" the prince said, with a chuckle. "I've never heard anything so ridiculous! Why, there's no one to succeed the King, there should be confusion. No one knows who should be the next. And the King, he's not married, so I don't see how it might pass to a wife of his."

Trevor held up his hands, ready to back out of this conversation. "I'm just relaying what I know. Use the information how you wish."

The prince backed off, muttering to himself. He began to pace round the clearing. Every so often he would raise his head, as if a brilliant idea had struck him, only to bow his head once again, clearly striking upon some insurmountable flaw.

The giant, John, with Horace at his side, stepped onto the scene. He looked over Yvonne, Zend, Plont and Trevor then said, "Me and my fellow Grotesque owe you everything for what you've done in helping us. Please, let us know if there's anything we can do to repay you."

Zend exchanged glances with Plont. "Well, we're planning on storming the King's—"

"Queen's," Yvonne said, correcting him with a sliver of a smile.

Zend continued, "We're planning on storming the *Queen's*

castle. You see, they've taken our children, and they want to turn them against us, make them into zombies to the crown."

John shook his head. "How terrible."

"Will you join us?"

Before John could respond, Horace cleared his throat and stepped forward. "There is one factor that you should probably take into consideration."

"Yes?" Zend said. "My ears are open for any kind of intelligence."

"Well, last night, don't you remember the witches and wizards are headed for the castle? Maxeth said that he wanted to become the first wizard king, and to allow magic to roam free in Ethereal once more."

Zend scrunched up his eyes. "Oh, come on, he wasn't serious about that, was he?"

"It might be best to err on the side of caution."

"Nah!" Zend said, batting his hand. "That's not what being a hero's about. We live for danger, we embrace it, it's what defines us. We're not afraid of a few magicians, not with Yvonne on our side."

Yvonne stirred. "What was that? I thought we had a deal, that after all this was over we'd all run off to some nice placid mountains to live happily ever after."

"That was before we found out that it was the King who'd taken our kids."

Horace sighed. "And that was before old John here"—he clapped John on his thick shoulder—"committed us to helping out with whatever Zend desires."

"Come on," Zend said. "We could really do with some white magic, with all that black magic bobbing about. You showed us all, back there, that you're a thousand times stronger than them."

Yvonne shook her head. "The only reason they couldn't fight me was because they couldn't see me. If they'd found out where I was rolling out those spells, then they could've ended me swiftly."

John flexed his muscles. "So what? We'll make sure we keep you hidden. There's enough of us."

Yvonne sighed. "I knew this was going to happen. This is what happens when you say 'yes' to one request, then, all of a sudden, everyone wants a white witch."

"Isn't this what you live for?" Zend said. "I mean, surely the whole point of you being part of Ethereal is so that you battle back against black magic."

"Well," Yvonne said, "it is and it isn't."

"But you'll come with us?" Zend said.

Yvonne surveyed them all, a thoroughly dour expression consuming her entire face. She jabbed her tongue into her cheek, sucked up some air and then spluttered it out. "Looks that way, doesn't it? This is just where having friends gets you."

"And where's that?" Trevor said, feeling a little left out of the conversation thus far, though glad that, everything considered, he would be back on the right track—heading toward the End of Time and, eventually, back to Earth.

Yvonne met Trevor's glance. "Having friends gets you killed, that's what."

AT LAST A WELL-MANNERED AND QUIET CASTLE

ALEXIS SURVEYED the courtyard from her window and considered that she had done a rather marvellous job with the castle so far. She had upped all the maintenance, had them add more plants round the place, she'd had all the walls washed to get rid of years and years of caked on dust and, finally, she'd upped the budget for the army, giving all the garrison fresh new uniforms to ensure that they'd stay onside despite the deposition of their previous leader.

So it was most unwelcome when, despite the warm summer's day, birds twittering in the trees and horses neighing in the stables, Jenson hurried into her bedroom, without knocking, and informed her that the entire platoon deployed in the Damned Forests had been 'misplaced.'

She looked him up and down. "What do you mean 'misplaced?'"

"Your Majesty, it's just that there's no sign of them. They've gone up in smoke for all I know."

"And what's being done to locate them?"

Jenson fiddled with the cuff of his long-sleeved tunic. "Nothing, ma'am, you see the men are afraid of venturing into the Forests—there's talk of magic afoot."

Alexis would've burst out laughing if it weren't for the terrified look spread out on Jenson's face. Although she had witnessed the King's illness she had never once, for a second, thought that it truly was witchcraft. Not really. Magic just didn't exist. But, she supposed, she had to play to her subjects' ingrained beliefs and superstitions.

"Well," she said, "I suppose we can give the trees a rest for a bit, they'll still be there once the men turn up, I'm sure."

Jenson continued to fidget away. "The men of the garrison, they're . . . they're a little restless, ma'am."

"What do you mean?"

"Ever since you had Frum put down in the dungeons there's been talk among them, that they need a new leader, and soon."

"Aren't they content to follow their queen for the time being?"

Jenson's eyes slunk off to a silver-backed hairbrush lying on Alexis's dressing table. "I'm sure they are, ma'am." His eyes found hers once again. "There are several matters needing your attention."

"All right."

Jenson continued, "There's the small matter of the academy."

"The academy? What's that?"

"It's a project put in place by General Frum to bring children through into your army."

"'Children?'"

"Yes, ma'am. They're taken away from their families and put into the training programme. Frum believed it would lead to much improved soldiers, better loyalty all round."

This was her chance to take action, to end all of these disgusting practices once and for all. She wondered how many other revolting secrets would crop up as she raked through the mess General Frum had left behind him. "How horrible," she said. "I'd like to disband the academy at once. Have those children immediately returned to their families."

Jenson lingered, something apparently still on his mind.

"What is it?" Alexis said.

"The thing is that, with the academy, the way we've been recruiting members has been to have a special group of soldiers sneak into villages at night and kidnap them."

And there it was, proof that things could get worse. "It's a wonder that there haven't been more rebels cropping up about the Kingdom when I hear things like this."

"Actually," Jenson said, "all the polls taken during King Fredrick's reign showed high rates of approval."

Alexis sneered. "And how did they ask the questions? Did they go up to peasants in the street, sword in hand, and ask them how they felt about the King?"

"Well, I was never really that involved in the polling process, but—"

Alexis held up her hand. "Look, this has nothing at all to do with disposing of the academy, does it?"

"No, ma'am, I suppose not."

"Then, please, if you'd be so kind as to follow my orders and disband the academy, to return the children to their mothers and fathers."

Jenson opened his mouth to protest again.

"No more excuses. I'm sure the men under *General* Frum's orders took great pains in his scheme to snatch the children from the villages and so I believe that they are quite capable of displaying a similar amount of guile when it comes to returning them. Or should I go down to the barracks myself to explain that to them?"

Jenson flinched at this suggestion. "No, ma'am, you certainly should not."

Alexis thought about leaving the conversation there, of returning to her—now daily—caking on of make up and squirting on of her lily weed perfume. But there was something in Jenson's tone which grated, some underlying problem that was being glossed over.

"Why shouldn't I go down to my barracks? Isn't it part of my kingdom?"

"Of course it is. But, you see, as I was saying earlier, there have been a few murmurs of discontent—nothing more than that I must add—but, I believe, that for the time being at least, you would be better served in leaving me as your representative when it comes to military matters."

Alexis was so outraged by this claim that she was of a good mind to demand that Jenson showed her down to the barracks right then and there, so that she could have out whatever back chatter there might be among the men of the garrison. However, before she committed herself to such a rash move, she wished to know more about the circumstances.

"What might the men do to me?"

Jenson raised his eyebrows. "'Do to you,' Your Majesty?"

"Yes, if I went down there and addressed them, what might be the worst that could happen?"

Jenson flushed, as if the very suggestion of the idea was unthinkable. "Really, they would do nothing, you are their monarch. You see, the problem, as I see it is that, um, er, how should I put this." He paused, fumbling for words. "It's just that they've never had a queen before, let alone a queen who has arrived on the throne in such . . . acrimonious circumstances, that is to say that the uncertainty of King Fredrick's true heir makes the matter a rather controversial one." He pursed his lips and gazed out the window. "The fact is, Your Highness, that it would be in everyone's best interest that the King's true heir is swiftly located and put into place."

"'Everyone's?'"

"Yes, ma'am."

"And I suppose you include yourself among those?"

Jenson didn't answer the question.

Alexis sighed. "Very well. I suppose that's the deal the King made with us, that together we were to oversee the transition, the passing of the throne."

"I might advise that you should reconsider your decision to take on such a burden for yourself. There are certain individuals who would be willing to take over, so that you shouldn't need to worry about such things."

The change in tone caught Alexis off guard and she almost tripped backward over a loosely-fitted tile. "And who might these 'individuals' be?"

Jenson licked his lips, his tongue flicking out like a serpent's. "The man you've had put down in the dungeons,

Your Highness. He would command the respect of the men of the garrison and any hint of mutiny would be completely obliterated. As concerns the disappearance of the King's men in the Damned Forests, he would take control of that too. You would, of course, retain your title and position in the castle, but—"

Alexis's cheeks warmed. "But, I would be a puppet."

Jenson ventured no further comment.

"Tell me something," she said, watching the flow of her sleek gown cling to her calves as she walked toward him. "Have you been speaking with General Frum, down in the dungeon? Have you been making deals behind my back?"

Jenson shook his head vigorously. "No, ma'am. Absolutely not."

"Then this idea just appeared in your head?" She clasped her hands together and then parted them. "*Poof!*"

"I'm merely thinking out loud."

"You promised the King on his deathbed that you would aid me however you could, so that the throne might pass to its rightful owner."

"And that's just what I intend to do. I *am* keeping my promise to the King and, to me, this seems like the most likely way forward in the matter—if you wish to avoid discontent in the castle, that is."

"My answer to them, all of them, is that they can do whatever they want. They'll need to drag me off my throne if they want rid of me. Should anyone try to take the crown away from me then I'm certain that the people would rise up against the army."

"Very well," Jenson said, stepping out the door. "If you ever have need of my counsel you have only to shout, as you would to a dog."

That last comment sent reverberations round Alexis's skull. She knew that Jenson had no basis to address her in that manner, but there was little she could do. He was one of her few allies in the castle.

Wanting something to take her mind off her own misery, she had her guards call for Arnold. She hoped that talking with him about his father, Lord Eversham, and concentrating on his grief, helping him get over it, would mean she could leave the matters of the Kingdom to one side for a moment.

Arnold arrived soon after. His eyes were watery and he looked much thinner, his armour hung off him and his sword looked more unwieldy than ever. The way he walked, with a slight sway, implied that he was hollow inside, merely an agent being blown about in the castle draught.

Alexis forced on a smile and stepped up to him, allowing him to plant a kiss on the back of her hand. She had the guard close the door to her chamber, something she never did when Jenson was inside her room, so that they might speak in confidence. "How're you getting on?" she said.

Arnold averted her gaze. "I feel like I'm going to die any day now."

"I know you must feel awful, angry inside, I can never begin to comprehend what it must've been like for you, to watch that happen."

"Then don't."

Over their past few meetings, Arnold had become increasingly contemptuous toward her, as if, somehow, it might've been her fault that Frum had literally stabbed Eversham in the back.

To be fair, she rather savoured the frostiness of his tone—it reminded her of her younger brother—and she relished the fact that they had grown closer than was prescribed by formality.

Arnold slumped onto a cushiony bench and brooded, staring at the lines on the palms of his hands. "I can't believe that he's gone. He was everything to me, and now I have no one."

"You have me."

"I don't have a mother or a father."

"Neither do I, at least not in Ethereal."

"What's Earth like?"

"Well," Alexis said, thinking how she might go about summing up the place in a few words, words which an early adolescent, raised on Etherealean educational policies might understand. "It's kind of similar to here, except we've developed quite a lot of science and technology."

"What's 'science?'"

This might prove more difficult that Alexis had anticipated. "It's the pursuit of progress through evidence and reason."

"Similar to alchemy?"

"Um, kind of."

Arnold sighed, obviously not all that interested in Earth. "All I ever wanted was to be a knight, like my father, I still had so much to learn from him."

"But, from what I've seen of you fighting with a sword, you look very good."

"I'm better than anyone else in the castle, that's for sure."

Alexis left this arrogant statement alone, knowing that Arnold needed a bit of TLC at present.

Arnold continued, "But I bet there's someone out there who's better. I train every day but there are some things you can never learn through practising them over and over again—the mental aspects, the mentality of the fight."

"Can't you speak to some of the men from the barracks?"

He shook his head. "No, they don't know what they're talking about. Not really. You see, they're sheep, like my father would always say, they have no concept what fighting really means. Oh, they'll shoot their arrows at a target pointed out to them or the swordsmen will rush toward the incoming enemies, but they don't think about the dance of duelling or the real craft of swordplay. They only learn the basic defences and attacks, and are content with those, knowing that they'll, most likely, never need to know any more than that to prosper on the battlefield."

All that made Alexis wonder what sort of queen she was, if she was merely going through the motions, enforcing what she needed to when she could really do more, be greater than she might originally have thought. And she was taken aback that these thoughts were being brought on by this twelve or thirteen-year-old boy. Then again, she was hardly a fully-grown adult herself at eighteen.

All this talk of fighting, discussing his craft, seemed to raise Arnold's spirits substantially, and he rose up from the bench and practised some techniques before her. Alexis clapped in all the appropriate places and, about fifteen minutes later, the display was curtailed by a tapping at her door.

"Come in, Jenson," she said, with a heavy heart.

However, when she turned to look at who it was standing in her doorway, she realised it wasn't Jenson at all. It was one of the men from the garrison. He had a sheepish look about him, like he was embarrassed to be there.

Alexis felt a touch impatient at him interrupting her talk

with Arnold—it seemed like such a private moment, a fragile, fledgling relationship. "Yes," she said. "What is it?"

The man from the garrison didn't reply, but he stepped into her chambers. Another man of the garrison stepped in behind him, followed by another, and another. Soon there were a dozen or of them, fully-armed with spears jutting up toward the ceiling.

Perplexed by this whole show, she got up and approached them. "What's the meaning of this? Who gave you permission to come into my quarters? I demand that you return to the barracks at once."

The men from the garrison just kept up their vacant expressions, fingers curled round the hilts of their spears.

"*I* gave them permission, Your Highness."

Alexis's heart bobbed in her throat. She looked down the corridor to see the unmistakable outline of Frum, leaning up against the wall, the visor of his helmet drawn down over his eyes, casting most of his face in shadow. She felt Arnold sidle up along side her, sword drawn and breathing rapidly. She reached out and touched his forearm, indicating for him to stand down, which he did so after a delay of several seconds.

"What're you doing out of the dungeon?" Alexis said.

Frum propped his visor back and trod down the corridor, a faint smile lining his lips. "The men decided that your order was incorrect, that I shouldn't be kept down there." He strode along the line of garrison men, inspecting each of them, not holding any reverence for the Queen's quarters. He pivoted on his heel and glared back at her. "Don't you find that just touching?"

"I find it treason," Alexis said, and then decided she needed to take a stand her, otherwise she would look ridiculous. After making sure that Arnold wasn't about the lurch forward and attack Frum, she turned her attention to the guards. "I demand that you take Frum back into custody, right at this moment."

Predictably, the garrison men didn't move from their positions.

Frum broke out in a full on grin. "They won't obey you, Your Highness, you see, they only take orders from those they respect." The heels of his boots clacked as he paced closer to her. "And they sure as hell won't take orders from some dizzy whore who was in the right place at the right time, and doesn't know when she's overstepped her mark."

Alexis steeled herself, forbid herself to stand down from this challenge. She met Frum's stare head on. "The people will never accept you as King of Ethereal, I might only have a cursory claim to the throne, but you have none at all."

"That's why I intend to leave you right where you are," Frum said, striding along the line of garrison men, inspecting their armour, as if this were just a daily army parade. "I'm not a particular ambitious man, unlike you I know my place, and I'm quite content in my role as General of the King's army. I don't have ideas above my station."

Alexis had a strong urge to land a hefty smack right across his face, but she knew that one of the garrison men would grab hold of her before she got the chance, and that might only serve to set off Arnold, who was already foaming at the mouth to get at Frum. And she had no doubt that Frum would not hesitate at any opportunity to have Arnold killed. She knew, realistically, that, for now, there was really nothing she could do—except from step aside gracefully and live to fight another day.

"So, Your Highness, what do you say to my proposal?"

"I really don't think I have any choice in the matter."

"I like to think that I keep my plans watertight."

Arnold's breathing got heavier and Alexis concentrated on consoling him, whispering for him to calm down, that this was just a minor matter, and that there would be another time for him to exact revenge.

Frum noticed the exchange. "What's that, boy? Would you like to take your revenge on me for what I did to your father? That seems a reasonable request, only that I would not lower myself to slaughter a child, for that is something which can never be forgiven, not by any of the gods."

"'Child,'" Arnold said, under his breath, "I'll show him what a 'child' can do."

Alexis snatched hold of the sleeve of his tunic, but he writhed out of her grasp and ran at Frum with his sword outstretched. The garrison men shifted from their positions, quickly forming a circle round Arnold, holding their spears to his throat.

"Drop your sword," Frum said, almost bored.

Arnold clenched the hilt tighter. "Stand and fight me like a man."

"And why would I do that?" Frum said. "Just after I've reclaimed my rightful position within the castle. If you have anything of your father's talent for swordplay then it would be a grave folly, indeed."

"Fight," Arnold said, through clenched teeth.

Frum clapped his hands and the garrison men moved in on Arnold.

"No!" Alexis said. "Leave him alone!"

Frum examined her and then turned his attention back to the garrison men, who were moving in on Arnold, ready to jab their spears into his supple neck. "Spare him for the moment. I suppose that, for all things to go on like normal, the Queen should have her personal guard."

The men of the garrison withdrew their spears.

Arnold fixed Frum in his stare. "We will duel someday, and until then I shall work harder than ever on my skills to beat you."

Frum chuckled. "If I were you I wouldn't bother. I don't doubt you could beat me on a level playing field right now." His features darkened. "But the problem, for you, is going to be in finding your opportunity. Because, if I'm nothing else, I'm an extremely careful man."

Alexis moved up alongside Arnold and put her arm round his shoulder. He resisted her at first, but soon he allowed her to lead him away, over to the other side of the room, to the window which looked out over the courtyard.

Frum smirked. "You can keep all this pomp, Your Majesty, don't worry about anyone taking it away from you. But remember that you're little more than a—how did I hear you phrase it?—that's right, a 'puppet.'"

She glowered at him and the noticed, just beyond the door, the frame of Jenson skulking there. She wondered how long he had been standing and watching the scene, no doubt with that trademark smug grin plastered all over his face. From now on she resolved to trust no one. She was only marginally better off than when she'd been down in the dungeons.

A HARD AND TREACHEROUS ROAD

SPIRITS WERE on their way down following the fabulous escape from Witney Branches and the black magicians. John supposed that was the natural order of the thing, because, as he noted, they were heading out on a hard and treacherous road, to the castle. But he still had every intention of seeing through his promise to Zend, Plont and Trevor, for their aid with their own cause. Aside from that, of course, he still had a chip on his shoulder concerning the castle, them attempting to turn him into a monster. If he could change things there so that there was never again such a savagery as the King's tournament, then he would've made a positive contribution—an achievement which he could be proud of looking back on his life, if he ever actually reached that stage and wasn't shredded into pieces by the garrison.

He looked over his comrades and was inspired that they at least had a chance. If nothing else, he was sure that they could at least be competitive, numbers-wise, with the garrison at the castle. The fact that they would be at a tactical disadvantage, attacking from the point of weakness, or that they would be fighting against well-trained men who would have weapons sharpened into killing form, only seemed minor hurdles at present.

They kept to the lowlands as far as they could, led along by Yvonne who claimed that she knew the territory of Ethereal better than anybody—telling them that their best chance of approaching the castle unnoticed was to go round the back. When they had no choice they headed up into the foothills where Yvonne told them to keep an eye out for dwarves who were notoriously jealous, and humourless, where their riamand mines were concerned—and not without good cause seeing as it was the most valuable mineral in all Ethereal. In fact, from where they stood, they could make out the elaborate marble structures jutting out of the hillside—the dwarves' mansions. John knew that with that level of opulence there would be security to match.

The first fireball landed about six feet off to John's left, and the second singed his eyebrows. When the third was hurled into the air everyone was already running. John reflected on the fact that, being the largest, and being construed as the greatest threat, he would always be picked out as the prime target. After all these heroics were over he would greatly look forward to a well-deserved resting place for him and the rest of the Grotesque.

Pretty soon after, fireballs lit up the entire sky, setting fire to the long, dry grass which surrounded them. The flare from the fires dimmed the sunlight. Their group kept up their march forward, with John grabbing hold of a couple of stragglers and carrying them over his shoulder. When they'd got out of the blazing fields, he examined his passengers. One of them was Yvonne and the other was that earthling, Trevor.

They did a headcount, checked everyone for injuries: light burns, singed eyebrows and general panic, all of which Yvonne patched up in no time, if not without a large amount of grumbling about this being an undignified task for her to involve herself with.

Only when they prepared to move on did they realise that they were surrounded, on all sides, by dwarves mounted on bivcheks—great big, ugly, mammoth-like creatures with bird faces. As their razor-sharp beaks clacked in their general direction, John noted that the bivcheks even towered over him, at least twice his height. He supposed that money could make up for a lot of things and, most importantly, in the dwarves' case, their little man syndrome. Not that he envied their success, of course.

One of the dwarves, dressed in non-descript animal fur and wearing a shiny purple broach which appeared to be made of pure riamand, dismounted his bivchek, using a handily-located rope at the side of its neck. With great athletic ability, he slid down the rope and then plonked himself right before them, bending his knees and hunching his shoulders as he landed.

John took in the dwarf's muscular shoulders and his tight tunic hardly able to contain his ripped chest. That was the thing with rich people—they spent their ample spare time getting themselves into shape, not having anything else to do with it.

The dwarf strutted before them, eyes narrowed and lips pursed. His hair was a chestnut brown, clearly expensively died, and it draped down over his face and shoulders. His beard, too, was well-kempt, with thick volume and a healthy sheen. His scent, a mixture of lavender and honeysuckle, wafted up John's nostrils. Someone was looking to make a good impression.

When the dwarf reached John, he scowled up at him, barely reaching John's knee.

John had the overpowering urge to simply cock back his leg and kick, thinking the image of a dwarf spinning through the air, clearing fields and swearing as he went, would be quite funny. Considering the situation, however, and particularly the beaks of the bivcheks, he restrained himself.

"My name is Herbert Shankle," the dwarf said, in an absurdly reedy, high-pitched voice.

John averted everyone else's gaze, knowing that others would be cracking a smile. He only managed not to by sinking his teeth into his lower lip and thinking about all the cruelness in the world.

Shankle strutted in front of them. "You are all trespassers on our land, you have exactly one minute to state your business and, perhaps, save your necks."

The very suggestion of this diminutive man threatening them would've been quite laughable, if it weren't for the bivcheks. To John's eye the bivcheks looked well-trained and quite dangerous. One of those beaks would make little work of piercing any of their chests, including his.

"Well?" Shankle said.

John looked over the faces of his companions and realised that this burden would fall to him, if for nothing else, because the rest of them seemed to be just about to roll about laughing. It was the combination of Shankle's other-worldly voice and the hysteria brought on by the spectre of death looming only a matter of inches away in the form of the bivchek beaks.

John had always believed that the best opening line of argument was the truth—at least it created the impression of honesty right off the bat. And so that was the angle he decided to go for here. "We truly regret having come upon your land, and we wish to leave as soon as possible."

Shankle scowled at John, as if he was unbelieving that John had had the nerve to be *that* big and to trespass on his land, seemingly just to insult him.

Unabated, John continued, "But we have a noble quest at hand. You see we are marching on the King's castle—"

"King's dead," Shankle said, with a humourless and dour tone.

"Sorry, I meant, the Queen's castle," John said, sensing that he wasn't going to be able to lighten the mood with a joke—even one of Sydney's limericks seemed destined to fall upon deaf ears. "Anyway, we've all got our reasons. Some among us have reason to believe that the King has stolen their children from them, to use in his army."

No response from Shankle whatsoever, a real shame for John, seeing as he had been banking with that statement stirring some kind of empathy within the dwarf's cold soul.

A little put off, John continued, "And then there's our friend, here"—he gestured toward Trevor—"he's come from Earth and he wants to get back there. It turns out that the portal is inside the castle walls, so he'll have to come with us."

Zend piped up. "Yeah, he can go back after he's helped us find our kids!"

"Right," John said, concentrating on Shankle, trying to look for some sign that he was being swung one way or the other on his deliberations over their fate. "And then there's me, well, I suppose I'm looking for a spot of vengeance. They wanted me to become the King's Champion and, well, they wanted me to slaughter a man to prove it. A Narbut."

At this Shankle hocked up a wad of phlegm and spat it out onto the dirt. He looked up, right into John's eye. "I blooming hate Narbuts."

"Oh, I see," John said. "It was the principle, really, nothing else. What I suppose I discovered about myself was that I just don't have the capacity to kill."

"That's a shame," Shankle said, grinning for the first time in their exchange—to reveal that his teeth were inlaid with several gleaming gems of riamand, "because we do."

On balance John thought that the dwarves' prisons were nothing short of spectacular. Granted, he'd only been able to get a quick look at the dungeons back at the castle, when he'd sprung Sydney and Courtney, but he was quite sure that, even if he had taken his time to really absorb the décor, it would have been nothing on this.

For a start their cells were generously expansive. John found that he could not only comfortably walk about in his, but he could also leap up and down, even do star jumps if he'd been so inclined. Second, they each had a fabulous view down the mountainside, where they could see finely-dressed dwarves wandering back and forth, in and out of their homes, all dressed lavishly, most casting a disparaging glance in their direction. And then there were the beds. Never in his life had he ever laid on a bed so comfortable. There was the mattress which was softer than mulched up leaves and then the sheets which felt like the inside of a rabbit's ear—perhaps a little like the inside of Rabbit King's ear, who was a few cells along, if he'd ever permit John to touch him. What John resolved after all this absorption of the luxury the dwarves had to offer was that the dwarves wanted even their prisoners, on death row, to experience their insurmountable hospitality—maybe so that it would be their final memory of Ethereal. A more cynical man might've believed that they wished to get into the gods' good books, with a bunch of recently deceased waxing lyrical about the delightful conditions the dwarves had submitted them to before snuffing them out.

As John suppressed a sigh at the wonder which confronted him in the form of a prison cell, he considered what Shankle had divulged to him on the way here, while they'd been shepherded over the hills with the threat of bivchek beaks to keep their minds on the road ahead. Shankle had informed John that he really had no beefs with the King, or his successor at all. In fact, as it turned out, Shankle was quite the royalist. He listed the various tax breaks the King had granted the dwarves and how, in exchange, they would send His Majesty the finest of their riamand jewellery as a gift each year. Although John had attempted to play the uncertainty card by suggesting that the Queen might be looking to change fiscal policy, that had only brought a frown onto Shankle's face, and John cursed their luck at falling into the hands of one of the few races who actually supported the monarchy.

Needless to say, when Courtney started sprouting off about how he was the true heir to the throne of Ethereal, Shankle got quite agitated, and after Courtney failed to shut up at the third time of asking, Shankle had his bivchek give him a little peck. That had only made things worse, as Courtney had chirped on about how much the bite hurt him, and that, when he was King, he would ensure that the dwarves would lose all their tax breaks and be drafted into the army. Although several of the dwarves had looked to be in favour of putting Courtney down there and then, Shankle had held them off, clearly reasoning that the man was already on death row and so should be granted some sort of reprieve. And they were all in the same situation now, awaiting Shankle's judgement on how they would be put to death for the heinous crime of wandering into the dwarves' domain.

John lay on his bunk, arms folded behind his head, looking out the window at the full moon in the sky. It was so bright up here, in the hills, that it was almost like a slightly dimmer version of the sun. He thought about his regrets in his life, how he'd never really got the opportunity to *really* travel and then, for about the thousandth time since it had happened, what might've been if he had killed that Narbut. Now he would be the King's Champion and, who knew, he might've managed to scout out that witch and brought her to the castle, and thus have saved the King and prevented the destruction of the Forests, which would've stopped the uprising of the black magicians.

Ho-hum, it wasn't worth thinking about it now.

A pair of dwarf guards paced up to the door of John's cell. They peered inside and John peered back. One of them said, "Boss wants to see you upstairs."

John wondered whether this was a request or command, and decided that he better treat it like the latter, if he was to have any hope of getting his friends, or at least some of his friends, out of this mess. If pushed he could always bargain away Courtney.

He eyed the axes the dwarves carried, getting another rush of nostalgia for the process leading up to the King's competition. He remembered Arnold, the boy who had given him the tips, and he wondered what he was up to now. No doubt he had got into the King's army and was being trained by the experts. If they ever managed to return to the castle he might be able to use him to their advantage—enlist Arnold's help to get them inside.

The dwarves led him up the stairs, not really seeming to be all that wary of him. John supposed that they would have no reservations in turning their bivcheks on him if he got out of line—with those kinds of animals about John could see how it might breed confidence.

They trod through several halls of polished marble with large tapestries unfurled on the walls, depicting various battles and, of course, lots of riamand. One of the guards leant into John and said, "Got all these done by Darguks."

"Cost an arm and a leg," added the other.

John had just been about to ask whether they had been done by school children, and he was glad he hadn't, although the subtext was that they could afford to pay anyone to do anything, which should've flagged up John's suspicions for what was about to happen next.

They emerged into a huge room with a blazing open fire place. The roof seemed to go up and up forever. John spied a turret at the very pinnacle, with windows letting in the moon-light. Just looking up at it gave him vertigo so he could only imagine what kind of effect it had on a dwarf. Shankle's familiar lavender and honeysuckle scent pervaded the air. The dwarf himself stood with his back to them, staring into the crackling fire.

The dwarf guards halted at John's shoulders and he took this as his cue to strut up to his host.

Shankle turned round slowly. He still wore the half-scowl, half-grimace from before, clearly appalled by John and his friends' presence not just on his land, but in Ethereal itself. Perhaps he was planning some kind of a portal to send them to another dimension entirely. "Do you know what my one weakness is, giant?" Shankle said.

"My name's John," John said.

Shankle flapped his hands as if it were just a technicality. "My one weakness in this world is gambling."

"'Gambling?'" John said.

"Yes, gambling."

John wondered exactly where this was leading. Had Shankle brought him up here merely to have some kind of heart-to-heart, was he really *that* starved for company in this place teeming with other dwarves?

"It's just the thrill of placing the stake, knowing that I could lose everything. I love that sensation, it sends butterflies fluttering in my stomach and blood rushing to my head. Do you know what I mean?"

John observed Shankle's expression, the lines that had appeared in his cheeks and the glimmer in his eye. This was the first time he had actually seen him enthusiastic about something. Again, John went with honesty. "I've never gambled, so I can't say that I do, no."

Shankle clucked his tongue.

John realised that he might've caused offence by implying that he didn't agree with gambling, so he stumbled to correct his error. "I've got nothing against it, though. Why do you bring it up?"

"You said that you were in the competition to be King's Champion, correct?"

"Yes."

"And that you would've won the competition if you had done as you were asked and killed that *Narbut*."

"That's right."

Shankle called out to one of the guards in their local dialect. Although it was rough sounding, it appeared to John that they'd attempted to smooth out the edges of the consonants, perhaps as a ploy to match up to the expectations brought upon them by their wealth.

The guard hurled his axe through the air and, without blinking, Shankle caught it by the handle. He passed the axe over to John.

Unbelieving that Shankle was actually giving him—a prisoner —an axe, he took it and held it at the hilt, unsure what he was supposed to do now.

"I have my little amusement here," Shankle said. "Something like that competition you described of the King."

Images of the Narbut on his knees flashed into John's mind. The stench of blood and sweat all round. The roar of the crowd. Holding the axe he felt like he was almost back in the arena, and it near enough paralysed him. He gripped the handle tighter, feeling the stretch of muscle over bone. And then his hand was seized by an uncontrollable shaking and he lowered the weapon. He shook his head. "No," John said. "I can't do it."

"But you haven't heard my offer yet."

"I can't fight in another tournament, not for anything—be put in a position where I'd need to take another's life—I'd rather you kill me."

Shankle made a groan of disappointment. "Not even if I were to free your friends in return for you fighting for me?"

The axe felt like a dead weight in John's hand, like it might tug him down to the ground and cause him to topple over. This was his chance, Shankle was giving him a chance, to save his friends and let them go on his way. "Explain the terms to me," John said.

"Quite simple, all that would happen would be you signing a contract to fight on my behalf and then I would let your friends go free." He sneered. "I'd have them accompanied to the borders of our land, of course, just to ensure that they don't sneak off with any of our riamand."

John stared at the axe once more. The guard kept it in good order: there were no notches or nicks in the blade, just as Arnold had taught him—to respect the weapon because it would often be the difference between life and death. Firelight shimmied across the face of the blade and he considered his chances of fighting his way through this place, knocking dwarves out of his path. But someone might get hurt, and if they did he would never forgive himself. In any case he would find himself confronted with those bivcheks. There was only one way out of this mess.

He passed the axe back to Shankle, who looked bitterly disappointed, and then said, "I'll agree to be your champion, but I want to watch my friends go safely across the land. I want to know you will keep your end of the bargain."

Shankle broke out into a grin, revealing two sets of perfectly white and straight teeth—that work must've cost several loads of riamand. "You and me, we're going to make a lot of money together. You have just made the best decision of your life."

John just stood there, staring into the flames, hoping that now at least his friends would have a chance of achieving their quest.

CHANGE OF HEART

HORACE HAD JUST FINISHED enjoying a substantial three-course meal consisting of a hearty meat broth followed by a spit roast, an entire suckling pig, curtailed with a plum tart. As he lay back on his bed, watching the sun dip behind the hills he mused that, if they were to kill him right now, he would die a happy man. He had to admit that he would go to the afterlife gushing all sorts of niceties about the dwarves' hospitality, if only one could overlook the rather draconian trespassing laws.

There was a rattle at the lock of his cell door—although it could hardly be called that, considering it comprised the finest oak and had polished up brass adorning. A dwarf guard strode into the room and declared Horace free.

"Free?" Horace said. "For how long?"

The guard shrugged. "Indefinitely, or until you go walking across our land again."

"Who says?"

"The boss."

Horace hung back, still frightfully suspicious. "Is this some ruse? I bet the moment that I step out of the cell you'll call out 'escapee' and all pile on top of me. It's something like that, isn't it?"

"Listen, Cyclops, if we wanted you dead there would be much easier ways to go about it. Heavens know you lot are all so docile that we'd simply have to say the word and you'd all be marching off in a neat line to the chopping block."

Horace was beginning to believe the dwarf. His argument seemed fairly robust in any case. He lingered back from the door, more with a touch of regret at having to leave his cell than anything else, and then he said, "Are we all getting out, then?"

"Yeah," the dwarf guard said, "all except for your thick-headed friend."

"John?" Horace said, frightened at what they might be doing to him.

"I don't know his name," the guard said, his tone growing impatient. "Hop along now, I've got other stuff to do, you know? And in case you hadn't noticed there's quite a few of you to get out."

Horace was about to say something else but he was prevented by the strong arm of the dwarf hurling him toward the exit. For a little person he really had some fierce strength on him. Horace supposed it came about from generations and generations of mining.

He stumbled into the corridor where he met with most of the others, who had already been freed. Most of them were smiling to themselves, exchanging hurried comments between one another. "They've taken John," Horace said.

The chattering stopped at once.

Susan emerged from within a group of freed Grotesque. "Where?"

"I don't know," Horace said, jerking him thumb back to indicate the guard, who was already working to open the next cell along. "He told me."

Susan brushed past Horace and approached the guard, just as he twisted the key. "What do they want with John?" she said.

The guard looked her up and down then arched an eyebrow. "What are you all, anyway? Is this some kind of circus sideshow?"

"We're Grotesque," Susan said, with a hint of pride.

"I can see that."

"Will you please tell us what's happened to our companion?"

"Boss wants him for his fighting tournament, thinks he's got a winner there."

Susan crossed her arms over her chest. "Why, John wouldn't hurt a fly."

The dwarf wiggled his nose and then yanked the occupant of the cell out into the corridor. "Doesn't much matter what he does or doesn't want to do. Fact is that once he's in there in fighting, it'll be either him or the other guy. I'm sure he'll learn what he has to do to stay alive."

Horace scanned the guard with his eye. "Has he . . . has he made some sort of a deal with Shankle?"

"That's none of your business."

"That's why we're going free, isn't it? He's offered himself for this dreadful fighting competition in exchange for our freedom."

"Actually," the dwarf said, "it was the boss that did the offering. Your man doesn't look like he's all that blessed in the bargaining department, those big ones never are."

Horace detected the tone of resentment in the dwarf's voice, like all the others which inhabited this hillside he supposed they didn't much like tall people—probably why they kept such fearsome animals, those bivcheks, around. "What's going to happen next?"

"I'm under orders to escort you to the edge of our territory, and then I'm letting you go. And I suggest in the strongest possible terms that you just keep on walking, without so much as looking back, because next time there won't be any stay of execution, we'll just turn the bivcheks right onto you out there in the fields."

"Thank you," Horace said, worried that his spectacular dinner might make a messy reappearance. "I think I get the idea. We won't bother you any longer."

"And definitely don't be thinking of coming back here to rescue your friend because that's just not going to happen. When we're done with him he'll be a cold-blooded killer. He won't know anyone or anything."

Funnily enough, rescue was exactly what Horace had in mind.

As promised they were marched out over the sumptuous glades, past several riamand mines and out to the very edge of the dwarves' territory. There was no emotionally-charged farewell. In fact, the guards simply turned on their heels and, without another word, strode back off along the trail. Horace supposed the threat was implied, so there was no need to repeat it over again for repetition's sake.

He thought there might be a discussion on what they were going to do with John, but the entire group moved off, apparently already forgetting John. The only ones who straggled were Sydney, one of the prisoners who John had saved from the castle, and, of course, Susan.

Horace managed a weak smile. "So you're in this with me, then? Ready to hang back and bust John out?"

Sydney and Susan exchanged glances, and then Susan said, "It was a wonderful thing that John did for us—sacrificing himself for our freedom. But you heard what the dwarf guards said about them not taking any second chances if they're to find any of us on their land. Besides, remember that John promised to help out with Zend and Plont's quest to free their children? Shouldn't you honour John's agreement now that he's not able to?"

"But there are lots of them. What difference will I or you or Sydney make to their quest?"

"Well, as far as you're concerned, you have that eye of yours. It could prove invaluable in scouting out terrain, to seeing any threat coming from a mile off. No doubt we'll need you when it comes to finding chinks in the castle garrison, working out where the soldiers are deployed."

"I wouldn't be that much help," Horace said, frustratingly already feeling that Susan was winning this argument. "I'm sure that Yvonne can use her white magic to see those kinds of things."

"We need you," Susan said.

"And John needs me."

The group had streamed away now, the last of them slipping from sight as they passed downward, through the foothills, back to level ground. Every nerve in Horace's body told him to walk along with them, to go down the incline to safety. But he knew what he had to do, he had to rescue John—after all the effort John had gone to in returning to help their escape, in finally managing to convince Yvonne to join their group, and thus save Horace's life, it would be cowardly to desert his best friend now.

Susan sidled up beside him and rested her cold fingers on his forearm. "He's got out of messes like this before, and I'm sure he'll be more than capable of doing it again." She tightened her grip on his arm. "Come on, Horace, let's go, leave all this behind. I've got a feeling that we will see John again very soon."

Horace resisted her tug and turned his attention onto Sydney. "And what about you? How do you feel abandoning someone who saved your life?"

Sydney blushed a little. "Come on, you don't think there's anything that three of us can do against a group of bivcheks, do you?"

No response seemed appropriate for Sydney's question because, deep down, Horace knew that he was totally correct, there was nothing at all they had, in the way of force, which could overcome those dwarves and their mean creatures. He allowed Susan to draw him away from the dwarves' territory and down the slope.

"That's it," she said, cooing as if she were reassuring a newly-joined Grotesque on taking their first steps in their monstrous state. "We've got other promises made that need seeing through. John can stand up for himself, he will be fine."

But, looking back over his shoulder, at the trail leading up to the dwarves' houses, Horace got the uneasy sense that John could not have been further from safety.

Perceived knowledge held that going downhill was much easier than going up—and so it proved. Before Horace had so much as put one foot in front of the other, he found the land beneath him flattening out and that they had emerged on a plain. He looked back over his shoulder to see the rolling hills growing out of the terrain, with a backdrop of snow-capped mountains. His stomach wrenched and he knew that he had left his best friend behind, left him in the lurch. But now, surely, it was too late to change his mind.

They set up camp soon after and the general spirit round the soon-blazing fire was one of optimism. They had escaped from a sure death and come down here, back on track with their quest, with only the loss of a single member of their party. And, Horace considered, that no one much cared about John Stonefield, beyond the fact that they had lost some of their muscle. Back at Witney Branches, John had mostly kept to himself. He would join in with celebrations like all the others, of course, but he never seemed to fully throw himself into matters. He supposed it might have something to do with his size—that because of it he had never felt quite at home in anyone's company except his own.

Plont turned out to be a masterful scavenger of the land and, in no time at all, he returned to the campfire bearing a bagful of trout, several bagfuls of wild berries and, much to Rabbit King's distaste, a dozen skinned rabbits. He did offer Rabbit King a sombre shrug by way of apology, but Rabbit King stormed off into the bush from which he returned soon after with some non-descript, and very unappetising-looking, roots which he toasted in the fire and then gnawed on, scowling at the others as they chewed on their rabbit flesh.

Horace kept to himself at the edge of the fire, feeling its warm glow on one side and the biting mountain breeze on the other. He continued to stare at the mountains in the distance, set in the moonlight, and he wondered what kind of torture John was going through right now. He wasn't a killer—he never had been. And Horace had hoped that after his escape from the King's castle that he would never again have to make such a despicable choice.

After everyone had eaten, Yvonne spoke in a hushed voice of what their plan for the next day would be. Horace's attention dipped in and out, unable to get his mind off John. While Yvonne went round all of them, asking suggestions, wanting to know whether they might have some kind of skill to offer on the way, Horace slipped away from the fireside and stood off at a nearby stream—about a hundred yards away.

Now he truly had a chance to let his mind wander, without all this talk of adventure, this wild plan of storming the castle. It had been a stupid idea from the start, a suicide mission. So what if the King's men had taken Plont and Zend's children, didn't they realise that witches and wizards had done much worse to the Grotesque, in alienating them from their families forever—forcing them to run for their lives lest they should be killed for being different? He supposed that no one could really under-stand without being a Grotesque themselves.

He cast a glance back at the faces in the flickering shadows, all sat round in a circle, and then he looked to the mountains, knowing that he only had one option open to him—just as he had known when he'd had to escape Witney Branches in search of help.

As he took off running, taking pains to keep his footsteps near silence in the tall grass, he hoped that this little piece of vigilantism wouldn't prove to be as disastrous as had bringing the black witches and wizards to Witney Branches. He had to save John, that was all that mattered now.

A BIT OF A KERFUFFLE

AS TREVOR STIRRED that morning, with bright sunlight glaring in his face, he considered how quickly he'd become accustomed to sleeping outdoors, and on just about any sort of surface. Take this hard dusty ground for instance. Back on Earth he never would've considered so much as spending a night in a tent, with a sturdy air mattress. Yesterday, while incarcerated in the dwarves' house / prison, he had been quite unable to get comfortable on that impossibly soft bed. Last night, though, he had got a decent eight-hour sleep and felt all the fresher for it.

He took in the rest of the camp and noticed that there were deliberations going on between Susan, Yvonne and Sydney. Still rubbing the sleep out of his eyes, Trevor paced toward them.

"Didn't you see him last night?" Susan said to Sydney.

Sydney shook his head. "Nope. Thought he'd gone to bed early."

Susan turned on Yvonne. "Isn't there some sort of tracking magic you can conjure up? Something you can use to sniff out where he is?"

"Sounds an awful lot like black magic to me," Yvonne said.

"And you can't bend the rules just once?"

"You don't get to be the whitest witch from 'bending' rules, you know?"

Trevor stepped into the group. "Who're you talking about?"

Susan glanced at him. "Horace. He went missing last night."

"Where do you think he's gone?"

"To rescue John."

"Why?" Trevor said. "What's happened to John?"

"Haven't you been paying attention?" Susan said. "Didn't you hear that he sacrificed himself so that we could all go free?"

"Must've missed that bit," Trevor said, extracting a twig which had become lodged in his wiry hair. "So are we going to go back for him, then?"

Zend strode onto the scene. "Absolutely not, there's simply not time. We have to get to the castle as soon as possible. Every word we speak here is another moment lost, another moment that our children are being held captive."

Sydney faced up to him. "He saved mine and Courtney's lives."

"And then he went all noble and decided to make that deal with Shankle. It's his own fault he's got himself into this mess with those dwarves."

Sydney backed up, looking to be standing aside in frustration, but then he swung back his fist and caught Zend with a mean left hook.

Zend stumbled, but caught himself before he fell, already

back on his feet and giving Sydney a counter punch. His fist smacked into Sydney's cheek.

Sydney let out an, "*Oof!*" and tumbled over.

Zend stood over him rubbing his fist. "Look, your hero's locked up now, he saved you once, that was very good of him, but if we waste any more time round here then it might be putting more lives in peril. What's worth more, the life of one or many?"

Stanley rubbed his bald head and winced in pain, but he had no reply.

"Good," Zend said, turning away, "then let's break camp and get a move on."

No one seemed to have any complaints about that.

If Trevor had got used to sleeping on the ground, he couldn't say the same about his feet getting used to all this walking. Blisters chaffed on every bit of skin covering his feet. He walked with an exaggerated limp, in the hope that someone would notice he was struggling and call the whole group aside for a rest. At one point he had got himself entangled in conversation with Yvonne and sounded out the possibility of her healing his blisters, but, once again, this had been condemned as bordering on black magic—a frivolous usage of magic—so he had been forced to let the matter lie.

The ground got somewhat squelchy beneath their feet and the first time Trevor's foot sank into a bog he found himself actually savouring the cooling sensation of the mud creeping into his boot. This was swiftly followed by the realisation that he couldn't get his foot back out again and it took a combination of Zend and Rabbit King to haul him out. And even after all that fuss he still didn't manage to get any kind of a rest.

Later in the afternoon, though, Yvonne did call them together, to give them a fifteen-minute breather. She took stock of their situation and declared their arms to be unsatisfactory.

Trevor thought this a reasonable appraisal, given that Zend only held a sharpened branch, while Rabbit King depended on rocks scattered about the path, something to hurl at any nearby foe. The Grotesque, of course, had nothing at all between them —being a peaceful people. Neither did Sydney or Courtney, having kept themselves on the right side of magic since their escape from the castle. In fact, the only person who seemed to be suitably armed was Plont, who had his bow and arrows which he'd fashioned back in the Forests—but he would need more arrows soon, considering he had expended several catching animals in the course of the journey.

Yvonne informed them that she had a friend called Leyton who lived within a day's walk, and that he kept an extremely professional arms dealership. He would be able to outfit them a reasonable cost. In fact he was quite happy to grant credit where heroic deeds were concerned. She informed them, by way of warning, that if they got Leyton talking about his past exploits, his quests, they would never manage to extricate themselves from his shop again.

So, with Yvonne leading them onward, they paced on through the Etherealean countryside.

Trevor first caught sight of the shack up ahead. He was quite proud to be the one to call out to the rest of the group, and then, realising that Horace and his telescopic eye had deserted them the night before, he felt decidedly less smug. There was a light skip in his step, despite the long day's march. It was funny the effect that the prospect of possessing a sword and shield could have on him—he supposed it drew on some childish imagining, long ago suppressed.

The chimney smoked away as they approached and Trevor considered why, if this Leyton fellow were really such a great arms dealer, he should set up shop in the middle of nowhere. He hoped it wasn't something sordid or, worse, dangerous.

As it turned out, Leyton had healthy crop of pink plants with bright yellow buds which grew round the back of his shack. Once they got closer, Sydney informed him that this was known as namtra and was highly controlled throughout the Kingdom of Ethereal because of its hallucinogenic properties. So that explained this out-of-the-way location. It seemed that they might be dealing with a middle-aged hippy—or whatever the Ethereal equivalent of a hippy was.

The rest of the Grotesque, led by Susan, stayed outside of the shack, while Trevor followed on the coattails of Yvonne and Zend, not wanting to get any trace of this 'namtra' on him lest there be some sort of check by the authorities on route to the castle. His thinking was that if he got caught with the namtra as well as being part of a group wanting to storm the castle then he would only prolong his prison sentence and never get home in a timely manner.

Trevor's first instinct, that Leyton must be some tucked away hippy, proved to be somewhat correct. There were incense stick-type-things burning away in the corner of the room, puffing a woody fragrance throughout the place. The smoke tickled

Trevor's nostril hair and he had to pinch his nose to stop himself sneezing.

Leyton himself had scraggy long grey hair which came down in waves. He wore a patched up quilted vest and a pair of trousers several sizes too small about the waist, evidenced by the fact that the fly remained open. He eyed Trevor and Zend with a glazed over expression before his eyes fell onto Yvonne and he broke out into a wide, idiotic grin. "Yvonne!" he said, stumbling toward her with his arms outstretched.

When he reached her, she did nothing to encourage the embrace, merely allowing him to wrap his arms round her and give her a squeeze. After he was finished with the overzealous greeting, she let out an unsubtle sigh. "Yes, Leyton, it's lovely to see you too. But this isn't much of a social visit I'm afraid."

Leyton waggled his finger in the air. "This calls for namtra all round." He crouched down and fished through a cabinet. "If only I can find my pipe then we can all sit round and get ourselves off Ethereal, just for a while."

"We're in a hurry," Yvonne said.

"This shouldn't take a minute," he said, still digging through his things, occasionally throwing something to one side.

A clay jug landed at Trevor's feet followed by a wooden spoon and then a rather nice, if a little rustic, ceramic bowl which—unfortunately following its careless treatment—cracked down the middle.

Finally Leyton straightened up, triumphant, bearing a jet-black pipe in his hand. "Success!" he said, eyes lighting up.

"Leyton," Yvonne said, sterner now.

Leyton bobbed across his shop, over to another set of drawers which he pawed through, before removing several pouches. He set them down, unravelled their drawstrings and then removed the crumbled up leaves from within—what Trevor guessed to be dried namtra. When he had finished filling the pipe, he jabbed the leaves down into the chamber and then stabbed its stem between his lips. He withdrew a pair of flints from his pockets and sparked the mixture into life. A purple-blue smoke wafted upward, hanging in the air a second before evaporating. His shoulders slumped and his eyes seemed to sink back in their sockets. He offered the pipe to Yvonne.

"No thank you," she said, batting it aside.

"Please," Leyton said.

Yvonne looked to the pipe and then to Leyton, who had taken on a hangdog expression, and then she snatched the pipe out of his hand. She put it to her lips and mimed taking a puff before handing it back.

Leyton wrinkled his brow. "Hey! You didn't have any."

"That's because I'm the whitest witch in Ethereal, and I haven't got there by smoking every pipe of namtra offered to me by drug-addled ex-heroes."

Leyton cradled the pipe in his arm and then brightened as he turned to Zend and Trevor. "You'll have some, won't you?"

Zend shrugged, took the pipe from him and toked it. He blew out a purple-blue smoke ring and then passed the pipe over to Trevor.

"Oh, no thank you," Trevor said.

Leyton puckered his lips. "Hang on, I know that accent anywhere. You're from Earth, aren't you?"

A little worried at what this admission might bring on, Trevor said, "Yes."

"Hmm, I visited a while back, didn't like it much. Quite

smelly. When I got back I had to wash everything I owned to get the stench out, and even after that it took quite some convincing to get any maidens into my bed." He winked. "If you know what I mean."

Trevor wasn't sure that he did, but he smiled all the same. As for Earth being smelly he could quite easily say the same about this namtra stuff.

Leyton whipped the pipe out of Zend's hand and shoved it into Trevor's chest. "Go on, have a pop."

"No, I think I'd rather not," Trevor said, looking to Yvonne for support.

Unfortunately for him, she was already meandering her way about the shack, pouting at various artefacts either strapped to the walls: swords, shields, bows and arrows, or lying about on surfaces: enormous eggs, unpolished jewels, jagged keys.

"Fancy that," Leyton said. "You've come all the way from Earth and you're afraid to have a little puff. The tiniest little puff. You know, I used to be like you, straight-laced. It took a quite fetching maiden to convince me that namtra really could open your mind to things. If I remember rightly it was just after I'd slayed—"

Yvonne raised her head. "Are you going to show us what you've got or not?" she said.

Leyton looked a little slighted by this abrupt remark, but his druggy daze seemed to prevent him from responding with a biting reply. He turned to Trevor. "Only when he has a go on the namtra. Then I'll show you my wares."

Trevor stared at the pipe, with no intention at all of 'having a go' on it. He glanced to Yvonne who, to his horror, nodded for him to take the pipe. He looked to Zend, who gave him the same assuring nod, then clapped him on the shoulder. "It's not like it's going to make you go blind or anything," Zend said.

All of a sudden, Trevor felt like he'd returned to his school days, that he was in a playground, round the back of the bike sheds while a circle of kids all implored him to take a drag on a cigarette. There was only one way out of this, and he knew it. He reached out and took the pipe from Leyton's outstretched hand and suckled on its lip.

He felt the rough smoke twitch down his throat and into his lungs, where it twitched about some more. Everything seemed to slow dramatically and the world became unwieldy and bulky. It was like someone had stuffed damp cotton wool in his ears. He realised that Zend was saying something to him only when he caught sight of his moving lips. And then he only made sense of the message Zend was trying to convey when Zend reached out and removed the pipe from his lips. "Breathe out," he was saying. "Breathe out."

The smoke vibrated inside his chest and, all at once, Trevor felt a splutter form at the back of his throat. He coughed up the smoke, giving it none of the admirable form which Zend had managed. His mind, however, still felt like it was drifting away from him—as if attached the string of a stray helium balloon.

Through the confusion he heard Leyton laughing hard, and then someone said, "Take him for a walk outside, that should clear him up. Just a little walk."

Someone touched the base of his back and guided him toward the door. Trevor allowed them to do so, not seeing any point in resistance. When he got outside, into the open, the blue sky was so overwhelming that he almost couldn't bear it—all he could think was that it just went on and on and on, without stopping. A dizzy spell caught him and he felt himself slip away from his helper and fall to the ground.

And then everything went black.

Trevor was roused by a damp cloth on the forehead. He tried his best to keep the forms straight which bore down on him, but they just kept slipping back before he could properly lock his gaze on them. He wanted to tell them to just keep still while he was getting his head together but words seemed to take on the texture of molten lead and his comments were lost in a bilge of moans.

And then, from above him, he distinguished actual, audible words. "First time he's taken namtra, is it?"

"Guess so," someone else said.

"Goodness, what I'd do for that first time again. What a rush!"

Trevor wanted to explain to them that it simply hadn't been his choice, that he had been pressurised into the whole business by Leyton refusing to show off his weapons unless Trevor had a puff—just a little puff. But that sort of delicate balancing of his central nervous system escaped him.

He blinked and looked beyond the two figures. The blue sky towered above and the sun was like a roll of fiercely burning magnesium. He was still outside, perhaps exactly in the spot where he had fallen. Maybe he had only blacked out for a moment or two.

Sure that he was regaining his human capacity, he propped himself up on his elbows and rubbed his aching head. He attempted to manipulate his mouth and realised that he could, indeed, move his jaw up and down—he continued to relish this simple action for the next few seconds, until one of the people said, "Do you think he's having a fit?"

Trevor eyed them again. He saw that one of the figures—his features now unmuddled—was Zend, no doubt the one reminiscing about his first time using namtra, while the other was Sydney. Still reeling off the success of managing to prop himself up onto his elbows, Trevor attempted to swing himself into a sitting position, which he managed almost too effectively—nearly swinging so hard as to land on his front, face first in the dirt.

Zend's steady hand clasped his shoulder. "You want to see the weapons now, with the rest of us? Or would you like some quiet time to get your thoughts together?"

Trevor found the notion of 'quiet time' so condescending that he mumbled something about being all right and immediately, with the aid of Sydney and Zend, rocked himself back onto his feet. After a brief bout of swaying he was back in control of his two legs and, for the most part, his arms. He even managed a stiff upper-lip grin to show that he was well on the road to repair. "Where to?" he said.

Sydney swung his arm out to point in the appropriate direction.

Trevor followed his finger to make out Leyton, smoke puffing away in his trail like some off-the-rails steam train. The Grotesque all followed on his heels like a line of lost missionaries looking for guidance from their leader.

"Think you can make it?" Zend said.

With a hefty swallow, which really did almost nothing to solve the dryness in his throat, Trevor said, "I'll do my best."

They set off after the others at a steady pace which Trevor was quite glad of. He noticed that both Zend and Sydney were keeping themselves level with his shoulders, in case he had the inclination to bob off to either side. He had to admit that he was rather glad to have someone like Zend forever grateful to him—for having saved his life from the tusks of a honey boar—it made situations like this pass much easier to have a strong hand ready to rely upon.

Leyton led them along a stony path which wound upward, into a cluster of hills behind his shack. For a second, Trevor had a horrible vision that he was leading them right back up to the dwarves, so that they might finish off their party, and then he realised that it was probably the lingering traces of the namtra making him paranoid.

They concluded their ascent when they reached the top of the current crop of rocks, with Leyton removing his pipe from his lips, taking a dramatic, and slightly paranoid, look round him before putting his back into shifting a boulder which blocked the entrance to a substantial cave.

The boulder shifted just far enough to leave a gap for Leyton to wander through, pipe now back in his mouth. Trevor was surprised to have observed great strength in someone who looked at least a decade or two older than him, then again, he supposed that all the talk about him having been a hero did have substance.

He lingered along the on the heels of the others as they streamed through the gap between the boulder and rock face.

Inside Leyton had already lit a torch and hung it up from the wall. When Trevor looked over the place, his vision went a little fuzzy. He shook his head a couple of times to lose the dozy sensation and then took in the various weapons, all hanging up on the walls: swords, shields, axes, javelins, bows and arrows, crossbows. It was a treasure-trove for adventurers. He noticed that everyone else in the group had been rendered into a similar stupor.

Leyton strode along the lines of weapons and gazed at them, with a wistful look in his eye. "Everything here is tried and tested in battle, all these tools have served me well, and so will they will serve you all." He waved his arm at the inventory. "Please, take whatever you need for your quest. I have no need for them now."

Through the numbness plaguing his skin, Trevor felt a tingle of anticipation, already eyeing one of the larger broadswords, hanging just around head height. He made for it with a smile on his lips.

NOT A COUP, BUT CLOSE ENOUGH

A LEXIS SAT in her bedchamber resting her head in her hands, staring out down into the courtyard to see the garrison marching back and forth for the sixth time that morning. She was sure that Frum was doing it merely to irritate her. Their first march had taken place just after five o'clock this morning, as she'd judged by the dim sunlight outside. If he seriously thought that she believed him when he claimed this was nothing personal, then he had another thing coming.

Needless to say, she had taken to her bedroom more and more over the past few days. At first, in the hours after Frum had effectively stripped her of her throne, she had made a conscious effort to get round the castle, to keep her head held high and to be seen by the courtiers, so they wouldn't think that she had retreated into hiding—taken this setback lying down. But, she had to admit, after her first few times out in the corridors, she had become unnerved by the looks of the garrison men, sure that they smiled behind her back or made snide comments out of earshot. Although she never caught one of them at business of this kind, she couldn't shake the suspicion, and so had decided not to go out at all.

Her single connection to the outside world had become Arnold and she had started, afresh, thinking of how she might escape the castle, and get back to Earth. It would be difficult, though, considering that the guards stationed outside her bedroom door doubled as Frum's eyes and ears, ready to report any shift in her behavioural patterns. Since it had been Courtney who had brought her to the castle in the first place, she would need to enlist the help of someone trustworthy, as well as being in the know, if she was to find her way back to the End of Time, from where she could return to her world.

There was a series of giggles and the ominous *clack* of heels along the corridor, and before Alexis had time to prepare herself she saw Cherry, leading the rest of the maidens, round her door with little more than a sneer by way of greeting.

Alexis had no intention of kicking up a fuss. She could tell by their behaviour that whatever they had in mind had the blessing of Frum, and she would only make things worse for herself—for Arnold—if she were to complain.

Cherry slunk over to Alexis's dresser, her face stretched into a manic grin. She slid open the drawers, one-by-one, and then turned to the others. "Help yourselves, girls."

Each of the maidens shot Alexis a wild look before digging into the drawers, alongside Cherry. With their heads bowed, their hands groping through the jewellery and fine clothes, they reminded Alexis of pigs at a trough. She knew that Frum had sent them here as another act of humiliation, to show her who was really boss. If only he would realise that she just didn't care anymore that, if he really wanted, he could have her throne—she was done with Ethereal.

Fine undershirts and finely-knitted stockings draped over the dresser, and filled the girls' arms. Their expressions were ones of hopeless ecstasy, like this were some deep and long-awaited dream for each of them. Alexis tried to summon a modicum of anger against them, but she only found pity.

Cherry jerked her head back to Alexis, holding up an undershirt which Alexis particularly liked—it was a powdery pink with silver lacing: feminine without being *too* girly, at least in comparison with the rest of her inherited wardrobe. "I'm taking this," she said, as if it weren't obvious.

"Okay," Alexis said.

Cherry studied Alexis with a sneer then folded the undershirt over her arm and pawed through the drawer to find something else which, Alexis presumed, would be more likely to get a rise out of her. She did her job well, plucking out a necklace of what, Jenson had informed her, was made of a mineral called riamand. The tiny purple gems glinted in the steady sunlight.

The maidens spent the next half an hour going through the entire dresser and, when they had finished there, they started in on her wardrobe, with the frocks all hanging up within. Cherry took exceptional pleasure in slipping Alexis's wedding gown off its hanger and giving it a lopsided glance before tossing it onto the floor, carelessly treading on it as she dug further into the wardrobe for something which did capture her attention.

Alexis looked at the bedraggled wedding dress beneath Cherry's well-heeled feet and she thought about how it really meant little to her. She had only felt beautiful wearing it, nothing else.

There was no emotional connection to her wedding day because the King had meant nothing to her. They had not been in love and, she was beginning to think after several years in Ethereal, that she never would find love. Not in this castle, not as a captive queen anyway. But, really, *love* was the least of her concerns right now.

The rummaging was brought to a dramatic halt, however, when Arnold invaded the room, sword drawn and eyes flaring. He waved his blade in the maidens' faces and demanded they leave at once. The maidens all fled from the room, shrieking, their arms filled with Alexis's clothes.

Arnold sheathed his sword and approached Alexis. "Who let them in here?"

Feeling empty inside, and unable to take her eyes off the rolling hills outside her window, the countryside beyond the walls of the castle, she said, "General Frum, I guess."

"Why didn't you call for me? I could've stopped them."

"They're just trying to get to me," Alexis said, still not breaking her gaze out over the plush green meadows. "It would've only been giving them what they wanted to have called you in to scare them away, and they'll only come back later, in the middle of the night, perhaps, when they can catch me unaware and unprotected."

He glanced over at her dresser, from which the clothes spilled out. "Would you . . . would you like some help in putting things back in order?"

She broke off her gaze outside and noticed the pink colour which had snuck into his cheeks. Then she realised that he was embarrassed because some items of her underwear were draped over the dresser. Often she forgot how young he really was—his reckless bravery and swagger suggested he was at least ten years older: a hardened knight rather than a callow teenager. She supposed he had learnt that façade from his father.

"No," she said. "I'll put all my things back later. I've got nothing else to do, so it'll be a nice activity to occupy my mind."

"Very well, ma'am."

"You don't have to address me like that, you know. I'm not really the Queen any longer."

"To me you are."

Alexis summoned a smile. "Thank you." Then she turned her mind back to what had bothered her throughout this day and longer. "Arnold? I was wondering if you know how to reach the End of Time from here."

"'The End of Time?' What's that?"

It seemed that she might be asking the wrong person. "Never mind. Is there someone knowledgeable in the castle, I don't know"—she searched her mind for the lingo—"a wise man or woman, someone like that?"

Another blank look and then, out of nowhere, a blazing grin. "Why yes, there's old Niddy, the librarian."

"Do you think you could take me to see him?"

Arnold smirked. "You don't think I'm going to allow any of these wretches to harm you, do you?"

Alexis's movement through the castle was greeted with all sorts of suspicious glances from both men of the garrison and courtiers. She reminded herself that she was Queen and she should not feel a stranger in her own domain. But it was one thing to think that in her head and to have to suffer all these looks in the real world. She told herself that she had brought this upon herself somewhat by closing herself up in her bedroom over the last few days—even taking her meals there.

They reached the library just as the sun was setting over the hills. They'd decided to come now since Frum would be down in the banquet hall, no doubt drunk out of his skull on whatever it was they were drinking tonight—perhaps with Cherry sprawled over his lap garnished in her purloined jewellery. Although this quest shouldn't have raised any suspicions in his mind, because if Frum was anything he was not a learned man—he probably didn't even know the castle had a library, Alexis wanted to keep a low profile more to keep Niddy from harm by his mere association with her.

The door to the library was open a crack and Alexis followed Arnold inside. They snaked through the overflowing stacks of books: hard-backed volumes with several bundles of yellowing paper only bound together with frail string. She breathed in deep, savouring the smell of paper and glue, and whatever else it was that gave libraries such a distinctive smell. Perhaps it had something to do with the sun warming the books throughout the day, bringing all those scents to the surface.

Arnold led her on, looking just as unfamiliar with the place as she was, and then he seemed to snap to some recognition and dragged her off down another of the aisles where they were brought nose-to-nose with a man with a fishlike face. He had slippery cheeks, wet with perspiration and hair slicked to the side. He had a weighty volume open before him and he read with his finger tracing the words, peering over the tops of his half-moon spectacles. He hummed to himself as he went and made no acknowledgement that he had noticed they were there. Old Niddy, Alexis supposed.

Whenever Alexis came across someone reading, back on Earth, she had always been struck with something of a reverential feeling. She never wanted to disturb whatever it was that that person was caught up with. So she, very slightly and with her hand over her mouth, coughed.

Despite such a delicate call for attention, Niddy almost fell right off his wooden stool, catching himself on the table before he tumbled over. He resettled his spectacles across the bridge of his nose and peered at them, at first with wide eyes and an open mouth, and then he improvised a bow, getting down off the stool and dropping to one knee. "Your Majesty! If I had known I would've swept the place up. I really had no idea. You see, the King, your predecessor, seldom—if not never—visited the library. I cannot apologise—"

"It's okay," Alexis said. "I'm not anything more than a puppet these days anyway. I've come here because I'd like some information about the castle."

"Ma'am, I will be at your service. I shall endeavour to fulfil whatever request it is that you wish granted, have no fear of that—"

"Terrific. I'm looking for a way to reach the End of Time. Do you know anything about it?"

"'The End of Time,' 'The End of Time,'" he said, tapping his chin, as if this were a standard request, something he got asked every day by people dropping in. "I do seem to remember that there is a volume on the place, it's somewhere round here, I'm sure."

"Do you think you could find it for me?"

"Right away, ma'am, of course," he said, diving off his stool and pattering along shelves, that sturdy index finger tracing the cover of each book as he went, only removing it from the skin of each book to readjust the glasses on his nose.

After about twenty minutes of searching, checking over the majority of the library, twenty or thirty stacks, he called out to them, triumphant. "Over here! This is it!"

Alexis and Arnold rushed over to where Niddy crouched, the volume open on his lap. He flipped through the pages, his finger tracing the information. Alexis got a glance at the language sprawling across the page and couldn't understand a word of it because, although the common language of Earth and of Ethereal were practically identical, their systems of notation were totally different—as she'd discovered when she'd attempted to write a letter to the King in her own language, and been laughed at for hours on end.

Niddy muttered to himself as he scanned the text with his finger. He reached a page, somewhere in the middle of the book, and then said, "Ah ha!" He shot a glance at both Alexis and Arnold then ploughed past them to a reading stand where he deposited the book on its back and pointed out what he had discovered. "Right here," he said. "This is what we're looking for."

Despite not understanding the language, Alexis could comprehend that the section on the End of Time was worryingly short, no more than a paragraph of five or six lines. It never ceased to amaze her that many people in the Kingdom of Ethereal knew of the End of Time but never thought of visiting it themselves—in fact never really thought of it full-stop. It was as if they just weren't all that interested.

"Shall I read it to you, Your Highness?" Niddy said.

Glad not to have to go through the routine of admitting that she couldn't read Etherealean notation, she nodded.

Niddy lifted the book up slightly and peered down on the page. "'The End of Time,'" he read, with eloquence befitting its elevated purpose. "'*The End of Time* is a meta-physical construct which marks the end of all worlds connected through the Nearite parallel.'"

Alexis felt that she was lost already.

Niddy continued, "'The End of Time presents itself to the eyes of beings as a series of graveyards, each of which holds various keys to different points in a particular world's history. The End of Time may be accessed through various portals, distributed throughout history, each of which works as a two-way system of passing through time or *time-travelling*.'"

Niddy slapped the book shut and blew off a layer of dust which had accumulated on the edge of the pages.

"Is that it?" Alexis said.

"Appears so, ma'am."

"But . . . but, it can't be. Something as interesting as that must have more information on it."

"Is it interesting?" Niddy said. "I suppose I'd never really given it pause for thought. Why anyone would want to travel *backwards* or *forwards* in time, or *between* worlds will forever remain a mystery to me."

"What I really wanted to know was how I might be able to get to the End of Time from here. Is there any way that I might access the place?"

Niddy scratched his temple and frowned. He tucked the large book beneath his arm. "Well, I remember a long time ago, when I was much younger, still the library assistant here, that there was something said about the Royal Graveyard round the back of the castle."

"Really?" Alexis said, thinking this promising as she recalled that graveyards seemed to have a lot to do with this time-travelling, world-hopping lark.

When Courtney had brought her to Ethereal, got her involved in this blithe mess, he had taken her through a placard in Rutsley Church and Burial Grounds. It seemed obvious to her now. What she needed to do was find the appropriate touchstone, the portal, in the graveyard here, and it would send her right back to the End of Time.

Hardly able to restrain her enthusiasm now, Alexis asked Niddy for a map showing the exact location of the graveyard. She had never visited, even during the King's funeral. It had been kept secret even from her, his nearest 'family.'

Niddy unrolled a map and spread it out on the reading table. He smoothed it out with his fists and then stood back to give her room. "It's up on the north side of the castle, a small patch of ground. Silly really when you think about it. Probably going to run out of space in a couple of generations' time."

Alexis checked over the space. It *was* small, and it was right opposite the barracks. She could tell with certainty that she would be seen entering. But, once she got inside, she could find the touchstone quickly and transport herself away before news even reached Frum of her entrance—or that was what she hoped.

She eyed Niddy. "Is there any sort of protection on the graveyard, other than the guards?"

Niddy scratched his nose. "I don't know. It's been a long time since I was down there."

"Just anything," she said. "Anything you can remember."

"Hmm, well, as I seem to remember there's a sturdy wall surrounding the place, and the door's got a lock on it, a big rusty contraption. But I can't say for sure. Sorry, ma'am."

Alexis smiled. "That's fine, you've been very helpful."

"I live to serve, ma'am," he said, giving her a gentle bow.

She thought that, if she managed to get her hands back on any sort of tangible control over the castle, she would do something good for Niddy. Someone who obviously such a humble and honest worker deserved more than to just be tucked away somewhere he wouldn't bother anyone else.

As she trotted back through the corridors, with Arnold at her side, she thought about how she was going to get her hands on that key. Thinking about it she was sure that it must've been kept somewhere in the King's chamber, her bedroom. That was where she would look first.

Her bedroom was just as she left it, which she supposed was a minor miracle given that the maidens hadn't had further urges to return. Perhaps Arnold had truly put on a terrifying performance, made them think that they might have to be content with what they already had. It would be one less thing to worry about.

With Arnold, she scoured the whole bedroom in search of the key. Several times she picked out what she believed to be the perfect hiding place: tied round one of the bedposts, high up where no one would see, stuck to the bottom of a drawer, beneath a loose bathroom tile, but she had no luck whatsoever. At one point she was certain that Arnold had found the key when he had bounded into the bedroom after foraging out on the balcony, but it had been only to inform her of an approaching group of people, a hundred or so, approaching on the horizon.

Alexis told him that they were—most likely—the missing men of the Forests, having turned up, not magicked away after all. They continued with their search, going over all the places they had looked for the second and then the third time before she called it off, and they sank back on her bed, both of them breathing heavily with sweat gleaming on their flushed faces.

She turned her thoughts back to the funeral, to who had accompanied the King's coffin to its final resting place. There was the priest, the four guards and . . . General Frum.

A chill crept up her spine and she knew that Frum had the key. He had to have it. There was no other explanation. But how in the world would she ever manage to get it off him?

BACK IN THE RING

THE ONLY SOLACE of this situation was that John knew his friends to be safe, from now on there would be nothing that the dwarves could do to harm them. That thought kept him warm during the nights, allowed him to get some fevered rest, to take his mind off the impending fights for just a few moments. He wished them well on their quest and that, in this wicked world, they would find a way through to the castle and have their justice.

If John's prison cell had been nothing short of paradise then he really had no words to describe his abode now. He inhabited a grand suite adorned with huge marble arches and pillars. His bathroom was big enough to house a small village, the bath tub nothing short of a lake in size—and all the water was warmed to a comfortable temperature. Whereas his view from his prison cell had been slightly ruined by the entrance of a riamand mine, here he had a panorama of the whole of Ethereal. There, in the distance, he could even make out the beginnings of the Damned Forests. At first, when he had looked round the room, he had thought it would make him feel more comfortable, more at home, but, in reality, it had only served as a reminder, nagging away at him. So he kept the blind pulled down to hide it.

Shankle had arranged for John to have a space to train using a specially-enlarged axe. He took the opportunities more out of a sense of wanting to be outside than to take any determined kind of practice for the fighting awaiting him. When he was outside he mainly listened to the birdsong and watched the dwarf children playing, singing their song in their dialect, pointing at him and gawping. Once again he was a freak.

At first he had studied his hopes of escape, taken notes on how the guards moved about their posts. How did he know that Shankle had really let all of his friends go, that he hadn't left just one of them down in the prisons to use as leverage were he to escape? The worst part of it would be that he wouldn't know whether or not Shankle had done that until he caught up with his group, and they could be anywhere by now. That unknowing would drive him crazy and it was beginning to look like there was no alternative than to take part in these fights, to win them so that, someday, he might have his freedom. He thought glumly that if he fought successfully enough then perhaps no one would want to fight him and Shankle would let him go.

Later on that morning one of the dwarf guards informed him that his first fight was scheduled for the evening, to be combined with a banquet being laid on in Shankle's honour. There was a tone in the dwarf's voice which suggested that John was expected to put on a show so that Shankle and his guest would be entertained—with the expectation, of course, that he would win, thus allowing his employer to reap his full financial award.

John took himself to practice, throwing himself more fully into a routine, knowing that his survival depended on him killing another being. He would find out who would win when it came down to him or someone else. And it frightened him to think that, tonight, he would have an answer.

Everything passed so normally in the time leading up to the fight. There was no special meal for John, although he wouldn't have been able to eat anyway. And there was no visit from Shankle or his invitee, which John had been half expecting—sort of a parading of Shankle's great warrior. When the time arrived the same dwarf guard who always brought him messages from Shankle arrived to escort him. John noted the guard had taken special care to press his uniform and polish the blade of his axe.

He followed the guard down the endless corridors, knowing that at the end of one of them he would be led into a dusty ring where he would be looked down on by the spectators and expected to kill. What was killing to them? Did it even matter? Had Shankle even thought twice when he had sentenced him and his friends to death for trespassing or had it been no more than a kneejerk reaction?

The guard brought him to a tiny iron, windowless chamber. Without a doubt the drabbest place in the whole establishment. He found his axe lying ready for him on a surface to his left and plucked it up, weighing it in his hand. Then the door slammed shut behind him and he was alone in the darkness.

He felt his chest rising against his tunic, the light chafe of the material against his skin. This was it. Whatever happened now his life was going to change forever. And then, near the back of his brain, the thought that there might be a way to escape struck him, remaining with him as the iron door leading to the ring slid upward, the mechanism of a pulley brought into action by unseen hands.

The light was blinding at first. A crowd muttered among themselves, far from the screeching hoards which had greeted his performance at the King's competition. He felt much calmer, almost like he had made peace with his fate and the feeling that all his worries would soon be behind him.

He held up his arm to shield his eyes from the bright light and then stepped forward, hearing the *scrunch* of the sole of his boots over gravelly ground. He tightened his fingers round the handle of his axe and looked up into the spectators' seats. He picked out Shankle, hard to miss as he occupied the box right in front of him, about a head and shoulders taller than John.

Shankle made no acknowledgement of John, remaining stern-faced and stiff-backed. There was a man sitting beside him of normal height—not a dwarf. A tingle of recognition passed through John and he realised who the man was. He scanned his features a second time, the matted hair braided together in clumps. The mean, steepled chin. General Frum.

The creaking of a gate ahead of John drew his attention away from Frum and back down to the arena. Muffled conversation broke out amongst the spectators. The whole atmosphere seemed totally eerie to John, as if he were about to do battle in someone's larder. He gripped his axe and raised it to his chest, keeping his muscles locked and eyes tracing the blade—just as Arnold had taught him.

His opponent, it turned out, was a Polnutch. He had never seen one before in real life, having only read about them in the book Susan kept in Witney Branches which detailed all the various races of Ethereal. He took in his appearance, the shaved head, the blotchy green patches on the scalp and the light-grey complexion, as if all the blood had been sucked out. He bore a scabbard, its blade jagged, like the teeth of a saw. As he walked he sauntered slightly, almost limped. From what John had learnt about Polnutches he gathered that they were an especially aggressive race, that often they attempted to mingle with men, who had interests in recruiting such a fearsome people into their armies, but it never worked. Polnutches didn't do discipline.

The Polnutch held up the scabbard in both hands and circled John. Already he was sizing him up, most likely not having known that he would be facing a giant before the fight.

John kept himself wary, realising that there had been no indication to start the fight. He looked about him for wherever the signal would come from and he picked out a large, gleaming bell above the hatch from which he had entered the arena. Just as he was about to look round for whoever would be officiating the contest, the bell struck a long and mournful tone. The vibrations passed through the air and trembled over John's skin. He brought the axe back behind his head and waited for the Polnutch to make the first move.

The Polnutch held back for about another minute, still slowly going round John, forcing him to turn round with him. All this circling was making John dizzy, but at least it was saving him from having to inflict pain on someone else—for the moment.

John cast a glance back up to Shankle's box. This time Frum glared back at him, lips pursed and hands gripping onto the rail. John wondered whether Shankle had made some sort of deal, if he wished to somehow offload John back to the castle. Now he saw the folly of having told Shankle that he had once been a King's Champion. It had probably saved his friends, but it might well be the end for him.

However, John had more pressing matters at hand, as the Polnutch leapt up to John's side and swung his scabbard. The blade caught John in the fleshy piece of skin beneath his upper arm and he let out an involuntary groan. The Polnutch was quick and danced round behind him, out of sight. John felt the blade pierce his lower back: the flash of pain followed by a numbness and then a dull ache. The last sensation was the warm blood dripping down into his trousers.

Out of pain, more than anything else, John jutted his elbow back and caught the Polnutch square in the nose, sending him tumbling to the floor of the arena. To begin with John couldn't appreciate this stroke of luck because of the pain searing through him. He tried to push it to the back of his mind, to tell himself that one way or another it would be over soon. He would either win the fight, and be patched up afterward, or die trying.

His arms trembled as he brought the axe up above his head and moved in on the Polnutch, who was still stunned from the blow to his nose. Just as John towered over him, the Polnutch rolled over and leapt back onto his feet, scabbard outstretched, ready to parry any blow. But John hadn't struck any blow. In fact he was frozen in the spectacle, knowing that he had had a chance to end the fight, to put his axe through whatever appendage of the Polnutch he could whomp. He had bottled it.

This fight was going to be just like the last. It would end with his failure to kill another being.

With this acknowledgement lingering over him, he squared up to the box and shot Shankle a glance.

Shankle remained impartial, not giving anything away. He had a good poker face—a good thing since he professed that gambling was his primary hobby. This fight to the death was just another bet for him.

The Polnutch chattered away in his dialect, his bronze eyes never leaving John. He knew the Polnutch thought it a simple matter of tiring the monster. If the Polnutch could only jab him a few more times, draw some more of his blood, then he would have a chance of moving in for the kill. As it was John, was struggling to keep his legs from trembling beneath him, from simply falling to his knees and gasping under the weight of pain.

With a cluck of the tongue, the Polnutch shrieked out and leapt through the air, scabbard pointing downward, intending to plunge it into John's stomach. Acting out of reflect more than anything else, John parried the blow with his axe, knocking the Polnutch back onto his feet, and then, again out of instinct, he swung his axe and caught the Polnutch first in the mouth and then on the hip.

A deep gargle emanated from the Polnutch's throat and blood bubbled from his lips. He almost dropped his scabbard, but clung on, eyes like a pair of smouldering coals. He was holding onto his life with mere strength of will—that famous aggressive streak John had heard so much about.

John braced himself for the Polnutch's next attack.

From within the spectators someone shouted out in the

common tongue. "Finish him off! He's there for the taking. Don't be a coward!"

John glanced over the spectators and realised that it had been Frum who had made the comment. Frum was on his feet now, hands clasped together, eyes wild with the prospect of blood. At least he appeared to be supporting John, rather than actively taking against him.

The Polnutch collected himself together, straightened up and, scabbard raised once again, he rushed at him. When got up close, John turned side on, like a matador, and the Polnutch skidded right past. John battered the Polnutch on the back of the skull with the handle of his axe, and the Polnutch fell to the ground, unconscious. The Polnutch's scabbard bounced off somewhere across the arena.

John stood and observed the spectators.

They rose from their seats, exchanging money between themselves, some of them shaking their heads and muttering dwarf curses under their breath.

The Polnutch lay where he was, his breathing coming quickly, but clearly in no fit state to continue the fight—not that night, at least.

John dropped his axe down to his side and let out a long, dreary sigh, glad that their encounter hadn't come down to a death match. His entire body ached. He felt the blood welling up around his lower back and dripping down from the wound in his upper arm.

Frum's distinctive, gravelly voice sounded over all else. "Finish him!"

John blinked back through the lights and picked out Frum

standing there. Shankle stood beside him, still looking bored watching on.

John shook his head and looked off to the side of the arena, expecting one of the doors to squeak its way open again, but they remained sealed off. He looked off up at Shankle's box and realised that if he wanted to get out, he could swing himself up over the railing. He would need to battle back both Shankle and Frum, if they put up a fight, but his exit path might well be open to him. If only he could set aside his pain, allow adrenalin to take over, all that he had feared ever since being this size—losing control, people getting hurt.

"Finish him!" Frum repeated.

That familiar doubt, that they might still be holding someone down in the cells—that they might kill them if John dared escape—returned to him. But he shook off the feeling, telling himself that it was now or never. If he continued to fight on, night-after-night, he would eventually be forced to kill some-one, or be killed himself, and so wasn't it justified for him to run now, to spare any more deaths at his direct hand?

As if Shankle had read his thoughts, he clapped his hands together, bringing the spectators back to a hush. The bell sounded again. A shudder passed up John's spine and he eyed the gate through which the Polnutch had entered the arena—it was rising once more.

Was he going to be allowed to leave? John had the distinct feeling that it was for quite another purpose. He needed to get some medical care. His blood pumped through him, and with each pulse he felt a little fainter, that he was getting colder and that his complexion was growing more pallid.

Indeed, just as he'd suspected, more fighters lurked behind the rising gate. This time he was surprised to note that they were four dwarves, all with axes, miniature versions of the one he clenched in his fist. They all wore the same purple cloak, the colour of their treasured riamand. John noticed that they had also set riamand into their axe handles. It glinted now in the harsh light of the arena. All the dwarves had long beards and weary faces, as if they had been forced down here on Shankle's orders and didn't much like it.

Another pair of dwarves, additional to the fighters, skittered out into the arena. They took sides of the Polnutch, counted to five in their dwarf language and then lugged him up, dragging him along the dirt to where the fighters stood, a brown trail of blood snaking its way in their wake. When they reached the entrance the fighters parted for them, watching the Polnutch leave with no little apprehension. The fighting dwarves padded out into the arena and the gate slid shut behind them.

John braced himself, holding his axe out before him, waiting for the dwarves to make the first move—that strategy had served him well with the Polnutch and he hoped for the same results here. He noticed the spectators hurrying back to their seats, cash passing between hands quickly, bets being doubled.

The dwarves, military-trained, in fact he recognised them vaguely as members of the guard, swarmed round him, their axes all straight in their hands, their eyes watchful of him. Soon they had got him covered from all angles, one in each corner of the arena.

John hadn't had much experience of situations like this, seeing as, during the King's competition, he had merely ended up being one of the last two left standing by virtue of his size. He managed to avoid these all-against-one scenarios. But now it was facing him, he had to deal with it, because, despite their size, all these dwarves had serious axes in their hands, blades sharp enough to do him damage.

When he took a step toward one of them, he felt a wave of nausea sweep through him. His grip on the axe faltered, but he clung on, got himself over the momentary dizziness, and then he gave a warning swing at his elected dwarf.

The dwarf, who had a bald patch the size of an orange at the centre of his scalp, leapt out of the way of the axe, and huddled off toward one of his companions.

John pivoted, expecting one of the other dwarves to be using this opportunity to sneak attack him from behind. But, when he looked back, he saw that the dwarves were still in the same position, both of them perspiring profusely, axes shaking in their hands. These weren't fighters. They were like John. He was certain they had never seen battle. Why would they ever have had to? With the combination of their limitless wealth, in the form of the riamand, and those bivcheks they had acquired for security, there was little need for dwarves to get blood on their hands. John took the decision.

He held out his arm and let his axe fall to the ground. Its muted *thud* reverberated round the arena and the spectators were silent—apparently unsure what this turn of events might mean for their bets. He eyed Shankle and said, "I won't slaughter innocent beings. There's no reason for it."

For the first time that evening, Shankle raised a smile. "You'll do as you're told, giant. Don't forget that I own you. You signed yourself to me, and you owe me your strength."

"I don't owe you anything," John said.

"What did you say?"

John had no intention of repeating himself. He gazed round him at the cowering dwarves, their axes clutched to their chests. Another wave of pain flooded through his muscles, made his bones feel like they might melt with the intensity.

Shankle raised his voice, obviously the situation was irritating him more and more by the second. "If you don't fight I shall put you to death."

Through all the colours waving round before him, the tinnitus whistling away in his ears, he managed a smile. "I'd like to see you try."

Shankle nodded to Frum beside him and retook his seat.

Frum shrugged off his cloak and unsheathed his sword. He sat on the ledge of the box and then dropped, his braided hair beating against the sides of his head as he did so. He fell into a crouch as he landed and bucked up onto his feet. He gnashed his teeth at John and roared forward with his blade aiming for his chest.

John ducked down and retrieved his axe, only just in time for him to beat off Frum's attack and, with pure, brute strength, to send him stumbling away from him.

Frum found his balance again quickly, but John had already spotted the box and decided that he was going to take his chances—he had no expectation of being able to match Frum's bloodthirstiness, and it would mean that he had no chance of winning the fight.

John tossed the axe in Frum's direction, not looking to hit him, only to distract him. Frum ducked the flying metal. John bolted for the box. He jumped up, feeling his blood pounding in his temples and his fingers found a grip on the ledge. As he hoisted himself upward, he spotted Shankle remove a dagger from his belt. John was ready when he launched himself into the box and he batted the dwarf's wrist away, to him it was no more than a baby's, and then he was away, escaping through the winding corridors, only a matter of paces from freedom.

Or so he hoped.

RETURNING TO AID A FRIEND

ORACE KEPT HIMSELF low on the landscape, making the best use he could of his monocular vision against the night sky. Soon he worked out a system. He would stop for about half a minute, scan the entire horizon, looking for any ominous signs, and then, not seeing anything, press onward. He was convinced that the only reason the dwarves had spotted them in their domain previously had been because they'd not been wary to their threat—not known to fear their surveillance. He wouldn't make that mistake again.

His boots crunched over gravelled ground and he knew he was drawing closer to the dwarves' main house—Shankle's mansion, or they called it. He kept his pace to a controlled rate, although he had to constantly check his excitement, realising that he was drawing closer to John. He couldn't wait to see the look on his face when he popped up to help him out of this jam.

There was a cough up ahead.

Horace ducked down in the tall grass.

Footsteps approached and then someone spoke. "When you do find him, and lock him up, I'd be most pleased to attend the execution. I never tire of witnessing the deaths of traitors to the Kingdom."

"Yes, sir, I promise you that."

The second voice was Shankle's—Horace would recognise that whiny tone anywhere. A shock of delight tingled through his veins and he knew that they could only be talking about John, who else were they holding prisoner?

"Good," the first voice said.

A horse whinnied and there was the leather-on-leather slap of one of them mounting—he supposed it was the man who had spoken first, seeing as Shankle surely had no reason to leave his home at this hour.

Now presumably mounted on the horse, the first voice continued, "I do regret that we didn't get much of an opportunity to discuss the new taxation, but I assure you that when I get some spare time on my hands—take care of whatever the trouble is back at the castle—then I shall be able to free myself to enjoy the pleasure of your hospitality once more."

"We would be most honoured, General," Shankle said.

"It's with utmost regret that I cannot aid you with the search for the giant, but I must prioritise matters of the Kingdom."

"Yes, sir, I understand that. Please, say no more about it."

"Farewell, then," the General said, giving his horse a snap of his whip.

Hooves crunched along the path, heading right for Horace.

Horace rolled over several times, hoping that he might be able to escape the horse's gait. As luck would have it, he managed to miss its hooves by a matter of several feet. He lay on his back, watching the horse disappear back into the gloom, apparently headed for the castle. Whoever that had been—that General—he had spoken with a tone of highest stuffiness, so he must've been important. It was intelligence like this, a leader being away from the garrison, that might well be invaluable to his companions' raid on the castle. But he had no way of getting the message to them right this moment, he had to save John first, and if he was free, as Shankle suggested, then it might not be quite the hardy task he had envisioned.

Once the General was clearly out of earshot, Horace overheard Shankle mutter in the common tongue, "Gods damned bloody bloodsucker. He'll gets what's coming to him if I have my way."

This was an interesting turn of events. Horace wondered whether Shankle might've been bluffing when he'd claimed absolute loyalty to the crown before. But now was hardly the time or place for a frank discussion.

Horace waited for Shankle to scrabble back off into his house before breaking cover. He shuffled along the path, keeping his eye peeled for any motion. Despite the escape attempt everything seemed quite tranquil, calm, in only the way swathes of riches could demand.

He stood before the house, looking into the porch. He eyed the railing where the General had kept his horse tied up, and wondered how different things might've been had there been a group of hungry bivcheks all waiting there. He supposed that they were trained to peck / maul first and ask questions later. Without seeing anyone around, Horace slipped into the house, keeping his back pressed up against the wall as he went, psyching himself up to bean a dwarf if it came to that.

As he worked his way along, he heard voices drifting down the corridor, among them he recognised Shankle's voice again, and he shifted onward. When he reached the doorway, he paused, telling himself that he had to stay calm and pick his moment lest he be seen.

Shankle was speaking to one of his minions in his own language, which Horace—not being a worldly Grotesque—had not a hope of comprehending. However, he picked out John's name several times during the conversation and, over and over, the words 'General Frum,' who he presumed to be one and the same as the 'General' who had just taken leave via horse. The tone was disparaging, plenty of spat consonants and hissed vowels, surely in keeping with his outburst on the porch just now.

Now seemed as good as time as any for him to get a move on with finding John, so Horace squeezed his eye shut and forced himself to make a dash past the threshold. As he passed by, he couldn't help but glance inside.

As he had imagined, Shankle, with his back to him, was barking at one of the guards. To Horace's horror, he saw the guard's gaze swiftly cross his, before snapping back to Shankle, parting his lips to warn him of the intruder. Luckily for Horace, Shankle ignored the guard's attempt to stop him in full flow and continued to sprout his vitriol. Horace trotted on down the corridor before the guard would get the chance to break his superior's lecture.

Horace soon crossed an area which featured a staircase leading down, and he recalled that this was the way he and his companions had emerged from the prison cells before heading along this very corridor and going to their freedom. He stared down into the gloom thinking that, if not for John, they would still be down there. Or worse.

He pressed on through the house, trying to extract some note of recognition from the labyrinthine, sprawling corridors, but that was futile, since he had spent no time up here. There was nothing for him to remember. And that was the reason why, Horace speculated, he ended up pushing open the door to the barracks.

Horace ogled the guards and the guards ogled Horace. He took in their neatly polished armour and axes. Several seconds passed before one of the dwarves cried out and Horace's brain reminded his feet that they should be moving, fast.

He sprinted off along the corridors with no destination in mind. Their yells bounced off the walls, snapping at his heels and pressing him on. He rushed past a few quite beautiful courtyards replete with fountains and marbled arched ways, but he had no appreciation for them. Not right now.

He reached the bottom of a spiral staircase. He snatched the railing and hauled himself upward, easily taking the dwarf steps three or four at a time. The top of his head brushed the steps above him and he caught his skull on a few of them, sending reverberations pounding through his brain. He heard the dwarves' steps patter along behind him and knew that, sooner or later, they would catch him, find a way to corner him, and he would be put to death, because there was no John to save him now.

He got to the top of the stairs and wheeled onward, noting the various rooms on either side of him and wondering whether he should duck inside one and hideout till the search died down. The most effective way to escape his pursuers would be to get out of the house and so he had to look for some exit, perhaps an open window to hurl himself out of. If he could get out he might be able to leave them confused, before they could prepare the bivcheks or those contraptions which shot fireballs.

When he looked behind him, he saw three dwarves running after him. Under other circumstances he might've found the sight quite amusing, their beards waggling and their already rosy cheeks impossibly flushed. But now he was struck down by abject terror and loathing that they might, somehow, get hold of him. And then a hand reached out of the gloom and grabbed him.

Horace's neck snapped back as he was drawn into one of the doorways. When he got his thoughts together, enough to look about him, and realised that it wasn't a dwarf that had got hold of him, he saw that, in fact, staring right back at him was John.

Blood stunk out their hiding place and when Horace looked John over, in the half-light, he saw that he had many wounds, all over his body. He wanted to ask his friend what had happened to him, whether or not Shankle had succeeded in making him fight or if he had been beaten, but he was distracted by the mumbling dwarves who now seemed impossibly close.

"I think they've found us," John said, just as a dwarf arrived in the doorway, his axe dangling from his fingers with a gurn plastered across his face.

It took seven dwarves to move them off down the corridor: two for Horace and five for John, with whom they obviously weren't taking any chances. As they made their way along Horace established that John *had* been forced into the fighting ring, but, against all odds, had managed to escape without harming anyone. That made Horace glad, even despite their capture and seemingly perilous situation, he was happy that his friend hadn't needed to sully his soul for their benefit.

Instead of taking them off down to the prisons, the dwarves bundled them off in the direction of the room in which Horace had seen Shankle. And, so it turned out, they were to be brought before Shankle, who stood with his hands on his hips and with his steely gaze, looking them over. First he glanced at John. "The big ones are never the brightest. I knew we'd capture you eventually." He examined his pristine fingernails, which looked like some poor manicurist slaved over every morning. "Most of those with your form learn how to fight, however, how to spill blood." He glared at John. "You really are a complete failure."

The words seemed to have no impact on John, he just kept up his directionless gaze, apparently at peace with whatever fate was about to befall him.

Horace, on the other hand, was seething that Shankle would dare make this remark to his best friend. He loosened his arms from the grip of his dwarf guards. "He's a better person than you'll ever be."

Shankle smiled faintly. "I am not a person, I am a dwarf."

Horace guessed he had a point there.

Shankle strutted from side-to-side, seemingly enjoying this situation, being able to play the villain—a part which became him. "You shall both face execution tomorrow morning, at first light." He sneered. "By bivchek."

Horace's stomach knotted at the thought of being pecked apart by those monsters. It was a horrible way to go, but he supposed it was really all the same in the end. He would have to die somehow, so why not by bivchek? There was the advantage that he would never remember the pain, after the whole horrid experience was over and done with.

Shankle spoke to the guards. His message turned out to be something along the lines of 'take them away,' since they were promptly hustled off in the direction of the corridor. Just before the guards could get them out of the door, Horace said, "We're just as against the new administration as you are. When our people are in charge there'll be tax breaks for all, especially dwarves."

Shankle chuckled. "You'll never be in charge. Tomorrow you'll be dead."

"We will be if that's how you want it, but our group are making their way to the castle with a white witch among them. They would help your cause if only you'll spare us. You could join with us. With your bivcheks you could greatly strengthen our hopes at bringing about a revolution."

Shankle barked an order and the dwarf guards brought the procession to a halt. He swaggered up to Horace and stared right into his eye. "I have always been a faithful servant to the King, whatever gave you the impression that I might be interested in committing such an act of treason?"

Horace kept calm, seeing that he had a golden opportunity here, that Shankle had shown something of his true emotions. He shrugged a bit more slack from the grip of his guards and said, "You're speaking as if the King's still alive, when he's dead and gone."

Shankle stared at him, his eyes calculating. "I still respect the crown."

"Even a Queen?"

Shankle's resolve cracked a touch, but still he remained humourless. He nodded to the guards who, in turn, dragged them along the corridor, down the stairs and into the familiar prisons.

As before, Horace and John were led to separate cells. Horace's newly assigned cell was nothing short of the standard of his previous one, in fact, in one corner, he noted that he had a bubbling hot spring, steaming away. His last hours on Ethereal would be comfortable indeed. Not having anything else to do, he stripped off and slipped into it, closing his eye and trying to forget that tomorrow he would be dead.

A little after dinner had been served—slices of spiced beef and tomato soup—he lay back on his ridiculously comfortable bed and watched the sun slink below the horizon, setting the whole hillside in a dashing pink glow. This would be the last sunset he'd ever witness, but he decided that he didn't feel all the sentimental about it. After he was dead life would go on. At least he had had a bit of adventuring, got to see the outside world, met some interesting people and creatures—some more blood-thirsty than others. The sun disappeared from view and, like a veil of coal dust, darkness draped over everything, snuffing out every last trace of light. He rolled over on his side and tried to slip off to sleep.

Three steady knocks at his door woke him with a jolt.

Horace rubbed his eye and stared into the gloom, realising that whoever was at his door was waiting for him to invite them in. Once again, he thought that if all prisons were like this then it was no wonder that people committed crimes, stole from each other, murdered. He gave his visitor permission and the door opened with a *squeak*.

Shankle, bearing a lantern, strode into the room.

Horace straightened up in bed, resting his back against the headboard. "What time is it?" he said, instantly feeling a little stupid for having asked the question.

"A few hours from dawn."

"Have you come to prepare me for execution?"

Shankle declined to answer. Still bearing the lantern, he trod across the prison cell and over to the window, where he looked out into the impenetrable darkness. "So you overheard my conversation with General Frum?"

Not really knowing what else to say, and quite glad at any opportunity he'd have to converse with Shankle and thereby, perhaps, manage to bargain his freedom, Horace said, "Yes."

"Hmm," Shankle said, continuing to stare out the window. "And you reached the conclusion that I might well be willing to work against the Queen's interest? To go against the Throne of Ethereal?"

"It was only an assumption, I apologise if I offended you in any way."

Shankle grunted, apparently satisfied at this.

Horace scratched up the courage to be direct with Shankle. "There's only one reason you're down here, isn't there? I mean, there's no other reason for you to visit a condemned man a few hours from death."

"And what reason is that?"

"You want to join us in storming the castle. You want to set things straight and assure your people's future."

Shankle laid the lantern down on the window ledge and planted his stubby arms on either side of it. Still with his back to Horace, staring out into the nothingness, he said, "My *people* have become accustomed to a particular way of life. The previous King was very much interested in the production of riamand, and was keen that we, the dwarves, should profit from our expertise at extraction. He was a fair man, whatever else people say—said—about him.

"As I understand things, the state of the Kingdom, there's a lot of confusion. It seems that there is no obvious heir to the throne and that there's great uncertainty in all parts. I believe, and this is just my own speculation, that General Frum has designs on the Throne. He wishes to take the whole Kingdom for himself. His visit here was supposed to be one of pleasure, with some gambling involving your big-boned companion, but it only served to plant more doubts in my mind. Both to Frum's intentions and the future of the Kingdom itself."

Horace could hardly contain himself, so swept up was he in where all Shankle's words were leading. He couldn't resist butting in. "So, you'll join us on our quest to the castle?"

Shankle turned round. A sliver of a smile passed over his lips. "I have always been a faithful subject, never wavering. But I must draw the line at tyrants and pretenders, I must not allow those other than the divinely appointed to occupy the Throne."

Horace's breath hitched in his throat.

There was a pregnant pause and then Shankle said, "I shall grant you a reprieve."

ON CASTLE ROAD

T REVOR WAS STILL fighting off the effects of the namtra days later. His feet felt like they were imbedded in blocks of lead and it was a constant battle to keep his eyes from folding down on themselves. Everything seemed to be a slog. The straps holding the new sword and shield to his frame dug into his skin. Whenever he reached the end of a day's hike and snuck off to a nearby stream to have a wash, he would observe the deeply ingrained red marks where the straps had rested.

During one such instance, just after he had finished with his daily inspection of the chafe marks and was in the process of draping his tunic back over his head, anticipating a delicious dinner of rabbit, prepared by Plont, would await him when he returned to the camp, he was caught off guard by the sight of Susan, on a bank, several feet downstream. She was totally naked and bathing herself. Totally naked, that was, apart from the many inches of fur which covered her entire body.

Just as Trevor was turning away, out of politeness, she called out to him. Reluctantly, he swivelled and gave her a limp-wristed wave.

She gestured for him to join her, to get back into the water.

Although Trevor could hear the crackle of burning wood back at the camp, he knew that he would still be in for a long wait before dinner was ready, so he didn't have anywhere else to be. After a brief pause, he shrugged off his tunic once more, a little self-conscious of his pasty torso and its various wobbly bits. Needless to say, he splashed into the water like time was going out of style and then swam, with his best doggy paddle, to reach Susan.

By the time he reached her, Susan was wringing out her hair —the hair on her head. "I caught you looking."

Trevor fumbled for words. "Oh . . . I . . . it's just—"

She giggled, the first time he had heard her laugh in days, ever since Horace had drifted away from the group on his mission to save John, then said, "The only reason I wear clothes is because I feel like I fit in more. But, like this"—she flapped her hands over her body—"I feel much more natural, there's no shame about being naked because I know that everything, for better or worse, is covered up completely."

"Right," Trevor said, "I suppose that is a point."

Susan floated onto her back, so that her hairy chest, beneath which were nestle her breasts, fobbed along the surface. She stared up into the evening sky. "Sometimes I wonder whether this curse was really a gift in disguise, you know? Before, when I was just a normal woman, I was so awkward, never sure whether or not I looked as beautiful as the day before. Now I know that I'm a freak so there's no doubt about it. I know that I'm not attractive."

Trevor felt that here common politeness called for him to make a comment. So he did. "Oh, I really don't know what you're talking about. I think you're really quite a charming lady."

She smirked at him. "That's very kind of you to say so, but I know that you don't really mean it. Don't feel like you need to hold any pretences with me."

Trevor kept quiet, knowing that nothing good could come of criticising a woman. Instead he chose to focus on the unnaturally clear water which washed against his body, reminiscent of that water the first day he had arrived in Ethereal. He decided that now was time to change the subject, and so said, "And what about Horace?"

The sparkle in Susan's eye dimmed. She shook her head.

"I suppose he'll be with John now," he said, not realising that, the way he put it, left open the possibility that they both might both be dead—with their gods in the heavens, or whatever they called the afterlife in Ethereal.

Susan brought her hand out of the water. Drops dripped from her fingertips, splashing onto the surface, sending off chains of tiny, interlinked ripples. "If Shankle finds Horace on his land, he will kill him."

Now thoroughly regretting having brought up the subject, Trevor attempted to steer the conversation into silence. "Hmm, yes, that might well be the case."

"But I don't think Shankle will find him. I've got a feeling that they're both going to be okay—it's something I can't explain."

"Magic?" Trevor said, trying to get with the programme.

"No, nothing like that. Something inexplicable."

Trevor thought that, of what he had seen so far, magic was relatively inexplicable.

Susan continued, "I just know that they're both fine, and that they'll return to us."

This was better than having to comfort a crying woman, so Trevor allowed her to relieve herself with these fancied imaginings. Being a pragmatist, and having witnessed first hand the truly diabolical nature of that dwarf, Shankle, he had grave doubts that he would hesitate for a moment to use extreme force against either of them: either those bivcheks or fireballs. The dwarves might conceivably lower themselves to the level of using their own axes to inflict the damage, but, if Trevor had learnt one thing of the rich over the years it was that they shirked physical violence whenever possible—in favour of delegating to one of their inferiors when the prospect of a blood-on-hands dilemma arose.

They floated about in the river for a while, until a steady voice, Zend's, called them for dinner. Trevor politely splashed for the shore so as to leave Susan with some semblance of privacy, no matter what she had just told him. There was more to privacy than not showing off private parts.

Even so, when he reached the bank, the one on which his own clothes rested, he glanced back over his shoulder to see Susan there, unmoving, lying on her back floating on the surface of the water, her hairy front exposed as she stared up into the sky.

As he squeezed his head through the narrow neck of his tunic, he wondered what she might be thinking about. He thought that Horace and John couldn't be far from her mind, so maybe she was colouring in her delusion of them, lying to herself that they were still alive and / or still had a hope of survival. Trevor considered his being an outsider as something of a 'gift and a curse,' as Susan had put it, as he was allowed a degree of detachment from all affairs, relationships and such—he could see things objectively, notice a no-hope situation when he saw one, as he did now with Horace and John. They were gone and, soon, he would be too—preferably back to Earth.

They trekked on into the afternoon sun. Damp patches broke out at Trevor's armpits and around the straps which held his sword and shield in place. As it had for the whole of their journey, it seemed like the others were going about a pace and a half faster than Trevor could manage. Just when his dejection and fatigue were getting the better of him, up ahead, at the front of the group, of course, Zend called out, declaring that they had come across Castle Road. When Trevor caught up, in his own plodding manner, he saw that Zend's assertion was correct. There was a stone brandished into the dusty path. Although Trevor couldn't understand the notation he was prepared to take Zend's word for it that it did indeed announce Castle Road.

Despite this, very literal, milestone, they made no event of it, continuing on their way, perhaps with a little added vigour in their collective stride. Trevor went through periods of feeling his whole body go numb and little muscles, that he previously had never heard from, tweaked and nagged. On the point of asking for them to take a recess, just for a moment, they popped up over a shallow hill to see a cottage in the valley down below, a tame stream running beside it, and Zend declared that they would ask hospitality of the owner and seek shelter for the night.

Apart from the pins and needles jabbing themselves into the soles of Trevor's feet, he found that the way down was fairly painless, since he had the knowledge that when they reached this cottage there would be no more marching for the rest of the day. And it would've been all the more simple if not for the inhabitant of the cottage slipping out of the door and proceeding to chuck plates at them.

The first dish whistled just over Trevor's head and crashed into fragments of crockery as it landed. Trevor turned his attention to the inhabitant of the cottage. He saw that the man was fairly young, perhaps in his mid-twenties, and he had quite a dainty frame which reminded him of a baby bird. However, without fail, the man was putting all his effort into each dish he hurled in their direction. Trevor had to admire his hardiness.

The man kept up this barrage of plates as the group, inevitably being thirty or forty strong, strode onward relatively unperturbed, down to his cottage.

One or two of the plates caught Grotesque, one even clipped Zend's shoulder. When it struck, Zend wasted no time in drawing his sword and waving it about in the air, declaring that he would have the man's head. Despite this threat, the man refused to give up his bombardment.

As they trickled down the slope and over the bridge, which led to the cottage, the man gave up the ghost and retreated into his home, leaving the remaining pile of dishes in an unsteady pile.

Trevor held back, not wanting to get himself involved in whatever violent activity Zend was about to involve himself. So, he picked himself out a nice flat rock and took a seat, glancing up in anticipation at the cottage, into which Zend disappeared, in pursuit of the fiend.

The rest of the group all waited along with Trevor, everyone mumbling among themselves, most of them wanting to know—like Trevor—what had been the motive of this deranged individual in throwing crockery at them.

Finally, Zend emerged from the cottage gripping the man by the back of the collar of his tunic, like a copper nicking a ruffian. He ruffled him up and then shoved him before them, standing to one side in expectation.

The man scratched his arm and eyeballed the ground.

"Go on, then," Zend said. "Explain yourself!"

The man delayed things further by appearing to pick out an especially interesting piece of ground, and to give it a particularly determined stare.

Zend tapped him on the arm. "Come on."

The man tilted his head back and examined the group of them, squinting a little. He looked over each. "I didn't realise there were going to be so many."

"So many what?" Zend said.

"You know, so many heroes."

Zend narrowed his eyes. "How do you know we're heroes?"

"Well," the man said, "you're all armed to the teeth and you're coming along here, Castle Road, what else are you? You don't think that just anyone would march on the castle. No," he said, shaking his head, "you're all definitely heroes."

"Actually," Zend said, "technically, that one over there"—he pointed to Trevor—"is the hero. The rest of us are just the support team."

Trevor's heart sank. What on . . . Ethereal was Zend doing in getting him mixed up with this weirdo? He interlocked his fingers and wondered what might be coming next, hoping that this wasn't going to be some sort of side quest. He had had enough of side quests. Now he was on his way to completing his own mission, getting back to Earth, and he could do without any further complications, thank you very much.

The man met Trevor's eye then gave him a curt nod. "Oh right, my apologies. He was the one that I was supposed to take care of."

"'Take care of?'" Trevor said.

"Yeah," the man said, sounding a little uncertain. "I'm the Dishwaster, you see? I was put here to stop any heroes trying to march on the castle, or at least delay them somewhat."

"And what're you going to do now?" Zend said. "Considering that you've failed to stop us."

The man rubbed his nose. "Oh, I don't know. I suppose I did my best." He looked round at the group once more. "It's just that I had no idea there'd be so many of you."

"May we use your cottage to make ourselves comfortable, then?"

The man shrugged. "All right. I don't see why not."

So, one-by-one, each of them visited the interior of the cottage. Still not entirely trusting this man, especially since he had just admitted that it was him he was after, Trevor stayed back from the others, quite content to forgo the grand tour. But, after everyone had been inside to have a look, the man emerged again then looked to Trevor. He gestured for him to come in, and Trevor, not wanting to be rude, relinquished his stubbornness and indulged the man.

As Trevor passed over the threshold, the man reached out and tapped him on the shoulder. "You're not from Earth, are you?"

A little taken aback by the directness of the question, Trevor blinked a couple of times then said, "Yes, how did you know?"

"Got that look about you."

"What look?"

"That dazed and confused one, beleaguerment really, like you're not totally clued up on what's going on."

"I hadn't realised it was that obvious."

"Taking a stroll in Rutsley Church and Burial Grounds, were you?"

Even more taken aback at this insight, Trevor said, "Yes, actually, how did you know?"

"Simple," the man said, grinning, "I'm from Earth too."

"Oh, I see."

It transpired that the man—or 'Dishwaster,' as he was known—had come into Ethereal several years before. In his previous life, back on Earth, he revealed that he had been a dishwasher, but not a particularly successful one. In fact, he had just been sacked from his job when a Time Nymph had offered him the job / kidnapped him from Earth and brought him here, and, before promptly vanishing, had outlined his new role as a permanent obstacle to heroes who might be making their way to the castle.

Not an effective obstacle, as it turned out, but an obstacle none-theless.

Trevor was rendered a touch speechless following the story. He rubbed his flaky scalp, even more flaky following the days and days of hiking in the hot sun. "Haven't you ever thought about returning, going back to Earth?"

Dishwaster reclined against his stove, on which a kettle was bubbling away, its sprout puffing out a steady jet of steam. "At first it was a bit of a change, sure, but to be honest I don't think that I've ever looked back. I mean look at this place," he said throwing up a hand to indicate the room. "There's an open fire-place, wood-burning stove, comfortable bed, nice and big, and there's fresh herbs out in the garden. If I want meat then I go out and hunt something. *This* is the life."

Trevor couldn't doubt that this place, when placed in comparison with washing dishes, did seem to have a lot going for it. And he supposed the mundanity and thankless nature of the task compared favourably with Dishwaster's previous occupation.

"So," Dishwaster said, hooking the handle of the kettle and pouring out some cups of tea, one for each of their party, which only served to shed light on the depth and variety of his crockery stash, "where're you headed?"

"To the castle, like you said."

"And what're you going to do when you get there?"

"Well, I'm just looking to find a way to get home really."

"Portal in the castle?"

"So they tell me."

Dishwaster reached the end of a line of mugs and then went back along the next, his forehead riddled with wrinkles as he concentrated on not splashing hot water all over the place.

Trevor thought it polite to ask, so he did. "Say, you wouldn't be interested in returning to Earth, you know, coming back with me, would you?"

Dishwaster let out a high pitched giggle—a giggle which revealed that he obviously didn't spend much time in the company of others. "Thanks, but no thanks," he said. "Ethereal's the only world for me. Oh, sure, I'll always have a special place in my heart for Earth, it's my home world after all, but it's just nothing in comparison with being here."

"But there's no medical care, or real infrastructure, and, well, magic's just sort of running loose about the place. Are you sure that you're really happy about being here?"

Dishwasher finished another line of cups and smirked. "Spoken like someone who's never done a twelve-hour dish-washing shift. Back there, on Earth, I have no prospects, a dirty old flat and a bunch of debt, here I've got my own idyllic cottage and I get to spend ninety-nine per cent of my time on my weaving."

Only now did Trevor notice the various tapestries adorning the walls, depicting flowers growing in the wild, a few of the river outside, and one—much larger—of the cottage itself, chimney smoking away cosily.

Dishwasher poured out the final cup of tea and then replaced the kettle on the stove.

Trevor wondered what sort of capacity that kettle had, and how it had been possible to pour so many cups of tea and then he decided that it must be 'bewitched' or 'charmed,' or some-thing like that, so he didn't bother asking the question.

"Give us a hand?" Dishwaster said, jabbing his fingers through the handles of the mugs, taking about six or seven in one go.

Trevor did help him to take the mugs outside where he took up a position away from the others, back on the rock he had sat on before. As he blew on his tea, sending up swirls of steam, he thought back to his life on Earth, what he would be missing. It seemed a long time ago now when he had sat on that wooden bench, munching on his sandwich and considering his impending retirement. His mind traced back to his wife, Mavis, and he wondered what she might be doing right at that moment. He recalled what he had been told about time not moving back on Earth while he was in Ethereal, that he could return home whenever he wished. Why *was* he in such a hurry to get back? Whenever he chose to go back, his life—or the small portion remaining of it—would be awaiting him. Then again, there was a significant problem here, in Ethereal, and that was that he had a large chance of being killed. Who knew whether he would still be alive by next week?

Right now he supposed that Mavis might be doing the washing up, moving so slowly as to seem to not be moving at all. Her hand gripping a mug, rubber-gloved hand sticking into it, bubbles slopping out over the side—the image in stasis. Out of the blue, he felt a tear prickle at the corner of his eye. He wiped it away quickly, before anyone could notice. Here he was supposed to be a hero and that was who he would be until such a time as he managed to get out of Ethereal.

Although Dishwaster's cottage was fairly spacious, there wasn't enough room for the entire party—not by a long shot— and so the set up camp on the soft grassy tufts surrounding the house. Dishwaster then invited a choice selection inside: Zend, Plont, Yvonne and Trevor.

As Trevor made his way toward the house, thinking fondly of that fire which would keep him warm all night, albeit on the floor, when he caught Rabbit King's eye. He didn't look mightily impressed by the state of affairs, no doubt a little miffed that he was not among the invitees. Trevor gave him a carefree shrug and then trailed along on the others' heels, into the house.

In the middle of the night Trevor heard footsteps and he stirred from where he slept on the floor. He looked to Dishwaster, who was already on his feet, looking out the window of the cottage intently, like a spooked guard dog.

Dishwaster caught Trevor's eye. "Looks like I've got a night-shift," he said, and stooped down to fish through the cabinet for a fresh batch of plates. Once he'd got hold of them he stole out of the house.

Not wanting to miss out on whatever it was that was happening, Trevor led on behind him, into the darkness.

Dishwaster crouched down low at the river, keeping a watch on the path coming down the mountain on the other side. He clutched a plate in his hand, ready to chuck it.

The people walking along the path didn't speak as they went, the crunching of gravel beneath their feet was the only sound in the otherwise silent night. Their forms were no more than silhouettes in the gloom.

Dishwaster leant into Trevor. "Take a plate if you like."

Trevor eyed the stack of plates, thought about it then said, "No, thanks, I'll just watch."

The people got closer, still silent. When they got within a few steps of the bridge, Dishwaster hopped up and tossed a plate. It whistled through the air and struck one of the people. Strangely, despite the *tinkle* of broken crockery confirming the strike, there was no other action from the people. No shouts. Nothing except for a hurried motion between them, a sense of panic rippling through the ranks.

Dishwaster was stunned for a couple of seconds before he got a grip of himself, then he got a grip on another plate and threw.

Again it found a target but, like the time before it, there was no sound whatsoever.

"Why aren't they screaming?" Trevor said.

Dishwaster looked wide-eyed, but his only response was to toss yet another plate, finding a third target.

The people were in a panic now, all of them rushing about aimlessly. Just as the first made to cross the bridge, Trevor made out the form and realised that it was a Beaverman, just like Rick, the one who had fled with them from the black magic.

Trevor tugged on Dishwaster's sleeve, unfortunately not in time to prevent him throwing another plate, and subsequently finding the luckless leader of the group, who went down on his knees, grasping his skull. He explained what was going on and that was the end of the dishwasting for the time being.

Trevor rushed back to the camp and roused Sydney who came running at the word 'Beaverman.' Together they returned to the riverbank where the Beavermen were collecting themselves together following the barrage.

"Can we get a light on this?" Trevor said.

Dishwaster mumbled something then stomped off to his cottage from which he returned bearing a lantern in his fist. He shone the light on the victims of his dishes. The four victims were all easy to identify since they were surrounded by their companions, all of them gesticulating wildly.

"I'll take care of this," Sydney said, skittering off to get among them, waving around and pulling all manner of faces.

"Is he all right?" Dishwaster said.

"I think so," Trevor said, not completely convinced.

Sydney spent a while with the Beavermen, clearly consoling them on what had just happened and, more difficult, trying to explain why it had happened. Several times he pointed off to Dishwaster and Trevor. That worried Trevor because—were it to turn ugly—they might mistake him as the culprit, rather than Dishwaster. However, Sydney had success in placating the Beavermen, as evidenced by the solemn nods being exchanged among the crowd. Sydney returned to them with a grim expression.

"What is it?" Dishwaster said.

"They've just come from the Damned Forests," Sydney said.

"Where's that?"

Trevor took it upon himself to explain the matter to Dishwaster, believing that his Earth view might afford more insight as compared with that of an Etherealean. It was quite strange to think that Dishwaster hadn't thought to venture any further from his cottage—to not go out and see the wide world. But, Trevor supposed, Dishwaster was content with his situation and never bothered with ideas of travel.

Once Trevor wrapped up his explanation, Dishwaster went

all doe-eyed, especially at the mention of magic, and then said, "Oh."

"My thoughts exactly," Trevor said, then turned matters back to Sydney who continued to relate the story.

"They say that the black magicians tore the whole place down, and that the Beavermen were forced to flee. They've been following this path for days."

"What about the dwarves?" Trevor said.

Sydney shrugged. "They said they have an understanding with them, they asked permission, talked to the right people."

Trevor wondered whether he might not have saved himself a great deal of fuss if he'd gone with Rick instead.

Sydney continued, "Anyway, I've explained that we're going to the castle and they'd like to join us. You see, they understand that the black magicians intend to march on the castle, that was where they were headed after taking care of the Forests. They hear that we have Yvonne, the whitest witch, among us and believe that she can lead them forward."

"She'll be thrilled to hear it," Trevor said. "Have they got any weapons?"

One of the Beavermen trod forward. Trevor recognised him as Rick, his distinctive mouse-like whiskers and beady black eyes. As if he had understood what Trevor had said, he pulled aside a coat of fur to reveal a rapier.

Trevor nodded. "Looks like we're all set then. We can use all the help we can get."

A KEY, AN ATTACK AND A QUEEN

B OOTFALLS SLAPPED down the hard corridor. Alexis waited with bated breath at her chamber door. She didn't dare look for fear that it could be one of the men of the garrison, come to take her down to the dungeons. She closed her eyes and prayed to whatever gods there were in Ethereal.

Arnold peeked in round the door. He was dressed in his armour, his sword hanging from his waist.

"Did you get it?" Alexis said.

Arnold rummaged in the breast pocket of his tunic and plucked out a key. He broke into a mischievous grin.

Alexis clapped her hands together then reminded herself that she had to keep her voice low, lest the guards standing at her door hear her and come to investigate what had agitated the excitement—she supposed that they had strict orders that she was not to have entertainment or leisure of any kind, that she was to remain miserable until further notice.

"What now?" Arnold said, eyes wild.

Alexis hadn't thought about what might happen to Arnold. She was sure that she wanted to escape this nightmare, get back to her real world: Earth, but could she really leave Arnold behind to face the consequences? The guilt would wrench her apart.

"Where do you see your future? Here in Ethereal or with me, at my side?"

"Why, ma'am, that's a silly question. Of course I shall serve at your side, until your death."

That was the answer that she had more or less been expecting, although the 'your death' part struck her as a little morbid. "You see, my world's very different to Ethereal."

"How so?"

Alexis really had no time to sit here and explain everything to him, but wouldn't it be unfair of her to force him into a decision without having laid out the full facts before him? Then again, Ethereal wasn't one of those places which bothered itself much with facts, so she thought she might be all right.

"Oh," she said, "just this and that. Small things."

Arnold grinned again. "As long as I'm by your side I know that my life's purpose shall be etched in stone. That is all that concerns me."

"All right, then, we'd better push on."

As they moved through the darkened castle, Alexis clasped Arnold's hand tight, steering him round the corners and keeping him close to her heels, worried that someone—one of the guards —might reach out and snatch him from her if she wasn't careful.

They got down the various staircases without bumping into any guards and they emerged into the courtyard, where she was aware of the men of the garrison up on the ramparts. As they had been over the last few days, though, they were facing outward, keeping an eye on the group which had been steadily approaching the castle across the plains. She didn't understand, if Frum was really all that worried about them, why he didn't just send a scout group to work out what they wanted. They weren't the men who had gone missing in the Forests, that was for sure. The whole castle seemed to be gripped in anticipation. The guards clutched their spears with whitened knuckles and were short-tempered with her.

Maintaining her caution, Alexis skirted the castle walls, keeping herself and Arnold within the shadows. She plotted the map of the castle in her mind, reminding herself that the grave-yard was located in the north. All she had to do was use the key to open it up and then feel her way through the gravestones till she found the one that sent her to the End of Time.

They reached the rusty iron gate and Alexis stuck the key into the aged mechanism then twisted. The mechanism groaned mournfully and she barged the gate with her shoulder. It remained stuck. She gave it another barge, then Arnold asked her to allow him to try. With his face contorted, Arnold rushed the gate and it sprang open, vibrating back on its hinges. It clanked into the wall with great force, and Alexis was sure that just about every soul in the castle had heard it.

She grabbed hold of Arnold and held him close to her, eyes skimming over the battlements.

One of the guards cried out and another shouted back in reply. There were several footfalls along the ramparts. Alexis considered running, but surely if she did that they would shoot first and ask questions later—claiming that they'd killed the Queen only by accident, for all its convenience in getting Frum onto the throne. Most likely no one would ask questions. No, Alexis and Arnold had to stay out of sight until the frenzy simmered down.

The guards continued to speak excitedly among themselves, still stamping their boots. Alexis established, after she had been standing there with Arnold for several minutes, that the guards were headed for the south side of the castle, in the opposite direction to where they stood. This was her chance, they were distracted by those invaders, surely the ones who had been camped out on the landscape. She grabbed Arnold tight and steered him into the graveyard.

Not seeing any other logical place to start with her search, Alexis touched the first gravestone she came across. Nothing. She looked over the rest of the graveyard. There were at least a hundred tombstones, kings and queens, perhaps some of their uncrowned children, she had to keep moving. She got onto the next tombstone. Again, nothing. The next yielded the same results. And the next. And the next.

"Should we split up?" Arnold said.

"No," Alexis said, with a harshness to her tone, "we have to stay together."

Arnold made no further suggestion as he bounded along beside her, still holding her hand.

Alexis heard the first crossbow bolt fire. She jerked her head upward to look, feeling that it had been shot right beside her ear, but, no, it was off at the south side of the castle, as she had suspected. That only strengthened her resolve to get out of Ethereal as soon as possible, to escape from this attack— although, on balance, the invaders surely couldn't be any worse than General Frum.

They kept on going through the gravestones, making their way through the first dozen, and then the next. Still nothing. Alexis wondered whether or not she was doing the right thing, if she had to mutter some magic words or something. She literally had to pinch herself, to remind herself that she wasn't in fact Alice in 'Wonderland,' but Alexis in Ethereal.

Muffled voices drifted up from the other side of the wall. Alexis looked round, to see if there might be men of the garrison above her, pointing their weapons down, ready to fire. But there was no one, which led her to the conclusion that those voices on the other side of the wall must've been the intruders.

She quickened her pace, zipping between gravestones, desperately waiting for that sinking feeling she had experienced so long ago before being whipped through space and time to Ethereal. With her other hand she clung onto Arnold, knowing that he would accompany her wherever she went.

Green-white light crackled through the air, illuminating the graveyard.

A shudder ran up Alexis's spine. Her mind told her to continue about her way, to keep on going through the gravestones, but she stood, transfixed. That light had reminded her of a firework, but in all her time in Ethereal she had never seen anything like it. So what had it been?

Arnold, too, was gazing up at the phenomenon as it faded. "What was that?" he said.

Alexis returned to her senses. "I don't know, but I think we'd better get out of here before we find out." When she dragged Arnold after him, he planted his feet, unmoving from the spot. "Come on!" she said. "There's not much time."

Arnold refused to move, however, still rooted in place.

She tugged at his arm and then, reluctantly, followed his gaze up to the castle wall, where a group of people stood, looking down on them. At first she was certain that they were the men of the garrison, but, as another rocket of light illuminated the gloom and she saw that they wore no uniforms, and that there were women among them. The invaders.

This did nothing to lessen her resolve, so she gave Arnold an extra strong tug, this time succeeding in yanking him from his daze, and together they stumbled on among the gravestones.

"I'd stop right where you are, if I were you."

It was a male voice, one of the people up on the wall. As instructed, as if spellbound, Alexis turned and looked up. She felt a knot form in her throat, swallowed it back then said, "I'm the Queen of Ethereal, in case you hadn't noticed, and I shall do whatever I please within the confines of my own castle."

"Who says it's your castle?"

Through the phosphorescent glow she made out his form: his tweed jacket, the black and green plaid trousers, the shoulder-length hair which draped onto his shoulders like cobwebs. She supposed this must be some villager, part of the intruders— perhaps peasants—who had come to take back what they had paid for with their taxes. Under any other set of circumstances, Alexis might've empathised with them. As it was, however, with her own neck on the line and desperately searching for some exit route out of Ethereal, she didn't.

Alexis elected to stay silent for the moment. Looking round at the graveyard she saw that there were maybe twenty or so more gravestones to try. If she just got a little more time she was sure that she would find the portal she needed.

"What're you doing here?" the man said. "Why aren't you up in your bedchamber being pampered by your various maids?"

Through gritted teeth, Alexis said, "They're taking a break tonight."

The man chuckled, then nodded to his companions. All at once, they levitated from their places and floated in the air, staying still a few moments as if giving Alexis the opportunity to appreciate this miracle. Then they swooped down the whole matter of forty or fifty feet, their hair fluttering in the wind, and landed right before Arnold and Alexis as if they had merely jumped the last step of staircase. The man at the front of the group seemed to be pleased with this display and he smirked at Alexis, saying, "They keep you cooped up here, don't they, Your Highness? Never tell you the real story about what's been going on in the Kingdom? How magic is going to rule over everything from now on."

From behind them, within the castle, there was a yelp from one of the men of the garrison, followed by a stampede of booted feet. When Alexis cast a glance upward she saw that, this time, the men were on their way, that they had noticed the intruders making their entrance into the castle. For the first time since being Queen she actually felt relieved at seeing her soldiers.

There were several of them, all armed with crossbows, some with their swords drawn, all of them looking down into the graveyard. "That's them!" one of the soldiers called out, indicating the people who stood before Alexis.

"They've got the Queen!" added another.

Alexis thought that much was apparent, but, then again, she didn't suppose men of the garrison were picked for their brains.

"Careful, Your Majesty," the first soldier said. "They're witches and wizards!"

She had just about established that too. The question was, though, how was she going to extricate herself from this situation and, more importantly, get her hands on the right gravestone?

The leader of the group held out his hand. "My name's Maxeth, very pleased to meet you, ma'am, all I've heard has been on the grapevine, but as I understand it you were previously the King's whore?"

Alexis glared at the outstretched hand. Who did this 'wizard,' Maxeth, think he was? Did he not realise that she had half the garrison at her back, no doubt getting him in their sights, preparing to let their arrows and bolts fly?

"That's the gist of it," Alexis said.

"And I understand that General Frum has taken it upon himself to install himself here as something of a de facto leader?"

"More or less."

"Ah," Maxeth said, with a nod, then he cast his eyes over the garrison men, all of whom had their weapons pointing at him. "Very well," he said to them. "Do you really want to fight us? Your physical force against our magic?"

There were murmurings of discontent among the garrison men.

"Where's your leader?" he said.

Louder murmuring, but no concrete answer.

Maxeth let out a sigh and then shot Alexis a glance. "You'd better hop along, I can foresee this reducing itself to blows. Things might get ugly."

Frantic, Alexis looked round the graveyard, at the gravestones. Just a few more and she would have the answer. No way could she leave. "I'm not going," she said.

"Please, Your Highness. To be honest I have no real beef with you, no intention of hurting you. Frum is the one we want, because once he's out of the way we'll be able to take all the power we need."

Alexis felt the weight of the collective gaze of the men of the garrison on her back. This was her opportunity to take a stand, to beat Frum once and for all, to show the men that she had what it took to be a leader, and she might as well leave them with a good impression before slipping back to Earth. "No," she said.

Maxeth sighed again. He raised his finger and wiggled it. Several white sparks danced around it before settling into his fingertip, which he then jabbed in Alexis's direction. Sparks shot out and wrapped themselves round her legs, forcing them to move up and down spasmodically. Before she knew it, Alexis's legs were marching her toward the exit of the graveyard and back toward the castle. When she glanced over her shoulder she saw that Arnold was following close behind, the same spell cast on him. She looked to the garrison men who were all open-mouthed, stunned by this display. She wished to order them to run but she knew that they wouldn't listen to her—not least because Maxeth had embarrassed her in front of them.

***

The magic continued to work away at her legs, driving her on, even when she got inside the castle. She assumed that Maxeth had got his hands on some map of the place as it seemed that she was making up the stairs, right for her bedroom. She heard the *snap* of Arnold's boot heels following her.

When she got onto the landing which led to her bedchamber, she felt the magic recede, its force loosen from her limbs. As she went further and further, the feeling of invisible hands moving her legs up and down disappeared to be replaced by a tingling sensation. She tried to stop herself walking and was successful. The magic had worn off. She turned to Arnold and saw that he too had regained control of his legs.

Her first instinct was to rush back down the stairs into the fray once more, but she told herself that would be a rash act—it would only get her into trouble. So, with Arnold trailing on her heels, she ventured back into her bedchamber, where she intended to wait the whole thing out. It was just a matter of time. Sooner or later all this political squabbling would be over and she could get back down to the graveyard.

As she set foot in her room, she noticed something didn't feel right. A shudder passed up her spine and her mind welled up. She looked round, trying to work out what had set her off and then, second time looking over her room, she saw that General Frum was leaning up against the window frame, with his back to her, looking out—almost motionless.

She took a step back and almost bumped into Arnold, who had drawn his sword. She reached out and touched his forearm, but Arnold kept his sword in his grip, eyes fixed on Frum. She turned her attention back to Frum. "What're you doing here?"

Frum flinched and turned to look, as if he hadn't heard them coming in.

She plucked a lantern off a nearby surface and lit it. The

bright flame licked the room. She noticed that Frum was pale. He seemed much skinnier. "They're looking for you."

"Who?" he said, his voice cracking.

"The intruders. The witches and wizards."

"Oh, I see."

"They're standing off with the men of the garrison. I think they'll kill them all if you don't go out there and show yourself."

Frum nodded, shaking as he did so, and turned to look back out the window.

"Did you hear what I said?" Alexis said.

No response from Frum.

Arnold bobbed past Alexis, holding his sword down at his side. "You've got not right being here! I demand that you get out right this moment."

Frum turned to look at Arnold—his gaze was faraway, like his mind was on something else entirely. He looked down at his belt and felt for a dagger hanging there. He rested his hand on the hilt. "You know, I came here to kill you, Your Majesty. I couldn't bear to lose this battle and think that you might have a chance of continuing on the throne."

Arnold held his sword up, the blade level with his nose. "And now you'll answer to me."

"Yes," Frum said, with a weak smile. "I suppose I will."

Alexis looked between Arnold and Frum, seeing the hateful stare Arnold held as compared to Frum's look of indifference. "Your role, General Frum," Alexis said, "is to lead the men of the garrison. I thought that, above all else, you were a man of honour."

"I am," Frum said, his voice so croaky that it was almost a whisper. "I was away, visiting the dwarves, when I got the news that the magicians were coming. If I'd wanted to I could've stayed there, but I chose to return here to do my duty."

"And so why don't you do it?" Alexis said. "They're going to kill the men of the garrison because of you."

"It doesn't matter," Frum said. "It's all over anyway."

"What is?"

"The reign of humans. Now that black magic has decided it has the right to rule, nothing can be done to fight back. They shall take the crown, give it to their leader—Maxeth—and we shall find ourselves stumbling back into another age of darkness."

Alexis wondered whether he was just being melodramatic—looking to her Etherealean gauge, Arnold, she saw that this little speech was having no effect in terms of diminishing his ferocity, but, then again, Arnold was just a boy and Frum had killed his father. Perhaps the gravity of his statements just refused to sink in.

"If you've given up," Arnold said, "at least permit me to be the one who kills you."

Frum, again indifferent, looked over Arnold, then back out the window, to the courtyard. "Very well," he said. "I've hidden my sword in the bathroom, beneath a pile of towels."

Still keeping his eyes fixed on Frum and his sword raised, Arnold stalked his way to the bathroom, paused to watch Frum for any further movement and then, not seeing any, ducked inside. He bobbed back out in a matter of seconds, bearing Frum's sword—with its blue hilt and its sharp edge. He arrived at Frum's side and offered him the sword.

Frum gazed at it, as if inspecting his reflection in its blade and then, without a word or meeting Arnold's eye, he took it from him.

Arnold took up his stance, sword held to his side, ready to bring it round and strike his opponent.

Alexis's mind just about caught up with the situation. She wondered whether she should make some attempt to stop it, to prevent more violence—more death—but how could she put herself in Arnold's shoes, when he had been the one who had been taken down to the dungeons on Frum's orders, had his father killed by Frum? Wasn't Arnold entitled to his revenge? Her words of protest dissolved in her throat.

Frum tore himself away from his beloved window and, still bearing his resigned expression, he held his sword in his hand, studying Arnold round the edge of the blade.

"This," Arnold said, "is for my father," before leaping forward and bringing his sword down.

Frum parried the blow, knocking Arnold off balance.

Alexis worried herself about how she would feel were Arnold to die. It would be all her fault for having offered him the role of her protector. She had instilled the confidence in him. If only she had left him to join the barracks, as surely he would've without her intervention, then right now he would just be another soldier—still filled with hatred and vengeance for Frum, but at least anonymous, left to brood on what might be one day. Now that she'd accepted him at her side he was filled with confidence, a knight of level-pegging with Frum.

Arnold caught himself on one of the bedposts and dodged Frum's counterblow. It seemed that the adrenalin of the sword-fight had done something to buck up Frum's attitude, to concentrate his mind away from the futility of their situation. With each of his blows he seemed to grow in confidence, parrying each of Arnold's strikes and pushing him back.

One thing was for certain, Frum was fighting much better than he had against Arnold's father—Eversham—he was going for all the opportunities, his feet moving quickly. Perhaps he felt that he had a point to prove, that he could've, if he'd wanted, beaten Eversham fairly. He had his second chance, redemption, in the form of Arnold.

Alexis was stunned at the resemblance of Arnold to his father, the smoothness of his action, the sweep of his strokes, how he kept moving his feet.

Frum backed Arnold up against the wall and drew back his sword.

Alexis's heart rapped against her ribcage. If she could've found her voice, she would've shrieked, but all she could do was watch on and hope.

With trademark nimbleness, Arnold dipped at the right moment, leaving Frum's blade to clang against the stone wall. Arnold took his chance, with Frum's weapon lowered, to strike him across the back of the shoulders. Frum crumpled to his knees and his sword rattled against to floor. Arnold's shoulders rose and fell with his rapid breathing. He held his sword over Frum's head, readying the killing stroke.

This time Alexis did find her voice. "No!" she said. "Don't do it!"

Arnold kept his gaze fixed on Frum, as if he might scuttle away given half the chance.

However, just as before, the battle was done. Frum was on his hands and knees, blood soaking the back of his tunic, trickling into an ever-growing manky pool beneath him.

"Lower your sword," Alexis said.

Frum glanced at her sidelong. "Don't get between us. The boy has every right to take his vengeance. Don't rob him of that."

Arnold remained totally transfixed and Alexis was sure that there was nothing she could say to stop him from doing whatever it was he wanted to do.

"I thought I might find you here."

Alexis swivelled round to look at the door.

Maxeth stood there, looking in. He was alone. "Didn't take too much to get the garrison out of the way, incredible how easily impressed humans are with some colourful lights and a touch of possession—it was enough for them to see their queen being led away by invisible hands, enough to bring them to their knees." He cocked his head to one side and inspected Frum. "My, my, whatever's happened here. If I didn't know better I'd say it looks like there's been a bit of a scrap."

If Maxeth tried to attack Arnold, Alexis resolved to leap into the way. She would take whatever hex or curse he intended to inflict on the young man.

Maxeth took a step into the bedchamber.

Frum was spluttering now, choking on his own blood as it pulsed up his throat. His hands and knees gave way and he collapsed onto the floor, face first, surely beaten.

Maxeth looked to Arnold. "Well? Aren't you going to apply the killing stroke?"

Arnold continued to stare at Frum.

"Speak when you're spoken to, boy!" Maxeth said, his tone harsher.

Arnold turned his head slowly, but failed to make eye contact with Maxeth. "No," he said, then sheathed his bloodied sword and walked away from the dying Frum.

Maxeth shook his head and puffed out his cheeks. "Dearie me, that's the problem with you humans, very few of you have that extra edge, that degree of ruthlessness to get things done." He stood over Frum, hands outstretched.

Alexis sobbed. "Please," she said. "Don't kill him."

Frum's bulging eyeballs searched her out. His mouth moved but he had no words. She liked to think that he was thanking her, but she had no way of knowing what he was trying to say.

Maxeth drew back for a moment and clucked his tongue. "Nothing to add to that? What would I have to gain by sparing his life? I've got a nice and obedient force of men at my side, men that—first and foremost—are true to their general."

Alexis sunk his teeth into her lower lip. "They'll . . . they'll obey you. I'll see to that."

Maxeth snorted a laugh. "Please, Your Highness, desperation doesn't become you. What makes you think that the men will listen to anything *you'll* say? They don't respect you or your rule, anyone can see that." He wriggled his hands and sparks swarmed round them, licking away at his skin. He focussed on Frum, his body ragged and beaten. "I promise I'll make this quick."

Alexis's mind felt like it had caught fire and, before she could fully absorb the scene, Maxeth stooped over Frum, she felt herself falling back and then landing with a solid *thump*.

FIRING UP THE CAVALRY

J OHN SUPPOSED it to be around midnight when he was
escorted from his cell and taken right back to his
bedroom. He asked them questions, but the guards were
unwilling to give them. When they made to leave him in the
bedroom he did manage to extract from them that he wasn't to
be killed at dawn after all, and he was left to be content with
that information.

The next day he got up with a slight crick in his neck. He
wandered about the room wondering whether he might be called
back into the ring, to be given another chance of fighting. And
then another, more dreadful prospect dawned on him. What if
Shankle was going to execute just Horace, and keep John on for
a second chance?

That possibility was too much for him to take and so he took
to bashing his fists against his bedroom door, until he realised
that it was unlocked. He trudged through the corridors,

intending to locate Shankle and get some straight answers from
him. He found him breakfasting in one of the large halls, with
the customary two guards at his shoulder.

John bustled in and slammed his fist down on the table,
sending the cutlery and porcelain bowls clinking. He took in the
breakfast: the multi-coloured fruits, the slab of salted pork and
then the pot of namtra tea steaming away. How could Shankle
just deal in death so calmly?

Shankle sipped at his tea and then glanced at John over the
rim. "What brings on all this fuss? Are you upset about keeping
your head for another day?"

"Where's Horace?" John managed to get out through
clenched teeth and without throttling him.

Shankle set his mug down and then set about cutting off a
slice of pork, which he subsequently popped into his mouth and
chewed delicately. "Horace is in his bedchamber, not quite as
nice as yours, I'm afraid, but hospitable all the same—if I do say
so myself."

All the pent up tension and fury moved to one side for a
moment. "Huh?" John said.

"That's right, I had Horace released last night."

John glared at him, still unable to quite comprehend just
what Shankle had said.

Shankle's eyes flickered over John's as he dabbed at some
stray fruit juice on his chin. "We made a deal."

"What deal?"

"Well, we decided that we have mutual interests at heart and
decided that we might be able to offer one another—"

"No," John said, "I know what a 'deal' is, but what were
the terms?"

"Quite simply we've agreed that we should join forces and march on the castle."

"What?"

"Do you have an objection to that?" Shankle said. "Forgive me, but I presumed that yourself and General Frum didn't much see eye-to-eye. Perhaps that was a hasty assumption. If so, I apologise."

John's brain felt like it was wading through an especially stodgy pool of treacle. "No, I mean, I hate Frum. He wanted me to kill so that I would become the new Champion of the King's army."

"Well then," Shankle said, getting to his feet, seemingly having lost his appetite, "you have nothing to worry about in that case."

John stood dumbstruck as Shankle slipped by him and out into the corridor. He snapped back to his senses before he got too far away and turned the corner. "Where . . . where's Horace?"

"Second door on the left, top of the staircase."

John burst into the room without so much as knocking. He caught Horace at breakfast, having had it brought to him on a well-polished riamand encrusted tray. "Would you please mind telling me what in hell is going on?"

Horace obliged him, outlining the plan he and Shankle had struck the night before. After he had finished, he looked at John then said, "You've gone quite pale, are you all right?"

Through his profound numbness, the aftershock at realising

that he wasn't going to be put to death and neither was Horace, he said, "When do we leave?"

"I was told directly after breakfast, but, I suppose, as soon as you're ready. As I understand it Shankle's just gone down to get the bivcheks saddled up and ready to ride out."

Just as Horace had outlined, Shankle was down with the bivcheks, chatting with several of what—John presumed to be—his generals. It was funny looking them all over, seeing how squat and dough-faced they were, and then to compare them with the sharp beaks of the bivcheks, and to know that laughing at the master of one of those would be an extremely rash course of action.

As promised, they saddled up, with Shankle finding an especially . . . well-built bivchek for John, which, Shankle claimed, could do with the exercise. When John observed its woolly-mammoth stomach, he saw that it hung only inches from the ground. Still, it had the mass to support John's mighty weight and, to John, who ever since his transformation had presumed that he would never get the chance to fulfil his dream of riding a horse, this seemed a decent compromise.

They rode out across the dwarf hillside, passing the riamand mines. It was a completely different experience to the first time they had crossed, when the fireballs had come raining down and their arrest had followed soon after. On balance, John thought this time was much more agreeable.

Once they left the dwarf territory behind, they broke into a steady trot, and then, as the foothills flattened out, they broke into a gallop, as instructed by Shankle. For the first few minutes of the gallop, John was certain that he would tumble to the ground in a heap at any second. He dug his knees into the bivchek's woolly flanks and snatched handfuls of its woolly neck. Several of the dwarves riding beside him took their opportunity to laugh. He recognised one of them as one of his opponents from the ring and shot him a quick snarl. That soon sobered him up.

He did get the hang of riding the bivchek about an hour or so later. Basically he just gave up caring about whether or not he would fall, and that seemed to do the trick. He took his newfound balance as an opportunity to check out their group. As he looked back over them he saw the lines of dwarves riding on their bivcheks snaked back for miles and miles, as far as he could see to the horizon. Shankle had his entire army out here. Whatever his reason was for rising up against the Throne of Ethereal, he supposed it must be meaty. He was quite surprised, later on, to discover from Horace that in fact it was over something so trivial as tax. Then again, never having held a job in his life, John had never really thought it an issue—and he had never had the responsibility of keeping up an empire of riamand mines, unlike Shankle.

In the middle of the afternoon, John sucked up the courage to ride his bivchek to the front of their column, beside Shankle. He thought that Shankle might order him to fall back, to fall in line with the rest of his soldiers, but, instead, Shankle gave him a hearty smile. An actual smile. That was when John almost *did* fall off his bivchek.

They came across a little cottage, with a smoking chimney later on in the day, and John was surprised to see a plate whistle past his ear and smash onto the stony path. He was even more surprised when he observed the scrawny little git who had chucked it, trying to hide himself behind the river bank. They soon had an apology out of him and John, with his dislike for any sort of bloodlust, managed to convince Shankle to spare this unfortunate man—clearly driven bonkers from living out here, so far from civilisation. What they did establish from him was that the Grotesque had passed through only a day or so before, and that they should be some way along on the path ahead. Once the man—who turned out to be called 'Dishwaster'—had stopped chucking plates at them he turned out to be quite hospitable, giving them all tea, bringing their bivcheks fresh cuts of meat to chomp on before offering the more senior members of their group shelter for the night. Shankle, however, being something of a obstinate fellow, demanded that they press on, not waste a single second, and so they did.

As night fell, Shankle barked for his soldiers to bring out their lanterns. They slowed the pace of their bivcheks to a trot and John relished the cool night breeze on his cheeks. Only a matter of hours ago he had been certain that never again would he feel such a sensation, and now he was back on the road, on his way to pay back the enormous debt he had accrued from those who had helped him during the rescue at Witney Branches.

They picked up on the Grotesque's tracks around midnight, judging by the position of the moon in the sky. Neither was this cause for celebration in Shankle's eyes, as he mercilessly kept his bivchek's head dipped to the track, driving it onward, keeping it going in the direction of the castle.

Sometime around dawn they lost the tracks and Shankle brought them to a halt. He got himself all flustered, in a bad temper, as only those who fail to sleep the night before do. His rosy cheeks and red-webbed eyes betrayed his frustration and he screwed up his eyes and fists as he dismounted his bivchek and stalked back and forth along the trail, trying to find the tracks.

John searched the horizon. They were now on the plains and all that stretched before them were green meadows. Castle Road snaked its way through the entire place.

Shankle rubbed his eyes. "They've left the road."

"Why would they do that?" John said.

"Maybe they found a shortcut."

John thought this over. He recalled that it was Yvonne, the white witch, who was leading them, so perhaps she had found a better way to go. He turned back to Shankle. "What should we do?"

"I reckon that we just keep on going, along the road, but stay aware."

"Do you think someone took them?"

"Out here that might be possible."

John couldn't imagine Yvonne allowing anything to happen to the group, but, then again, hadn't they got captured by the dwarves when she'd been in charge? Hadn't they all been sentenced to death? Now he wasn't feeling so sure about this.

"Couldn't we, you know, have a look round for them?"

Shankle shook his head. "I can't risk that. We came to take down the castle, Frum, that was the deal we made. If something has happened to your friends that's your business."

A flash of anger passed through John. "And what if we decide we're going to look for them?"

"Then I'll turn my bivchek on you before you've gone ten paces."

John met Shankle's eye, but the only look there was one of a tired man, looking to reach his destination, take care of business and then go back home. John looked round him again, trying to pick out some clue as to the Grotesque's route, but there was nothing to find. Reluctantly, he climbed back up onto his bivchek and rode on with the others.

The ride was torture for John as he tried to keep his mind off what fate might've befallen his companions. If he reached the castle and they weren't there then all this, the entire journey would be for nothing, since he had agreed to go on the quest in exchange for what Zend had done in freeing his family. Or would it? Even if it turned out that his companions had been captured, or worse, wouldn't the best thing he could do for their memory be to storm the castle and return their children to their rightful homes? He kept that thought close, to keep him warm and to guide him on his way.

They proceeded along Castle Road which, despite its grand name, failed to have any really distinctive features at all. In fact, contrary to the daring nature of their quest, John found himself dropping off to sleep on the back of his bivchek. He had missed a night's sleep after all.

He was roused by a whooping call from Shankle to the others. He blinked the sleep from his eyes and noticed, spread out before him, ten or so acres ahead, the castle—the home of the *Queen* of Ethereal. He eyed its structure, the stone ramparts, the deep moat surrounding the plot and then the drawbridge, from which he, Sydney and Courtney had escaped. Still stuck in his dreary state, he felt angry that he hadn't taken up the initiative of going after his friends, making more of an effort to find them. But they were grown men, they could take care of themselves.

Shankle called out something to his dwarf soldiers who, John saw, covered the land on their bivcheks, which tossed their heads and snarled. The soldiers pulled their axes from their backs and held them up, awaiting their leader's orders.

"What now?" John said.

"Now we attack," Shankle said.

EASY DOES IT

TREVOR SAT on the fringes of the trees, looking down on the castle. They had taken a longer route through a narrow valley when Yvonne had sensed black magic in the air. Following their previous brush with black magic, back at Witney Branches, Trevor didn't blame her one bit.

Down below, he could make out a large group, which he had watched advance throughout the afternoon. Only now, as they were only a few fields' length away from the castle, did he notice they were all mounted, and then, when they drew closer still, he realised that they were dwarves, and that their mounts were bivcheks.

He scrabbled to his feet and rushed back to the camp, where a fire smoked away, and several rodents which Plont had hunted from the forest roasted away on spits. He was breathless when he drew up to the fireside and had to double over, to get his breath back, before he could relay the information.

Yvonne looked the most alarmed of all of them. "But, the dwarves, it can't be. They've always been well-allied with the royal family. Never would I believe that they'd take up against them."

Trevor wiped the sweat from his brow, a little annoyed that his eye witness testimony was being questioned. "You can go off and have a look if you like. I can assure you that they're all there, bivcheks and all, ready to march on the place."

Yvonne rose and writhed her hands. "Or, might it be that they've come to the Queen's aid? That they've heard of our attempt to march on the castle?"

"Your guess is as good as mine."

Zend stared into the crackling flames. "Does this change our plans at all?"

"I shouldn't think so," Yvonne said, shaking her head. "It doesn't change my protective spell, in any case. By morning I shall have regained sufficient strength to cast it."

"Good, good," Zend said, with a sly smile.

Trevor stood there, feeling thoroughly useless, but, at the same time, wanting to unburden his mind of his own conjecture. "What if the dwarves want to join us?"

Blank stares greeted this comment.

"You know, as our allies," he said, as if that clarified the matter.

Yvonne frowned. "And why would they do that? Have you been paying attention to the fact that they wanted to execute us, that the only way we escaped those paranoid mercenaries was by bargaining away one of our group?"

Now that Trevor thought about it, he felt quite stupid for having mentioned it at all. He decided now was time for him to quiet down and let the grownups talk. So he sat down on the log and accepted the small, roasted animal that was presented to him, munching on it as he considered that tomorrow he might well have to use his sword and shield. His strategy would be to stay as close as possible to Zend and Plont—they at least had some stake in keeping him alive, if it was only to return him to their village as, ostensibly, their 'hero.'

After everyone had eaten, they all lay down beside the fire, each to their own little patch of ground, and all went to sleep. Trevor, however, couldn't. That wild idea about the dwarves just wouldn't leave him and, as he felt a gentle breeze on his cheek, he thought he could hear the clanging of metal on metal and the splintering of wood. He told himself that it was merely anticipation, that he was all worked up about the following day and that his mind was playing tricks on him. But, after tossing and turning for the best part of an hour, he ventured away from the fireside, back through the forest to where he had looked down on the castle earlier.

As he approached the same spot he had been that afternoon, he noted the blaze of light encapsulating the castle and, next, he saw the dwarves, surrounding the castle, throwing ropes up the walls, the bivcheks whinnying and screaming. He observed that some of them had made it up onto the ramparts and were, right at that moment, doing battle with the garrison. Needless to say, he returned to the fireside sharpish, already feeling himself filling with a degree of smugness. When he delivered the news he expected Yvonne to immediately disband the camp and for them to head down the slope to the castle, to help out with their apparent allies. However, her response was much more measured than that, in fact she simply rolled over and went back to sleep.

"But we've got to help them!" Trevor said, unable to keep his voice level.

"Out of the question," Yvonne said. "My powers won't be up to protecting you, not until morning."

"But this might be our chance. What if the garrison drive off the dwarves by morning? With them by our side victory's assured. Have you seen the beaks on those bivcheks?"

"The answer's still 'no,'" Yvonne said.

Trevor just stood there, still unsure how he was going to proceed with this new information, then he eyed Zend and knew what he had to do.

Zend was wide-awake a second after Trevor had completed his potted report of the movement on the castle, and he rushed to get Plont up—who had fashioned himself a hammock from some vines and slung it up between a pair of trees. With Plont and Zend at his side, bright-eyed and bushy-tailed, they tried Yvonne once more. But the answer was still the same.

"Just get some sleep," she said. "I'm telling you that I won't have the power to keep you all safe, not till morning. Can't a witch get her beauty sleep round here anymore?"

Zend cast off this matter with a wave of the hand. "Then we'll march on the castle without your protection!"

It was testament to Zend's persuasive enthusiasm that he managed to rouse just about the entire camp and get them to listen in to his plan of early attack. Trevor noticed that he elided the small matter of the protection spell, but he reasoned that by the time they got down there, had climbed the wall, it would probably be morning anyway. Zend's argument ran along the lines that if they were to wait until morning for the attack, then the dwarves might invade the castle, take control and act with just as much hostility as if they'd been trespassing on dwarf territory—they'd want to know how they'd so conveniently shown up only hours after they'd vanquished the garrison, and things might get nasty. Trevor, at least, was convinced.

And so the entire group, minus Yvonne, who slept on apparently oblivious of their departure, moved out of the camp, through the trees and down the hill, onward to storm the castle.

Trevor had been caught in such a daze, just moving along with the others, that Zend had to remind him to draw his sword and ready his shield, which he did. As he took his sword in his hand, the first time he had ever really wielded it in anything resembling anger, he noticed how heavy it was, how improbable it would be that he would be able to prevent himself from toppling over when he swung it let alone strike an intended target.

They reached the moat in no time at all, and to no resistance and no sign of any dwarves. It seemed that Zend's prediction of the dwarves already having taken the place over had proven true. Not even a bivchek remained outside. Everything seemed so quiet. There were none of the revelries which Trevor would've expected to hear following the storming of a castle. But, then again, he supposed it might well be some sort of cultural thing, an Etherealean thing, not to go completely berserk at a moment like this.

As a group they rounded the castle, getting into the front section, where they found the drawbridge had already been lowered. Zend got a little twitchy at this sight and, in a kind of shouted whisper, announced for the others to hold back while he led an advance party to determine what the state of play was. Sydney translated for the Beavermen.

Trevor would've been quite content to hold back and let Zend and Plont lead the way to their diplomatic meeting, but he found himself being tugged along with them. He glanced back over his shoulder at their gathered forces, the torches their held in their hands glowing against their faces: the Beavermen and Grotesque all armed, their eyes quivering in their sockets in anticipation of the fight.

They plodded onto the drawbridge, hearing the *creak* of the wooden planks beneath their feet. Zend and Plont kept casting their gaze upward, to the battlements, searching for any sign, but there was none to be found. Trevor just held his sword tighter, more as a comfort blanket than as a means of defence.

In the courtyard there was still no sign of the dwarves or the garrison. Where had they all gone? Trevor bucked along behind Plont and Zend. "Where do you think they're holding the children?"

"In the barracks," Zend said, then glanced off to his side and pointed to a large wooden gate. "I'd think it's over there, that looks the most likely."

The whole atmosphere was eerie and oppressive, it felt like the silence would crush them beneath its weight. Zend, however, seemed unaffected by its sensation or, at the very least, he hid it well, as he trod up to the large gate, grasped its large handle and turned. It opened with a rusty *groan* and they filed inside, going into the darkness.

Trevor felt for the wall and guided himself along. He was reassured that Zend led the way and that Plont brought up the rear. When he was with these two he felt well-protected. For all their melodramatic heroism, they were dependable and competent.

The gloom played tricks on Trevor's eyes, making him see shapes form before him and then disappear just as quickly. He felt a tingle up his neck, similar to static electricity. He recalled the sensation as being similar to when he had watched the black magicians hurl their hexes and curses at Horace back at Witney Branches. And that was when he had his second brainwave of the morning. Keeping his voice low, he said, "I think they're here."

"Who's here?" Zend said, with a little irritation.

"The magicians."

"Guess we'll have to be careful, then," Zend said, moving on through the dark.

They headed down a gentle slope. Trevor could taste moisture in the air and, from somewhere, hear a dripping pipe. He thought that they must've been below the moat by then. He felt the tiles beneath his feet grow slippery, some of them were loose in their sockets and he almost tripped up a couple of times.

A dull light appeared up ahead. Trevor felt his eyes strain to gain a focus. He kept up his pace behind Zend, moving along more quickly now. Their footsteps echoed round them, coming back at them as a series of wet *slaps*. They reached the source of the light, a sole lantern propped up against the wall. Trevor was gazing at it when he heard Zend call out in glee. He looked up to see a room stretching out before them, seemingly hundreds of bundles of rags spread out on the floor. Only when some of them stirred did he realise they were human beings—that they were children.

Zend crept up to one of those huddled on the floor. He prodded them with his toe. "Hey!" he said. "Wake up."

The bundle of rags shifted and a dirtied child's face squinted up at them.

"Where're you from?"

The child said a name which Trevor couldn't understand, let alone pronounce.

Zend ruffled the child's hair and then moved onto the next, asking the same question. He got through about an eighth of the room before he found a child from Gotnot, who he swept up in his arms and hugged to his chest, as if they were no more than a ragdoll. His eyes glittered through the darkness and he picked out Trevor. "This," he said, "is my younger brother, Thwock."

All of a sudden, met with this emotional scene amid the heightened tension, Trevor found himself welling up.

Plont, too, stalked through the sleeping children, asking the same questions, only quieter, and getting his own little collection of Gotnot children. He seemed to have his own attachment to one of them, but he made no effort to elaborate on their relationship. Soon, after they had checked through the entire hall, they had got twenty children between them. They returned to where Trevor stood looking on.

"Let's go," Zend said, holding a couple of the children's hands, while the others all linked hands in a chain behind him.

"What about the others?" Trevor said.

"They're from other villages."

"But we can't just leave them here."

"Who says?"

"It's just not right, that's all."

Zend exchanged glances with Plont, then looked back over

the children gathered there. "It'll be hard enough getting our own children out, let alone the others. What if one of them cries out?"

But, without waiting for Zend's reply, Trevor had already started to nudge children awake and to help them, dopey-eyed, to their feet. It took them half an hour or so to get all the children up and together. The children hardly made a sound, which Trevor supposed to be a consequence of them having been locked up down here for so long—that their senses had become dulled. A quick dose of sunlight and a hike through the country should go some way to solving that.

They filed out the way the had come in, with Zend looking decidedly twitchy. When they got back out into the dawning day, the children blinked in the sun, held up their arms to shield their eyes. Their rags appeared more wretched in the daylight, the bronze muck on their brows more luminescent and their eyes more matted.

Having emerged from down below, Trevor was taken off guard by the fresh smelling air confronting him. He sucked it into his lungs and savoured it. He clenched the hands of the two children at his sides and steered them toward the drawbridge, through the still deserted castle. Whatever had happened here, Trevor had the sense that they would be best advised to get away as quickly as they could.

Just as they approached the drawbridge, passed through the outer courtyard, a voice drifted down to them from up on the ramparts. All of them stopped and stared, out of surprise more than anything else.

An elderly man stood up there. He had long grey hair and wore a tweed jacket with green and black plaid trousers. He cocked his head to one side and said, "And just where do you think you are going?"

Trevor recognised him as the dark wizard: Maxeth, the one who had attempted to turn Witney Branches into kindling.

It was Plont who broke into a sprint first, with Zend and Trevor soon snapping to their senses. Trevor gripped two of the children's hands in his and dashed toward the drawbridge, no longer feeling the days and days of fatigue which plagued his body. Only one thought occupied his mind, that he had to escape the castle, get away from Maxeth.

They got within a few feet of the drawbridge before it swung up, driven by invisible hands, and slapped shut against the stone pillars alongside. They were forced to come to a halt and to look back to Maxeth—completely at his mercy as to what would happen to them next.

Maxeth rubbed his hands together. "If you and your children wish to live then I'd advise you to round the castle walls, and come to meet with the rest of the party." He set off walking up on the ramparts, not pausing to see whether they would follow.

Trevor eyed the drawbridge. It was easily thirty or forty feet high and there was no way they would manage to scale it—he couldn't have made it himself, let alone shepherd children up it. He looked to Zend and Plont who appeared to be distinctly out of ideas. "I guess we have to do as he says," Trevor said.

Both Zend and Plont looked glum, but they set off after Maxeth, following the path that he outlined for them.

The children were still stuck in their daze so they made no

comment about where they were being led, merely rubbing their eyes and trudging along.

They followed the curve of the castle walls and arrived where Maxeth stood up on the wall overlooking them. Down in the courtyard there was an enormous bubble which contained the collective forces of the dwarves and the men of the garrison. All of them were slumped down, trapped, waiting for something to happen.

Trevor recognised a pair of the Grotesque within their numbers: Horace and John. It was little consolation now that he had been proven right, that the dwarves had come to fight for the same cause as they.

"Into the bubble, then," Maxeth said.

Plont and Zend hung back, and so did Trevor.

Maxeth let out a sigh. "You're not going to make me use my magic *again*, are you? You know it does take it out of me some-what." He glanced over his shoulder, back over the turrets to where—Trevor imagined—the rest of the invading force waited. "When your allies decide they're going to come in too, I'll cast another of my spells to keep them occupied so, don't worry, I'm going to keep order whatever happens."

"We're not going inside!" Zend said, glaring up at Maxeth.

"Very well," Maxeth said, then wiggled his fingers—sparks swarmed over his hands, consuming them completely and then a ice-white ray darted out and danced round Zend.

Apparently losing control of his own movements, Zend broke out into a jig. Still holding tight to the children at his side —who screamed out at the sensation—he skipped into the bubble to join the dwarves and the men of the garrison. Once they got inside the effects of the curse subsided, Zend regained control of his body and strutted up to the bubble, bashing his fists against it. Although his mouth was clearly animated, shouting out insults to Maxeth, he remained silent, unable to make a sound from within. Now Trevor saw why the castle had been so quiet when they'd entered.

Maxeth turned to Trevor and Plont. "What about you two? Are you going to go willingly or do I need to bother myself with magic again?"

Trevor looked to Plont and then held out his arm. "After you," he said.

A BUBBLE IN THE COURTYARD

ALEXIS PACED back and forth at her window, occasionally looking down into the courtyard where the giant bubble encapsulated the entire garrison, along with some intruders—dwarves, from their appearance. And now they had been joined by a group of children—those children which Frum had intended to become soldiers, before his demise—and another three unfamiliar figures, including a portly looking man in his fifties or maybe early sixties. Maxeth continued to stalk along the battlements, looking out on the plains leading up to the castle, as if in expectation. If he was expecting something or someone she had no idea what or who it could be.

She looked to Arnold who perched on the edge of her bed, his sword resting across his lap. He pressed his fingers to his temples and stared at the blade. What he was thinking about she could only guess. He had watched Maxeth finish his greatest rival. Did he feel that he had got his revenge or was he more afraid that he had missed an opportunity to take care of an even greater evil in Maxeth?

She turned away from the window and sat beside him. "You know that Maxeth would've destroyed you if you had dared try and strike him. You wouldn't be here now to protect me."

"But I could've tried," Arnold said. "You've seen them all, down there in the courtyard, I could've stopped that happening if I'd just been braver, picked up my sword and confronted him. If all this ends with black magic taking up the Throne of Ethereal then history shall remember me as a coward."

Alexis thought of mentioning that if the black magicians managed to seize power of the Kingdom, that they might deign not to bother recording any such 'inferior' human history, but this, perhaps, wasn't the right time to kick the boy's ego while it was down on the floor, writhing about, fighting for its life.

She got up and shuffled back over to the window. The sun was high in the sky now and she could feel its heat on her cheeks. She basked in its warm glow and then turned her attention back to the graveyard. All she had to do was get back down there and resume her search for the right gravestone. She knew that if she continued to just hover round her bedroom then, sooner or later, Maxeth would come for her—to officially take her crown as his own. But it wouldn't be easy for her to sneak out. Maxeth had informed her that his followers, the other black magicians, wandered the corridors in search of any stragglers, ordered to kill on sight. He had also implied that they wouldn't pause to ask questions or show any sort of reprieve for royalty. She was damned if she stayed and damned if she went.

Out the window, she noticed Maxeth moving off round the ramparts. She followed him with her stare, his prancing round.

There seemed to be a new tension in him, he held his shoulders stiff, his gait was steady and determined rather than being lazy and stodgy. Whatever had caught his attention he was treating as a very real threat.

She went to the next window along, which looked out over the front gate and the drawbridge. When Maxeth got to his position, he stopped and looked down, speaking with someone. She noticed that he writhed his hands down by his side as he spoke—irritated by something. And then, all of a sudden, a white-haired woman—a witch—burst upward into the air and confronted him on the battlements.

Alexis's heart bobbed in her throat. She called out to Arnold, who came up alongside her. "Who's that?"

Arnold steeled his gaze, turning it away from Maxeth and onto the woman. His mouth propped open. "Why, that's the White Witch."

"The 'White Witch?'"

"I . . . I never thought that she was truly real but seeing her there, seeing her now, I can see that all they've said is true."

"What's true?" Alexis said, growing increasingly frustrated with all this assumed knowledge, feeling like she was constantly two steps behind.

"There was an old myth, when I was a boy, that declared when black magic rose to rule against the powers of good, there would be an equal response from white magic, and she has come. There she is."

Maxeth and the White Witch were deep in conversation, their eyes locked together.

Alexis opened the window wide, hoping to hear their words.

As they talked, Maxeth and the White Witch hurried along

the ramparts. Maxeth backed up, and Alexis thought of the prospect of him slipping off, falling backward to his death in the courtyard. Then she remembered that he could just as easily fly so such a misstep would hardly be disastrous for him.

They drew closer, both of them now above the bubble. When were they going to start fighting? Alexis stomach dropped as she thought about what the consequences would be if the White Witch were to lose.

From the drawbridge, she heard the *thuds* against the wood. When she turned her head to look she saw that the wooden planks were buckling. There were more intruders trying to get into the castle—were they the White Witch's allies? She could only hope.

Maxeth's attention was distracted for a moment, and that was when the White Witch took her chance. Similar to Maxeth, her hands glowed, but instead of a beam shooting out from them, a waft of steam settled in over him. Maxeth clawed at the air round his head, screaming out, apparently in pain. The White Witch continued to speak her spell, to weave her words and send Maxeth into deeper and deeper fury.

Alexis observed Maxeth's witches and wizards burst out into the courtyard. They spilled out, throwing their curses in the White Witch's direction. The White Witch backed down from her confrontation with Maxeth, taking to the air to avoid the various beams and sparks. Alexis was certain that one of them would catch her, but she always seemed to avoid them by a hair's breadth. She fluttered her way over to Alexis's windowsill where she perched right before her.

A shudder ran through Alexis and she backed away, feeling Arnold draw his sword beside her. She watched on as she saw

Maxeth also take to the air, fly toward her, eyes fierce and teeth bared. He had barely got within a few feet before he was reduced to grabbing his skull and screaming out once more. Whatever it was that the White Witch was casting upon him it was having a notable effect.

Alexis felt great well-being and calm flush through her. She knew, instinctively, that it could only be because of her proximity to the White Witch, whatever magic she cast it was having a cleansing effect on her. Her eyesight took on a crystal clear quality and her brain felt sharp.

The witch and wizard pirouetted through the air, each of them taking turns at holding the upper hand. Whereas Maxeth constantly attempted to unseat his adversary with fizzing hexes, the White Witch's defence seemed to be wholly passive, that she was somehow striking Maxeth inside his brain, toying with his very senses. They battled on.

At one point in the battle Maxeth's witches and wizards grew weary of merely watching the fight and rose into the air. But, seconds after they had risen, they were sent spiralling back down, with looks of ecstasy on their faces. Some were rendered into giggling fits as they rolled about down on the tiles of the courtyard, while others bashed their fists against their skulls as if trying to break a monster out of their brains. The upshot of this was that the White Witch and Maxeth fought on in peace, *mano-a-mano*.

As they battled on, they swung through the air and burst through Alexis's window. Maxeth caught the windowpane and sent glass tinkling onto the floor. Alexis backed up against the wall, dragging the seething Arnold alongside her.

The White Witch got Maxeth caught up in an especially

divine fuss, and he dropped to his knees, shouting for the voices to get out of his head. She took her time, watching on, apparently waiting for him to cede the fight.

Arnold held his sword and was ready to rush in and finish the job. His teeth chattered together and Alexis could feel him shaking beside her.

The White Witch turned to Arnold then said, "You, hero, are you going to finish him off, or what?"

Arnold froze, sword still stuck in his grip.

With a roar, Maxeth lurched up once more and flew at the White Witch, catching her with a hex in the cheek. The White Witch tumbled down to the floor, her body twitching as she went. Maxeth stalked above his victim, grinning from ear-to-ear. "Looks like I've got you just where I want you now. Any last words?"

The White Witch looked dazed, her eyes bulged in their sockets.

Alexis snatched hold of Arnold's tunic and shook him. "Now," she said. "This is your chance. You've got to finish him now."

Maxeth remained totally oblivious to anything else passing in the room, concentrated on the White Witch, his smile growing wider as each second ticked by.

"Do it!" Alexis said, gritting her teeth.

Still Arnold remained still, frozen by the spectacle.

With Maxeth muttering some ruthless curse to himself and holding his hands up above his head, no doubt preparing for an especially nasty killing strike, Alexis slipped the sword from Arnold's hand and rushed up behind Maxeth.

She brought the blade up high and then, as she drove it

downward, Maxeth turned. But he was too late. As he released his curse, she stuck the sword through his stomach. The blade emerged on the other side, having passed through his spine, coated in blood. Maxeth emitted a hollow gargle and his empty eyes lolled about in their sockets. His curse bounced off the roof and flew right out the window where, judging by the piercing shriek, it found a target in one of his witch or wizard followers.

Alexis let go of the sword and watched Maxeth fall back to the floor of her bedchamber. As he plunged onto the neat rug, with the adorned green triangles she'd always quite liked, his arms sprawled. He lay there, on his back, with the sword sticking out of him.

She turned her attentions to the White Witch, who looked bemused at what had befallen her. Her eyes settled onto Alexis and she said, "You must be the bravest mortal that I've ever met." Her eyelashes fluttered and then closed. With a final, pained breath she said, "I *am* glad that humans have triumphed over magic, it was time for it to happen."

Alexis's whole body trembled and she watched the White Witch's chest go still—notching up the fourth person she'd seen die. She backed up from the body and looked to Maxeth, who, despite having expired also, was continuing to bleed all over the rug. This did look as if it would be a costly clean up.

Soon after Maxeth was beaten, the bubble down in the courtyard burst and its prisoners were freed. She was expecting them to take up the battle where they had left it off, but she watched on as the men of the garrison shook hands with the dwarves and turned their swords onto the remaining witches and wizards who, with a few exceptions, gave themselves up right away, and allowed themselves to be led off down to the dungeons.

The intruders bashed their way in through the drawbridge, a race of men who looked a lot like beavers, an astute judgement as she found out later that they were called Beavermen. The rest of the day passed with jovial festivities, much honey liqueur was consumed and a band was dug up from somewhere.

As for Alexis, she was surprised to find Sydney and Courtney among the numbers of those who stormed the castle with the Beavermen. What surprised her more was that she was actually fairly pleased to see them—she gave each of them a hearty hug. When they'd backed off she looked to Courtney, the one who had brought her here and got her involved in this mess in the first place.

Courtney bowed. "My queen."

She found herself flushing at this show of deference and took a few moments to store it for later, so that she might enjoy it again and again, then she said, "Actually, I think I should pass the crown to you, since you claim to be the rightful owner."

Courtney beamed at her. "I knew you'd see sense."

Sydney coughed loudly. "I think you're overlooking a minor point, which is that there's no proof that Courtney is in fact the true heir to the Throne of Ethereal."

"*Prince* Courtney."

"Yes," Sydney said, rolling his eyes, "that's exactly what I'm talking about."

Henrietta appeared in the doorway of Alexis's bedchamber. Alexis wondered how long she had lingered there, and when she had arrived. In contrast with the cheer and good spirits seeping through the castle, Henrietta remained guarded, unsure of herself.

Alexis presumed this was because of what had happened before, with her seemingly going along quite willingly with Frum's, and then Maxeth's, regime—although there really wasn't much she could've done during the latter. Alexis bounced up to her and pecked her on both cheeks. "Please, Henrietta, don't feel bashful at all. Whatever happened is all history now."

Henrietta summoned a weak smile for Alexis but turned her gaze onto Courtney, who she approached.

Courtney, a little taken aback at being the centre of her concentration, looked about in panic, as if she might be concealing a knife and be about to stab him through the heart right before he got his perpetual wish.

When Henrietta got within a few paces she stopped and placed her fingers to her lips. "My goodness," she said. "You look so much like him."

"Like who?" Courtney said, frowning and eyeing up the sword—freshly cleaned—which hung from Arnold's belt.

"King Tyron, your father."

Courtney brightened at this fact. "So, what you're saying is that you can acknowledge that I am the true heir of Ethereal?"

She nodded in reply.

"And what about my mother?" he said.

Henrietta shook her head. "She was killed, I remember, the same night as your father, when the attackers came to pillage the castle. We all feared that we should die until your uncle, King Fredrick, returned to restore order. He believed you all dead. I was given the responsibility of handing you over to another, so you would be taken somewhere safe. King Fredrick, he made to understood you'd all died, but he saved us."

"Yes," Courtney said, arching an eyebrow. "I suppose he was good for something after all."

Alexis supposed that that was the closest Courtney would get to praising his uncle and so decided not to press the matter any more.

Courtney bulked up his shoulders and glanced round the room, looking down his nose at everyone without exception. "And that only leaves the matter of my queen." His gaze fell on Alexis.

"Oh no," she said, backing up, with her palms raised, "you can find someone else who wants the job. Really, I'm not interested."

"Ah," Courtney said, as if this were only a minor obstacle, then he looked to the door, where the maidens, led by Cherry, were looking in on them. He narrowed his eyes. "You then," he said. "Would you like to be my queen?"

Cherry stared back at him then jabbed her, sizeable, chest with her chubby finger. "Me?"

"Yes, you."

She broke out into a wide smile and then nodded profusely.

Alexis breathed a sigh of relief.

Once the marriage was complete, Alexis announced her intention to leave Ethereal. She had had enough of this world and was ready to return to Earth, for better or worse. So she said her semi-emotional goodbyes to the members of the court, including a curtailed half-smile for Cherry, a pat on the shoulder for Jenson, then she bucked off to the graveyard to continue her search for the portal. She noticed that one of the old men, part of the invaders' force, had joined her. She glanced to him. "Are you all right? Are you lost?"

"Oh, I just heard that you're on your way back to Earth."

"And what of it?"

"Well, you see, I'm from there too, and I was looking to get back."

Alexis studied him, thought about whether or not he was telling the truth—then decided that, really, she didn't care. If he was truly an Etherealean who wanted to escape the Kingdom, Courtney's rule, then she couldn't really blame him. Together they ventured into the graveyard in the late afternoon sun.

The more difficult decision was with Arnold, who had been following at her heels like a lost puppy for the entirety of her trip here. She looked to him now and examined him. "You know," she said. "I'm not the Queen any longer, so you may consider yourself freed of my service."

"You mean, you don't want me to go with you?"

"Well, it's just that Earth's very different from Ethereal, and back there I really have nothing to offer you. You might find that you're more at home staying here. I'm sure that you could put in a good word with the King, and he might find a place for you amongst the army."

Arnold jabbed his tongue in his cheek as he considered this. He looked to the other man with her then back to Alexis. Without warning he lurched forward into her arms and plunged his head into her breast.

She only realised that he was crying when his tears dampened her skin. When she held him back from her she noticed that she was too. She gazed into his sparkling eyes then said, "I know you'll make an excellent knight here, you'll honour your father's memory."

"I'll always remember you," Arnold said, backing up.

"And I'll remember you too."

Arnold got up to the entrance of the graveyard, cast another glance at her and then rushed off, back into the castle, to mingle back among the festivities.

Alexis eyed up the man then nodded to him, and together they searched through the gravestones until they found the magic one which whisked them away, back to the End of Time.

Divus, one of those who guarded the End of Time, and who was conveniently standing right by the portal to Ethereal, looked between the two of them. He held up his hands. "Really, don't tell me what happened, I don't want to know. Just follow me, please, and we'll say no more about it."

Alexis exchanged glances with the man, who it turned out was called Trevor, and they followed Divus to the portal leading back to Earth, a placard emblazoned onto one of the buttresses of the dilapidated church. Under Divus's watchful gaze, they both touched it and Alexis felt the nauseous swirl grab hold of her stomach and lead her downward, through the floor.

They emerged in Rutsley Church and Burial Grounds into the bright midday sun. She and Trevor exchanged pleasant smiles and then set off in their separate directions, she back toward school, where she should've been at that moment, and Trevor back to wherever he had to go.

She received a scolding upon arrival, five minutes late back from lunch, and that afternoon she had double biology—which she hadn't done her homework for—so it didn't get much better. She daydreamed through most of her classes, thinking about what might be going on in Ethereal at that moment—realising that time would be passing quickly by, perhaps a generation had already slipped away, and along with it everyone she had ever known. She never had quite got the hang of the timing.

As she trotted off back home, she thought about her life here on Earth and considered that, on balance, she was better off. She might not be a queen, but at least she could be a teenager again, soon she would be going off to university and that would be a whole other adventure. She peeled back the front gate and jogged up the garden path. When she stuck her key in the door she found that it worked just like before.

AND EVERYTHING WAS WELL AGAIN

J OHN STUMBLED over a dwarf and apologised profusely, using the phrase which Shankle had taught him. He would be the first to admit that the honey liqueur had shot right to his head, and now he was faced with fighting off this dizzy spell. After he slipped through a group of Beavermen, he continued on to the interior of the castle, where he located a toilet to deposit his excess liqueur. Once he had done so he ran into Courtney who was lingering about in the corridor, still wearing his groom's tunic, following his snappy wedding to Cherry. His tunic had a large stain at the collar where he'd missed his mouth with his cup of liqueur. Courtney gestured to John, beckoned him close to him, and, when he got him close, dropped his voice to a conspiratorial whisper. "Never did thank you properly for busting Sydney and I out of those dungeons." He leant in even closer so that if John had held a naked flame to the air, it would've soared into a fireball, egged on by Courtney's breath. "I've got an offer for you," Courtney said, with a hiccup. "If you're interested."

"What kind of offer?" John said, struggling to hold himself upright, and then realising that he was supposed to add, "Your Majesty," he did so.

Courtney slapped John between the shoulder blades, which took some effort, considering he had to hook his arm back round his back and hop to reach the spot he was aiming for. Anyway, he managed it, then said, "I'd like to make you General of the King's army."

"What?"

"That's right," Courtney said, with a grin. "With you in charge of the men there won't be so much as a sniff of discontent throughout the Kingdom." He eyed him. "So, what do you say?"

John thought about it. He really hadn't thought about anything, what would happen, past the invasion of the castle, and now he had achieved that he realised that, really, he didn't have a plan at all. "Uh, can I have some time to think about it?"

"Of course," Courtney said, then, "Take all the time you need!" before strutting off, back into the courtyard where several servants waited—looking slightly anxious at the state of their king, no doubt already wondering what sort of a drunk he would make.

John pressed his back against the wall, in the vague hope that stasis might sober him up a touch. After a minute or so he felt much better and ventured back out into the courtyard where he ran right into Zend and Plont. Right away he could see, from the flushed cheeks and marinated eyeballs, that Zend was steaming. Plont, on the other hand, looked rather restrained, looking out for his friend, making sure that he wasn't going to get into any sort of trouble. Zend pointed at John's chest, his finger wobbling all over the place. "Say, *giant*, have you seen our Earth friend about here anywhere?"

"You mean, Trevor?"

Zend closed one eye, obviously bothered about looking at several versions of John, then said, "Yeah, that's the one."

"Last time I saw him he was with Alexis, and they were heading off to the graveyard, to go back to Earth."

"What?" Zend said, stooping forward.

Plont reached out and supported him with a steady arm.

John shrugged. "That's what I saw."

Zend went a puce colour and promptly vomited. When he was finished, he straightened up and wiped his mouth with the back of his hand. He continued to address John as if their conversation hadn't been interrupted at all. "He told us that he was going back with us to Gotnot. He was supposed to be the whole hero of this thing. How're we supposed to celebrate properly now?"

"Well," John said, feeling distinctly sober now that he was confronted with someone in such a state as Zend, "maybe when you go back to Gotnot it'll give you two the opportunity to be heroes. Won't that be better?"

Zend seemed to analyse this logic for a while, and to have problems comprehending it entirely, before he broke out into a drunkard's grin. "Hey! You're right." He lurched forward and gave John a wobbly jab in the upper arm. "You're all right, *giant*."

Feeling woozy, John said, "Thank you."

"Now!" Zend said, sticking his finger in the air, as if to test the direction of the wind. "Which way are they serving?"

"Over there, I think," John said, pointing in a vague direction, not quite knowing himself.

Zend nodded with a little pout. "Very good." He slapped John on the arm as he passed by. "I'm sure we'll be seeing more of you. Do stay well, won't you?"

The teetotal Plont winked at John, then guided his companion away, onward for more drinking.

John headed on through the crowd until he was stopped again by Sydney, who was standing with Rick—the Beaverman. In this situation it turned out to be something of an advantage to have a silent language, consisting only of broad gestures, since voices could hardly be heard over the romping music.

Sydney put as much of his arm round John's waist as he could manage, then communicated some message to the Beaverman, before turning back to John and saying, "I was just telling him about the time that you broke us out of the dungeons, that you're a hero."

"Oh no," John said, "really it was nothing. I can't take much credit for it. If I had taken another turn then I never would've come across them."

"But you did," Sydney said. "And you most likely saved our lives."

Again, John felt himself blushing. He really would've liked to get away from the thrall for a while, to have some time to himself, to reflect—especially to think about the offer which Courtney had made him. Now he had the opportunity for a career, to make something for himself in the big wide world, no longer would he be considered a mere freak: a Grotesque.

"I'll see you later," John said, accepting Sydney and the

Beaverman's handshake, before searching out his companions, as he had been trying to do for most of the past hour.

In all the revelry it was really difficult to pick out any individuals, and then he sighted Horace, up on one of the ramparts, to one side of the drawbridge, with Susan standing beside him. They looked quite morose, pensive as they glanced out over the land which led up to the castle.

Just as he reached the steps, he was cuffed by Shankle, who left his group of dwarves to come and talk with him. "I wanted to speak with you."

"Right," John said, still glancing up at Susan and Horace, wanting to speak with them.

"I just wanted to say that I've heard the King's plans for you, that he intends to make you General of his army."

"Oh, news travels fast."

"It does," Shankle said, keeping his eyes fixed on him. "I just wanted it made clear that you will hold your promise to us, you will be true to your word where the previous general was not?"

"Of course I will," John said.

Shankle brightened and held up his cup of liqueur. He took a sip. "Good. Then one of these days we must talk prices, make some sort of a deal."

John realised that, if he did take the job of General, he would have to learn a huge amount, he would need to dedicate himself fully to it. There were so many aspects that he would need to absorb and take care of. He managed a smile and then wished Shankle well, before, finally, being allowed to haul himself up the stairs and to emerge out onto the ramparts, where Horace and Susan were waiting.

He strode up to them and rested his elbows on the wall,

joining their collective stare, out over the plains. "It seems that everyone's heard about the offer before I did."

Horace and Susan smiled weakly at him.

"So what do you think I should do?"

Horace eyed him. "Why, you should take the job, of course. You'd make a brilliant general."

That vote of confidence meant the world to John and he raised a smile to it, then he turned his attention to Susan, who didn't look so convinced. "And what about you?" he said.

Susan plucked at some loose pieces of fur on the palms of her hands and then, all of a sudden, looked up at him. "You know that we have to hide away, we need to find another place like Witney Branches. Perhaps the King has changed but people's perceptions haven't. We are slaves to the Kingdom just like before."

John considered her comment. He thought about how she had taken him in, how the Damned Forests had become his childhood home, and how it hurt him horribly to think that they were now destroyed. The only solace was that the agents who had caused that destruction—the black magicians—had been taken care of. And then the perfect idea struck him. He looked back at Susan. "Why don't the Grotesque make up their new home here, in the castle?"

Susan glared at him. "Have you gone totally crazy? That's completely the opposite of what we need. I mean . . . people will see us . . . everyday."

"That's the point, though, isn't it? We've got to change people's perceptions, make them see that we're not some outcasts, that we can be positive contributors to society. There's no way we'll change their minds by hiding ourselves away."

Susan flinched.

John turned his attention to Horace. "What do you think?"

Horace blew out a long stream of hot air. "I don't know, John. We came up here because we felt uncomfortable, you know, being down there with all those people. It just doesn't seem right for us to live with everyone else."

John waved his hand at the courtyard. "But look at the others. They're doing just fine."

Down below many Grotesque danced with dwarves and men of the garrison. Rabbit King hopped in and out between them, already looking like he—the one who had been the greatest outcast of all the Grotesque—was fitting right in. Jenson, who he remembered from his stint as King's Champion-elect was now making hasty conversation with Shankle. Everyone was smiling and laughing, knocking back their liqueurs as they went.

Even Susan couldn't deny this sight, and she turned back to look at John. "So, what you're saying is that you intend to take the role of General in the King's army? You think that's what you really want?"

John stared off into the distance, to the horizon, the line of trees which lay on their sides—all that remained of the Damned Forests. There was no home for them to go back to, and he wondered whether this—all *this*—had just been fate nudging the Grotesque in the direction of humanity, trying to get them to leave their comfort zone and reach out to the bigger world. Being here, in the castle, among other people, just felt right. He couldn't deny that.

"Well?" Horace said.

When John turned back to them he noticed that they were both staring at him intently. He gave them a broad grin. "Yeah,

I'm going to take it." He looked back out over the plains. "If we find that the people can't accept us then we can always leave, find somewhere else to hide ourselves away, but, for now, we should make the effort, try to make it work."

They all stood there on the ramparts, in silence, for several minutes, before John suggested that they re-join the party pulsing down below. And when they descended, got back among the others, had a wonderful time, drank and made merry, John couldn't believe that there was any other way to live.

AHEAD, A GLORIOUS RETIREMENT

T REVOR WHISTLED as he paced along the street. Life
was great. He had managed to return from Ethereal
without losing his life or getting lost, and he was heading for
retirement. When he had reanimated back on Earth he had
found himself back wearing his jacket, complete with his notice-
of-retirement pay out in the inside pocket—he supposed that
time and space somehow bargained for sticky re-entries. He
would've thought it all a dream if he hadn't been standing beside
Alexis—the ex-Queen of Ethereal—when he'd turned back up in
Rutsley Church and Burial Grounds.

He returned to the office for the afternoon, to see out the
rest of his time. He was shocked to see the array of dismal faces,
the crouched postures over computers, as they tapped away,
worried about their own jobs. Didn't they see this as a great
opportunity? If only they could reach out and grab something
with their settlements then this redundancy might well have

been the best thing that had ever happened to them. Far be it from Trevor to ram that philosophy down their throats, though, he was content that, for the first time in his life he would really appreciate having time to himself, and being secure in doing what he wanted.

He ducked into his boss's office and gave him a vigorous handshake before ducking out, waving goodbye to each of his ex-workmates. Several of them gave him askew glances, surely wondering whether they were going to flip on the evening news that night to find that he had thrown himself beneath a train or similar. To be honest, Trevor couldn't care less what they thought because he was happy.

Deciding to take a shortcut on his way home—why should he waste even a moment of his life?—he passed through a play-ground. He usually avoided the playing field, not wanting to get mud on his shoes. But what use were his shoes now that he didn't have a job?

The playground was empty at the moment. He presumed that all the kids were having their tea at that time. As he got about halfway across the field, with the wooden gate which led to the path round the back of his house in his sights, he noticed a strange crackling off to the side of him. He thought about running but realised that he wasn't in Ethereal any longer —the only real danger was from muggers, and they didn't tend to broadcast their presence with crackles. He was surprised to see a girl standing there—apparently having popped out of nothing.

She had black eyes and delicate features. It looked like her nose would break with a good, solid tweak. Her black hair was in a pixie cut, which Trevor had noted in some of his younger, female co-workers, and her hair shimmied as she cocked her head.

"Um," Trevor said, "are you all right?"

She ignored the question and produced a clipboard from—seemingly—mid-air. "I'm a Time Nymph."

"A 'Time Nymph?'" Trevor said.

"That's right."

There was a long silence and then Trevor said, "You mean you're come from the End of Time?"

"I do some work there." She broke into a smile. "My name's Pixibob."

"Uh huh," Trevor said. "Have I done something wrong?"

"'Wrong?'" she said. "No, nothing 'wrong.' Please don't worry, this is all just procedural, we do this with everyone who uses the End of Time, to get their feedback on the process, see how we might improve things. To check"—she paused then flicked a ladybird from her forearm—"to check whether or not you are truly suitable to this world following your foray into other worlds."

"Kind of like a survey?"

"Yes," she said, with a chirpy tone. "That's the word I was looking for." She turned back to her clipboard, to study the page there. "Now," she said, "first of all, 'What impact, if any, do you think your voyage beyond this world has had on you?'"

Trevor hands grew clammy. What was it she had said about him being 'suitable' to continue living on Earth? What had she meant by that? Would she take him back to the End of Time, to some sort of 'time prison' if he answered incorrectly? One thought stuck with him and that was that he had to take care with his answers if he wanted to get home in time for dinner.

He stretched his mind and thought long and hard for moral or reason. After some hard seconds thinking he thought he had something. "Well," Trevor said, staring up at the perfect blue sky, "I suppose that, after all my adventures, the life and death situations, I've come to value my life here on Earth a bit more."

Pixibob scrawled away on her page, then peered over the clipboard. "Right, the next one—"

"Wait!" Trevor said. "Was my answer okay? Did I say the right thing?"

She smiled at him. "There're no right answers."

"But there are wrong ones, aren't there?"

Her smile remained and she ploughed on. "'Have you felt any overriding numbness or nausea following your arrival back to Earth?'"

"Well, I don't think so."

"You 'don't think so,' or you haven't?"

"I haven't."

"Good," Pixibob said, scribbling that down. She glanced up at him. "Almost done here, just one more question to go. 'Which world do you prefer: Earth or Ethereal?'"

On the face of it this seemed a relatively easy one. He supposed, through the not-so-thickly veiled façade that this was being used to determine whether to permit him to continue on Earth or to toss him right back to Ethereal. Then again, he wondered whether that might be the idea, to lull him into a false sense of security. If he badmouthed Ethereal in favour of Earth might they see through it and believe him to be bluffing? He formulated his words carefully, checking them over and over again in his mind before he dared say them out loud. When he was ready, he met Pixibob's eyes and shot from the hip.

"Well, there're good things about both places."

She raised an eyebrow. "Such as?"

Trevor licked his lips. "For example, in Ethereal there are lots of wide open spaces, lots of nature, it's a beautiful place, everything just seems to have a glean to it." He caught himself before he got to waxing lyrical—that might just talk him back there. "But, then again, there are some things which I could do without. You know, there's a lot of brutality about the world. Everyone seems like they want to kill each other, like—"

"And is that much different to Earth?"

Trevor thought about it a moment. "In a way, no, but it's just not the same thing, is it?" He rocked back on his heels and tried to steady his breathing. "What I like about Earth is the decent amount democracy and the fair standard of basic welfare among its people."

Pixibob flashed her eyebrows at him.

Trevor was getting a little frustrated here. What did she want him to say? He bundled onward, convinced that he really couldn't dig himself a hole any bigger than he had already. "And, well, I suppose the last point I'd make is that Earth's my home, that it always has been and I feel like I belong here, whereas, in Ethereal, I don't know, I just felt like an alien the whole time."

"From what I heard they made you a hero."

"Yes, they did."

"Not everyone gets made a hero, you know? That's something really quite special over there."

Seeing where she was going with this argument, he attempted to head her off. "Really, it was a misunderstanding more than anything else."

"And you saved someone's life, a resident from Gotnot Village: Zend Gloot."

"Yes, well, a honey boar rushed at his throat. It was an impulse, really."

"Don't do yourself down, from the answers you've given I've good reason to think that you would do wonders in Ethereal. What makes you so sure that you're suited to Earth? From what I've got here in my notes you've spent almost all your life at a cubicle, tapping away at a computer."

Trevor reached inside his jacket and touched the envelope nestled there. He closed his eyes and then withdrew it. "Because of this." He handed the envelope over, then said, "This means my freedom. From now on I'm going to do whatever I want with my life. Please, I just want to be left in peace to live out the rest of what I've got left, what do you say?"

Pixibob opened the envelope and slipped the typed page out from within. She read it, her eyes darting from one side of the page to the other, extremely quickly—more quickly than he'd ever witnessed anyone reading anything. Then she handed it back.

He took it from her, not quite sure she'd really taken the time to absorb its meaning, folded it in two and replaced it in his inner pocket.

She tore the sheet off her clipboard. "I'm going to recommend that you be considered for relocation in Ethereal—"

"No! Please!"

She gave him a warning look, then handed him over a thin, blue piece of paper. "This is your carbon copy, for your records, it lists the answers to your questions as well as giving other information on your trip to Ethereal. Don't lose it."

He took the paper from her then scrunched it into a ball and let it drop to his feet. "You've got to listen to me. I can't go back there, somehow I managed to get through, to return here, but it was really touch and go. If you send me back it's as good as executing me. You wouldn't execute me, would you?"

"Your case shall be duly considered and you shall receive your answer." She glanced down at the crumpled up ball of blue paper. "I would pick that up, if I were you, from what I've heard this park dishes out fines of a thousand pounds for littering."

Trevor, always the conscientious citizen, did as he was told.

Pixibob remained where she was, still smiling inanely. "Have a good day."

"When do I find out what's going to happen to me?"

"Oh, some time this evening, maybe."

Trevor had to be content with that answer. He trudged his way back home, feeling all his enthusiasm and joy at being back leak right out of him.

***

And so it was with mixed feelings that Trevor wiped his feet on his doormat. He could smell a nut roast wafting about and his stomach churned. He looked down at the statue of a cat which sat on the doorstep. He had always thought it an ugly, nonsensical thing, but now he felt envious of it, knowing that it didn't have its own worries for its place in this world—that it wouldn't suddenly slip away from all this, like a carpet being tugged out from beneath.

He walked into his house, slipped off his work shoes and told his wife what had happened at the office—that he had been made redundant. Just as he had been, when he had first been told the news, she took it as a shock, and then, as he outlined all the plans he had for their future, that now he would *finally* have time for all he wanted to do, she caught onto his enthusiasm. But he found his spirit somewhat tapered by the knowledge that, at any moment, it would all be snatched away. He resolved to enjoy the prospect of his future while it lasted and not to think too hard about how he would feel if it were taken from him.

After dinner his wife proposed that they drink champagne. Trevor, meanwhile, would've rather drunk just about anything else, knowing that his impending journey through space and time, back to Ethereal, would bring it all back up. But he played along with the charade, waiting for the moment when it would all disappear.

They finished the bottle between them and he saw that it was nearing midnight, by the kitchen clock. He excused himself from the table, taking the empty bottle in hand, and he headed out into the cold night. He watched his breath steam in front of his face as he traipsed along his garden path to his wheelie bin. There was no one around the street, of course, it being a week-night, and this being a respectable neighbourhood, so it was a lonely moment as he flipped the lid and tossed the bottle in. As he padded back up the path, headed for his front door, he caught a figure standing in the shadows, looking at him.

The man had a pointed face, with eyes like glass marbles. He wore a strange robe, nothing like that from Ethereal, but certainly nothing that had been made on Earth either.

Trevor felt the champagne tingle in his throat, then he said, "I suppose you've come to take me away, haven't you?"

"Yes."

"Who are you?"

"I'm Frank, Master of Time."

Trevor scoured his mind, going back to his first passage through the End of Time—he recalled Divus mentioning something about him.

"Pixibob told me that you're having second thoughts about returning."

Blood rushed into Trevor's cheeks. He dug his fingernails into his palms. "This is my world—I just don't understand how it can be decided that I'm to go back, who could possibly make the judgement about where I'd be better off?"

"In all my time in the job I have to say that I've never seen someone with a record quite like yours. From what I can see you'd make a wonderful difference to Ethereal, make it a better world."

Again, Trevor explained that it had all been luck, that he had found great companions to guide him back to Earth—the only place he had ever wanted to be.

Frank considered this, cocking his head to one side. "There is one stipulation concerning your transfer."

"And what's that?"

"I can't wilfully send you somewhere you might be likely to do yourself in."

"'Do myself in?' Whatever do you mean?"

Frank shrugged. "You know, kill yourself. Get all depressed about being sent somewhere you desperately don't want to be. Are you telling me that's the sort of stuff we're talking about here?"

Again Trevor considered a dual motive, that Frank might be

testing to see whether or not he was really desperate to get out of whatever contract he had unintentionally signed. But, he decided, the best recourse was simply to play it straight and tell the truth, lay out the story just as it had happened, leaving no room for confusion. So that was what he did.

Frank listened without uttering a word. He cleared up any of the disparities in Trevor's story, making sure he got things correct. At one point, Trevor wondered whether he was recording all this somehow, such was his attention to detail, and then, when Trevor wrapped up the tale, Frank nodded his head and said, "Well, I can't say that you won't be a great loss to Ethereal, but I hear what you're saying. While I'll never get retirement myself that's no reason to deprive you of it. From what you've outlined it sounds like a truly wonderful thing."

"So," Trevor said, with baited breath, "I can stay here, on Earth?"

Frank gave him a solemn nod and then promptly disappeared into thin air.

It took several seconds for this news to truly sink in and, when it did, Trevor actually managed a leap into the air, although he failed to tap his heels together. When he landed there was a little twinge in his back, but, truthfully, he didn't care.

He dashed back into the house, giving himself up to his glee fully now. He ran into the kitchen, where his wife was doing the washing up. He turned the radio up loud and danced her all round the room. They cracked open another bottle of champagne and discussed their plans late into the night.

Once, while Trevor was refilling his glass, he was sure that he saw someone outside staring in through a gap in the curtains. He recognised the face: Frank, the Master of Time. He wondered whether Frank got any pleasure from this—from seeing him happy, or whether it had been a mere objective, business-like decision. However it had come about Trevor couldn't have been happier.

As he lay in bed that night, staring at the ceiling, feeling the world swaying slightly all about him, he tucked his hands behind his head and told himself that everything was going to okay. There would be no more questing or dwarves or Beavermen or Grotesque or black and white magicians. There would just be the small matter of seeing out his normal, unremarkable and mundane life. And that was just how he wanted it.

THE END

AUTHOR'S NOTE

Thank you for taking the time to read one of my books. If you would like to hear about my latest releases you can sign up for my newsletter here: www.raymondsflex.com

Thanks for reading!

Raymond S Flex

Ethereal
A Long Way Home Novel

Copyright © Raymond S Flex, 2014.
Published by DIB Books
All rights reserved.

Cover design and layout copyright © DIB Books, 2014.
Cover art copyright © Dariush M/ Shutterstock, 2014.